PRAISE FOR

'Step aside, Stieg Larsson, Holt is the queen of Scandinavian crime thrillers' *Red*

'Holt writes with the command we have come to expect from the top Scandinavian writers' *The Times*

'If you haven't heard of Anne Holt, you soon will' *Daily Mail*

'It's easy to see why Anne Holt, the former Minister of Justice in Norway and currently its bestselling female crime writer, is rapturously received in the rest of Europe' *Guardian*

'Holt deftly marshals her perplexing narrative ... clichés are resolutely seen off by the sheer energy and vitality of her writing' *Independent*

'Her peculiar blend of off-beat police procedural and social commentary makes her stories particularly Norwegian, yet also entertaining and enlightening ... reads a bit like a mash-up of Stieg Larsson, Jeffery Deaver and Agatha Christie' *Daily Mirror*

ANNE HOLT

A GRAVE FOR TWO

Translated from the Norwegian
by Anne Bruce

CORVUS

First published in hardback in Great Britain in 2019 by Corvus,
an imprint of Atlantic Books Ltd.

This paperback edition published in 2020.

Originally published in Norwegian as *En grav for to*. Published by
agreement with the Salomonsson Agency.

This translation has been published with the financial support of NORLA.

10 9 8 7 6 5 4 3 2 1

A CIP catalogue record for this book is available from the British Library.

Paperback ISBN: 978 1 78649 851 9
E-book ISBN: 978 1 78649 852 6

Printed in Denmark

Corvus
An imprint of Atlantic Books Ltd
Ormond House
26–27 Boswell Street
London
WC1N 3JZ

www.corvus-books.co.uk

A GRAVE FOR TWO

SELMA FALCK

If Oslo were a body, then this would be the city's backside. This particular apartment.

This arsehole of a living room.

The tiny room was icy-cold. The grey-brown textured wallpaper had peeled off at the corners, and the cheap laminate flooring was spattered with stains. Especially beneath the windows. Selma Falck hunkered down and gingerly dabbed at one of the dark half-moons. The crust loosened with a sticky, disgusting sound.

The tram had rattled past every fourth minute since she had started to carry in the boxes. The windowpanes were covered with frosted vinyl film, possibly to deter prying eyes. It could just as easily have been to prevent them from falling out, since distinct cracks were silhouetted behind the plastic. The room grew noticeably darker each time trams or heavy trucks passed by outside. It was growing late. Despite someone having used parcel tape to seal the cracks around the windows in addition to the plastic film, an increasingly irritating miasma of exhaust fumes assailed her nose.

The boxes were stacked in two towers by the bedroom wall. Darius squatted on top of one of these, glowering at her, crouching as if ready to pounce, his tail swinging slowly from side to side.

Selma Falck sat down on the only item of furniture in the living room, a red settee from the sixties. It had already been here, and smelled vaguely of heating oil and cheese puffs. At least she hoped it was cheese puffs. Darius suddenly arched his back and hissed angrily, but remained on top of the rickety pile on the other side of the room.

Three weeks and three days had gone by. Since then, Selma had continually caught herself glancing at the time for no good reason, as if she could make it stop with a mere look. Or preferably turn it back. This coming Monday, exactly four weeks since Jan Morell, with unaccustomed gravity, had entered her office, the deadline he had given her would expire.

There were only four days left.

She would soon be on target to lose almost everything she had ever owned.

Apart from her car, which she would never give up, and the cat that Jesso had browbeaten her into taking with her. Darius leapt down from the tower of boxes and slipped soundlessly into the bedroom. Something toppled over in there. Something had broken.

Selma closed her eyes as an ambulance speeded past. The siren tore through the wall. She clutched her ears but it did not help in the least. When she opened her senses again, Darius was standing in the middle of the living room.

His eyes glittered. His tail was still swishing belligerently from side to side. In his mouth, the animal carried a mouse with enough life left in it that its naked tail was twitching convulsively. The cat yawned, and the poor creature dropped to the floor where it lay convulsed with spasms.

Selma Falck had not wept since Saturday 13 December 1986. In six days, that would be precisely thirty-one years ago, and so she was extremely taken aback when she thought she could feel the suspicion of tears on her left cheek. It ought to be a physical impossibility. The surprise made her rise to her feet to find a mirror.

She had listed the medal from that period on eBay a fortnight ago. Not a single soul had shown a scrap of interest. The Olympic medal from two years later would probably have been a surer bet, but she had hesitated to part with it for the time being.

She was not crying, according to the mirror she found in her handbag.

It was impossible for her to live here.

She had to live here. In this rat's nest. Or mouse's nest, as already demonstrated, and when she peered up at the ceiling for the first time, she spotted such an enormous greyish-blue stain that she gagged.

And threw up.

The vomit matched the living room carpet.

Within the time limit Jan Morell had given her, she had managed to sell valuables to the tune of just over 13,000,000 kroner. Of that, she was now left with 23,876 kroner and 32 øre, without the slightest notion of when she would be able to earn any money again.

Fortunately no one had any idea where she was. Not Jesso, who apparently couldn't care less anyway. Not the children, who had both made it clear that they never wanted to see her again, ever, when she had picked up some bits and pieces and filled the boxes from Clas Ohlson before driving off in a delivery van she had borrowed from the Poker Turk. None of her friends knew where she lived, although rumours of illness had apparently spread, leading to fifty-two text messages and unanswered calls in only the last couple of days. Selma Falck did not have cancer. Not as far as she knew. Inadvertently, or actually mostly in desperation, she had been forced to overplay her hand a little when incredulous

3

partners were unable to fathom why she had so suddenly been forced to sell out. She had not used the c-word, but from what she had told them with eyes full of sorrow and a trembling lip, it was not so strange that the others had drawn the wrong conclusion. The thought made her gorge rise again. She shook her head vigorously, swallowed and decided to forget the mirror and instead find something to get rid of both the dying mouse and the green muck on the carpet.

No one must know where she was.

When the doorbell rang as she reached halfway across the living room floor, she gave such a forceful start all of a sudden that Darius arched his back again. The half-dead mouse crawled helplessly towards the door, as if it thought rescue was at hand out there. Selma padded quietly in the same direction, though she had not entirely made up her mind to open the door.

Someone was knocking loudly and impatiently.

No one knew she was here.

The doorbell rang yet again.

THE CELL

T he days were no longer his own.

The room had no windows. An LED light on the ceiling was turned on twenty-four hours a day. No visible cables. Nothing he could rip out. The bed was made of cement and formed part of one wall. He didn't even have a mattress, just some straw that had already become thoroughly matted and had started to smell.

He hadn't been given a blanket either. Not even clothes. He wasn't cold, it was warm in here, but he still hadn't grown accustomed to sleeping without anything either over or under him. Dozed a little now and then.

Never slept.

Still too terrified.

He obtained water from a hole in the wall. No larger than that he could use his thumb to close it off, he guessed it to be a half-inch pipe. It dribbled continuously. Since he had no cup, he had to slurp it from the wall, where the perpetual trickle of moisture had left a yellowish-brown trail. It was starting to get slimy. Right beneath the spring, on the floor, a grate was fastened over a drain. He pissed there. Had a shit too, at the times when it was possible for him to squeeze something out. The bars on the grate were wider in the middle. Sometimes he was lucky and hit the target. Other times he had to poke at his own excrement with his foot to get rid of it. Push it, and sometimes even force it down.

Occasionally he received food, through a hatch in the metal door. Bread mostly. Bread rolls, sometimes with a spread of some kind. Never anything hot, never something that had to be served on a plate or eaten with a fork or spoon.

The days had gone by. Nights no longer existed.

The light bothered him and had stolen time. He could have been there for a week, a fortnight, or a year.

Not a year.

But a long time. A few days, at least; he should have tried to keep count of time from when he woke with no idea of where he was. He did not know why he was there. Had absolutely no clue. He screamed at the unknown figure that brought his food. Yelled and battered his fists until they bled on the grey steel of the closed door. Out there it was always silent, and the hatch was too small to discern anything except shadows on the other side.

The man must know him. It had to be a man. When he woke and found himself a prisoner, he felt pain beneath the tendons of his knee and at the top of his back, as if someone had carried him. Dragged him for a stretch too; his heels were sore. It must be a man, and he must know him.

There was nothing in here he could use to kill himself.

He wanted that more than anything; he would prefer death to this and had tried to ram his head into the wall with all the strength he could muster. Several times. All he had achieved were cuts and bruises. He had stuffed his mouth full of straw, but kept coughing it all back up again. A reflex, he assumed. He had wet the fucking grass, made it soaking wet and crammed it into his nose and throat, as hard as he could; he had almost succeeded, but just as the room went pink, his head became light and he sank down on to the bed, he had been overtaken by fits of coughing and had spewed it all up again.

Every time.

Whoever was holding him captive must know him.

Whoever had imprisoned him must know that he would choose death rather than this. And the worst thing, the very worst thing, was that each time the stranger had delivered some food, only now and then and in a pattern that was impossible to work out, that scraping, mechanical noise came from behind one wall.

It then moved closer and made the room steadily smaller.

THE SKIER

In the long series of more or less meaningless events that comprise a life, this day would be included as forgettable, no big deal, Hege Chin Morell thought. In time, she would look back on these days, these weeks that lay ahead of her and this surreal moment, and shrug with indifference.

Just a bump in the road. An annoying but surmountable obstacle on the road towards a brilliant Olympic Games in PyeongChang.

She was twenty-four years old and had decided that everything going on at present had actually not happened. It was too absurd. So obviously untrue. Something had gone wrong, and that something would be identified. The negligence would be corrected. It was simply a question of time; she'd tried to convince herself in the three days plus that had passed since she had received the incredible information.

Every minute of this hell on earth was sixty seconds too many.

The people facing her had become a greyish-blue, noisy mass. She closed her eyes gently and concentrated on picturing herself in her mind's eye, triumphantly crossing a finishing line. A Christmas tree; a swallow dive into salt water. Her mother's face, less distinct as the years passed, the smile that Hege could no longer completely catch except in fleeting retrospective glimpses. Mum's blue eyes and her long, pale blonde curls, so different from Hege's black, coarse hair that mother and daughter had woven a zebra plait of both their locks when she was little and was allowed to fall asleep in the crook of her mother's arm once the nights grew too dark.

The most important thing of all, of course, was something she did not remember. Someone, probably her birth mother, had left her outside the absolutely correct children's home. There was a photo of Hege, barely two months old, in a basket, with scabs in what little hair she had. She was wrapped in clean rags and had a green bear made of hard plastic for company. If she had ended up in some other place, at some other time, it would not have been Jan and Katinka Morell specifically who some months later would have brought that pale baby, suffering from eczema, home to Vettakollen in Oslo on the other side of the globe. Her biological mother, or whoever it had been, had left her early one morning under a half-dead willow tree outside the old mission station, a lucky chance in life, and little Chin would eventually learn to ski.

Her birth mother had made it worth coming into the world by abandoning her.

Four Olympic titles and almost ten thousand hours of training later, Hege knew that life brought ups as well as downs. She had learned to take them both with an equanimity that disconcerted the Norwegian public.

Hege Chin Morell knew there were great moments in life. And small ones too. Life was a chain of strong and weak links, of good and bad, of apathy and historic occasions and everything that existed between birth and death. The chain was long, and this particular moment, this absurd press conference, would just have to be endured. Hege had to stay on her feet, and she straightened her back yet another notch at the thought.

Something was completely wrong, and it was going to be cleared up.

She opened her eyes again and stared at a point high above the heads of the almost forty assembled journalists and photographers.

Four serious men sat lined up beside her, three of them with hands folded and downcast eyes. The table was covered in a dark-blue tablecloth that matched her sweater, a garment that for the first time in six years was stripped of the sponsor's name. Even the manufacturer's logo was covered with a piece of tape. The usual fruit bowls, smoothie bottles and bottled water, that as a rule were strategically laid out on the table to be captured by the camera lenses, were conspicuous by their absence too. A solitary, nameless jug sat on the tablecloth. Only Hege had been favoured with a glass.

It was empty.

An intense tumult, filled with speculation, had suddenly ceased the moment she entered. The cameras zoomed and clicked, some people went on whispering, but the President of Norway's Cross-Country Skiing Federation, Bottolf Odda, did not have to raise his voice when he fiddled with the microphone and cleared his throat.

'Welcome to this press conference,' he said. 'We'll come straight to the point.'

A photographer tripped over someone else's leg and sprawled his full length. The president paid no attention to him whatsoever.

'The reason Norway's Cross-Country Skiing Federation has called this conference is that Hege has had ...'

He swallowed.

'A situation has arisen,' he began again. 'Earlier this autumn, Hege Chin Morell gave a drug test sample that has proved positive.'

Now even the cameras fell silent.

'Which must be a mistake,' the cross-country skier herself said loudly. 'I haven't taken drugs of any kind. There must be something wrong with the tests.'

The photographers went berserk again.

THE FATHER

The stairway smelled indefinably dirty. An earthy odour combined with heavy traffic, Jan Morell thought as he waited for someone to open the door.

He thought he could hear sounds, but it was difficult to know whether they came from the apartment or from the noisy city outside. He was tempted to put his ear to the door. The two uneven, apparently sticky, stripes of indeterminate colour that ran diagonally across the timber deterred him from doing so.

It had been unusually difficult to track down the address. That sort of thing seldom took more than half an hour. Jan Morell's private detective, or security consultant as was stated on his payslip, had spent a day and a half laying his hands on a Norwegian Turk in Ensjø. The guy ran a car wash and repair workshop in an obscure establishment by day and a poker den by night. He had been obstinate, the brief note said. Jan Morell preferred not to know what the security consultant had done next. He turned a blind eye. The main point of the report was that Selma Falck had been permitted to rent this apartment for three months for next to nothing. Strictly speaking, it was really a loan. The Turk was a former, and obviously extremely grateful, client of hers.

Exactly like Jan Morell. If he wasn't especially grateful these days, he was at least decidedly former.

No one opened up.

Jan Morell thought he heard a cat meow. He hammered loudly

on the filthy door and rang the doorbell again. Now he heard footsteps.

Someone inside touched the door handle. The security chain rattled. In a slender gap between the door and the frame, Selma's right eye and the corner of her mouth came into view.

She said nothing. Just stood there, as if she needed time to comprehend that he had found her. He glanced down. A cat's face, he concluded. The animal looked as if it had been involved in a head-on collision: its nose was like a flat button just below its ice-blue, over-large and fairly prominent eyes.

'Open up,' he said brusquely, nudging the door with his elbow. 'I have an offer you can't refuse. One last, substantial wager.'

Resolutely, he shoved open the door and strode inside.

THE TUBE

Hege was at home alone. In the small cul-de-sac outside the house in Vettakollen, behind a tall hedge of Serbian spruce, a pack of journalists and photographers had set up camp. Earlier that evening she had heard them and their vehicles, left with the engines running. The police came. Called by the neighbours, she assumed. The photographers, who had squeezed through the hedge and come terrifyingly close, were shown off the premises by four uniformed men with barking dogs.

It would soon be ten p.m.

Her father had driven her home after the press conference. Neither of them had spoken a word. They had parked at their neighbour's house further away and walked along an icy footpath to their own back garden before entering through the patio doors. Once inside, her father had remained tight-lipped. He checked all the entrances twice over before he stopped, took her hands in his and said: 'I'll put everything right.'

With emphasis, as if there were a full stop after each and every word. Then he dashed off out again the same way they had come.

This was what he was like. He was someone who put things right. He wished more than anything else in the whole world that someone would put things right. Clear up a horrendous misunderstanding. Find the mistake. Find five mistakes or ten or however many there were that had convinced Anti-Doping Norway that she was a drugs cheat. That she had used an anabolic steroid that right now she couldn't even remember the name of, even though she had read their letter over and over again for three days in a row and anyway, knew of it from before.

Hege wanted someone to put things right, but on this particular evening she wished her father hadn't left. That someone had been there with her. Someone other than Maggi, who presumably sat in her apartment in the basement watching Polish TV.

She walked through the almost pitch dark rooms. Her father had drawn all the curtains, thoroughly and systematically, before he left. Switched on the odd lamp that he had flicked off again on his second round. Hege stopped in front of the fridge. Opened it. She hadn't eaten since breakfast, but didn't want anything. Nothing except for her father to come home.

And that her mother would rise from the dead.

And that someone from Anti-Doping Norway would ring the doorbell with a broad smile and apologize for the dreadful misunderstanding. She certainly had not given a positive drugs test and would have to forget the terrible scene in front of the press corps when she managed to hold back the tears until her father had led her through a maze of corridors down to the basement car park. Someone else had driven out in her father's Mercedes with the smoked glass windows to fool the journalists for long enough to enable the two of them to follow unnoticed in a borrowed Honda.

She quickly slammed the fridge door shut again.

It was four days since the World Cup race in Lillehammer. She had been knocked out in the semi-final of the classic sprint, but won the skiathlon the next day. Usually she got a lift with someone for races in Norway and Sweden. Teammates or coaches. Physiotherapists or even the national team doctor. This weekend, however, she had driven herself. On her own, in order to listen to an audiobook.

She had almost finished Elena Ferrante's fourth novel.

It was always Maggi who packed for her. Packed and unpacked her travel bag. Maggi washed the clothes as well. The home help had been with them since Hege's mother had died, and on the whole attended to most of the chores she and her father found tedious. Changing the bedclothes. Cleaning. Tidying. Preparing food. Following strict instructions, certainly; a dietician, commissioned by her father, had put together an all-year diet Hege stuck to as if her life depended on it.

And it did, of course, in a sense.

It was a matter of optimizing the possibility of winning, as her father said.

Since Hege had collapsed into bed when she came home on Sunday evening, and then woke to the news that she had failed a drugs test, she had not noticed that her bag had been emptied, the contents washed and everything put back in place. In the following days, Maggi had sneaked around like a kind, but deferential and almost invisible, ghost.

Hege ran down the stairs, taking three steps at a time. She dashed into her own room and flung open the double doors of her wardrobe. The light came on automatically. On one side of the seven square metres of storage hung her training gear. It was impossible to say if anything was missing, but the bag was empty and in the right place on the floor beside the bathroom door. She let her fingers slide across the row of hanging clothes. Stopped and tugged at a sleeve. She had worn that jacket on Sunday.

For a moment she stood deep in thought.

There were the pull-on trousers she had packed at the bottom of the bag; the zip was faulty and needed to be fixed.

Everything was here. Maggi had done her job, as Maggi always did whatever she had to. The big toiletry bag, with extra room for her carefully measured asthma medications, should be placed in the top drawer under the bathroom basin. She only used it when travelling. It contained everything she needed, and lest she forget anything on a trip, she had a double set of everything. Hege opened the door into her own bathroom and pulled out the drawer. The toiletry bag was where it should be. She picked it up, placed it on the counter beside the basin and opened it.

Deodorant. Approved by the national team's doctor. Make-up. Approved by the national team's doctor. Toothpaste, hairbrush in a plastic bag, mint dental floss. The perfume her father had given her at Christmas, examined and approved by all the expertise with which her father always surrounded himself. Three inhalers. A packet of Paracet, unopened.

She stacked the items one on top of the other in the wash-hand basin. The toiletry bag was soon empty.

The unfamiliar tube lay at the very bottom. In a rectangular white box with green and black writing. Together with some sort of 'no admittance' mark in red, fairly large, stamped above the words 'BANNED SUBSTANCE' in black.

TROFODERMIN was the name of the medication.

Hege dropped the box on the floor.

Her ears were ringing. She tried to blink away the black dots dancing in front of her eyes. She grabbed her inhaler, applied it to her mouth, pressed and took a deep breath.

Open-mouthed, she continued gasping for breath.

She was well aware what Trofodermin was.

On the other hand, she had no idea how the package had ended up in her toiletry bag, in her luggage, after a successful World Cup weekend in Lillehammer.

Absolutely not the foggiest, and the world had stopped spinning.

THE GLASS PALACE

H e was freezing.
Arnulf Selhus knew it wasn't cold in the large room. The temperature and air quality were controlled by an installation so modern that only two years ago, when the king had formally opened the building, it was the only one of its kind in the world. All the public rooms were set at 20.00 degrees Celsius, right down to the decimal point. Nevertheless his teeth were nearly chattering.

Sølve Bang apparently noticed nothing.

'This is a scandal,' he shouted. 'A scandal we simply can't afford, Arnulf. Taking drugs is completely unacceptable!'

The platitudes sent a shower of fine spittle across the oak table.

'Of course,' Arnulf Selhus said apathetically, covering his face with his hands. 'You've said that several times now. But what the hell can we do, eh? Kill the young girl?'

'That might be an idea,' was the quick riposte.

Sølve Bang stood up just as abruptly as he had dropped into the pale-blue designer chair only two minutes earlier.

'She's never been really popular. That goes without saying. She's far too ...'

'Give over. Cut it out.'

'Well, she's certainly created a catastrophe now. She's responsible. Someone is responsible. Nothing here in this world happens without someone being responsible, Arnulf. It's a betrayal. A dreadful betrayal of us all. Of the Federation, of the other team members, of …'

'Of you,' Arnulf mumbled into his own hands, so softly that he hardly heard it himself.

'What did you say?'

'Nothing. But now you should really calm down. Strictly speaking, this doesn't have anything to do with you, Sølve. We have procedures for this. Protocols. Rules.'

'Rules? Protocols?'

The small, corpulent man's voice rose to a falsetto. He began to trot back and forth across the floor, parallel to the glass wall that on some days let the whole of the Oslo Fjord reveal itself out there. Now, as usual for the time of year, a peasouper of a fog weighed down on its huge, cold expanse.

Arnulf Selhus raised his eyes again. Sølve Bang walked with short steps, had a pendulous paunch and a nose so long that it almost touched his upper lip. His eyes, normally slightly protruding, had begun to look cross-eyed in his agitation.

He didn't look much like a former skier.

Maybe not much like a writer, either, Arnulf thought, although admittedly writers came in all shapes and sizes.

The yellow memory stick hanging round his neck, on a narrow chain of the same material, bounced up and down on his tie as he trotted around. He continually touched it with his fingers, on hands that could have belonged to a girl. Arnulf Selhus had known this man since 1982 and had never particularly liked him. But right here and now he felt an unfamiliar, new sense of loathing.

Or fear, it suddenly struck him.

The room was filled with dread. It lurked in the corners. It hid behind the straight, pale curtains he felt an almost irresistible urge to close. Even outside the ridiculously large windows, between the dark spruce trees that flanked the car park, it looked as if an indefinable, dark-grey presence threatened to force its way in through the glass and seize him.

Arnulf Selhus had difficulty breathing deeply enough.

Sølve had enough on his plate and still noticed nothing.

That a man who had won one measly World Cup race thirty-five years ago was permitted to behave as if he owned Norwegian cross-country skiing was beyond Arnulf's comprehension.

Sølve Bang had even managed to steamroll through this damned building, this glass monument on the slopes of Holmenkollåsen. With himself as head of the jury when the architecture competition was advertised, and later in charge of the building committee.

Many people thought when cross-country skiing had broken free from the Norwegian Ski Federation in 2008 it had been an example of sheer hubris. Arnulf Selhus among them. Classic short-sightedness as he had both thought and said at the time. The administration of cross-country skiing in the Norwegian Ski Federation had landed an exceptional sponsorship contract with Statoil, adding petrol to the flames for those who regarded cross-country skiing as the very jewel in the ice crown of winter sports. Remarkably enough, the agreement was entered into for a period of twenty years, an eternity in sponsorship terms. Alpine skiing could go its own way, was a comment muttered ever more loudly in the corridors after the deal had been struck. In truth, it was only a tiny group of adherents that bothered about Telemark skiing. Similarly with the loopy snowboard fraternity – anyway, it was populated by individuals who had never really understood the meaning of organization. Freestyle skiing was for teenagers and had barely contributed one iota since Kari Traas's time.

Norway was cross-country skiing, and Norwegian cross-country skiing could stand on its own two agile feet.

The Cross-Country Skiing Federation was now only nine years

old, and its independent status had failed to be the picnic that Sølve Bang and his many followers had anticipated.

Neither had they anticipated a top athlete being caught up in a drugs scandal.

Clapping his hands to his face, Arnulf groaned.

'We have to talk to the sponsors,' he said. 'They can't just ...'

'That's exactly what they *can* do,' Sølve snarled, taking hold of his memory stick as he approached his companion. 'All sponsors have a drugs clause. Statoil's is unconditional and strict. They have every right to pull the plug on us, Arnulf!'

'We still have the state sponsorship. Lottery funds. Volunteerism. The smaller sponsors, such as MCV. We can still ...'

'Volunteerism? Do you think this ... this ...'

He let go of the memory stick and spread his arms.

'Do you think the Crystal Palace was built from money raised by *selling waffles*? Do you think it's the old biddies shuffling around out there ...'

His slender right hand waved uncertainly in the direction of the grey windows.

'... holding jumble sales and making hot dogs and whatever else they ... Do you think it's *volunteerism* that has made it possible for the NCCSF to grow to such heights? What? Do you think ...'

All of a sudden he subsided on to a chair, clutching his forehead and blowing slowly out through his nose.

'And with that unstable, incompetent cow in the Ministry of Culture the prospects for lottery funding don't look too good either,' he added bitterly. 'That's how it goes when people in here have eaten and drunk their fill and travelled business class and then ...'

'Those accounts have been buried,' Arnulf Selhus broke in sharply. 'Everything before 2015 has been settled by Parliament. That's for definite. After Sochi, things don't look so bad, and those are the accounts the world will respond to. Only those.'

Silence ensued. The fog outside grew even thicker, if that were possible. When he abruptly rose to his feet and stood facing the window, the lights down in the car park were reduced to vague cotton wool dots of lighter grey against all the darkness.

'But let's take one thing at a time,' he concluded, tugging at his tie. 'We have enough on our plate with Hege right now. And anyway, neither you nor I will be the ones to deal with this situation. I'm going home.'

He turned around again.

Sølve Bang seemed deaf to the world. He sat lost in thought, with eyes unfocused. One hand was holding the memory stick, which he clicked in and out of its cover in a nerve-wracking rhythm.

'I'm going,' Arnulf Selhus repeated as he headed for the door.

The other man still gave no answer. He clicked and clicked, and as Arnulf Selhus put his hand on the door handle, it dawned on him that neither of them had given a thought to how Hege Chin Morell must be feeling after the revelation.

'Well, not as fucking awful as me, anyway,' he muttered inaudibly as he closed the door behind him and left Sølve Bang to sit alone in the spacious conference room which King Harald – in person – had honoured with the name 'Golden Girls'.

THE BET

'It's not connected,' Selma said, pointing at the black TV screen. 'I haven't seen the news for ages.'

'Well, you have a mobile.'

As Jan Morell scanned around, his expression looked as if he was standing in the midst of a landfill site. His previously narrow nose turned into a straight line.

Selma sat down on the cheese puff settee and made a gesture of invitation to indicate he should do likewise. He remained standing.

'It's about Hege,' he said without making any comment on the apartment apart from a look that continued to scour the room. 'She's failed a drugs test.'

'What?'

'Anti-Doping Norway claims she's somehow taken Clostebol. Of course, she hasn't.'

'Clostebol?' Selma repeated. 'That's an anabolic steroid, as far as I recall?'

'Yes, one I knew nothing about. Until three days ago. It's obviously a misunderstanding. A mistake. Sabotage, at worst. That's what I want you to find out.'

'Me?'

She picked up a yellow cushion and put it behind her back before continuing.

'You've given me a deadline of Monday, Jan. This Monday! I

was at the bank this afternoon, so that's already taken care of. Thirteen million kroner have been returned to your account. You'll just have to wait for the last three. I quite simply can't cough up any more. Give me two years for that part. I'll also hand in my licence to practise law, as you've demanded. On Monday. If you think I can get to the bottom of something as complicated and serious as a drugs charge by that time, then you overestimate me.'

'You can work without a licence.'

'As a lawyer?'

Selma smiled joylessly, pulled out the cushion from behind her back and punched it lightly before clutching it to her chest. It had grown noticeably colder in the last hour.

'No,' Jan Morell said tersely, now at least turning to face her.

Until now he had been speaking into thin air. Now he sought eye contact.

'You can never have access to other people's money, Selma. We've discussed that. You can't have a licence to practise law with your ... predilection. The matter is over and done with.'

'Then I can't help you.'

'Not me. You can help Hege. And you'll do it as a consultant. Working for me.'

Selma felt her pulse race. She breathed more quietly, concentrating, and regained control.

'That's sheer madness, Jan. We have an agreement. One: I pay back the money.'

She used the fingers of her right hand to count on her left.

'Two: I hand back my licence to practise law. Three: I must never gamble again. Nothing. At all. The quid pro quo is that you don't report me. Quite a ...'

Darius leapt on to the settee, circling himself soundlessly a couple of times before lying down.

'... rough deal,' Selma rounded off.

He opened his mouth and she held up her palms to stop him.

'Strict,' he nevertheless went on to say. 'But fair.'

She placed the cushion as a buffer between her and the cat.

'Fine,' she said, with a note of resignation. 'But an agreement like that makes it totally impossible for me to work for you. You'll realize that, if you think about it.'

'Look on it as a bet,' he said sharply. 'Your very last one. If you find the explanation for how and why an honest, clean, elite athlete has quite inexplicably tested positive and risks losing the greatest experience of her life, then you'll get your money back.'

'PyeongChang.'

'Yes.'

'No cure, no pay?'

'Yes. Only then will it really be a bet. You have until the very last selection date. 24 January 2018. If you succeed, the money's yours. Sixteen million. Many of your problems could be fixed for sixteen million kroner, Selma. Especially since three of them represent debt you have nothing to show for. If you don't succeed, then both you and I will have wasted our time.'

'But why me?'

Jan Morell gave a faint smile.

'Look at yourself in the mirror,' he said with a touch of contempt. 'Read your own CV. If anyone is able to get to the bottom of this, it's you. A top athlete. A top lawyer. You took on three famous drugs cases and won two of them. Into the bargain, you're one of Norway's most famous faces and admired role models.'

'Former top athlete,' she corrected him. 'And from Monday on, also an ex-lawyer. Probably also a far less famous face. From now on, at least.'

Holding out his hand, he pretended not to hear her.

'Do we have a deal?'

Selma got to her feet. Stared at his hand without taking it in hers. Darius jumped warily down to the floor again, with his eyes fixed on the mouse, now lying stone dead in the middle of the floor.

'I don't even know where to begin,' Selma said hesitantly.

'By coming with me,' Jan Morell told her, retracting his hand and heading for the door. 'You have to speak to Hege.'

Only now did he catch sight of the mouse and stopped short.

'What kind of place is this?' he exclaimed, taking a step back. 'And what the hell's that cat doing here?'

'It's a long story,' Selma said curtly, circumnavigating the mouse cadaver as she went to collect her outdoor clothes. 'I have to do something first. I can be at your place in a couple of hours.'

A swift glance at the Rolex. Yet another item she would try to keep for as long as possible, it struck her. In reserve, of course: a watch like that would fetch a good price on eBay.

'Before midnight. OK?'

'Yes.'

'And ...'

'Yes?'

'You'll have to cover all expenses.'

Irritation, possibly anger, crossed his face.

'Within reasonable limits,' he finally said. 'Do you take the job?'

'I accept your bet. With no particular belief that I'll be able to win. Have you considered at all that she might in fact be guilty?'

'She's not. I know that. Anyway, you forgot one point.'

'What?'

'In our agreement. Point four. You'll provide me with written confirmation from a licensed psychologist or psychiatrist that you're receiving treatment.'

Now Selma was the one to freeze.

'That point will have to be deleted.'

'Out of the question.'

She hung her jacket back on the hook. The tiny hallway was unlit. Only the open door into the living room made it possible for them to see the contours of each other's face.

'I'll never consult a psychologist, Jan.'

'Yes, you will. Ask Vanja Vegge for advice. Isn't she a good friend of yours? If you don't do that, I'm happy to inform you that the formal complaint is ready and waiting in my safe.'

She stared at him. Was met by a blue gaze, brimming with success, arrogance and wealth. Despite being scarcely five foot eight, Jan Morell was a man at his full height. He usually got his own way.

'No,' she said firmly.

'Your choice,' he said brusquely, putting his hand on the door chain. 'The formal complaint will be delivered on Monday.'

The door slammed behind him.

Darius meowed.

Selma Falck hesitated for a few seconds. Grabbed her jacket and dashed out into the stairwell.

'Jan!'

Fortunately, he had waited for her beside the mailboxes.

THE HIDING PLACE

The first thought that came to Hege, when she no longer felt she had to throw up, was to call her father. The second thought struck her before she located her phone:

What one person knows, nobody knows. What two people know, everybody knows.

It was her father's mantra. Ever since she, as a tiny, deadly serious bundle, had been collected from China, Jan Morell had instilled in her that she should never trust anyone. No one. Except for him and Katinka, Hege Chin's Norwegian mother.

You can never trust anyone except the people who put you before themselves. No one other than those who love you. Only Mum and I do. Remember that.

Mum had always smiled indulgently, rolling her eyes slightly, and tried to make him listen to reason. Most people were dependable, Hege should know. On the whole, people wished one another well. That was how she lived, Katinka Morell. That was what she was like, and that was how she died after a hospital blunder her widower pursued at great lengths through the legal system. Eventually receiving three million kroner in compensation. The money was invested in a trust for Hege, who was eleven years old at that time. Not that she would ever need it, as Jan Morell's only child.

The writing on the box shone out at her. She had perched it on the edge of the wash-hand basin. It crossed her mind that she had touched it, and she picked it up with a hankie and began to rub away the fingerprints that must be all over it. The packaging fell apart, becoming flat and misshapen, and the lid opened up at one end.

The text was in Italian.

Hege had been to Italy. With the national team. At the end of August, beginning of September.

The tube itself slid out of the package and fell to the floor.

What one person knows, nobody knows.

Dad and Hege were as one. It was always the two of them. In a sense it always had been, at least after Mum's death when the skiing had taken the upper hand for them both. They had used training to eradicate their sorrow. Tried, at least. Skated through Nordmarka in winter, ran in summer, used roller skis, treadmill, weights and a stopwatch to flee from a death neither of them had seen coming and also never succeeded in running away from.

They were two sides of the same coin.

But Dad always thought on his feet. He was so quick thinking, so fast that he always stole a march on everyone else and for that reason he was always allowed to choose the trail. He was proud, almost boastful, of being called Pathfinder as a child, when he was the best at skiing among all the youngsters in his neighbourhood, despite using old wooden skis with Kandahar bindings far longer than all the others.

He was going to do something. At once. Move heaven and earth to find out who had compromised Hege's luggage. He would take one look at the tube of ointment, bark out some specific questions and dash to the door again. Dad always did something. Took action. PDQ and on the double.

Hege didn't want anything to be done. She wanted the tube of Trofodermin to disappear by itself. All this should just vanish, and she picked up the tube. The lid unscrewed with a barely audible click. After turning the cap, she pierced a hole in the foil seal over the opening. She lifted the toilet seat lid and squirted the ointment down into the bluish, fragrant water. She used her finger and thumb to squeeze the tube three times from bottom to top. Carefully, to avoid getting any on her fingers. The sticky mass disappeared down into the blue void, and when it proved impossible to press out any more, she flushed three times. Vigorously deployed the toilet brush and flushed yet again.

Her breathing was steadier now.

She fetched a lighter from the small table with candleholders in the living room. Back in the bathroom, she held the packaging above the toilet bowl and set it alight. Let it burn until it singed her fingertips. Dropped it. Flushed it away.

The tube was made of metal. Perhaps it could be melted at a high temperature. In the fireplace, maybe, but none of the fires were lit now. Following a period resembling winter at the beginning of November, mild weather had set in, turning their existence grey and wet. Even up here on the heights. The fireplaces, both the one in the kitchen and the big hearth in the living room, were never used unless it was really cold. That was also a change since Mum died; Katinka Morell would even light the fire to roast marshmallows in the middle of summer.

Dad had a more practical bent.

The purpose of the fireplaces was to heat up the rooms, and now and again for decoration when they had company.

She would have to wait. Without giving much thought to what she was doing, she put down the toilet seat lid, stepped up on top of it with the empty tube in her hand and unhooked the ventilation grille. When she was younger, she had hidden her diary in here, a notebook so full of trivialities that it now lay in the drawer of her bedside table, with nothing being written for years on end. She hurriedly thrust the tube into the round duct, as far inside as possible, and put the grille back in place again. The catch had loosened, she noticed; in her early teens she had gone in there on a daily basis.

Dad thought the bathroom should be renovated. Until now Hege had flatly refused. The room would soon be completely antiquated, he argued, and something should be done in consideration for the value of the house. But there was still a bit of Mum about the bathroom, something Dad failed to notice. A heart, neatly painted in nail varnish on a tile just beside the door. Hege's height marked on the doorframe. Lines with dates written in various pens with big exclamation marks when she'd had a growth spurt.

If the bathroom were renovated, Hege imagined, she might sneak the empty tube into the floor cement.

She gave herself a slap on the ear at the idiotic idea. This couldn't wait. The tube would have to be disposed of as fast as possible, but in the meantime it could stay where it was. She would think of something.

What one person knows, nobody knows.

No one knew that she could have been caught red-handed with a banned medication in her toiletry bag, traces of which substance had been found in her own body. She let the water in the basin run until it was red-hot, and held her hands under the flow until they were crimson.

Maybe she had done something terribly stupid. It wasn't really possible to ingest drugs through an ointment for wounds. But, technically speaking, of course, it was. From a formal point of view, traces of this ointment could bring her down, and the tube could be the proof she needed at least to be able to blame something. Something far less damning than systematic use of a performance-enhancing drug.

The problem was simply that she had never used that bloody cream. An even greater problem was that someone had tried to make it look as if she had done so.

She should, of course, have gone straight to Dad.

Now it was too late, and she went down to the basement to run on the treadmill.

THE DOWN-AND-OUT

He lived in a cardboard box from IKEA.

It was large and had contained a settee called Stockholm. To tell the truth, Einar Falsen lived in several boxes, of varying sizes, in four different places around Oslo.

This particular abode was situated under the Sinsen interchange and was his usual haunt during Advent. The other shacks made of cardboard, scrap wood and bushes were dotted around the wilderness region of Oslomarka, two of them pretty close to populated areas, one of them close to the Katnosa Lake. He headed there during good weather in summer and could stay there for weeks at a time. He got by on what he found. Both in the landscape and at picnic spots, it was really unbelievable what people left behind, even so far inside Marka that only really experienced hikers ventured here. One or two outdoor fanatics eventually got to know him and slipped him a sausage or a few slices of crispbread on their way home through the forest.

Approaching Christmas he settled every year beneath Norway's busiest traffic machine. More than a hundred thousand vehicles thundered above his head twenty-four hours a day, which he found soothing. This hiding place behind the colossal piles of aggregates and boulders had belonged to him for many years now. It had seemed under threat when the Roma people made their entry into Norway in 2013. Politicians were enraged and set the cops on them. Einar Falsen was allowed to stay as soon as the young, gruff uniformed officers understood who he was. That pre-Christmas period was good, because they brought him coffee prior to repeatedly chasing the gypsies off to a series of different night shelters. Last year some of the seedy Romanians returned, but they kept a safe distance with all their bags and baggage down by the new football pitch at Muselunden.

Einar Falsen was seldom cold.

Cardboard and newspapers, an old sleeping bag, layer upon layer of clothes he regularly fished out of damaged UFF second-hand clothing containers. Aluminium foil and an enormous hat with earflaps. The sum total normally kept out the cold.

But he was hungry. It was fairly late, he thought – the rumble of heavy traffic above his head had abated somewhat. Selma should have been here by now. He pulled off his mittens and took the old mobile phone out from his chest, close to his skin, packed in an old sock wrapped thoroughly in three layers of silver paper to ensure the phone didn't kill him.

The mobile was an old Nokia 1100, and he'd received it as a present. It contained one saved phone number, and he used it very rarely. Selma was the one who had insisted on giving him the opportunity to contact her. Cordless phones were dangerous, he was well aware of that, but Selma had guaranteed that this particular model was safer than any other. It was nonsense, of course, since in the first place mobile phones emitted cancer-producing radiation, and secondly they were under surveillance by the Norwegian security services and the CIA, one and all. After a great deal of persuasion, he had nevertheless gone along with 'taking care of it', as she had put it; it could hardly cause any harm when he almost never switched it on. She should have been here at ten p.m., the message confirmed. It was now twenty-three minutes to eleven.

Selma was the only one he had.

And there she came.

Einar loved the way she walked. Supple, as if she were constantly ready to break into a run. In the glow from the Maxbo billboards at the foot of the interchange and the floodlights on the football field to the north-east, he could see her nimbly jumping from one boulder to the next. They were slippery these days, he had experienced that for himself last night when he had fallen and given himself a nasty knock on the way home from a round of begging, but Selma moved like a dancer.

She was born in 1966, he knew. Fifty years old last September. Selma moved as if she were twenty-five.

'Hi, Einar. Sorry I'm a bit late.'

'I'm not going anywhere,' he said with a smile. 'At least you came, Mariska.'

She returned his smile and began to root around in the bag she carried in her right hand.

'Here. A fully charged power bank. Give me the empty one, please.'

Einar produced the heavy little energy supply for his mobile phone and gave it to her in exchange. Both the empty one and the full one were encased in bubble wrap and a sock.

'And here you are,' she said, sitting down as she unpacked a sandwich from Deli de Luca. 'Cheese and ham with an extra dollop of red pepper. Sorry, but I didn't have time to fill a thermos of coffee, so ...'

She handed him a giant-sized cardboard beaker wrapped in napkins and sealed with tape.

'Probably not hot any more.'

'Doesn't matter. What's wrong?'

'Wrong?'

'Yes. You've been so stressed out lately. Now there's definitely something bothering you.'

'No, there's not.'

'I recognize that look of yours. Is it something at work?'

He guzzled down half the contents of the beaker without waiting for an answer.

'No, of course not,' she said casually as he drank. 'Just lots to do.'

'And the family?'

'Absolutely fine. The kids are so busy I hardly see them. It's only Johannes living at home these days. He's got a lot on his plate. You know how it is.'

Einar Falsen stood up, unsteady through rheumatism and eleven years as a down-and-out. He stretched his arms up into the air with a grimace before shaking his legs, one at a time.

'This isn't us, Mariska. We don't sit here lying to each other. If there are things you don't want to talk to me about, that's fine. But don't tell lies.'

'I've been given a case,' she said quickly.

'I assume you get cases all the time.'

He sat down again, on a pile of newspapers and with the rolled-up sleeping bag at his back.

'It's actually not as a lawyer that I've received this particular case,' she said, taking a bottle of cola from her pocket. 'I've to be more of a sort of … investigator, in a sense.'

'You? Investigate? You're a lawyer, damn it.'

Chuckling, he shook his head and sank his teeth into the sandwich.

'What's it about?' he went on with his mouth full of food.

'A drugs case.'

'Boring.'

'Not necessarily. It's to do with Hege Chin Morell.'

The chewing stopped momentarily.

'That Chinese girl? The cross-country skier?'

A slice of red pepper trailed from the corner of his mouth. It looked like a dribble of coagulated blood. He swiftly poked it in again with a finger covered in ingrown grime. Selma handed him the cola bottle.

'She's not Chinese, Einar. She's Norwegian.'

'Yeah, yeah. But originally Chinese. No surprise that she was never popular.'

'She is popular. She's a winner.'

'No. She's tolerated because she wins. Admired. That's something else entirely. And now she's gone and taken drugs into the bargain. Sic transit gloria mundi.'

'She claims it's not true. That it must be a mistake.'

'They all do.'

He was still talking with food in his mouth. The sandwich was soon all eaten up.

'Good,' he said, swallowing and putting his hands back into a pair of enormous construction workers' mittens from Mesta, black with yellow reflective stripes. 'Thanks.'

'They all don't.'

'Almost,' he insisted, stashing the cola bottle between two rocks. 'There aren't many penitent sinners. Even I don't repent. And I killed a man. With my bare hands.'

He lifted the mittens up in front of his eyes and stared almost in bewilderment at them before adding: 'That's far worse than taking drugs. In the eyes of other people, I mean.'

'Well, judging by the media attention, that's debatable.'

Selma waved her iPhone, which immediately began to light up.

'Hey! Keep that murder weapon away from me!'

He half-rose and drew back on the large boulder. The cardboard box behind him wobbled. Selma returned her mobile to her pocket.

'Einar,' she said gently. 'Where do I begin? I mean …'

Reassuringly, she patted the jacket pocket into which the phone had disappeared.

'Switch it off,' he ordered.

Selma complied.

'If we assume she's telling the truth,' she began again. 'Just for the sake of hypothesis. It seems incontrovertibly correct that she provided a urine sample that showed a tiny amount of the banned substance Clostebol.'

'Sounds like a cleaning agent.'

'Where do I start?'

'On what?'

A police car advanced along Trondheimsveien with sirens blaring. The sweeping blue lights did not reach into the darkness beneath the bridge. The noise did, however, and they sat in silence until the vehicle accelerated towards Carl Berner and disappeared.

'There are actually only three possibilities,' Einar said quietly as he drank the rest of the cold coffee. 'If we take for granted that she's telling the truth.'

He took off the mittens and carefully broke the cardboard beaker open along the seam. He licked the dregs from the inside and folded it up neatly before tucking it into a well-used plastic carrier bag from the Rema supermarket chain.

'First of all, there could be some mistake with the tests.'

'That doesn't seem to be the case. Her father, Jan Morell, you know ...'

'I know who Jan Morell is.'

'For a man with no internet connection or fixed abode, you're remarkably well informed, Einar.'

'Newspapers,' he said tersely, shifting his backside a little. 'Great things. They're lying about all over the place and can be used for so many purposes. Just because you get to know most things hours after everyone else, doesn't mean you don't know.'

Selma smiled. Einar liked to see Selma smile. He persuaded

himself that she kept this particular smile just for him, a mixture of admiration and love he had once encountered from so many people, but after all that had happened, now only had the strength to accept from her and her alone.

'Hege learned of the case on Monday,' Selma said. 'Her father has used the time since then wisely. With his money and energy a lot can be resolved PDQ. It doesn't seem that there's anything wrong with the tests.'

'Then we're down to two scenarios. Either she ingested this substance by accident, through her own fault or someone else's, or else she's been sabotaged.'

Silence reigned between them.

Einar Falsen felt a headache coming on. It was just his luck. After four good days when only his rheumatism had grumbled a little, especially his left hip, it was as if barbed wire was tightening around his head. It must be that blasted phone she always had with her, even though she had switched it off.

'An accident is the more likely scenario,' he said, closing his eyes. 'Sabotage the more exciting.'

She did not reply.

'You have to start by freeing yourself,' he said slowly.

'What do you mean?'

'Empty your mind. Pretend you don't know anything whatsoever about the Chinese girl or her father. Begin with a completely blank sheet of paper.'

'That could be a bit difficult, since Hege's the best cross-country skier in Norway and has received wall-to-wall coverage for years and years.'

'A blank sheet, Mariska,' he said, opening his eyes again. 'A completely blank sheet. When you speak to her for the first time, you have to try to wipe the slate completely clean. Ask the obvious questions. Even if you think you know the answers. You're not going to put a roof on the building yet. You must first dig down into the very foundations.'

He began to open the bags that lay in some kind of systematic order around him. Eventually he found what he was looking for, at the bottom of a blue IKEA shopper.

'Take this. I have two of them.'

She accepted the small, dog-eared book he handed her.

'*The Investigator's ABC*,' she read aloud. 'What's this?'

'It's *The Investigator's ABC*,' he replied, grinning. 'A book I wrote in 2002. Just before everything went haywire in my life. Published by a real publishing company, to boot. I was told the following year that 169 copies had been sold. Lucky dogs, all 169 of them, if you ask me. It's worth its weight in gold.'

He nodded contentedly at the book.

'Read it. I think you'll have to go now. That phone of yours will be the death of me before too long. Don't you notice anything?'

Selma got to her feet. She tried to find room for *The Investigator's ABC* in her pocket, but it didn't fit. So she tucked it under her arm as she fished out a one-hundred-kroner note and a twenty kroner coin from her purse.

'Take a trip to the Tøyen Baths,' she said, placing the money on his mitten. 'You need a wash. Phone me if you need anything.'

'Don't be a stranger,' he said with a smile. 'You know where to find me without me having to send you a message. Don't let too much time pass.'

'Do I ever let too much time pass?' she said, smiling back at him.

'No. And you know what?'

'No, what?'

Even in the semi-darkness in here he could see that her shining eyes were brown, almost black.

'I did the right thing, didn't I? It was right to kill him?'

And she came back, as she always did, before she left him every single time, she crouched down over him and gave him a hug and whispered in his ear through that huge cap of his: 'You did the right thing, Einar. The bastard deserved to die.'

VETTAKOLLEN

J an Morell's home showed signs that someone had left in a
hurry.

Some time ago. The old things were lovely. Not only the
antiques, of which there was an abundance in the house. A large
rose-painted chest in the hall, embellished with the date 1782,
looked as if it had never been spoiled by renovation. A rocking
chair, equally unmistakably advanced in years, sat in one corner
of the living room, with beautiful damask cushions and a pile of
books stacked on a small sideboard on the right. Here and there
the furnishings looked like small enclaves of cosiness and solici-
tude, items chosen with care to suit the exposed log cabin walls of
dark-stained, heavy timber.

The rest was hi-tech.

The living room was all black leather and steel, placed on a
chalk-white shag-pile rug. Two settees were arranged facing each
other, with a table of polished concrete between them. On the
north wall hung the biggest TV screen Selma Falck had ever seen
in a private home – it must have been around eighty inches wide.
A panorama window had been carved into the south-facing wall,
in absurd violation of the house's original architecture. Selma
guessed that the view would be magnificent on a good day.

Now it had started raining in the darkness.

Katinka Morell still existed in this house: in the bookcases and
the ornaments, maybe even in the carefully arranged knitting left

on the rocking chair, as if on display. It didn't help much, though, because the living room seemed chilly. Maybe especially because the hearth on the other side of the TV was an enormous, dismal, black hole that dominated the room. It should really have been constantly lit, Selma thought as she found herself shivering.

Hege Chin Morell stood in the doorway of what must be the kitchen. Selma could hear someone in there, and the rattling of china being unloaded from a dishwasher. Jan Morell had already taken a seat on one of the two settees.

'Sit down,' he told Hege.

She remained on her feet. Selma approached her with out-stretched hand.

'Hello. I'm Selma Falck.'

Hege's handshake was cool and fleeting. She nodded briefly, mumbled her name, let go her hand and headed for the settee where she sat facing her father. Selma chose to sit beside her. The sliding door into the kitchen slid shut with a peculiar sound.

'You can tell Selma everything,' Jan said. 'But before we start, I just want to say this.'

Leaning forward, he spread his thighs, plumped his elbows on his knees and folded his hands. He stared intently at his daughter.

'You're allowed to make mistakes,' he said. 'I've always said that, and you know I mean it. Everyone makes mistakes. We all do stupid things. Nasty things, some of us even do cruel things at times. We all deserve a second chance. I've messed up too, before I met your mum, and ...'

'I don't know much about that.'

'Whatever,' he said, brushing her off. 'This time it's not about me. And if you've done something stupid, something illegal or something detrimental, then you have to say so now. There's always a way to move on, Hege. Always a way. OK?'

She nodded.

'Good,' he said in a clipped tone, as he leaned back. 'Go ahead and talk.'

'I don't know where to begin,' Hege said. 'It's a bit difficult to grasp what you ... what on earth you might be able to do. I've submitted a positive drugs test despite never having taken drugs. Everyone says, and not least writes, that there's no hope now. Dad has ...'

Until now she had been looking down at her own hands that were fiddling with a loose thread on her sweater. Now she looked up and straight at Selma.

'So there's nothing wrong with the test. That seems clear. Dad's already looked into what's ...'

'I'm continuing to follow that aspect,' her father said. 'Even though it seems futile. Tell Selma about ...'

'Jan!'

Now Selma was the one doing the interrupting.

'Either you stay silent, or else you leave the room. If there's any point at all in this conversation, I have to be the one in charge of it. OK?'

The man lethargically raised his hands in the air.

'I choose to believe you,' Selma continued calmly, looking at Hege. 'And if you haven't consciously taken drugs, then in all honesty there are only two possibilities. Either you've ingested this banned substance inadvertently, or you've been exposed to sabotage. If it's been an accident, you're in the soup all the same. To avoid suspension, you have to be entirely blameless. For all practical purposes, it's only sabotage or something in that direction that can save your skin. So we'll go for that one, OK?'

She smiled in an effort to be encouraging, but it didn't feel particularly successful.

'You've been through the Cross-Country Skiing Federation's anti-doping course, I take it, and know that objective responsibility is ...'

'I've never done it.'

'What?'

'That course. I've actually never ...'

'Isn't it compulsory?'

'Yes, but there hasn't been ... time for it, really.'

Selma licked her lips and took a deep breath.

'OK. I see.'

'But I know about objective responsibility, of course. That I'm the one who has to prove I'm completely innocent in the case, rather than the drugs authorities having to prove I'm guilty.'

'Exactly.'

'But I'm absolutely, incredibly careful! Maggi arranges everything for me. Dad has had a detailed list compiled of all I can eat, drink and take by way of dietary supplements. Maggi prepares everything. Heavens above ...'

For the first time Selma could discern an underlying desperation in her voice. Until now she had been pretty subdued, almost apathetic, as if she had already given up.

'How many travel days do you have?' Selma asked.

'Eh ... between 220 and 240 a year? Something like that.'

'Does Maggi accompany you on these trips?'

'No, of course not.'

'Then that's the point. You have to be really precise when you're talking to me, Hege. I do believe that Maggi takes good care of you when you're at home. But, you see, you're not here for most of the year. You're travelling. You stay in hotels. You're on planes, buses and cars. Lots of different people make and serve food for you. You also use medicines.'

Nodding, Hege continued to play with the loose thread. Her sweater was about to unravel completely.

'If we regard this case as a bet of sorts, then I'd say the odds are ...'

Selma waved her hand back and forth, hesitating.

'One in a hundred,' she finally said. 'Two in a hundred. Somewhere in that area. If you're not one hundred per cent truthful and specific when you're talking to me, then we're closer to one in a million. Those are extremely high odds. Which means bad odds, for everyone except for the bookmaker.'

She paused. A thought had crossed her mind. Hege had at last left her sweater in peace. Now the young woman was picking at her watch, an Omega Constellation with mother-of-pearl face and diamonds instead of numbers.

'Naturally, I have a professional duty of confidentiality,' Selma said, fixing her eyes on Jan Morell. 'As a lawyer, I have that. Even if Hege is going to use Hjorth & Co for the legal part of the case, it's best if we decide here and now that I'm also her lawyer. With a different mandate. Don't you think, Jan?'

For some reason the man was always suntanned. Now, however, a distinct blush suffused his cheekbones, and his jaw muscles were taut.

'Don't you think?' Selma repeated. 'It's best that I'm Hege's lawyer, if not in fact then at least in name? That protects us both.'

'OK,' he said softly, after a pause so long that Hege seemed nonplussed. 'For as long as you remain a lawyer.'

The blush had spread to his neck.

Maggi entered from the kitchen, carrying a tray with three mugs, a teapot and a plate of chocolate biscuits that looked home-baked.

'It's too late for coffee,' she said with an obvious accent. 'But maybe something to warm you up?'

She placed the things on the table, tucked the tray under her arm and disappeared just as noiselessly as she had come. The sliding door into the kitchen closed with an almost inaudible swish, almost like the doors on the USS *Enterprise*. Selma caught herself wondering if it was motorized. In all honesty, this was a remarkable house, but the bet had already started to pay dividends. In the meantime, it would be unnecessary for her to hand in her licence to practise law.

One-nil to her.

'Let's begin with the active ingredient,' she said in a loud voice, grasping her mug with both hands. 'Clostebol. Do you have any knowledge of it at all?'

'Yes. It's a steroid. A synthetic anabolic-androgenic steroid. Also known as 4-chlorotestosterone, since it's the 4-chloro derivative of the natural hormone testosterone. Used especially by athletes from the old Eastern Europe. Clostebol has been on the World Anti-Doping Agency's list for ages.'

'Yes, that's right. And you say you haven't gone on that course?'

Selma thought she noticed a hint of embarrassment in Hege. A double blink of the eyes, and a forefinger drawn quickly down her nose.

'One of its uses is in a cream you can buy in Italy,' the young woman said, her voice louder now. 'For cold sores. Well, probably for lots of other things too, but certainly for cold sores.'

'What?'

Jan looked as if his daughter had made a full and extremely surprising confession.

'How on earth do you know that?'

'Because ... when we were in Central Europe in late summer, then ...'

She lifted her face and leaned her head back, as if fighting tears.

'We shouldn't really talk about it.'

'What's this? What is it you shouldn't talk about?'

Jan Morell sat hunched forward, with legs spread and elbows on knees.

'Go out,' Selma told him. 'Now. Please leave.'

Jan's face darkened again, but he gritted his teeth with an audible click and remained seated. Selma made up her mind to give him one last chance. After all, he was the one in possession of the sixteen million kroner she'd been given an opportunity to win back. Sixteen million and a little of her old life.

The old life was fairly high on Selma's wish list.

At least some parts of it.

'What are you talking about?' she said, placing her hand on Hege's lower arm.

'About Hedda Bruun. She's plagued by herpes, you see.'

This was a gross understatement. For several years, Hedda Bruun had been one of the best skiers in the Norwegian national team. Blonde, blue-eyed and gorgeous. Whereas Hege Chin Morell was as athletic as a heptathlete and most renowned for strength, toughness and stylish skiing, Hedda Bruun was small, explosive and displayed a rhythm change Hege had never been able to match.

Hedda Bruun was a poster girl for all things Norwegian, but her lip was a constant, horrid nuisance.

'Sun and arduous training,' Hege went on. 'The cold. Any kind of stress. All of these can make her break out in sores. And when we were in Italy, it looked dreadful. Big and painful, and they split open at night. Her pillow was covered in blood.'

'You shared a room, didn't you?'

'Yes, almost always. That's why I know.'

'Know what?' Jan broke in before, quick as a flash, drawing an imaginary zip across his mouth.

'That Hedda got a tube of ointment called Trof ... Trofodermin. From Stian Bach. The national team's doctor. Her usual ointment was empty, the sore had been there for days, and the doctor had forgotten to bring more.'

'Forgotten?' Selma exclaimed. 'He'd forgotten something as elementary as that?'

'Yes. So he went to the nearest town. Livigno, I think it was. He bought the cream at a pharmacy there and gave it to Hedda. We were in our room when he came with it, it was quite late. Most people had gone to bed by then. Hedda asked Stian if the cream contained any of the ingredients on the banned drugs list. He said no and told her she could use it.'

She put two thumbs in the air.

'That's what he did. Thumbs up. And then he left. But Hedda, she's ...'

Hege hesitated. She leaned over the plate of biscuits and reached out her hand before changing her mind and straightening her back.

'If possible, she's even more paranoid than me. So she checked the packaging. That's to say ...'

A solitary frown became visible above her flat nose.

'The tube didn't come with any packaging. It wasn't in a box, you see.'

'Should it have been?' Selma asked. 'Do you know that it comes in a box?'

'Maybe not,' Hege said quickly, and hid her face in the steam from the big mug. 'But there's usually accompanying instructions for use. They're usually inside a box. Aren't they? Anyway ... Hedda read what was printed on the tube. One of the things it said was that the ointment contained Clostebol. The ending of the word freaked her out ... bol, you see! It took only a few seconds on the internet to confirm that she'd been only a hair's breadth from catastrophe.'

'And this was something the national team doctor had given her? Really?'

Hege nodded.

'Hedda was raging. She screamed so loudly that I was afraid she'd wake everyone around us. It was about eleven o'clock at night. We had a long session planned for the next morning, so I got pretty stressed out.'

'What happened then?'

'Hedda wanted to go to the president of cross-country skiing. To Bottolf. Bottolf Odda. At once. I've never seen her so furious. The sore on her lip burst open from all her ranting and raving. She looked like ...'

A rare smile crossed her face. Hege Chin Morell was a beautiful woman, with regular features and large, narrow eyes, but she smiled far too infrequently. Even after winning, she was serious and sober in interviews. At the beginning of her career, this had been used against her by sports journalists, especially reading between the lines, but eventually as the medals came rolling in, her lack of visible pleasure was taken as a sign of concentration and dedication. For the first time, Selma noticed she had an alluring dimple just beside the left corner of her mouth.

'Dracula. She looked like a vampire. Blood was trickling down her chin.'

'And then?'

'I managed to calm her down a little. Offered to fetch Bottolf, since she was so upset. And then I did that. Luckily, he was awake.'

'Was he on his own?'

'Yes ... yes, he was. He was dressed and alone and came with me at once.'

The sci-fi sound of the kitchen door made them all turn their eyes.

'Do you need anything else?'

Maggi had taken off her apron.

'No,' Jan said curtly. 'You can go to bed. I'd like breakfast at six a.m.'

The Polish home help nodded in acknowledgement before

disappearing into the hall. Selma assumed that the stairs down to the basement went from there.

'Goodnight, Maggi!'

Hege waved at her back, like a little child.

'And then?' Selma asked once the home help had gone.

'Bottolf listened to Hedda. Examined the tube. He agreed, absolutely, that Stian had made a mistake. A massive blunder. He praised Hedda for being vigilant and then asked us to keep our mouths shut.'

Jan Morell looked as if he would leap up from the settee on the other side of the highly polished concrete table. Now his face was deep red. The look Selma gave him forced him back into his seat.

'What do you mean, you should keep your mouths shut?' she asked Hege.

'In Bottolf 's opinion, no damage had actually been done. Since Hedda hadn't used the ointment. And if other people got to know about this, it would all come out. To the press. Become public knowledge, you know. A whole gang of journalists had been there a few days earlier. To suss out the lay of the land, so to speak, a couple of months before the start of the season. But they had gone. If we just said nothing, no one would know anything about it.'

'Who would gain by that? Stian Bach?'

Hege let her ponytail slide through her left hand. Her hairline drew a straight, almost diabolical, V across her forehead. A lot of hair had come loose from the elastic band in the course of the evening, thick, black strands that were plastered to her neck. She seemed sweaty, even though the temperature in the uncomfortable living room was on the cool side.

'No. It would be best for Hedda, he claimed. If this got out, her name would come up in conjunction with a doping case. On the internet, you know. When people did a search on her name. Bottolf said it was vital not to tell a soul, and he'd take care of the rest.'

'Search on the internet?' Selma said, perplexed.

It was completely illogical. If you conducted a search on, for example, 'Ole Einar Bjørndalen' and 'doping' in the same field, then it was dead certain that you'd end up with a shedload of results. Because he'd been staunchly opposed to that kind of thing. Not because he'd been suspected of or caught cheating.

She fished out her mobile and rapidly keyed in three words on Google.

'Look at this,' she said, holding the display up to Hege. 'More than 1,100 hits on my name cross-referenced with 'doping'. Because I've dealt with drugs cases, both for Anti-Doping Norway and the Court of Arbitration for Sport. No one has ever, on any occasion, accused me of taking drugs for that reason! Did he really say that?'

'Yes.'

'And you both went along with that?'

'Yes. What should we have done?'

Selma slumped back in the settee. With a loud sigh.

'What about confronting the doctor? As far as I know, he's still the national team doctor. Do you know what consequences this had for him? If any?'

'No. Apart from Hedda refusing to have anything further to do with him. Me too, for that matter. To be on the safe side.'

'Has nobody ever reacted to that, then?'

'No. Hedda went home from Italy before the rest of us to receive treatment for her herpes sores. When we got back, another doctor had already been appointed to the team. Both Hedda and I have used her ever since.'

Something occurred to Selma. Her fingers tapped in another search on her mobile.

'19 September,' she muttered before raising her voice: 'The Norwegian Cross-Country Skiing Federation has employed Vibeke Stenshaug as a new assistant national team doctor. "This consolidates our efforts at every level," commented Bottolf Odda at a press conference, and continued: "Vibeke will contribute to the further professionalization of the medical care provided for our athletes in a steadily more demanding and physically exhausting sport." My God. They buried the whole foul-up.'

Jan Morell sat bolt upright. Without a word, he crossed the living room to a door. Selma had no idea where it led.

'You're phoning no one,' she said sharply at the top of her voice. 'Jan! You're phoning no one, do you hear me!'

He came to a sudden halt.

'Listen to me,' she said, rising to her feet. 'This is a really interesting story. What it has to do with Hege's case, we've no idea as yet. Possibly nothing. But the fact is that we now, only a few hours since you asked me to take a closer look at what might have happened, have stumbled upon something highly irregular. This is an ace up our sleeve. If we reveal that we have it, it loses its value.'

'This case isn't about Hege,' he said. 'It's about cronyism. It's about our whole bloody system being based on the idea of protecting one another. So that they can swan around with VIPs and ...'

'Jan!'

Selma took two steps towards him, stopped and spread her arms in a gesture of dismay.

'You know the Cross-Country Skiing Federation better than me. But I'm a better player, don't you think?'

As he opened his mouth to answer, with a sharp retort if his expression was anything to go by, she corrected herself loudly: 'More experienced. I've more experience in gambling than you.'

He didn't answer. Didn't nod. But at least he stood still.

'Don't show our hand, Jan. This is only the first card. We have to collect a few more if we're to have any chance of winning. Don't toss this card down on the table just yet.'

After a brief pause, encouraged by the fact that he still hadn't made a move, she added: 'Please.'

'OK. Fine. But now I have to turn in. You can leave now.'

'Promise me you won't do anything.'

He murmured something that could be interpreted as a promise, and then he was gone.

At the same moment, Hege wilted.

Cowering on the settee, she sat with her arms tightly curled around her legs and her face partially hidden behind her knees.

Selma couldn't understand her.

In the outside world, Hege Chin Morell was polite to everyone, loyal to her teammates and friendly towards spectators. Especially if they were children. In 2016 she had been named a UNICEF ambassador and, instead of two World Cup races during the pre-season period, had chosen to give reports from a refugee camp in Greece linked with a fundraising campaign on TV2. To the obvious disapproval of the Norwegian Cross-Country Skiing Federation's senior management, although it didn't affect her in the least. In such cases she was determined, almost headstrong, while at other times she could appear so evasive that she seemed immature. Spineless, even, Selma had thought on a couple of occasions. Hege Chin was a regular target for racist trolls, especially on far-right pages where the kindest name for her was 'Ching-Chong'. To the equally regular questions from the press about her reaction to that sort of thing, she never gave a more forceful answer than some reference to freedom of speech. And then she made herself scarce.

'I'm convinced someone has sabotaged me,' Hege said all of a sudden, staring straight at her. 'We're not talking about an accident. Neither by me nor by anyone in my circle.'

'Yes?'

'I just can't comprehend who would be interested in doing that. I mean ...'

Her voice cracked.

'Who am I? I go skiing, Selma! I move as fast as I can with metal runners under my feet and poles in my hands. I pick up a few medals and dress in red, white and blue. It's sport. When all's said and done, it's a game. Who in the world has any interest in sabotaging a sportswoman?'

Selma was tempted to mention Tonya Harding.

'What makes you so sure?' she asked instead.

'I'm so careful. At least as careful as Hedda. She managed to safeguard herself, thanks to her own vigilance.'

Suddenly Selma felt dizzy.

It was late. She couldn't remember the last time she had eaten. On reflection, she couldn't fathom what she was doing in this dismal mausoleum in Vettakollen at all. The girl on the settee could expect six months' suspension or something of that order, from what she herself had called 'just a game'. She didn't feel sorry for Hege. In truth she, Selma, was the one there was reason to feel sympathy for. She was the one who had lost everything. Her husband and children, house and home and the whole fucking business.

Anine. Johannes.

Don't think about the children. Don't.

Selma tucked her hair behind her ear and swallowed. At least the children knew she wasn't ill. She wanted to say something, but knew her voice would barely carry.

'Dad said you used to be an Olympic champion,' Hege said.

'Then he's lying,' Selma said, clearing her throat. 'I got silver in the Olympics. Twice. Eighty-eight and ninety-two. And a World Championships bronze in eighty-six.'

'And then you won *Shall We Dance?* last year.'

Now she was smiling again.

'*Shall We Dance?* was harder to win than you'd think. But I have to go. We won't get any more done tonight. It's Friday now. I'll make the train if I get a move on.'

Hege followed her out into the hallway. Selma put on her jacket and scarf and remembered she'd left *The Investigator's ABC* on an old telephone table beside the front door when she arrived.

It was still lying there. She drew on her gloves and tucked the book under her arm before letting Hege open the door.

Outside, a fine layer of snow had enveloped everything. Not enough to make the ground white, but a grey coating of slush had settled on the lawn, the footpath leading to the road and the bottom three granite steps.

Someone had been here. Very recently. The footprints were obvious. A person, a man to judge by the size of the prints, had come up from the road. He had been on the steps. The top steps were sheltered by an awning and were free of snow, but at the foot you could see that the person in question had walked up and down the steps before making what had to be a circuit of the house. At any rate, the footprints clearly traversed the lawn in a south-east direction and disappeared around the corner. From the south-west, the prints made a return. In the end the stranger had crossed the lawn diagonally towards the hedge at the bottom of the property.

There was no one to be seen. It was remarkably quiet.

'Does the doorbell work?' Selma asked crisply.

'Yes. At least it did earlier today. I can test if ...'

Selma just managed to stop her hand on its way to the substantial brass button.

'Don't disturb the others.'

'But someone's been here! Somebody's ...'

She pointed at the footprints on the grass. The figure had stood at a distance of only five or six metres from the vast panorama window. A slushy patch of one square metre or so was completely trampled.

'He's been staring at us. From there you can see right into the living room. Why has he ... Why didn't we spot him?'

'It's light inside and dark outside,' Selma said, more brusquely than she'd intended.

'We have to call the police.'

'The police? To tell them that someone's taken a walk around your house? I don't think that's a good idea.'

'But ...'

Selma turned on her heel and gripped Hege by the shoulders. She caught her eye in the light from the exterior lamp on the overhang above them.

'It's most likely been a journalist,' she said as calmly as she could. 'Those people know no boundaries, not at all. Don't be afraid. Go to bed now. There's no danger, OK? Only a journalist. You know what they're like. Jan said they were here in force earlier this evening. The police were here too, I understand. With dogs and the whole shooting match. To chase them out of the garden. One of them has just been a bit more persistent than the others. Even bolder.'

'He's been watching us. In my own living room. He's been staring at me! They'd all gone, every single last one of them, before you arrived, and I opened the curtains because they were no longer ...'

'Hege!'

Selma gave her a shake.

'Listen to me. It was a journalist, OK? Off you go to bed. Now. Draw the curtains, and then they won't bother you again. You have to make a list. Of absolutely everyone you can think of who could lay you open to sabotage. Through food. Contact. Drink. Medicines. Voodoo, for that matter. A list. Can you manage that, Hege?'

Selma saw that the girl was shaking. Carefully, she pushed her into the hall, giving her the most reassuring smile she could muster, and closed the door without waiting for an answer. She took her mobile from her pocket and began to follow the stranger's trail around the house in the light from the pocket torch function.

The prints were surprisingly clear. Selma had been mistaken. The man, or woman in big shoes, hadn't just been here. At least an hour must have elapsed. The prints were made in soft slush, which had frozen to ice immediately afterwards. The edges were knife-sharp.

Size forty-six, Selma guessed after holding her hand over a particularly distinct print. She took three photos of it, one of them with her keys neatly arranged beside it as a measure, and straightened her back.

Naturally, it could have been a journalist.

Selma had come across many journalists in her life, and they sometimes sported strange footwear. All the same, she had yet to meet a journalist at work in such expensive ski boots.

To be more precise, Fischer RCS Skate Boots, she was certain.

In fact she had the same boots herself.

As had almost all members of the national cross-country ski team.

THE MANUSCRIPT

101 OFFICE INTERIOR, OSLO CITY CENTRE, DAY

Open windows with curtains fluttering. Obviously summer. A MAN sitting on a settee. He is holding both hands around a mug of steaming tea. A WOMAN is seated on an office chair, with a sideboard beside her, where there is also a teacup. She has a notepad on her lap, but has put down her pen. She is swinging quietly from side to side, with her legs crossed.

WOMAN: How can you be so sure?
MAN: The story fits. The skis ...

(PAUSE)

WOMAN: Lots of people had skis like those.
MAN (somewhat discouraged): Not at that time. Besides, I Googled it. Searched through the archives. Afterwards. After they were there. At the Ski Museum. Everything fits.
WOMAN: Does it mean anything?
MAN: You're asking if it means anything?
WOMAN: Yes.
MAN: Of course it means something!

The WOMAN looks down at her notepad. Closes it. The MAN drinks the hot liquid. He suddenly bends down to the floor and puts down the cup. Looks around, spots a used cup on the desk. Picks it up and puts it down at the other side of his feet, in exact symmetry with the first one.

WOMAN: What does it mean, then?

MAN (obviously upset): Everything! Of course it means everything! I've been talking to you for nearly a year now, you have to appreciate that this is important!

WOMAN (nodding calmly as she leans back in her chair): So you say, but I'd like you to elaborate. After all these years, how can this be so significant?

MAN: Well … you see … then it wasn't my fault.

Tram brakes screech. There is heavy traffic outside.

MAN (cont.): I feel liberated. More settled. It's as if I've really succeeded at something, at last. I've searched for them for such a long time.

(LENGTHY PAUSE)

WOMAN: Have you really? Searched for them?

MAN: Yes, definitely. Not physically as such. That seemed so impossible. But in a way I've been searching. Coming to you has been a way of finding them.

WOMAN (smiling): Is that so? I wasn't the one who showed you the photo from the Ski Museum!

MAN: No, but you're the one who made me stronger. More aware. More certain of what I have to do now. You said it yourself: I have to distinguish between what is in my power to change, and the factors that lie beyond my control.

WOMAN (nodding): I see. What is it you now have the power to do that wasn't possible for you to do before?

A door slams outside the office.

WOMAN (cont.): Can you give a more detailed description of what this sense of relief feels like?

The MAN sits still for a few seconds, and shrugs.

WOMAN: What has changed?

MAN: Everything. Everything has changed. Things can come into balance. Everything can be different.

WOMAN (smiling): Everything, no less. That's good.

MAN: They've owned me for such a long time. Now I'm the one who owns them. The tables are turned. I call it karma.

WOMAN (distracted): That's good.

The WOMAN looks at her watch. The MAN gets to his feet.

MAN: Yes, it's good that everything's going to be different now. At long last.

THE LYNX

The animal was eighteen months old and at the beginning of his first whole winter without his mother and siblings. He was unusually large. His fur had been soft and reddish-brown in summer, but by late autumn it had thickened up into a greyish-white, thick coat. After loping several kilometres through pouring rain, he now merged into the winter-shrivelled landscape, almost bare of snow.

His mother had taught him that days were for rest. The evening was the lynx's hunting time, he knew, even though he often broke the rule. He had the sight of an eagle and moved soundlessly, even in pitch darkness. And he was curious.

His mother had given him a cuff on the ear every now and again.

Whereas his two sisters were naturally shy and drew back at the least sign of danger, his urge to explore led him into more problems than his mother could countenance. By February she had chased him away. This was before she had mated again; her cub was still too young to manage by himself, and for all she knew, he might have perished before he had lost the scent of his old family.

He had not.

He had wandered south and seen many things. Fewer than sixteen hours ago, he had brought down a one-year-old roe deer in Nordmarka, beside the hill that bore his generic name. There was plenty of wild game in the forest here, and he intended to settle down. The urge to mate had started to trouble him, but something deep inside told him that must wait for another couple of months yet. The world was still too dark.

He hadn't come across any bitches yet anyway.

That could wait.

Pedestrians were the only things that bothered him about his newly established territory. Even deep within the forest, where the tracks were narrowest, the paths criss-crossed the terrain and human beings used them constantly. Down here, beside the biggest track of them all, he had never ventured. He stood between the spruce trunks, a safe distance from the road, where he saw a car drive past. The engine noise made him draw back, but not far. He was a courageous lynx, and when it grew quiet, almost completely silent, he dared to move out again.

He spotted prey in the stream.

A human, he realized when he caught the scent on the light breeze from the west. No more of those noisy machines came along, and after a few minutes he padded quietly down to the stream bed, exactly where it disappeared into a concrete pipe beneath the road that bisected Maridalen lengthwise.

It smelled dead. The blood, however, still tasted fresh when the lynx lapped it up, just below the dead man's hard skull. The carcase was lying on its stomach, with its face in the water. The scent of blood burned his nostrils, but most of all the rank smell of human being.

The lynx was still replete after the prey he had felled and eaten before daybreak. Besides, he preferred to kill his own meat.

Carcases were emergency rations.

He slurped down even more blood. Lingered for a few seconds in front of the dead human's feet as he sniffed inquisitively at the peculiar sticks attached to each of them. The lynx snatched at one of these, but it was stuck fast and didn't taste good. When a little wheel began to spin, even the most courageous of lynxes was startled.

The rain was still pouring down, swelling the stream.

The lynx withdrew into the forest at the top of the road.

He disappeared into the moss between the wet trees and never looked back.

THE MESSAGE

'You can't mean that, Selma.'

Vanja Vegge stared indignantly at her over her red wine glass with a stem so long and slim that Selma feared Vanja's rage would cause it to break.

'That would be a conspicuous breach of professional ethics!'

She stopped the glass on its way to her mouth and put it down again as she shook her head.

'In the first place I wouldn't be able to take you on as a patient no matter how much you needed it. You don't treat your closest friends, Selma. Secondly, anyway, I can't possibly issue any declaration that you're receiving treatment from me if that has no basis in reality! What's more, there isn't anything wrong with you. What would you need me for? Other than as a friend? Have you gone ...'

Selma took a deep breath and let the air ooze out through puffed cheeks.

'Fine. Forget it.'

She grabbed the Pepsi Max glass and drained it in one. Her restlessness made her twirl the empty glass on the table. Didn't want to, but had to. Put it down with a bang.

'Fabulous food. Thanks a million. I have to think of leaving now.'

Vanja Vegge put her hand, rattling with five bracelets and huge rings on all her fingers, on top of Selma's.

'What's going on with you? What's actually happened?'

Selma pulled her arm away and camouflaged the dismissive gesture by picking up the napkin and wiping her mouth.

'Nothing.'

'Nothing? I've been trying to get hold of you for a week! Your office says you've left. Left! Sure enough, your secretary gave me the run-around, but in the end it seemed as if she was saying that you're ill. Seriously ill, Selma! Is that true? You don't look even the slightest ill to me, but it's ...'

'I'm not ill, Vanja. I'd be grateful if you could spread that news. It's all due to a misunderstanding, OK?'

'That's great, then! But all the same ... Jesso is grumpy and won't say anything at all. I've tried to contact Anine for three days now, but all your only daughter has said by way of reply is a text message asking me to tell you to go to hell if I find you. What ...'

Selma put down her knife and fork.

Don't think of Anine. Nor of Johannes. Don't think about your children.

'Selma, you're crying!'

Vanja's voice dropped a notch and her words came more slowly.

'You can't cry, Selma. That should be physiologically impossible. What's happened?'

'Nothing. Absolutely nothing. I'm not actually crying. Look!'

She leaned forward and opened her eyes wide. Vanja mumbled something inaudible. Selma forced a smile and blinked quickly.

'There really are no tears. Just a bit moist, which is fine.'

'Why have you moved out? The only thing Jesso would tell me was that you're no longer living on Ormøya. Where are you living, then? It was fine for us not to talk about this while we were eating, but now I really must insist that ...'

The doorbell rang.

Hesitating, Vanja looked in irritation at the clock.

'Wait a minute,' she commanded as she got to her feet. 'Don't go.'

Selma did not go. She was in no fit state to leave. She was hardly able to do anything at all. She'd been at Vanja's for more than two hours now without talking to her. Of course, she had chatted nineteen to the dozen. Selma Falck was good at small talk, best of them all; she had prattled her way through a long and extraordinarily successful life. On the other hand, she could barely recall the last time she had talked to anyone. About what should really be talked about, but for which there were no words. The situation had forced out of her bits and pieces of the story about everything that had led her here. It had been impossible to avoid. Jesso had to know something of the truth, of course; she had practically hounded her husband into losing everything and owed him some sort of explanation. The children, too, the nineteen-year-old who still lived at home to some extent and the twenty-three-year-old daughter who was studying law and planned to marry next summer. Selma had revealed very little to her husband and children, a tiny scrap of the true story, hardly anything at all, but enough to have Selma disinvited on the spot from Anine's forthcoming sumptuous wedding.

Stop. Don't think about them. Not about the children.

'You have friends, Selma. Unbelievably many friends who wish you well.'

Vanja's voice drifted through from the hallway as she apparently fumbled with the lock.

'And I'm the best of them all. Now we're going to have a heart-to-heart. We've the whole night ahead of us. I'm not letting you leave!'

Selma shut her eyes.

Took a deep breath, and tried to make her face resume its usual contours. She wanted to be her usual self. The competent, glib, popular Selma Falck that everyone knew, and who had been selected as the country's best dressed woman as recently as 2015. Now she could smell her own body odour. Only faintly, and partially camouflaged by the Penhaligon's perfume and an ancient hoodie with NORWAY emblazoned on the back, but noticeable all the same. The bathroom in her temporary apartment was, if possible, even more repellent than the living room, and she hadn't showered for the past two days.

She knew of a poker group in Ensjø. They usually began around midnight.

She had to go.

She stood up unsteadily, with both palms resting on the table. With her feet planted well apart, without shoes, she saw now that she was wearing one black and one grey sock, and she had shot up from her chair when she heard Vanja scream.

At first she did not understand what it was. The sound was so unfamiliar and unexpected that her brain needed a few seconds to confirm that it was a human scream she had heard. Then the sound had to be placed in context: it came from the hallway in Vanja and Kristina's excessively colourful apartment.

From Vanja's throat.

Selma broke into a run.

'What's up?' she said when she came to a sudden halt in the doorway of the long, narrow hallway.

Two men.

One was from the police, an older guy in uniform. An inspector, Selma could tell from the stripes on his shoulder. Experienced, she saw from the appropriately mournful face and the hefty hand on Vanja's shoulder. The other man was far younger. He was wearing a dark suit and clerical collar. His glasses were threatening to slide off his small snub nose.

'Is that you?' the pastor blurted out. 'Selma Falck?'

The policeman's eyes darkened.

'Unfortunately, there's been an accident,' he said quietly. 'Is Kristina Holm here?'

Vanja tore herself loose from the inspector's grasp.

She had started to howl.

'No,' Selma said, approaching Vanja with purposeful steps. 'Kristina's in Tromsø this weekend. What has happened?'

The howl became a shriek. Selma only just managed to catch hold of her friend as she began to fall. The wail grew gradually weaker and higher, like a band saw as it became hot.

The pastor seemed alarmed and pressed himself against the wall.

'We asked to come in,' he bleated. 'It wasn't our intention to talk about this out here in the hallway. Maybe we should sit down and ... She just knew!'

Selma looked at the police officer. The police officer looked at Selma. His pale-blue eyes were as old as the hills, with a greyish film behind one pupil.

'There's been an accident,' he said again. 'I'm sorry to tell you that Haakon Holm-Vegge is dead.'

Vanja fainted, but Selma held her tightly and would never let go.

THE TIP-OFF

It was only by a whisker that the young journalist – newly appointed to a six-month temporary post in the *Dagens Gang* newspaper's sports section – even checked the text message on his mobile when it buzzed. The woman he had brought home from the city centre around eleven p.m. was already naked, and he himself was only in a sweater. Things were going well.

'Wait a minute,' he panted, reaching out towards the coffee table.

'Forget that for now,' she groaned, pulling him towards her with a firm grip on his buttocks.

The temptation was irresistible.

'Two seconds,' he said nevertheless. 'Just two seconds.'

One minute later he was heading out the door.

And almost fully dressed.

SATURDAY 9 DECEMBER 2017

THE PRESS CONFERENCE

S elma quickly realized she shouldn't have come.

Despite not being a journalist, of which everyone was well aware, she had been able to enter without difficulty one of the biggest conference rooms in the Norwegian Cross-Country Skiing Federation's glass palace below the Holmenkollen national ski complex. The room, named the Dæhlie auditorium after the famous cross-country skier, Bjørn Dæhlie, had windows facing north-west. A December storm had roared in from that direction several hours earlier. The vast glass panes were now monochrome grey and dripping wet, and they were visibly moving with each powerful gust of wind. As more journalists kept swarming into the room, a young woman in an overly tight skirt struggled to make the mechanical curtains work.

Without success.

As soon as Selma sat down in one of the furthest-back seats, a microphone was thrust into her face.

'*Dagbladet* here! Who do you represent, Selma Falck? What's the reason for ...'

She pushed the microphone carefully away.

The night had lasted a lifetime, and she had not slept.

The pastor had disappeared from Vanja's apartment when Selma asked him to. The police inspector had stayed until he had contacted a doctor. The doctor had arrived, talked to Selma in hushed tones, left three pills in a small envelope and then left with the policeman.

Only Selma had stayed until morning came.

At ten a.m., Kristina had landed at Gardermoen airport, just in time before the entire airport was closed because of the bad weather. She was chalk white and red-eyed, with a shapeless mouth distorted by crying. During the night, in quiet spells while Vanja dozed, Selma had contacted their closest friends. Two of them had booked plane tickets, met Kristina at the airport and brought her home. In the meantime, several of them had silently set up camp in their apartment. Most of them old teammates, and they had come for the long haul. Selma could finally leave.

Only after 2,000 metres in the swimming pool at the Tøyen Baths had she felt somewhat restored. She had gone home and picked up some clothes from the only box Darius hadn't yet peed into, and felt presentable for the first time in ages.

'Selma Falck,' whispered a middle-aged man in jeans and an orange padded waistcoat.

He had assumed a sympathetic expression, but nevertheless failed to disguise his curiosity.

'Condolences. Truly. Haakon was your godson, wasn't he?'

Selma didn't want to answer. But Selma Falck always gave an answer.

'Yes,' she said softly. 'And thank you.'

She really shouldn't have come.

Vanja became Selma's friend on Monday 20 August 1973. In the photograph of the new Primary One class, they both had red satchels with white seams. Pigtails. And each with a ball under her arm, which the teacher hadn't discovered until after the photo had been taken. Selma had defiantly got her own way and was wearing trousers. Vanja was dressed in a skirt and white lacy blouse, and they were placed side by side in the classroom to remain seated like that for ever afterwards. No matter what the teacher said. Many years later they both ended up in the national team, and Vanja would find Kristina. Selma met Jesso and got married, something Kristina and Vanja were unable to do until times changed when Haakon was three years old.

Selma made up her mind to leave before the press conference was under way. She had no business being here. It had been restlessness that had brought her here, she figured: an intense agitation and a hope that she might learn something more than the policeman had been able to impart last night. Bottolf Odda had moved into sight out there on the podium. He was waiting for something or someone, with his hands folded and his eyes cast down. Pale, and wearing a dark suit and tie, Selma could hardly remember ever seeing him dressed like this.

Two enormous vases of flowers were on display. Something that might be a book of condolence had been set up on a small table at the front corner of the room, with a lit candle beside it. This promised to be more of a memorial service than a press conference.

Selma stood up to leave before it all kicked off.

Indecisive, she sat down again.

It was Saturday, a storm was raging outside, and it wouldn't be long until Christmas. She still hadn't bought a single present. It didn't matter; she didn't even know where she would be at Christmas. It wouldn't be on Ormøya, so she had hoped that Vanja and Kristina would invite her now that Vanja had discovered a tiny sliver of Selma's secret.

That would hardly happen now.

Haakon was dead.

At the age of almost twenty-seven, Vanja and Kristina's son had somehow inexplicably run off the road. On roller skis, during one training session of an endless number of training sessions. Up by Skar, to all appearances, he had turned and embarked on his return journey down to the city. It was not far. The details surrounding the accident were still extremely unclear, as the policeman had explained last night. Haakon had sustained a head injury and apparently fractured his arm, but neither of these was sufficient to kill anyone. The stream he had been lying in was barely half a metre deep at most, but his body had been found face down. Drowning was the probable cause of death. That was how it looked at present, the inspector had carefully and repeatedly maintained.

We would have to wait and see.

Selma stood up again and tried to make her way out. It was difficult; the surge of journalists and photographers and other people with more or less loose connections to ski sports was never-ending. The ubiquitous Sølve Bang traipsed around at the front, adjusting the bouquets of flowers, and speaking in a quiet, earnest voice to the people seated in the front row.

A caricaturist had once depicted Sølve Bang as Batman's arch-fiend the Penguin. The drawing was so like the original and so exquisitely malicious that the artist had been sued for defamation. The conflict had fortunately never reached a courtroom. It didn't even get to the stage of reconciliation.

It had just evaporated, after Selma had explained as calmly as she could, one or two things about freedom of speech in general and caricatures in particular to her exalted as well as offended client. Sølve Bang had never paid her for that work. But he had at least given up.

Selma was not the only person who had difficulty understanding the man's influence at the Norwegian Cross-Country Skiing Federation. He had one or two formal duties, such as being on the Selection Committee and the Ethics Board, but none of these corresponded with his true position and power.

The way he looked now, no one would believe he was once one of the world's greatest cross-country skiing talents.

At the age of sixteen years and nine months, Sølve Bang had won a World Cup race for seniors. Ahead of Koch, Wassberg and Harri Kirvesniemi, the best skiers of the 1982 season. The three veterans had all been slightly miffed that the young lad had even been allowed the chance to have a start number on his chest. He was far too young.

For the rest of that season, Sølve Bang had participated in the age-appropriate classes. And won most of them. His next season was not so glorious, and when he turned eighteen, it looked as if it was all over. He wasn't injured, and he had trained tenaciously, but it was as if he had shot his bolt. All at once, in an explosion of effort, in the later fabled race in which a rosy-cheeked boy with fuzz on his upper lip had shown the elite of the world how to ski a fifteen-kilometre course.

When he retired at the age of nineteen, the skiing fraternity shrugged their shoulders. History was full of early bloomers, talents that never became any more than that. However, they had not quite managed to forget his name when that same autumn, only a few months after hanging up his skis, he made his debut as a novelist with a book that was sold to thirty-two countries and snatched up most of the existing literary prizes in 1985 and 1986.

Forgotten Tracks was the name of the book, a historical romance about the unknown, extremely young Birkebeiner Sturla Tryggvasson, supporter of Norway's King Sverre, the true hero of the race to bring the king's son, Håkon Håkonsson, to Nidaros in 1206. *Incredible invention!* cheered the reviewer in *Dagens Gang* when the book was published, while others gave it top marks and splashed it on the front pages.

That mostly took care of things.

So far, so good.

Since then Sølve Bang had produced a book around once a decade, without ever repeating the success of the time when he hadn't yet turned twenty. All the same he had established a name for himself, or perhaps more accurately retained it, as one of the major figures of Norwegian literature. Selma Falck did not know why, but then she didn't have much of a clue about books.

About sports, on the other hand, she was fairly expert.

Fortunately Sølve had not caught sight of her, and she tried to duck down in her chair. It was too late to make a serious attempt at escape. The lady with the tight skirt had closed the door and stood sentry there, rigid and serious.

Silence fell.

Bottolf Odda picked up the microphone.

'Welcome,' he said in a sombre voice, and cleared his throat. 'The Cross-Country Skiing Federation has called this brief press conference to mark the tragic accident yesterday evening in which our national team member, Haakon Holm-Vegge, lost his life.'

It grew even quieter in the Dæhlie auditorium, if that were possible.

'At this time, our thoughts go first and foremost to Haakon's close family. His partner Elise and their one-year-old son William, of course, and also Haakon's parents, Vanja Vegge and Kristina Holm. We. Share. Your. Grief.'

He seemed about to break down. The pause was so lengthy that it would have been embarrassing in any other circumstances.

'As you know,' he continued at last, 'Haakon was struggling with a minor shoulder injury that had prevented him from travelling to Davos this weekend. The rest of our women's and men's teams are there for the World Cup races today and tomorrow. It is up to each individual whether or not to continue. Those who wish to do so will be permitted to travel home as soon as possible.'

It was no longer just as quiet. The sound of fingers racing over keyboards combined with the rumble of the storm that had eased in the past half-hour.

'We do not intend to provide any details about what happened in Maridalen. The police will make a more comprehensive statement at the appropriate time. Today I shall simply give a brief explanation of the consequences Haakon's passing will have for the national team, both in the days that lie ahead and for the remainder of the season. After all, Haakon Holm-Vegge was Norway's best cross-country skier of the past two years, and we had all been looking forward to seeing him in PyeongChang in February.'

Once again he had to take a moment.

'But that is not going to happen now,' he mumbled and cleared his throat.

Someone sniggered. Others shushed.

'Well.'

The man straightened his back, took a deep breath and prepared to launch into another speech. That lasted for exactly three minutes, but then he was finished. However, he had not been particularly informative. It was unclear both whether and how this would influence the composition of the team that would travel to Toblach the following weekend. No decision had been taken about how the NCCSF would mark the young skier's far too early death, other than that all skiers would wear black armbands this and next weekend. It was still too premature to set a date for the funeral. That the Crown Prince would, however, be present was something that Bottolf Odda, obviously moved, was pleased to announce.

Selma was far from certain that Vanja and Kristina would allow anything of the kind.

Bottolf Odda had finished speaking. He patted his breast pocket, for no apparent reason, and opened the conference to a brief round of questions. Twenty or so hands shot into the air. The questions that followed were uninteresting, and answered in an even more boring fashion. Finally Selma made a serious effort to stand up and move towards the door.

'Carl Ole Hansgård here, *DG Sport!*'

The journalist's voice was lighter, higher and far more insistent than the others had been.

Selma stopped and glanced over her shoulder. The man who had got to his feet was young and fairly short in stature, with red hair, close cropped to a couple of millimetres over his entire head.

'Will the Federation request a drugs test be carried out on the body of the deceased?' he asked.

'What?'

The Cross-Country President stared at him, uncomprehending.

'We've received ... we have information that Haakon Holm-Vegge may also have ingested a banned substance, the anabolic steroid Clostebol. The same as Hege Chin Morell, in fact. Will this be checked? And if so, when can we expect a result?'

Bottolf Odda had not had a chance to answer when Sølve Bang leapt up from the first row and seized the microphone.

'These are malicious rumours none of us have heard until now,' he said sharply, without a moment's hesitation. 'Haakon Holm-Vegge was one of the loudest voices against drug misuse in the whole world of cross-country skiing. Besides, this is neither the time nor the place for this kind of wild speculation. Out of respect for the bereaved, and not least for our recently deceased close friend and colleague, we will now draw this press conference to a close. Thanks for coming.'

A piercing, high-pitched squeal followed – the woman assigned practical details obviously also had problems with the sound system. The red-haired young man was suddenly popular, but clearly had no intentions of speaking to anyone. His fleeting smile should really be triumphant, Selma thought, but most of all it appeared uncertain. She now stood at the exit. As he passed her, he stopped for a second and greeted her by moving his head back in a gesture of recognition.

'Selma Falck,' he said, quite unnecessarily.

'Yes,' Selma replied, holding out a business card.

To be on the safe side, she had hastily scored out her office number.

'I'd appreciate it if you'd call me at your earliest convenience. On my mobile.'

'Yes of course,' he answered. 'Maybe.'

Hesitated. Tucked the card into his back pocket and moved on through the crowd.

Selma lingered. Only when the Dæhlie auditorium was almost deserted and the woman in the tulip skirt bloomed with impatience at the door, did she shrug on her coat. She didn't quite know where to go. Or could go. The apartment in Toftes gate would never become 'home', but the cat needed to be fed. Maybe she could go to the cinema; as far as she remembered she had fed the animal before she had gone to Vanja's the previous evening. One possibility was going to see Vanja and Kristina, but she didn't feel up to that right now. Tonight, perhaps. Tomorrow. She should actually ring Hege Chin Morell, but since she hadn't moved forward by as much as a metre since the day before yesterday, there was scarcely any point in that either.

Maybe see to Einar.

Something or other.

She had to think of something. It was no longer possible to lie to herself about why she had made the trip up to Holmenkollen.

She had nothing to do there. The truth was that after her sleepless night with Vanja the urge to log on was worse than it had been at any time since she had given up four weeks ago. It was no longer a matter of the usual restlessness that always came sneaking up on her when she had abstained for some time. Not only the pressure inside her head, the discomfort of being unable to concentrate, the agitation that she could easily shake off because she knew what it took. Now the craving felt physically painful, a tight ache in her diaphragm, soreness in her arms and legs, and she could barely manage to stand still.

She was far too close to giving in and so she headed back to the Tøyen Baths and swam another 2,000 metres.

THE MOBILE PHONE

DG Sport's short-term temp Carl Ole Hansgård had scarcely left the Cross-Country Skiing Federation's premises when an older colleague from the same newspaper grabbed him by his jacket shoulder and literally hauled him into his car.

'Are you a total idiot?' he snarled. 'Do you have a brain at all? Is it possible ...'

Lars Winther slammed his fist so hard on the steering wheel that he grimaced.

'... to be so cack-handed? Where did we drag you from? A rubbish dump somewhere, or what?'

'I ... I just meant to ...'

'Shut up. You're so fucking stupid there should be a bounty on your head. Keep your mouth shut.'

Carl Ole fumbled with his seat belt while his experienced colleague fired up the engine, engaged drive and sped out of the area far faster than the weather and driving conditions merited. He skidded wildly as he pulled out on to the road and was forced to slow down a little. They drove on for a minute or so. The foul weather impaired visibility, and Lars Winther had to crane forward to check his bearings as he approached the first possible parking spot.

'What the hell were you talking about up there?' he asked crossly once the car was stationary.

'I asked if they were going to do a drugs test on the body. If they ran such ...'

'I was there, Carl Ole! I heard what you said. But why on earth did you say that?'

'Because I was wondering about it, of course! You'd better cut this out!'

The older journalist closed his eyes. Breathing slowly and heavily, he held the wheel with rigid arms.

'One, two, three.'

Pause. He opened his eyes again.

'OK. But what was your reason for asking if Haakon Holm-Vegge was going to be tested for drugs post-mortem, then?'

'I received a tip-off.'

'A tip-off?'

'Yes. By text message last night. Before we knew he was dead.'

'Eh?'

'At half past eleven. Take a look.'

Quick as a flash, Carl Ole keyed the code into his iPhone and handed it to Lars.

'Here.'

The message had come from a concealed number, Lars noticed before he read aloud: *The skier Haakon Holm-Vegge has died in an accident. If the autopsy is thorough enough, traces of the banned substance Clostebol will be found in his body.*

'Do you see?' Carl Ole asked eagerly. 'I had to ask! This is huge, Lars! Why would anyone send me a message like that if ...'

'Idiot. Shut up.'

He handed back the phone and stared out at the rain with unfocused eyes.

'Messages like that can never be taken at face value just like that, Carl Ole. It's more likely that someone's pulling your leg than that Haakon Holm-Vegge has taken drugs.'

'But ...'

'No, now you have to keep your mouth shut and listen to me. Got it?'

A nod.

'When did this message arrive? To the minute.'

'23.32. Just after half eleven.'

'And the accident took place at some time between eight p.m. and half past, correct? But wasn't made public until after midnight?'

Yet another submissive nod.

'When I got to the *DG* building, there was nothing about the accident anywhere. But before I had a chance to investigate, the news agency issued a press release.'

Lars Winther stretched out his hand to take yet another look at the phone. He forwarded the message to himself, and took a photo of the display with his own phone into the bargain.

'This instant, you must get hold of one of the IT guys. Let them take a closer look and see if it's possible to track down the sender. ASAP, right? More to the point, ask Agnes. She's the best, and I know she's in town this weekend. Get a new phone from her, and tell her to ring me as soon as she's got something.'

'OK. And then what'll I do?'

Lars started the car, flicked on the indicator and drove slowly out on to the road again.

'You'll learn that press conferences are not the place to take up things like that. Write it down on a sheet of paper. *Press conferences are not the place to tell our rivals what you know.*'

The roar made his colleague shrink into his seat.

'A thousand times,' Lars said after a brief pause, braking at the sight of an oncoming lorry that took up almost the entire road. 'Write it a thousand times on loose sheets of paper. And then write down: *When I receive a tip-off that might be a major scoop,*

I tell an experienced colleague or my line manager. A hundred times should do.'

Carl Ole gave a sheepish grin as he tucked his mobile into his inside pocket.

'Sure!'

'Yes, sure. By hand, mind you. Have the bundle on my desk by Monday. And I'll have that business card.'

He switched the windscreen wipers on to max and held his right hand, palm up, towards his passenger.

'The business card,' he repeated. 'Did she say anything?'

'Selma Falck?'

'Yes, who else?'

'She said nothing. Or ... that I should give her a call. Should I do that?'

Lars waved his hand impatiently. Carl Ole raised one buttock and drew the card from his back pocket. Hesitating, he placed it in his colleague's hand.

'No,' Lars said. 'You won't do a bloody thing after handing that phone to Agnes. I'll deal with this.'

'But ...'

'Listen.'

His voice was gentler when he opened the glove compartment, flung the business card inside and snapped it shut.

'Why do you think you were the one to receive that message?'

Silence.

'And not me or someone else on the paper?'

Still silence.

'Let's say this isn't a bizarre joke,' Lars went on. 'Let's say there's actually something in what's claimed in this message. Then it's a bit strange, isn't it, that the person in question chose you rather than anyone else? From the start-off, so to speak? How many stories have you had published with your own by-line? Three? Four?'

'Three of my own. And one with Andreas.'

'Precisely. You reek of new beginner, and you work at the most powerful sports desk in the country. What conclusion do you draw from that?'

He hit the brakes as a jogger suddenly darted into view five metres in front of the vehicle.

'Jogging in this weather,' Lars muttered. 'What do you think?'

'I'd have chosen a treadmill myself, yes.'

'Imbecile.'

'That it had an ulterior motive,' Carl Ole said quickly. 'He wanted me to ... make a fool of myself.'

'Exactly. He or she, whoever sent this message, wanted to cause a rumpus. Didn't want days and weeks of checking and slogging and undue secrecy behind closed doors from us sports guys.'

'He wanted immediate action,' Carl Ole murmured, obviously embarrassed. 'But ... why would he want that?'

'No idea. And with that dilettante behaviour of yours, it could be pretty difficult to find out.'

Carl Ole did not understand. On the one hand, he realized the blunder he had made. Of course he should have shown Lars the message or one of the others who had turned up at the sports desk at first light on Saturday morning. It had just been too tempting to give it a miss. The sensation of rousing the entire press conference out of its reverential atmosphere had gone to his head.

Crazy, he knew, but why it should be so completely destructive was harder to comprehend. After all, he hadn't said much. Just ignited a spark, so to speak, speculation about what information DG might have that no one else knew.

A ping made him take out his mobile again.

'Stop,' he said sharply.

The car stopped. In the middle of the road.

'Look,' Carl said, handing over the phone.

Lars read aloud: *Haakon Holm-Vegge was on drugs. Don't give up. More info to follow.*

Then he reread it another couple of times before thrusting the phone into his own pocket.

'I've changed my mind,' he said. 'I'm taking over.'

Neither of them uttered a word for the remainder of the drive.

THE WALL

No. No!

He wasn't sure whether he thought it or yelled it. The only thing he was focused on was the wall, the wall facing him, the one without the bed and the water hole that wasn't made of brick.

The room mustn't get any smaller.

It was already too small, too stifling; it shrank threateningly and had become a coffin he had to escape from. Or die.

His food had just come. He paid hardly any attention to it, didn't even pick it up. The man out there didn't wait long. After a few seconds he had pushed the bread roll in through the rectangular hole in the door and let it fall on to the floor before he slammed the hatch shut and locked it.

The mechanism was triggered. The low, rumbling noise sounded distant and yet uncomfortably close at one and the same time.

No. No. No.

It was impossible to breathe. The air felt like water, thick and suffocating; he gasped for oxygen. He stood with his back to the wall and stretched his legs out to the floor as far as he could. He spread his arms out with his palms on the boards he knew were made of plaster, since he had already torn off a lot of it. Although it hadn't helped in the least, the rough planks below were solid and impossible to break loose. His fingers were sore with splinters, several of which were becoming infected.

He pressed against it.

The machine won.

The wall moved another ten centimetres.

The cell was killing him.

THE LIST

The summary was far longer than Hege had anticipated. The support set-up alone filled a whole page. After all, the physiotherapists treated her constantly. As a rule Knut Nilssen, the best and oldest of them all. The two others had also had the opportunity to get close to her on a host of occasions. The same applied to Stian Bach, at least prior to the incident in Italy, and later the assistant doctor, Vibeke Stenshaug. The wax technicians, seventeen of them in total, were often in close proximity and moreover they had an enormous bus full of chemicals.

It was impossible to sleep after Selma Falck had left her just after midnight the day before yesterday. The footprints on the lawn had really terrified her. Yesterday morning, long before daybreak, and while Maggi was preparing an early breakfast in the kitchen, she had gone outside to examine them more closely. They were gone. The temperature was fluctuating, and alternating frost and thaw had transformed Oslo into a skating rink.

Hege yearned for snow. For real snow, the natural snow that made it worthwhile living up here on the heights where it was only a matter of fastening on your skis and zooming out into the woods.

Last night too she'd had difficulty sleeping. She hadn't been training as much as usual. Twice yesterday journalists had turned up on the street, but none of them had taken the liberty of ringing the doorbell. Or planting footprints around the house.

Since she was under suspension, she couldn't go to the team headquarters. The exercise studio in the basement was at least as good, but she was tired, unfocused and lacked motivation for anything other than a stint of running on the treadmill.

Yesterday evening she had finally embarked on the list Selma Falck had requested. When she woke two hours after bedtime from a nightmare she could not remember, she had surfed haphazardly on her phone.

Haakon was dead.

Going back to sleep was out of the question. The newspapers could not say much more than that it appeared to be an accident during training. Normally Hege would have phoned someone. She could rouse Hedda Bruun at least. Previously. Before the allegations. But not now. People she usually associated with had vanished from the scene in less than a week. Without a sound, and lacking specific facts, they had disappeared, almost as they had when her mother had died and everyone became remarkably silent every time Hege approached.

To pass the night, she had completed the list. Only to appreciate that it was worthless.

'Why is that?' Selma Falck asked.

The lawyer had arrived unannounced. She seemed restless and distracted, but looked a lot better than she had on Thursday. Her agitation could be connected to Haakon's death, Hege thought, and she had offered Selma her condolences at the door. A number of online newspapers had emphasized that Selma Falck, the dead skier's godmother, had been present at the Cross-Country Skiing Federation's press conference.

'Because it can't be exhaustive,' Hege answered with tears in her eyes as she suppressed a yawn. 'I've just really been fooling myself, thinking that I had everything under control. That the Federation had everything under control. The fact is ...'

She pushed the list, which ran to two pages, towards the settee on the other side of the polished concrete table, where Selma was seated.

The two pages still lay on the table. Selma Falck hadn't even glanced at them. She sat twirling her wedding ring that appeared too large. In every sense. It was slack, Hege noticed, and also seemed unfashionably broad.

'As far as the medical side is concerned, until the episode with Hedda I'd thought we were completely secure. Now it appears this was wrong. Food and suchlike? Beverages?'

Around her wrist she had an elastic band. She gathered up all her hair and fashioned a ponytail with deft, practised motions.

'I've really always thought they had things under control. Every single one of us, and of course, the Federation. But on reflection, it's easy for anyone to sabotage us. After all, we sometimes eat in restaurants. We buy food. Even if we have our own cooks with us at the major championships, we're not exactly kept in prison. If anyone really wanted to do us harm, it stands to reason that it's incredibly simple to sabotage us. Through our food. Through what we drink. Our medicines. I can see that now. So I'm actually left with just one single question.'

She clammed up, waiting for a sign that the other woman was paying attention.

'Who would be interested in harming you?' Selma said. 'That's what you're wondering.'

'Yes.'

'Have you come up with an answer?'

Selma pulled the two sheets of paper towards her and held them outstretched as she squinted at them.

'No,' Hege said. 'I can't fathom it. I've no enemies.'

'Everyone has enemies.'

'Not me.'

Selma's smile was impossible to read. It was slightly lopsided and did not reach all the way to her eyes. Maybe she was making fun of her. Maybe it was just that she was as discouraged as Hege herself. She resembled someone Hege could not bring to mind. There was something about those dark, almost black, eyes and the mouth with the unusually wide Cupid's bow, as if she had been born with a harelip that a true artist had put heart and soul into repairing. Her dark hair was coloured, in Hege's opinion – Selma Falck must be at least fifty years old.

She reminded her of someone.

Someone on TV.

'Racism,' Selma said in a loud voice. 'We have to go there, Hege.'

'I'm not a target for racism.'

It came as an automatic response. And it was almost true. Hege Chin Morell had lived in Norway for all of the twenty-four years she had spent on this earth, apart from the first six months. Her Asian facial features had never been a problem. Not at nursery. Not at school, at least no more than one or two casual remarks her parents had prepared her to tolerate. She was far from the only adoptive child in the neighbourhood and school catchment area, and she had toddled through her very first ski lessons in the company of a boy from Ethiopia and a tiny little girl born in Colombia.

'Not at all,' she added firmly.

Selma stared at her. Cocked her head. Her eyes narrowed.

'We live in tough times,' she said. 'I keep up with it on the internet, Hege. I keep myself up to date, despite my age.'

That smile again. Crooked, maybe ironic. Or possibly merely distant and distracted; her physical restlessness was tangible. Her left leg was trembling, and it appeared that Selma might be bothered with eczema. She kept scratching, her elbows, her knees and sometimes even her face.

'I don't pay any attention to those keyboard trolls,' Hege said.

'Smart move.'

'I don't experience any other racism.'

'I see.'

'You must be feeling very sad.'

'What?'

'About Haakon. Maybe it would be better to talk about this another time?'

At last Selma sat still. She exhaled loudly, slowly, and clasped her hands on her lap. Her eyes were turned to the side, as if contemplating something or other.

'I read the online newspapers just before you arrived,' Hege said.

Selma did not react.

'It said that a journalist came out with a question about Haakon and drugs. At the press conference. Where you were.'

Now Selma at least looked up, but she had started to scratch her left elbow again. Beneath her sweater, it looked as if a lively ferret was playing a game of hide and seek.

'It also mentioned that on the internet,' Hege said by way of explanation. 'That you were there, I mean.'

Selma nodded, still silent.

'What was that about, actually?'

'I don't know. The journalist was interrupted.'

'Haakon didn't take drugs. That's a certainty, at least. He was one of the most gutsy when it came to demanding severe action against drugs in sport. His post-mortem will show that he was clean.'

'Yes. If he hasn't been sabotaged, you know. Like you. Maybe the entire national team has been subjected to a colossal sabotage operation.'

Hege stood up.

'Come here.'

Selma looked at her with raised eyebrows and did not stand up.

'Come here,' Hege commanded, so loudly that the kitchen door gave a soft, long sigh and slid open.

Maggi's sad figure appeared.

'Everything's fine.' Hege waved her away and headed towards a door at the far end of the living room, behind the bleak, enormous hole where a fire should have blazed.

She registered that Selma was following in her wake.

'This is Dad's home office,' Hege said, opening the door and stepping inside.

Selma was still following her.

The room was spacious and square, with a huge desk in the middle of the floor. A dead iMac was placed in front of a black leather office chair. The desk surface was tidy, almost bare, and there was a faint smell of aftershave and furniture oil.

'That's Mum and me,' Hege said.

She was pointing at a picture. It was hanging on a wall covered in photographs, old and new, black-and-white and colour, big, small and many sizes in between. This one hung in the centre and was largest of all.

'I was eight,' Hege went on. 'That was three years before Mum died.'

A girl with dark hair and slanted eyes narrowed with laughter. Crooked, pearl-white smile; one of the big front teeth had still not emerged, the other still had a ragged edge. The woman was around forty, and just as fair as the youngster was dark. She had her arm around her daughter and her forehead tilted towards the girl's hair.

The mother was smiling.

'It was Dad who taught me how to win,' Hege said. 'But it was Mum who taught me how to lose. Dad taught me to ski. Mum taught me everything else. I ski for Dad. I try to be a good person for my Mum's sake.'

Suddenly she caught hold of Selma's hand. It was cold and slightly clammy.

'I haven't taken drugs,' she said in a soft, urgent voice. 'And it's bloody awful that so many people believe I did. I can't sleep, all my routines have been broken, my whole life has been turned upside down, and Dad is in the depths of despair. My career as a skier shouldn't be over for years yet. All the same ... all the same ...'

She let Selma go. Covered her face with both hands.

'All the same, that's not why it's important for me to be exonerated,' she said, her voice almost non-existent behind her hands. 'Totally exonerated. I can probably manage without skiing. It's not as if we're hard up exactly ...'

Her hands fell and she looked around the room.

'... and I did well at senior high school. I can continue my education. Do something conventional. But you see ...'

'Your mother would have been so sad.'

Selma's voice was different now. Her eyes were moist, as if on the verge of crying, but Hege had read somewhere that she couldn't shed tears.

'Yes, Mum would have been absolutely devastated.'

'She would have known that you haven't done anything wrong, Hege. She would have had confidence in you. Mothers are like that. Most mothers, anyway.'

'Yes, but all the same. It's important for me to be cleared. For many reasons, not least for Dad, but most of all for Mum's sake.'

A movement outside the window made them both wheel around.

Out there, in what remained of the grey afternoon light, under an apple tree only five metres from the house stood a roe deer. It was looking straight at them, with its ears pricked. Its jaws were working from side to side, rhythmic and incessant.

'Dad leaves out carrots,' Hege whispered. 'And then they eat the half-frozen windfall fruits.'

They stood there, motionless, for several minutes.

'I believe in you,' Selma said softly and slowly.

'Thanks.'

'The problem is that I'm completely at a loss. I've no idea what your father thinks I can do for you.'

The roe deer outside froze. Its jaw movements stopped abruptly. Its ears flicked from side to side before the hind took long leaps in flight from whatever had scared her. In the distance they could hear three harsh barks and a car parking.

'Are you unwell?' Hege asked. 'Is that why you can't help me?'

'No. Unwell? Not at all.'

A door slammed on the other side of the house.

'Come on,' Hege said. 'Dad's home.'

Selma walked towards the door. Stopped and bent towards another photograph. Three young men, teenage boys in a colour photograph, faded to pastel by the passing of years. The boy in the middle was Jan Morell. He had a wide, self-assured smile and had turned up the earflaps on a knitted ski helmet that had then been in the bright colours of the Norwegian flag, but in the picture had turned to pale-pink and baby-blue.

'That's Dad and his pals,' Hege said. 'Come on.'

'Arnulf Selhus, isn't it? The Finance Director of the NCCSF?'

'Yes, they were best friends.'

'Were?'

'Were. We have to go now.'

'What about the third man?'

Selma leaned closer to the picture.

'That's Uncle Klaus. He and Dad still see each other, from time to time. We have to go now, Selma.'

Hege was quickly out the door. Judging by the sounds from

the kitchen, her father was already there. He could enter the living room at any time, and he didn't like anyone going into his office. Even Maggi had to give him warning twenty-four hours in advance if she intended going in there to clean.

'Klaus? But isn't that Morten Karlshaug? The photographer?'

'Yes. Klaus is his nickname. Come on.'

Hege had just managed to close the door to her father's office and move all the way to the fireplace when her father entered the living room. She gave him a lame smile and hoped Selma didn't notice how relieved she was that he hadn't come in seconds earlier.

Apparently she was safe. It looked as if Selma had enough on her own plate today.

More than enough, in fact.

THE MANUSCRIPT

201 OUTSIDE, STREET IN OSLO CITY CENTRE, DAYTIME

The MAN walks along the pavement. His thick, silver-grey hair flutters in the wind. Sunshine. The MAN opens a heavy gate, goes inside. The gate slides slowly to behind him.

202 INTERIOR, OFFICE IN OSLO CITY CENTRE, DAYTIME

The WOMAN sitting on an office chair. She is restless. Swings from side to side. A notepad and pen are on an adjacent sideboard. The MAN is seated on a settee. Leaning forward, eager.

WOMAN: I think we've reached the end of the road. You don't have anything more to gain from this.
MAN: Could you stop swinging on your chair? Please.

The WOMAN sits completely still, with her face turned directly towards the MAN.

WOMAN: As I said, we're at the end of the road.
MAN: The end of the road? No way! It's now that it begins, you see. It's to your credit that I've come this far at all.
WOMAN: Come where? Where do you actually think you've come to?

MAN: To my liberation! At last I can start to do something. Sort things out, as you well know. Put things right!

WOMAN: And how are you going to do that?

MAN: In lots of ways. I'm writing a script for a TV series, for one thing. That could be great. There's a possibility for symmetry in all of it. Balance.

WOMAN (looks at the clock in a far from discreet manner): I think …

MAN: It's twenty minutes since I arrived … Honestly.

WOMAN: You can manage on your own now.

MAN: No. Now is when this starts to become important.

(PAUSE)

WOMAN: I'm really finding it difficult to see where you want to go with this. Can you try to explain?

MAN (rather overwrought): YOU'RE the one who explained to me that Mum and Dad's reaction was normal. Dad grew silent, and Mum blubbered. They separated a year later. Fairly commonplace, according to you. Normal. I stayed with my father, something that was NOT usual at that time, in fact. He pulled up all the roots I had and moved away. New place, new people. Mum re-married, I ended up with two half-siblings, and Dad grew increasingly silent. Mum's new guy didn't like me. At their place I was superfluous. At Dad's I was alone. My brother was gone. Everything was off balance.

(LENGTHY PAUSE)

WOMAN: Yes, as I've told you many times before, your parents' reactions are …

MAN (angry): Off balance. Do you hear?

WOMAN: Yes, I hear. Your parents' reactions to the death were pretty normal. The subsequent developments too. Of course this would have felt chaotic to a small child. Chaotic and therefore threatening. That's absolutely normal, it's just …

MAN: … I'm the one who's abnormal, then. Eh?

WOMAN: No. As we've discussed so many times before, there's nothing normal or abnormal in a human reaction to …

MAN: You used exactly that word a minute ago. Normal. About my parents. But not about me.

WOMAN (with a loud sigh): You were seven years old.

MAN (quietly): Yes, I was seven. And the only one who paid a price for what happened. A fucking high price. An unfairly high price for a seven-year-old. It's time to take something back.

WOMAN: By writing a manuscript?

MAN: That too. And other things. I've got a few plans.

The MAN stands up abruptly. Remains standing, scrutinizing the woman for several seconds. The WOMAN obviously feels ill at ease.

MAN (cont.): You're right. Let's draw a line under things here. For this time. See you next Thursday, same time.

WOMAN: As I said, I think we've reached the stage where we can say we're …

MAN: I'm the one who'll decide when you and I are finished. It's important to maintain balance between us as well. You're the therapist. I get to decide when we're finished.

The door slams behind the MAN. The WOMAN remains seated, restless again, for a long time.

SUNDAY 10 DECEMBER 2017

A STROKE OF LUCK

The second Sunday in Advent was six and a half hours old when Selma Falck opened the door into the apartment in Toftes gate.

She was humming an ABBA song, and the first thing she did was to give Darius some food. Then she unpacked the cat litter tray she had bought on Thursday, and filled it with sand. In the course of the next hour she had sorted out clean and dirty clothes from the cardboard boxes. There was a relatively new washing machine in the bathroom; at least it worked. After using two bottles of bleach to scrub the walls and porcelain, she tore down the shower curtain and threw it out. She showered for a long time, washed her hair, noticed that Darius had devoured all the food and had crapped in the box. She vacuumed the whole apartment, connected the TV without switching it on and scoured the kitchen until it at least smelled acceptable.

To round it off she put on a machine load of underwear.

Last night, when it was no longer possible to resist, she had taken out 9,000 kroner from the ATM. That was almost half of all she owned.

When she was let out of the Poker Turk's dive just after six that same morning, it had started to snow. Selma had 29,500 kroner in her handbag. Divided into three envelopes, with 1,000 kroner notes in one, 500 bills in another and small denomination notes in the third.

For more than six hours she had experienced peace. Not given a thought to the children. Not to her office, not to Haakon, Vanja or Kristina. And certainly not to Jan Morell or his daughter. Selma had won nearly all the time, been lucky and skilful and on top of everything.

She would buy a new bed with some of the cash.

Besides, there was another poker session on Monday.

The stakes were higher there, and if she shopped at IKEA, she wouldn't need to touch what was left in her bank account. She put a clean sheet over the cheese puffs settee, placed a pillow at the head and let Darius curl up at the foot.

Selma had taken a night's respite from herself, for the first time in almost four weeks. She was still humming an old hit song when she lay down. She had money. Far more money than yesterday. She was doing well. On the front foot. And best of all, she thought as she closed her eyes, was that she had woken from something that only yesterday had been heading for the skids.

That was good, because now she knew precisely how she was going to start searching for the explanation as to why Hege Chin Morell had submitted a positive drugs sample without having done anything wrong. It was a night like this she had needed, and as soon as first light, she would seriously begin on the assignment Jan Morell had given her.

With a smile, it crossed her mind that she was well into overtime.

Then she drifted off to sleep and did not wake until nine hours had elapsed.

THE DELUXE EDITION

The apartment was enormous, but that was really all it had going for it. At least if you discounted the address, which was also a plus factor.

Sølve Bang had inherited the place, all 200 square metres of it, from a great-aunt in 1997. Gudrun Bang had been a librarian all her life, and the literary halo on her nephew's son shone even more brightly at that time, if that were possible. The inheritance was a welcome solution to the still relatively young man's chronically catastrophic financial situation, but caused a rift between him and his siblings so wide that no one had attempted to patch things up ever since. As both his parents were dead and his brother had lived in the USA following a student exchange visit at senior high school, Sølve was as good as on his own. Partners had come and gone six times since the time when the apartment in Thomas Heftyes gate was furnished throughout in the Biedermeier style.

The women in Sølve's life had not entirely appreciated the bourgeois late empire trappings. Each of them had brought something to the place and pushed out something else. A mahogany writing desk and a dining room set in stained beech with chair covers of silk damask were first to go. Subsequently chaises longues and sofas, beds and paintings, as well as the heavy curtains below beautifully decorated pelmets had all disappeared, to be replaced by the occasional piece of furniture from Expo Nova and Møbelringen, from IKEA and Skeidar and a suite from the flea market at Ruseløkka school into the bargain. The problem was that these women eventually vanished from the scene. Along with their goods and chattels they took some of their items of furniture, and in the end increasingly obvious gaps leered at Sølve in every room. Of course he could have bought replacements – his finances weren't in such a bad state – and there were ways of furnishing an apartment for less than 200,000 kroner. But that wasn't how he wanted it. Sølve Bang liked expensive things. Biedermeier, for example. When he had gone along with the women's demands for dilution of all the heavy brown furniture, it was primarily because the pieces had given him a necessary financial lift each time they found their way to the Blomqvist auction house and new owners.

His great-aunt had known a thing or two about Biedermeier.

The desk was among the few pieces he had kept.

It was actually a dining table, and it had pride of place in the centre of one of the three drawing rooms. Facing the windows, and with the door to the almost clinically bare kitchen behind it. The chair was new. Sølve Bang bought a new chair once a year, and then he normally did not stint. This one had arrived in early autumn when he was short of funds, a Kinnarps Capella uphol-stered in anthracite-grey wool. It was the first time in years he had not gone for leather.

He didn't like the chair: to his mind, it looked cheap.

He didn't care for the calculation that appeared on the computer when he asked for a fourth word count, either.

The contract from Statoil had been impossible to turn down. Almost five years ago, Sølve Bang had been offered the opportunity to write the history of Norwegian cross-country skiing. There was plenty of reading material about skiing in Norway, of course, but he was going to write The Book. The standard work.

The saga, the highly literary, but nonetheless widely accessible description of the nation's most important and popular sport.

No one had qualifications like he had. The skier who became a world famous author before he had reached the age of twenty, was to receive 5,000,000 kroner divided into five annual instalments for undertaking the task. He pretended to hesitate, but had made up his mind as soon as he realized what they meant by 5,000,000. The money was for him. As remuneration. A fee, no less, 1,000,000 per year and all expenses paid. The payments arrived on the twelfth of every month.

The original deadline had expired last summer.

The picture editor had completed his work. The dust cover was clinched: the skier from the rock carvings at Tro, evidence of the sport's Norwegian origins from approximately 5,000 years ago. The motif had been used before, both as the starting point for the icons of the Lillehammer Winter Olympics and on a postage stamp issued during the Skiing World Championships in Oslo in 1966.

Embossing and foil. Clothbound spine and corners. Silver edges in the same tones as the spot gloss on the rock carvings. To top off the exclusivity, ribbon bookmarks in silver. With tassels.

No expense had been spared. Everything was ready.

Apart from the text.

When the manuscript should have been delivered, Sølve had simply extended the deadline by sending chapter headings and a table of contents, together with three disconnected extracts. The structure was plausible, the texts well written. As the new deadline approached in October, Sølve Bang was let in on a business decision so secret he could hardly sleep that night at the thought that he had been entrusted with such a secret. Statoil was to change its name. Neither the state nor oil was any longer considered particularly representative of the colossal company.

A bit too 1970, it had been decided. Reactionary. On the other hand, Equinor pointed crystal-clear towards something greater and better, a name that, according to the firm's senior management, both said something about where the oil giant came from and where it was headed.

OK, Sølve had thought, rather at a loss since the new name mainly aroused associations with horses, but the change of name involved a glorious postponement of his personal contribution. The book would now be launched two days before the Winter Olympic Games, on 7 February 2018. The same day as public disclosure of the company's new name.

The absolutely final deadline for delivery of the manuscript was fixed for Christmas Eve. The unusually short time span between submission and publication, especially for a deluxe edition of this type, would make it a close call, but it would work.

If only he could meet the very last, and very final, deadline.

The book was estimated at around 600,000 characters. In an ordinary novel, without illustrations, this would be the equivalent of 400 pages. Since *Cross-Country Skiing in Norway – Historic Tracks into the Future* would be published in large format, but also be fully illustrated, it was reckoned that the final result would be around 500 pages in length.

He had to have 600,000 characters by Christmas Eve. There was exactly a fortnight left until then.

Sølve stared in dismay at the word counter.

69,562 characters. Including spaces. That was all he had.

The text didn't even hang together.

In the next fortnight he would have to write more than 530,000 characters, that is, more than 37,000 characters per day. Which was quite simply not possible.

Not for anyone. At any rate not for anyone in his literary league. On a good day he could come up with 2,000 characters.

His record was 2,492, and that had taken him eleven unusually inspired hours.

He rose from the Kinnarps office chair and moved into the kitchen. The floor tiles in there, from 1934 and therefore lacking underfloor heating cables, made his footsteps resound on the bare, ice-cold walls in the overly large room.

Sølve Bang never wore slippers. He used indoor shoes.

And now he was incredibly thirsty.

The pipes groaned when he turned on the old mixer taps. He let the water run for a long time. Grabbed a glass from an enormous overhead cupboard and filled it to the brim.

When Hege Chin Morell was caught taking drugs, Sølve had been furious. He felt his entire book project was in impending danger, and with that the next payment due as soon as the following Tuesday. Statoil had, like all other sponsors, a strict drugs clause in their contract with the Federation. No one could overlook the fact that Hege's drugs allegation might poison the atmosphere between the two parties so emphatically that the whole project regarding the deluxe edition ran the risk of falling through. So incensed had Sølve Bang been, for three days in a row, that he had completely forgotten to give closer consideration to how the contract between Statoil and himself had actually been worded.

He drank. Filled the glass again and drank half of it as well.

During the contract negotiations, he had used a friend as his lawyer. Someone from BAHR, one of the best known and most international law firms in Norway, an old school friend from St. Sunniva's, who at the outset had cost 6,000 kroner an hour. When the invoice had arrived, Sølve had put the paper at the bottom of the dirty laundry basket before sending a text message to his friend, partly offended, partly hurt.

No reminder ever appeared.

His friend was an excellent lawyer. Brilliant, in fact.

Sølve slammed down the glass and returned to the drawing room. For a moment he stood thinking, half squinting at the curtain-less windows where December scudded past with sleet and gusts of wind. Suddenly he turned on his heel and walked on towards the bedroom. One wall was covered in practical, out-of-place wardrobes by the name of Pax. They had been left behind by partner number four who had been unusually fond of clothes. Sølve's wardrobe was far less comprehensive.

It took him a second or two to find the document. He kept his belongings in pedantic order, and all his contracts had been systematically filed in ring binders stored in the cupboard furthest off.

Three minutes later he sat behind the Biedermeier desk giving thanks to a God he had never believed in. With his eyes closed, his hands folded and his body tensed.

His friend from St Sunniva's had safeguarded him.

If he withdrew from the project, or did not manage to complete it, then the majority of the advance payment would have to be paid back. The contract specified an exponential scale. The further into the project, the greater the percentage to be repaid. With a rapid mental calculation, Sølve discovered he would have to shell out almost 350,000 kroner if he himself decided to pack it in.

That was money he by no means possessed.

Not without selling the apartment, which was out of the question.

On the other hand, if Statoil were to withdraw, the situation would be completely different. In paragraph 11.2 of the agreement, it emerged that Sølve's interest in Hege Chin Morell's drugs case suddenly became of major import. A breach on the oil company's part, regardless of reason, implied that Sølve Bang, named

The Author in the contract, would be able to keep all monies paid plus a sum approximating to three months' remuneration. Furthermore he would retain the rights to his own intellectual property.

It was too good to be true.

Sølve read the clause three more times.

The good news was actually true.

He placed his hands behind his neck. Fixed his eyes on the stucco between the wall and ceiling, which was dark with dust and yellowed with age. He released his hands and slammed a fist down on the table. It was painful.

Hege's affair might not be sufficient. Statoil might possibly consider it all to be a one-off occurrence. An occupational accident. A side-track that could be bypassed. Hege had never really fitted in anyway: Sølve himself was struggling to insert the dark-haired foreigner into a beautiful book about Norway and cross-country skiing.

But then there was that little journalist. At the press conference, where he had more than hinted that Haakon Holm-Vegge might also have been involved in drug-taking.

If both the best female and the best male Norwegian cross-country skiers were exposed as cheats, it could signal the end for the Federation. At least in the short run.

'In the short run' also included the Winter Olympics. Only a few days ago, the International Olympic Committee had excluded Russia from the games in PyeongChang. If the weirdo from *DG* really had anything to go on, and hadn't just been on a crazy fishing expedition, that could lead to chaos. And a rupture between Statoil and the Cross-Country Skiing Federation.

Sølve touched the mouse. The screen lit up. The word count box still told him that the manuscript so far contained 69,562 characters. His plan was to spend all evening and much of the night knitting together some of the fragments he had already written.

It didn't work. He was too restless. Overexcited, almost, at the thought that he might be able to avoid submitting anything at all.

It was certainly worthy of a good dinner, he thought all of a sudden, and put the computer into sleep mode. He hung the yellow memory stick around his neck, and before he reached as far as the hall, he had already decided on a restaurant. The Statholdergaarden, Oslo's gourmet restaurant, always had a table for him whether or not he had a reservation. Even now in the pre-Christmas season. For a moment he considered phoning someone, but then dropped the idea.

There were plans to make, thoughts to think, and maybe everything would go his way for once.

It would be high time.

THE MANUSCRIPT

301 OUTSIDE, OSLO CITY CENTRE, DAYTIME

The MAN goes through a gateway from a busy street. Looks down, is preoccupied with avoiding stepping on the lines on the pavement. A scattering of dry, yellow leaves indicates that autumn has just begun. The MAN stops at a closed door.

He rings the doorbell and from habit places his hand on the door, as if he is used to it opening immediately.

WOMAN'S VOICE (metallic): Yes?

MAN (smiles): You know who it is.

WOMAN'S VOICE: Didn't you get my message?

MAN: What message?

WOMAN'S VOICE: I sent you both a letter and an email.

MAN: Saying what?

WOMAN'S VOICE: I can't discuss that with you here on the entry phone. I suggest you check your letterbox. And your email.

MAN: Can't I just come up and … Let me speak to …

WOMAN'S VOICE: No. Sorry.

A sharp click, the conversation is over. The MAN hovers for a few seconds before ringing the doorbell again. No one answers. The MAN hesitates briefly and then returns to the entrance door and disappears with hurried steps.

QUI BONO

'I think you're absolutely crazy. Do you know what time it is?'

'Yes. But you probably don't, Einar.'

It had only just become Monday.

Selma Falck had rounded off the weekend by going for a walk with Darius. An embarrassing idea. Someone or other, probably Anine, had stuffed a cat harness and neon-coloured chain into one of the boxes. It had taken Selma an eternity to get the contraption on the recalcitrant animal. Under cover of darkness, with a woollen hat and scarf covering half her face, she had carried the cat under her arm down to Sofienberg Park. There, she had let it toddle around for twenty uncomfortable minutes before dragging it unwillingly behind her back home again. A stray Alsatian had almost acquired an evening snack along the way, but Selma had surprised herself by delivering a well-aimed kick to the mutt's nose.

Suitably hard.

After sleeping all day it was pointless going to bed. Her elation after the night of poker playing was dwindling, and Selma was far from being as cocksure as she'd been when she fell asleep. Her phone displayed six missed calls. Five of them seemingly from Vanja and Kristine. She ought to call them back. Jan Morell had also tried to contact her.

The only person she wanted to contact was Einar.

He was asleep when she approached, but woke before she reached him.

'Around ...'

Einar Falsen scrambled up from lying on his side in the cardboard box between the boulders under the Sinsen interchange. He tilted his head and ran his mitten over his face.

'Half past twelve,' he said firmly. 'I can tell by the sound of the traffic.'

It was in fact twenty-five minutes to one, and Selma sat down breathlessly. She had been running. Clouds of condensation wafted around her when she took off her running top. She pulled out a folded down jacket from a small Camelbak rucksack, along with a thermos and a blue lunchbox. She poured coffee into both of their plastic mugs and opened the lunchbox before placing it on a stone in front of Einar.

'A midnight snack.'

'Thanks.'

'I've made a list. And also some choices. Thought I could discuss them with you.'

Einar sat up, leaning on a rock, still enveloped in his sleeping bag. A rank odour of sweat with a hint of urine was thrown off by the rifle-green sleeping bag when he pulled it up to his waist as he grabbed a sandwich with butter and brown cheese.

'Good. What kind of list?'

'Of possible perpetrators.'

'Perpetrators? Have you already established that the girl was sabotaged? What was it I said to you about an open mind? Guilt, innocence. Sabotage, accident, deliberate attempt at cheating. You can never decide in advance, Mariska. I told you so.'

He attacked the sandwich as if he intended to murder it.

'Of course.'

Selma tried to find a comfortable position on the jagged stones. It was never easy.

'I tried that,' she said. 'But it was pointless. I'm too short of time. I simply have to begin with the hypothesis that she's been sabotaged. I have to take any shortcuts going. If she wasn't sabotaged, but has taken drugs either intentionally or by accident, I won't be able to get her exonerated anyway. At least not in time for the Winter Olympics.'

She licked her lips. Hesitated.

'And then I found an interesting chapter in that book of yours.'

Einar smiled broadly with his mouth full of food.

'*The Investigator's ABC*,' he said triumphantly. 'Brilliant! What are you referring to? Which of my many pearls of wisdom did you find interesting this time?'

Selma Falck didn't read literature. She'd barely opened anything other than textbooks all her life. Seldom went to the cinema. If she had a free evening, something she rarely had, she watched TV. Eight years ago she had come across the first season of *The Walking Dead*, a post-apocalypse series so full of action that she actually succumbed to its fascination. Deeply enough that she had watched every season since, twice over, and she had an expensive figure of Michonne on her office desk. Purchased in London and brought home with a good deal of loot. When Selma had read in a newspaper article somewhere that the series was strongly inspired by Albert Camus's *The Plague*, she had bought a novel for the first time ever. And never got further than page six.

If she wasn't keen on written fiction, she was nonetheless good with facts. She had completed her law degree in the normal length of time in parallel with a handball career, and had ended up among the top ten per cent in her year.

That had won her 50,000 kroner in a bet with her brother.

Selma knew her professional literature, and *The Investigator's ABC* was a piece of junk.

Muddled and unfocused, repetitive and pretty badly written into the bargain. She suspected the so-called publisher of being a kitchen worktop affair. Even Einar's spelling mistakes had survived editing and correction. Since Einar Falsen had undoubtedly been a competent and clear-thinking policeman, Selma assumed that his illness had already affected him at the time the book was issued.

'Qui bono,' Selma said.

'Who benefits,' Einar replied, nodding. 'Marcus Tullius Cicero's speech in defence of Titus Annius Milo. Who was actually convicted, despite Cicero's efforts.'

Tossing the rest of the sandwich into his mouth, he chewed it up and washed it down with the scalding-hot coffee.

'Have you brought any dessert?'

Selma handed him a packet of Smil chocolates she took from the bottom of the Camelbak bag.

The Investigator's ABC was full of platitudes. In the chapter on the significance of motive, Einar had dealt comprehensively with the most obvious causes of crime. Revenge, money and sex. Or a combination of these three. An apparently self-drawn graph also showed that most cases of homicide in Norway were deplorably uninteresting: murders committed in the heat of the moment, usually when drunk, and committed against family, friends or acquaintances.

Selma picked up a thin cushion and a Co-op carrier bag. She pulled one over the other before tucking the bundle under her backside.

'This afternoon I tried to track Hege Chin Morell's life as well as I could,' she said, catching herself on the point of taking out her mobile to show him the documents she had produced.

Einar ripped open the Smil packet. Three chocolates fell between the stones. He swore under his breath and emptied the rest into the Mesta mitten.

'And to make a long story short, I think we can ignore sex in this case.'

'Oh? Don't you think the Chinese girl has sex, Mariska?'

'I've no idea, and it's none of my business. I just mean it's difficult to imagine her being mixed up in any drama of that sort. She's been linked to romantic liaisons only twice. The gossip magazine *Se og Hør* reported on an alleged relationship with an Austrian three years ago. He was a skier too. Only a year ago there were rumours circulating that she was involved with one of the wax technicians. As far as I can see, both of them were wrong. All the same ...'

Her coffee had finally become lukewarm enough to drink.

'As I said I don't have much time and I have to take a few chances. I'm going to forget sex.'

'Now you're getting bloody confused,' Einar said, plunging his hand into the mitten full of chocolates.

'Yes. I'm no good at this.'

'You're starting at the wrong end.'

'Almost certainly.'

'You have to look at the crime. If a crime is involved, but then you're assuming that, aren't you?'

'Yes ...'

Einar seemed totally preoccupied with the chocolates. He stuffed more into his mouth before he'd swallowed the first ones. Sucking and chewing, he swallowed and went on sucking. It took him less than two minutes to finish the whole packet.

A thick layer of chocolate coated both corners of his mouth.

'You're working from a hypothesis that she was drugged without knowing for sure,' he mumbled, peering down into his mitten with one eye. 'That someone has deliberately harmed her as a skier.'

He turned the mitten over and shook it.

'You don't have any more, do you?'

'No. And not necessarily. Someone wanting to harm her as a skier, I mean. Cross-country skiing is her whole life. If someone wanted to harm her, regardless of the reason, using drugs to sabotage her career would be particularly effective. We can see that. She's completely shattered.'

He no longer seemed to be listening. He was twisting and turning the mitten, already stiff with dirt and perspiration, in his search for more chocolates.

'Back to qui bono,' she said, placing her hand on the bony knee that jutted up inside his sleeping bag. 'That chapter's actually good.'

'The entire book is good.'

'Yes, of course, but that part in particular was ...'

'Who gains from the crime?' he broke in. 'Who benefits from Hege Chin Morell not going to the Winter Olympics?'

'All the other female skiers in the whole world.'

Einar grinned.

'Then you've got quite a job ahead of you.'

Selma did not answer. Einar was still smiling. More of a grimace, really: lopsided and with three missing teeth on the side of the mouth that hadn't quite managed to take part in the smile. His beard was unusually unkempt, even for him. The chocolate on his face was beginning to solidify. His cap was askew, with the earflaps mournfully teetering on his shoulders. His brown eyes looked sideways with crow's feet so deep they divided his face in two.

He reminded her of an aged cocker spaniel.

'Yes,' Selma said, sounding discouraged. 'That's why I made the list.'

She thrust her hand down into the rucksack.

'Mariska.'

'Yes?'

'If I ask you the question the other way round ...'

'The other way round?'

'Yes.'

She remained seated with her arm in the rucksack.

'Who loses by Hege Morell not coming to the Olympics?' Einar asked.

'Er ... she does, of course. And the Federation. Norway, for that matter, if we presuppose that we want to win as many medals as possible.'

His head gave a jolt, and he clutched at his ear.

'Fuck,' he said softly. 'Have you brought that bloody phone with you?'

'No!' she lied. 'Word of honour, Einar. I left it at home.'

She showed him two open palms, as if that might prove something.

'Who loses most of all?' Einar asked, still with his eyes tightly shut and a hand clamped like an ear defender on his left ear. 'Absolutely most of all?'

'Hege.'

'Are you sure of that, Mariska?'

'Yes.'

All of a sudden he looked at her again. He stretched out to the arsenal of plastic bags and carriers between the stones and rummaged around until he located a bundle of newspapers.

'I've followed that girl Hege,' he muttered. 'Who hasn't? And in the autumn there was an interview ...'

He leafed repeatedly through the papers.

'What do you call that kind of thing?' he murmured. 'Those interviews where there are two ...'

'A double portrait.'

'Yes. A double portrait, that's it. Of the Chinese girl and her dad. Here!'

He handed her something that might be a copy of *A-Magasinet*, the weekend supplement from *Aftenposten*.

'Read that.'

Selma did not reply. She did not accept the magazine when he handed it to her.

'Selma!' he said angrily.

She could not recall the last time he had called her by her correct name.

'Read the interview!'

'I *have* read it,' she said. 'Shh.'

The interview was from the autumn and was one of more than twenty she had skimmed through when she had finally awoken some time in the afternoon.

But they were not what had struck Selma with astonishment all of a sudden.

It was the thought of yesterday's conversation with Hege in Jan Morell's home office.

Selma Falck knew what it took to be a winner.

Handball in the previous century could not, of course, be compared with cross-country skiing in 2017, but the principles were the same. You had to train. And train. Put up with pain, put up with boredom, repetition and more pain. You had to sleep. Eat. Recover. Miss out on most of the things that did not have to do with this one, single, overriding concern: to be the best possible athlete. All the time, and constantly improving. Better than yourself, and better than all the others.

Selma herself had cheated. She had quite simply trained too much. More than was good for her, more than her coaches allowed. She had sneaked away when her teammates were finished, both at her local club and the national team. Run and pumped iron. Always more than the others. Trained too much, trained in and out of the injuries that had afflicted her. At her best, between the World Championships bronze and the first Olympics silver, she had realized that she was partly driven by compulsive thoughts. If she just punished herself enough, she would be the best. If the others used indoor treadmills in November, she would run through the woods. Beyond the paths, in varying terrain, faster and faster, increasingly steep, at first until she grew hot and on until she felt so cold that she quite literally couldn't flex her fingers.

For more than fifteen years of her life she had been driven by something she later appreciated was founded in self-loathing. You had to be over the top, or else you were nothing. Run on Christmas Day. Do strength training as usual on birthdays and Norway's National Day; even on the day of her grandfather's funeral she had felt nauseous at the thought that she had missed a hard session. In tests, the incessant tests, with maximum pulse and lactic acid up to her ears, she always managed more. Ten more minutes. Five. In two more minutes of intense pain she would be the very best.

Otherwise she was nothing.

You never skipped anything. You played on with blisters as big as 20-kroner coins and hoped that no one would find out. There was a deep sense of satisfaction to be gained from having the strength to do it, especially if no one saw it, especially when the sacrifice and self-control were only her own; she was in charge of herself, she owned her body through what she could make her five foot eight frame and more or less constant sixty-eight kilos withstand.

Only in this way could she become the best handball player in the world.

She never made it, but she became really, really good.

'Everything comes from within,' she said into thin air.

'What?'

Einar finally replaced the *A-Magasinet* in the bundle.

'The enthusiasm for training. The will to make sacrifices. When I played handball. It was all about a deeply rooted, inner ... desire? Need? I don't entirely know. But it comes from inside you.'

'I suppose it must for everyone. Performing well at international level must be bloody boring more than anything else.'

Selma nodded as she struggled to make herself more comfortable on the cushion inside the Co-op bag.

'Playing ball is always fun. Strength training can be OK. Cardiovascular is ... pretty awful, really. Boring, essentially, you're right there, but also painful at times. Extremely so. And it must ...'

Once again she interrupted herself. She had started to feel cold. All the same she remained seated, with her eyes half closed and unfocused.

'Hege's will to win comes from external forces,' she said slowly, as if she didn't entirely believe what she was saying. 'She wins for her father. It's his dreams she's fulfilling. Not her own.'

Selma tried to recollect exactly how their conversation had gone. Word for word. She couldn't manage it completely, but for some reason she had been left with the impression that Hege Chin Morell was more upset on her father's behalf than her own.

And her mother's.

Her mother had been dead for fifteen years.

Einar shook the sleeping bag and drew it all the way up to his armpits.

'I can't make out how you know that,' he said, refilling his mug from the thermos flask. 'But if you're right, then you're on to part of the most interesting aspects of casuistic victimology.'

Once again Selma recognized the peculiar expression from *The Investigator's ABC*. It must be one of the many turns of phrase he had quite simply made up. She got to her feet and slapped her thighs. It was probably plus one or two degrees Celsius here underneath the bridge, but the air was raw.

'You know,' Einar went on without noticing she was gathering up her belongings in order to leave. 'People think an investigator's only task is to find a perpetrator. But it's not like that. Cheers!'

The man must have mucous membranes made of thick leather. He drank down all the coffee in one gulp. Wiped his mouth with his sleeve and let off a loud fart of satisfaction down into the sleeping bag.

'Sometimes, Mariska, it's not obvious who is the victim of a crime. Most often, qui bono is a sensible question. Who gains from the crime? But sometimes, Mariska, you have to ask yourself ...'

He lifted his arms out to one side, as if preparing to deliver a speech to an enthusiastic assembly.

'... who loses most by the result of the crime? If you find the answer to that, you'll find the real victim in this case.'

He dropped his arms abruptly.

'Are you leaving?'

'Got to run. Home. It's late.'

'Are you running all the way to Ormøya now?'

Selma did not answer. She stuffed her running jacket into her rucksack – it was too cold to change.

'You'll be back soon?' Einar asked.

'Of course I will.'

'And, don't forget ...'

'Yes.'

She slung the rucksack on her back and fastened the belt before leaning over him and giving him a hug.

'I did the right thing,' he murmured into her shoulder. 'Didn't I? It was right to kill him?'

'You did absolutely the right thing,' Selma whispered in return. 'That bastard deserved to die.'

THE WALL

The room had grown even smaller.

He had paced it out several times. When he first woke in here, not understanding anything, and with no idea what had happened, the cell had measured six paces in length and four wide. The door with the hatch was on the long wall, just beside the pipe where the water trickled out and down into the nauseating drain where his excrement now at least slipped easily through the grate. He had constant diarrhoea.

The cell had become square. Four paces in each direction. One of what had been the end walls, the moving wall, was now almost all rough board. He had torn off all the plaster. Last night, or earlier today – it was impossible to know what was what – he had been wakened by walking in his sleep. He had been squatting beside the heap of broken material, chomping on a piece of plaster, when he suddenly realized he was awake.

In the last few days, or hours, he had tried to work loose the rough boards in the corner where the most dangerous wall met the one constructed of brick. There was a gap of a couple of millimetres in that spot, so that the wall could move forward each time the infernal machine was activated on the other side. However, it was useless.

His hands were aching. His backside was sore, and he had problems sitting down. He never slept for very long, he imagined, even though it was difficult to know for certain. His sleep was filled with dreams, most of them about being in a desert, fleeing from incredible monsters that finally caught him, when he was wakened in panic by his own screams.

The second-worst thing about this place was that it was locked.

The third-worst was that there were no loose objects there, apart from his food, some straw and himself. Nothing to use. Nothing to hold. Nothing to move, no movement to follow with his eyes.

The fourth-worst was being naked.

He still had no clue about what had happened.

Even now, he did not know what he had done.

What's more, he could not recall anything except being on his way to his car in the garage in Ivan Bjørndals gate in Sagene when all at once his world had gone up in smoke.

The very worst thing about this place was that the room was getting steadily smaller and could presumably collapse to almost nothing.

The machine came to life again out there, and he began to cry.

MAGGI

The little heart beside the doorframe was so beautiful. Painted with red nail varnish, at a six-year-old child's eye level. Maggi had spotted it the first time she had cleaned in here, only a few weeks after the lady of the house had passed away. Her initial impulse had been to scrape it off. She would prove herself worthy of the job. Even though she had come with good references, Jan Morell seemed both sceptical and strict. She was given a three-month trial period, and the bathroom had to shine. Just as she was about to remove the hard lacquer from the surface with a stove scraper, she changed her mind. Instead she covered the heart with a length of sticky tape and scrubbed down the rest of the room.

She had continued to do that.

She also took care of the doorframe. While the rest of the bathroom was always washed down with water and detergent, bleach and other chemicals, she merely wiped the doorframe painstakingly with a dry-fibre cloth over the wood where Hege's growth chart was drawn in pens of various colours.

Maggi enjoyed being with the little Morell family. Before she was employed there, she had been in Norway for six months. She'd had cleaning jobs with eleven families. All paying on the black market. Only one of them had bothered enough to learn her name.

Magdalena Wajda.

It was eleven-year-old Hege who had shortened it to Maggi, which had delighted Magdalena. And the little girl's father had paid her wages. Proper wages, into her bank account each month, in accordance with a contract that they had renegotiated every second year. The pay was good. If somewhat less than illegal casual workers received, she had in addition free board and lodgings in a cosy bedsit in the basement. She acquired a pension. She had rights to sickness benefit, though she had never taken a single day off work. With preparing food and washing clothes as well as cleaning the house, her work was varied and far less physically demanding than driving from address to address to scrub floors for people she never met.

Maggi loved Hege.

Jan Morell was strict and sometimes condescending, even though he treated her fairly. The man had seemingly never been attached to any new woman after becoming a widower. If he had, then he kept her at a distance, and that was just as well. The timber house in Vettakollen was Maggi Wajda's domain. She took a fortnight's holiday in her homeland every summer, plus a Christmas break with her sister in Wroclaw, but otherwise stayed put in the little cul-de-sac up on the fringes of the forest.

Hege was a quiet child. Mild-natured. When Maggi met her for the first time, she kept two hamsters in a cage in her room. They were called Kavring and Jonatan, even though they were both females. The very first night, after a slightly taken-aback Maggi had agreed to put Hege to bed, the little girl had come in to her with the cage. Kavring and Jonatan would stay with Maggi for three nights. To bring her comfort and keep her company in this new, strange house.

The youngster had been used to being read to. Obviously not by her father. Maggi's Norwegian language skills consisted of around one hundred words when she arrived, so for the first few months the eleven-year-old had read to her. After six months, they swapped roles.

Hege became the child Maggi had never had. She knew that she had by no means replaced Katinka Morell, but that didn't matter. Hege often demonstrated her fondness for her with the occasional hug and lots of smiles. A few confidences, at least in her teenage years, and little signs of thoughtfulness. In the initial period, Maggi received drawings, home-made Christmas decorations and little notes with hearts attached to her bedsit door with something Hege called 'teacher's chewing gum'. Later, when her skiing career took Hege around the globe for two-thirds of the year, she always brought some small gift home. Never to her father. Always to the home help.

Maggi worked in silence, lived a quiet life and felt an unassuming, deep love for a young woman whose mother she was not. She didn't often plan more than a couple of months ahead. Now she was approaching sixty years of age. Occasionally, especially when she had switched off the light to go to sleep, thoughts of life as a pensioner crossed her mind. As a rule she managed to shrug these off, and fall asleep.

The heart in the bathroom had faded after all these years. Even though Maggi looked after it well, it was unavoidable. At one time she had tried to freshen it up with a new coat of nail varnish, but fortunately realized in time that it looked awful. She managed to remove the new varnish before it hardened.

Hege had not done anything wrong. Maggi knew that. It wasn't only the Norwegian media that had gone berserk over last week's revelations, for some of the Polish newspapers had also covered the story extensively. Justine Kovalčik, the senior member of the Polish women's national team, had found a fresh opportunity to cast malicious aspersions at her Norwegian competitors.

That riled Maggi.

Not that she knew much about either cross-country skiing or Kovalčik, but she knew her Hege Chin. Not on her life would she do anything wrong. Hege didn't even cheat at Monopoly when she was aged eleven.

The bathroom *did* need to be renovated. Jan was right about that. The grout in the shower alcove had begun to loosen a long time ago. Maggi suspected it had started to get waterlogged behind there, since it did not take too many hours after each wash with bleach solution for it to smell a bit musty. The silicone seal between the basin and the wall had yellowed, with tiny spots of something Maggi assumed was some kind of mould. It couldn't be eradicated, no matter how much she scrubbed.

She heard rhythmic, faint thuds from the basement. Hege had been exercising for nearly two hours down there and would soon come up for a shower. Maggi would have to hurry.

The grate on the air vent had fallen on the floor.

That had happened a couple of times before. Really, this bathroom would have to be upgraded soon. It was at least twenty years old: she could read the date on the window trim.

Maggi put the metal grate in the basin, finished off and returned the detergents to the cupboard. Taking hold of the grate, she stepped up on to the toilet seat and prepared to do something she'd had to do from time to time before.

Attach the damned grate.

She saw that there was something inside it.

There shouldn't be anything in the air vent. Once a month, she vacuumed both the grate and the round pipe inside, as far as she could reach before it curved upwards. In the past, when Hege was younger, she had hidden her diary in here. Maggi had always put it back after cleaning, and never said a word. Nine days ago, it had been clean as a whistle in there.

And empty.

Without a moment's thought, she thrust her arm in and took out the offending object.

It was a tube. It looked like an ointment. Or cream. It was practically all used up. Maggi could not fathom how it had ended up there. The writing on the contents list was so tiny that she had to screw up her eyes.

She understood immediately. Clostebol. The name of the active ingredient had been mentioned in both the Polish and Norwegian newspapers.

Her mind felt blank, and she pushed the tube into her apron pocket before clamping the grate in place and hopping down from the toilet seat.

She was so dizzy she had to put her hands flat on the wall.

She tried to think clearly, but the incomprehensible discovery made that impossible. Her pulse hammered in her ears, and a sour taste forced its way up through her gullet, making her feel queasy.

She heard footsteps in the living room. Not the skipping, fast, running dance of before. One week ago, life had changed dramatically for Hege, and therefore also for Maggi. She rushed from the bathroom, through the bedroom and into the hallway, and had just managed to reach the kitchen before Hege entered from the living room.

The girl looked at her. Her training session had painted red half-moons on her cheekbones.

'Thanks,' she said quietly.

'For what?'

'For cleaning the bathroom.'

Maggi forced a smile.

'For being here,' Hege said, heading for the fridge.

She opened the door, picked out a bottle of water. Snapped off the lid and drank.

'I'm the one who should say thank you,' Maggi answered so softly that she did not know whether Hege heard her.

At any rate she had no idea what to do with the tube that was burning a hole in the pocket of the well-worn apron Hege had sewn at school when she was in Primary Seven.

THE VIEWING

This room was filled with love, and Selma felt ill at ease.

Vanja and Kristina had chosen to have a viewing.

Haakon lay in a coffin placed on two black trestles in the middle of the living room. The lid was off and the red lining looked like silk. The corpse was dressed in a jogging suit from Lyn, the club Haakon had joined as a four-year-old and had never left. Red-and-white jacket with a logo and dark-blue trousers with zips along the sides. His hair looked newly shampooed. Blond and combed back. His eyes and mouth were closed. The newspapers had mentioned a head injury. Someone must have disguised it with make-up. Since there were still a number of unexplained circumstances surrounding the accident, Selma couldn't entirely understand why Haakon's body had already been released to the family.

But it had been.

From a distance he looked undeniably dead.

Or like a not too successful wax doll, it struck Selma as she carefully wove her way through all the stools and wooden chairs set out for the guests. An inanimate object, something that had never been alive.

There must be at least twenty people present, on a Monday morning, and the room was cold despite the fire being lit. A window was slightly ajar. People moved away from the icy draught. Selma assumed that this was what made it possible to have a dead body on display in an ordinary living room.

When the message about the viewing had arrived by text, Selma had been considerably upset. She knew she would have to go, but she did not want to. She had never seen a dead person before. Not even her own parents. Her father had taken a tumble on a business trip when Selma was thirty-two, and she had had no choice. Her mother had died after a short illness. Pancreatic cancer, it was all over within six weeks, and Selma had made sure to be in Nice with three girlfriends when the end was near. Her holiday was interrupted, but her mother was securely placed in a closed coffin by the time Selma arrived home for the funeral. She had given a firm 'no thanks' when the undertaker from Jølstad's funeral services had offered to open the lid.

There was something theatrical about a scene such as this. Something artificial, Selma felt when she looked out at all the people sitting with bowed heads and hankies in their hands. So typical of Vanja and Kristina.

Everything was so over the top with them.

Always so lively. The apartment was a horn of plenty filled with bizarre caprices. Nothing matched, which in some peculiar way meant that everything went with everything else. An eclectic style and vivid colours made the place so unusual that most people laughed when they entered.

Now no one was laughing, although to be honest, a cadaver in running clothes was pretty absurd.

Selma took a lighter from a woman she had never clapped eyes on before, and lit one of the many candles on a table beside the coffin. Most were already lit, maybe thirty of them, slim as cake candles, in tiny candlesticks. The flames flickered in the draught. People came and went.

Selma already wanted to leave.

Vanja and Kristina sat on the other side of the coffin, by Haakon's head. They glanced up when she approached. Vanja sobbed silently, with Kristina's hand clasped in hers. With the other she stroked Selma's cheek gently. Without uttering a word. Few people were. One or two in hushed conversation and the hum of the December traffic in Pilestredet were the only sounds to be heard.

Selma recognized most people here. Not a single skier, she noted. No one from the Federation. Elise and little William, Haakon's son, hadn't come either. Most of those present were well over forty. Just Vanja and Kristina's people. Some of them were well known to Selma, other friends, and several of them approached to speak to her. Two hours ago, the *Dagbladet* newspaper had published a short article stating that Selma Falck had unexpectedly sold herself out of the law firm Falck & Partners ANS. It also suggested that they had been unable to contact Selma herself for comment. Fortunately it did not mention anything about a serious illness.

They would scarcely come here, the journalists, and the occasion also did not lend itself to intrusive questions from the others.

Selma really wanted to get away from here as fast as possible.

This was new. All the time, no matter where she was – with the exception of the Poker Turk's basement joint – she felt a strange urge to flee. As soon as she had arrived anywhere, she wanted to turn around. This bewildered her. All her life she had been drawn to others and had felt that others were drawn towards her.

For someone unable to really love anyone, she was actually incredibly social.

And popular.

Selma Falck filled her life with other people, and had been more alone in the past four weeks than the last ten years. Until Monday 13 November, when Jan Morell had confronted her with the continuous embezzlement from his client account, she would have taken a gathering like this in her stride. She would probably have arranged it. Ordered food and organized drinks and been the person who had made the sign in the hallway requesting everyone to switch off mobile phones and put them out of sight.

Before she had been exposed, she would have walked quietly around a room like this. Chatting. Tidying up. Making sure that Vanja and Kristina had everything they needed, at a time when they really wanted nothing except to turn the clock back three days.

But that was before.

Now she felt enveloped in a cocoon of sorrow and great love. In Selma Falck's life there was no room for any of that. Her inability to cry had always suited her down to the ground. During the World Championship Bronze Final against the DDR in the Netherlands in 1986, with the score at 21-11, she was hit on the nose by a goalkeeper's elbow. The injury was more serious than it had first appeared. Three operations later, her nose looked fine again, but her tear ducts were destroyed.

Selma could not shed tears, and she was the only one in the room who was not doing so. She stood apart, staring at her deceased godson in the hope that everyone would leave her in peace.

Haakon had been a longed-for and carefully planned child, in every sense of the word. He was loved from the date of his conception, and was still equally adored by his mothers as he lay in state in the most colourful living room in the world.

Selma's children were born because offspring were part and parcel of a marriage.

She was fond of her children. Admittedly, she liked Johannes better than Anine, but that didn't matter. Her daughter was just so difficult to understand. Even as a tiny baby Anine had seemed so strange. As soon as she was old enough to hold a ball – Selma had been so looking forward to this and had managed to get one with the Bækkelaget logo on it – the little girl had put the ball to sleep in her doll's cot and wrapped a little quilt around it and started to sing a lullaby.

Anine and Johannes were the nearest Selma had come to loving anyone.

Maybe she did actually love them. She didn't know for sure, but doubted it. She didn't especially miss them. She never had done. Neither on her own travels when they were little, nor when they themselves went on trips once they grew older. She was glad they existed, and she was sometimes anxious when she didn't know what they were doing. It pained her that they hated her now. She tried as hard as she could not to think about them. It was difficult, even though, deep down in her heart of hearts, she did not believe any of the furious messages they had sent her recently. They were just so angry on their father's behalf. It would pass. In time. Maybe.

Don't think of the children. Don't.

Once in a while she tried to imagine what it would be like if they died. The thought terrified her, but the dull sorrow that overcame her then was so different in intensity from the life-affirming, overwhelming energy it gave her to risk something. To take chances. To compete.

To gamble.

Selma herself felt that it must be some kind of defect, even though she never spoke to anyone about it. In her brain, perhaps. It was called oxytocin, the love hormone, and it was impossible for her to produce enough of it. She was concerned about people, she experienced empathy and felt deep pleasure from friendship. She had been a team player from a young age, and she had liked the fact that in their early years, Jesso had admired, loved and wanted her.

It was just never particularly reciprocated.

Kristina and Vanja had been so head over heels in love that Selma didn't really understand what became of them at the time they moved in together. She married Jesso because he was kind. They had a good life together, for a long time: he gave her space and was already earning a good salary when they set up house. Since Selma considered children to be a natural consequence, it wasn't insignificant that Jesso was a fine figure of a man, smart, and also exercised almost as much as she did.

Jesso had good genes, and was a good dad in every way.

Selma had, however, never been in love with him. They had just lived together for almost quarter of a century. The only person she had ever been infatuated with was Morten Harket. By the same token, she had never met him. There was some kind of connection here that she had never really bothered to grasp.

Nils Holm, Kristina's older lawyer brother, had approached from behind her without her noticing.

'Hello,' he said softly, almost whispering.

'Hello.'

Her eyes were still fixed on the corpse.

'I've been here all weekend,' he continued. 'Expected to see you here.'

'I was here all Friday night. And Friday evening too.'

She tucked her hair behind her ear and tried to look emotional.

'When the police came.'

He nodded.

'I heard that. Thanks.'

Selma did not reply. Merely nodded. It must be possible to leave now.

'There are rumours,' Nils said. 'That you've sold up. Suddenly.'

She finally turned to face him. Gave a sad smile.

'It would be nice to have a chat with you, Nils. To catch up, you know. But this is hardly the time, don't you think?'

He hesitated. Studied her.

'You left us suddenly as well,' he said.

'Yes, a long time ago. A very, very long time ago.'

The doorbell rang.

'I'll open it,' Selma said quickly, gesturing to Vanja and Kristina that they should remain seated.

Not until she was on her way to the door, relieved at escaping from her very first real employer, did she remember the sign someone had attached to the door.

Don't ring the bell. Just come in.

Of course, it could have fallen off. She emerged into the deserted hallway and took three deep breaths before putting her hand on the heavy brass knob and opening the door.

'Bottolf Odda,' she blurted out. 'So good of you to come. Come in.'

'Selma Falck,' he replied, sounding surprised. 'Oh. Hello.'

The NCCSF president poked his head in and glanced towards the living room.

'Is there ... some sort of ... party going on here?'

'A viewing.'

'What?'

'A wake, if you prefer. A lot of people are here to grieve.'

'Wa ... no, no. I just wanted to ...'

He retreated a couple of steps.

'Are his mothers here?'

'Yes, of course. We're holding a viewing, as I said. Come on in.'

Selma opened the door wider and spread her arms out in a gesture of encouragement.

'No,' Bottolf Odda said firmly. 'I'm not invited. I just came to ...'

He ran a rough hand over his unshaven face. His suit hung badly on him and raindrops glittered on his shoulders. His red tie had a dark stain and he reeked of fast food.

'I just wanted to give them a little ...' he began, '... warning. A heads-up, so to speak.'

'I see. What about? Or isn't it a bit silly of us to be speaking out here in the hall?'

He brusquely grabbed her elbow and steered her out into the stairwell.

'This is probably best,' he mumbled.

'What is?'

'That I tell you. Then you can tell them.'

His hand was raised lethargically towards the front door that had almost slid shut behind them.

'OK,' Selma said, nodding obligingly. 'I'm a sort of family lawyer, you might say. What's this about?'

'The A-test,' he whispered.

'The drugs test? On Haakon? Was a sample really taken?'

'Yes. It's ...'

'He died on Friday,' Selma interrupted. 'Surely there aren't any results yet? It usually takes at least a fortnight!'

'Jan Morell,' he said so softly that she had to ask him to repeat it. 'Jan Morell! He has so many strings he can pull that it's really scary. As soon as the rumours began to do the rounds on Saturday, after the press conference, he started to work his magic.'

Bottolf Odda pushed his hand under his jacket.

'Now we're doing all we can to delay the B-test.'

'What? Are you planning to sabotage ...'

'No, no, no!'

He waved his left hand about while the right hand was still fumbling for something that was apparently tucked into his inside pocket.

'Not sabotage. On the deceased's behalf, we have requested analysis of a B-test. To prevent this becoming public knowledge before the funeral. Or cremation. What is it to be?'

Selma did not answer. She grasped one side of his jacket and held it out.

'What is it you want to show me, Bottolf?'

'This.'

He handed her an A4 sheet, and she opened it out. Read. Read yet again.

'Clostebol,' she murmured, running her tongue over her lower lip. 'Extremely minimal quantities. But obviously present.'

She calmly folded the sheet of paper and gave it back to him.

'The same substance that Hege has been caught using,' she said. 'This is starting to turn into a real crisis.'

'Yes,' he nodded, his voice breaking so much that his answer became a squeak. 'Not only for Hege and for Haakon's posthumous reputation. But also for ...'

His hand rested under the left side of his jacket for so long that Selma feared momentarily that he was about to have a heart attack. His face was grey and damp, but the moisture could be from the rain outside.

'Are you all right?' she asked.

'Bloody hell,' he said, stroking his face. 'Bloody hell, Selma Falck. This is primarily a crisis for the Norwegian Cross-Country Skiing Federation. Death and drug-taking. Damn and blast.'

All of a sudden, he inhaled loudly. Almost gasped for air, and then repeated: 'Death and drug-taking!'

His eyes were brimming. His lower lip trembled before he abruptly straightened up, adjusted his jacket and tie and ran both hands over the few wet strands of hair he still possessed.

'And less than two months till the Winter Olympics,' he said in an exaggeratedly light tone of voice as he forced a grimace that might resemble a smile. 'I've got enough to do, you might say. Thank you very much.'

'Thank you.'

He began to move towards the stairs. Selma stood there watching him.

'Now it's come to me,' he said suddenly, turning around. 'Who you look like. A bloody strong likeness, really.'

'I know.'

His smile was wan, but now at least it seemed genuine.

'You must have heard it. All the time.'

'Yes.'

'It's really striking. I like it, by the way. The series. And the actress.'

He turned up his jacket lapels and trudged down the stairs.

THE CONVERSATION

'This is actually impressive.'

Jan Morell was a man of few compliments. He had grown up with a single mother who told him every morning, always equally dispassionately, that he would never amount to anything. Just like his father, she said, although Jan never really knew what had become of him. Then his mother tossed in a line or two about Jan being the reason for everything painful and difficult in her life, before lighting a cigarette and going back to bed. Not until he was seventeen years old did Jan meet anyone who spoke nicely to him. Her name was Katinka, and he made up his mind to take care of her for the rest of her life.

She died twenty-five years later.

Jan Morell was a man of action. He had fought his way through his childhood, when he was not skiing or skating with equipment that was old-fashioned and heavy as lead. He bought it himself, with hard-earned cash from bottle deposits, at the Stampen second-hand store in Prinsens gate. Or at a flea market. His mother hadn't got him so much as a proper cap: for eight winters in a row he had roamed around in a knitted ski helmet he had been given by his hero Knut Johannesen, better known by his nickname Kupper'n, one time when as a little boy he had sneaked on to a tram and a bus all the way to the petrol station in Bøler to get the old speed-skating star's autograph.

His teenage years, after Katinka came on the scene, became

something quite different. He had spent some time in the sin bin at junior high school before they met, and knew little about anything other than playing sports. For two years he re-took subjects he had previously failed, and managed to pass his senior high school exams as an external student. That was in 1981. He was not accepted as a student at the Norwegian School of Economics, but after a year of study at correspondence school by day and working by evening and night, he ended up in Edinburgh. Only ten years later Morell Clear View, MCV, was the eighth-largest consultancy company in Norway.

Today it was the second-largest.

Jan Morell owed nothing to anyone. He had not reached as far as he had through inappropriate boasting, neither about himself nor others.

'This is really impressive, Selma. As usual, you're unusually systematic and efficient.'

Jan had spent almost twenty silent minutes leafing through the ring binder she had filled in the course of the night. Although her apartment was a dump, and he scratched himself at the thought of having been there, the block had at least splashed out on broadband provision. Since Google had given her nearly a million results on Hege Chin Morell, most of the work had obviously gone into sifting and sorting. Muckraking and golden nuggets, biography and travels. Rumours, myths and facts. Selma claimed it had taken her ten consecutive hours on the settee with the laptop on her knee and the printer on the floor. He was happy to believe that. Then she had taken extracts from articles that were worth something, and placed them in chronological order in a green, thick ring binder. In addition she had drawn a relationship chart of everyone mentioned on Hege's own list. The vast majority of these were connected to the NCCSF in one way or another. A summarizing chapter was provided after every section, and finally a conclusion that ran to three pages.

It was unnecessarily long, and actually extremely simple: it appeared that no one really wished Hege Chin Morell any harm.

'You arrived at that too.'

He carefully closed the ring binder.

'Which means she might not be the intended victim,' he went on while Maggi arrived from the kitchen and put coffee cups and buttered bread rolls in front of them.

He waited until she had set out everything.

Selma seemed uncomfortable, sitting there on the settee opposite, constantly pulling her cardigan more snugly around her. Leaning back, he entwined his fingers behind his neck and studied her closely.

'Or what?' he asked once the kitchen door had slid shut again.

Selma tilted her head to one side.

'That thought had struck me too.'

'That was why I was so set on having Haakon's sample analysed.'

'How did you manage that? In such a short time, I mean?'

'I can manage most things,' he said gruffly.

'Yes, but ...'

'When the rumour started to circulate that Haakon might also have fallen foul of drugs, I realized that this could be a straw for Hege to clutch.'

Selma did not react. She gazed at him, searchingly, with her body locked down. Her arms folded over her chest and her legs crossed.

Selma Falck looked like an athlete. Even after so many years. Jan had followed the fourth season of the reality TV show, *Champion of Champions*, in 2012, primarily because a friend was taking part. A rapid mental calculation told him that Selma must have been forty-six when the series was filmed. She had ended up in fourth place, as the best woman. And was far more fascinating to follow than Jan's friend, who had won. Selma was tall and possibly a kilo or two heavier than in her prime. All the same there was fluidity in her movements and strength in the way she conducted herself that did not entirely chime with her real age. Her face was broad, her chin almost square; there was a trace of masculinity that disappeared each time she smiled with wide, full lips that were obviously not the result of any cosmetic trickery.

She had not smiled since her arrival.

Her eyes were slightly too far apart, he noticed now for the first time. Almond-shaped, a little crooked and so dark that in this dim light he could not distinguish the pupils from the irises.

'What do you mean?' she said in the end.

'Look at this,' he said, pushing a sheet of paper towards her.

She picked it up. Read. A frown bisected her forehead.

'Haakon was tested six days before he died,' she said without looking up.

'Yes.'

'And you've managed to come up with those results already.'

Jan sighed. He leaned back again and clasped his hands behind his neck.

'Don't sound so surprised, Selma. I was your client for nine years. You know I can pull strings. You know I never do anything illegal. It gets a bit tedious if you're going to make a song and dance about it every time I ...'

Suddenly he leaned forward and grabbed his coffee cup.

'... get things moving. What else do you notice about that?'

He raised his cup and tilted it carefully towards her before he took a drink. The coffee was too hot and he put it down again before adding: 'As you see, the sample taken just before he died was absolutely clean. But the post-mortem sample shows a concentration of Clostebol of three nanograms per millilitre. What does that tell you?'

Selma was still staring at the sheet of paper.

'That he can't have taken the substance to achieve any kind of performance-enhancing effect,' she said slowly. 'Clostebol has, as far as I remember, a half-life of eight hours. He was clean at the start of last week, and with such a low concentration as this only a few days later, he can't possibly have been on ...'

At last she looked up.

'... any kind of systematic drugs regime,' she rounded off, pushing the sheet of paper back across the table.

'Exactly. Hege's concentration was also low. Seven nanograms per millilitre, so higher than Haakon's, but all the same totally insignificant amounts. Unfortunately for me ...'

He raised the cup to his mouth and tried again, as if the liquid could have cooled down in a mere thirty seconds.

'Unfortunately for Hege,' he began again, 'it was more than three months since she was last tested. In other words, she hasn't the same ...'

He hesitated for so long that Selma gave him some assistance.

'Alibi,' she said. 'Haakon has a watertight alibi. At least the earlier test gives a strong indication that he hasn't consciously been taking drugs. That wouldn't prevent him from being suspended, but it could have been important in terms of how long he was barred from competing.'

Jan nodded.

He had thought for a long time that he had a good knowledge of her. Smart and capable. Social. Outgoing and easy to understand. An efficient lawyer, with a network of contacts even he envied. It seemed as if she knew the whole of Norway.

Norway definitely knew her.

So when he began to suspect that there were substantial sums missing from the client account in his name, he simply could not believe it. As a rule, Jan Morell believed in himself. Always, in fact, but untypically he had chosen to hope that there might be an alternative explanation as to why he was unable to access his money, when out of the blue he received an offer of a favourable investment.

She had admitted everything immediately, as she should. Did not plead for mercy. On the contrary, she told him sotto voce that it had all started around six months ago. A small amount now and then, usually repaid within a short time. Then something must have gone seriously wrong. What had been until then a continuous fairly easily camouflaged misappropriation of funds had turned into regular theft. It took him longer to learn what the money had been spent on than to obtain a confession.

She liked to gamble, was what she had finally admitted. On everything, apparently, without being willing to go into details.

The meeting in Selma's tasteful office in Bogstadveien had taken place four weeks ago. She changed abruptly. She was still her usual smiling, pleasant and correct self to others, he noticed. But not to him.

He had begun to realize that she was actually extremely lonely. As he was.

The difference was that he had chosen it. Just as he had decided that his life should take a sharp turn when at barely seventeen he had met Katinka, he had chosen another new direction when she died. For a quarter of a century he had been permitted to keep her, and the loneliness after her death was a way of still being together.

But in the case of Selma Falck, it was completely different.

On Saturday evening, while the rest of the house slept, he had Googled for pictures of her. She had been everywhere during those years, and her internet archive ran to almost 200,000 photographs. In sweaty running gear and elegant evening gowns, at the palace, on a climbing wall, on ice rinks and in court. She seemed equally well dressed in all of these, even in her lawyer's robes. In some photos, especially when she was dressed to the nines, she was with her husband. Jess Olav Mork was his name, also originally a lawyer, but he had now been the MP for Venstre for the past twelve years. He had held his seat by the skin of his teeth in that autumn's general election. One of the most recent images was from Thursday 26 October, only a couple of weeks before Jan had exposed Selma's crime.

The photograph had been taken as the guests arrived at the annual parliamentary dinner at the palace. Selma was wearing a midnight-blue evening dress that, according to the blurb, was designed by Ove Harder Finseth. The neckline was plunging and her arms were bare. Her long, dark hair was half up, half down, and she was looking straight at the camera with the same broad smile as everywhere else.

Her husband, on the other hand, was staring directly at her.

Of all the pictures Jan Morell took the time to peruse that evening, in the company of three glasses of whisky and finally a cigar on the doorstep, there was only one photo that showed eye contact between Selma and Jess Olav. That one had been taken in 1988 at the Olympic Games in Seoul. The final was just over and lost, and the image from *Aftenposten* depicted the young couple as they were about to kiss.

Almost thirty years ago.

'The Cross-Country Skiing Federation,' Selma said, picking up a roll. 'You think someone's out to destroy the NCCSF. Per se, so to speak.'

Jan nodded.

'So you think that ...'

She examined the bread roll and took a bite. Chewing silently, she swallowed and then said: 'That the Russians have sabotaged the Norwegian national team by sneaking drugs into the bodies of our best male and female skiers? Or maybe you suspect Sweden? Or maybe it's our friends the Danes who are pissed off about having only one skier among the million best in the world?'

She took yet another bite of the snack and chewed slowly. Watching him.

'Not necessarily them,' he said acerbically. 'It doesn't have to be foreigners.'

'Have you any other suggestions? Our Telemark skiers?'

He had never known her to be sarcastic. Her eyes narrowed and even though she was chewing, he could see that she was smiling.

'Have you been in contact with a psychologist?' he asked.

She did not answer.

'The deadline runs out today. In ...'

He drew back his sweater and peered at his wristwatch.

'... five hours. You don't have much time.'

'I've spoken to one,' Selma said. 'I'm meeting him tomorrow. Word of honour.'

'That's a few hours too late.'

'He couldn't see me today.'

'Selma.'

He reclined, placing both arms on the back of the settee and his right foot on his left knee.

'I have a philosophy in life,' he said, raising his voice. 'And that is to give everyone a second chance. That's what people get from me, Selma. My employees. My friends. My ...'

His hand made a gallant gesture in her direction.

'My lawyers. One more chance. That's what life gave me. An opportunity to correct my own mistakes and misdeeds. Never more than that. Never two. If you've been in touch with a psychologist today, however, I'll temper justice with mercy. You've met the deadline halfway. A written declaration that you're receiving treatment for your compulsive gambling must be on my desk by five o'clock tomorrow. OK?'

Selma put down the half-eaten bread roll on a plate. Brushing away some invisible crumbs from her deep-red jacket, she looked straight at him. Every trace of irony had vanished when she calmly said: 'You do have a point, Jan.'

'Yes or no? By five tomorrow.'

'Fine. Promise. And you do have a point.'

'I see.'

'This unexpected turn of events with Haakon, this ...'

She got to her feet. Stood for a few seconds, with her hands on her hips and a faraway look as she concentrated.

'It might all be a coincidence, of course. There doesn't have to be any kind of connection between Haakon and Hege's cases. But there are some striking factors here that make it absolutely worthwhile to find out whether they might both have been sabotaged. And let us take first things first.'

She crossed to the bare fireplace, but turned all of a sudden in the middle of the room.

'Clostebol, then, is a synthetically manufactured anabolic-androgenic steroid,' she said. 'The androgenic effect has to do with typical male characteristics, such as production of semen and beard growth.'

'As if Hege could have ...'

'However, athletes are looking for the anabolic effect,' she interrupted him. 'Increased building of bones and skeletal musculature. Just like the testosterone that occurs naturally in our bodies, but administered to patients for a pretty broad spectrum of illnesses. The point is ...'

She moved on towards the fireplace, crouched down and began

to set a fire in the deep hearth. The logs in a woven basket on the floor were so old that they had gathered dust.

'Clostebol isn't found in any of the medications available on the Norwegian market,' she said. 'And why it should be necessary to include Clostebol in the ointment Hege told us about, the one that Hedda Bruun was given for her sore lip, is incomprehensible. The ointment also contained neomycin, which is more logical. That's an antibacterial substance. Do you have matches?'

Jan pointed at the mantelpiece. Selma tore up an old newspaper, tucked it well under the wood and lit the fire.

'So why Clostebol in particular?' she asked, straightening up.

Jan, assuming that the question was rhetorical, did not reply.

'WADA's list of forbidden substances is pages long,' she went on. 'And getting longer by the minute. All the same, there are only a few of these that are particularly relevant for use by cheating athletes. For cross-country skiers, the most obvious would be EPO or traditional blood doping, as well as anabolic-androgenic steroids. AAS. You might also imagine that stimulants, primarily amphetamines, would have a certain desirable effect during a fifty-kilometre ski race. But I've never heard of skiers being caught for that sort of thing. Have you?'

'Er ... no. Or yes, I have. There was a suspicion that the Italians used it, both in Chamonix in 1937 and later. At that time they used all kinds of strange things. Naphtha. Even strychnine.'

'OK. But in modern times?'

'No.'

'Exactly. Besides, the effects last a relatively short time, and races can be very long. However, it's beyond doubt that AAS can have a real performance-boosting effect. But then again: why on earth use Clostebol of all things? Precisely the same substance that a totally innocent Hedda Bruun was so close to ingesting in Italy? In an incident that has been hushed up ever since?'

Now she was standing in the middle of the room.

'I've checked, Jan. If Hedda had used the ointment as the doctor advised her to, she'd have fallen foul of a drugs test taken within a reasonable length of time afterwards. She had terrible sores, and the active ingredient would have gone straight into her bloodstream.'

'Do you mean ... do you really mean that the national team's doctor might have deliberately tried to administer the drug to Hedda Bruun?'

'No idea. I don't know Stian Bach, and for all we know, the whole thing might have been an inexcusable blunder. But don't you see?'

Suddenly she grabbed her bag and fished out her mobile. She keyed in to the home pages of Anti-Doping Norway, hesitating for a second before pressing one or two buttons and then sitting down beside him.

'Here. This is the list of banned AAS preparations.'

'It's long. Very long.'

'Yes.'

She sat so close to him that he could smell her scent. Faintly of perfume, more strongly of what he assumed to be shampoo. At any rate the fragrance was stronger when she tucked her hair behind her ear and continued.

'Clostebol has actually only been popular in one place,' she said, more quietly now. 'In a particular era. In the former DDR. We remember, don't we, what their athletes looked like. It's a relatively weak anabolic steroid, and in recent years it hasn't been available on the legal market in pill form. Nor in liquid form, for injections, which are what athletes prefer when they decide to cheat. However, the derivative is found in a number of creams, as well as in a vaginal tablet, whatever that might be good for. There's also a nasal spray. In saying that ...'

She stood up again. Jan would normally have been annoyed by this restlessness. Now, however, he was concentrating so fiercely on what she was saying that she could have done handstands without provoking a reaction from him.

Clearly she was fit enough to do that too.

'... it's certainly possible to get hold of the stuff on the black market,' she went on. 'You can find most things there. I've done some cruising around websites from the weightlifting world, the less legitimate parts, and those guys seem to think that the stuff's for wimps. Not strong enough, except in large doses, which are difficult to administer. Clostebol is quite simply not an especially suitable drug nowadays, with the control regime sport has to put up with. More than seventy cross-country skiers worldwide have been caught taking drugs since the legislation was introduced. Not one of them for use of Clostebol. Not a single one. Until now. There have been a few cases, of course, including that of a cyclist in Italy who had used Trofodermin on a rash. But it's far from the most common substance found by the anti-doping authorities.'

The wood had burst into tentative flames. Selma used the poker to introduce more air between the logs.

'But then, all of a sudden, we come across Clostebol three times in a short period,' Selma continued. 'First in the story from Italy. Then in Hege's sample. And today in Haakon's.'

Jan was following her movements with his eyes.

'So you think the cases are linked? All three of them?'

'I don't think anything. I'm just establishing that it's all a bit of a coincidence. And if we're going to have the slightest chance of exonerating Hege before the Olympics deadline date, we need to chase up the few connections we catch sight of. We just don't have time for anything else.'

Now Jan Morell also got to his feet. He moved towards the huge panorama window. It had stopped raining, and a grey strip of daylight was dwindling in the west. Beneath the apple tree, beside the sparse pile of old carrots, stood an elk. A bull calf, he saw, born this year, with distinctive nodules on its forehead where the antlers would grow when the animal was older. The mother was nowhere to be seen.

'He's so beautiful,' Selma said under her breath, as she came to stand by his side.

She was just as tall as he was. They stood, in silence, both with their hands on their backs and feet slightly apart, like two soldiers on guard.

'Why does no one come to her defence?' Jan said in an undertone. 'Fight for her?'

'I'm doing that. You're doing that.'

The calf raised its head. Turned its broad muzzle towards them. Sniffing the wind, then listening before it continued to chew.

'It's so obvious that she hasn't cheated,' Jan said. 'Such tiny amounts of Clostebol couldn't make her into a better skier. Bloody hell, Selma, she was already the best! Why are people so … ready to find fault?'

'Give a wide berth to social media and reader comments.'

'Is it because she …'

He checked himself. She finished for him: '… isn't wholly Norwegian? Maybe. She doesn't think so herself.'

'I know. We decided it should be like that. That racism shouldn't be our problem. It never has been either. It can be different with adopted children. They become Norwegian in a different way. Than …'

He let the comparison hang in the air.

'Maybe,' Selma replied. 'Or maybe not. What did people always say about Marit Bjørgen?'

'A lot. That she shouldn't have quit in the spring. That she should have postponed having a second child. That she should have continued for another season and competed in PyeongChang in February, for example.'

He suspected that Selma was giving a genuine smile at last, even though they were both still staring out at the lawn, where the elk calf was quickly clearing the area of carrots.

'Yes, of course. But I was referring to how Norwegian she was regarded. So down to earth and easygoing. Let nothing go to her head. So gloriously Norwegian! As people said.'

The calf was replete. It began to wander across the lawn, slightly hesitantly, as if the food station were too valuable to leave. The two people at the window stood gazing at the graceful animal, which abruptly pricked up its ears, picked up speed and disappeared into the fringes of the forest bordering the property.

'And what have people always said about Petter Northug?' Selma asked, turning to put more wood on the fire.

'It depends what you mean by people.'

'He's so terribly un-Norwegian.'

Selma drew quote marks with two fingers on either hand.

'So full of himself. So self-assured and egocentric. Brash and cheeky. So accustomed to victory. In other words: un-Norwegian. That's how we divvy up our skiers, Jan, into the many Norwegians and the few 'terribly un-Norwegian' ones. But they're always from Norway all the same. They have names such as Haakon and Martin and Petter. Marit and Ingvild. None of them have that little "Chin" added as a disturbing element in their names.'

Jan opened his mouth to say something, but hesitated so long that she went on: 'You mustn't forget that this is the most Norwegian of all sports. The real primeval sport. That unifies radicals and racists. That makes even the most ardent anti-nationalist go wild. And into the bargain, the only sport we have all taken part in ourselves, so to speak. As outdoor recreation, most of us, but there's scarcely a Norwegian who doesn't have a pair of skis or five in storage in their basement.'

'The ethnic Norwegians amongst us.'

The fire had begun to crackle.

'Spot on,' Selma said, tossing yet another log on the flames. 'The ethnic Norwegians amongst us. Cross-country skiing is an identity sport. Measured globally, it's a tiny, minority sport, in which probably a hundred Norwegians could go straight into one of the national teams. Three million of us who could have qualified for all the national teams as well as the six or seven best skiers. Have you ever heard anyone say of a handball player that she or he is so "gloriously Norwegian"?'

Once again she drew quote marks in the air, more animated now.

'For us Norwegians, cross-country skiing is a matter of national pride. It's about being Norwegian. About our great society. Of course it can't be said about Hege that she is "gloriously Norwegian". Because she's not. And yet you certainly couldn't assert that she was un-Norwegian. That would be stretching things. In that respect Hege was always a rare bird on the ski trails. Not to her teammates. Not to the Federation. But to those who lay down the real foundations of popular sports: the majority.'

'The men's national football team has lots of …'

'Cut it out. Football is a world sport. On the football field, the spectators have scarves, banners and noisy rattles. And traipse around in their team colours. Along the ski trails, what do you see there? Knitted sweaters, plus fours and Norwegian flags, Jan. Markers of national identity. Flag upon flag upon waving fucking flag! All over the place. Any ordinary Sunday at Holmenkollen looks like a seventeenth of May parade on rotten snow. This year a gang of women from Bærum had even put on national costumes. National costumes! On a ski trail!'

A furious blush had spread from her neck upwards. She was really unrecognizable.

Selma Falck had built her career as a lawyer and celebrity on the basis of never taking a position on political questions. A kernel of the strictly politically correct was all she ever allowed herself to express. She had fronted several fundraising campaigns, but only to benefit totally uncontroversial causes. Save the Children and UNICEF, as Jan could recall. He had read one solitary interview in which the journalist had pressed her harder to find out where she stood. The only thing she would say, after a great deal of pressure, was that she had never voted for the party her husband represented in parliament.

Selma Falck was known for her direct manner, forthright character and no-nonsense approach. But if you analysed interviews with her, listened more closely when she spoke on TV or radio, it was as if the real Selma Falck was well hidden behind the armour of threadbare phrases and invulnerability.

There was only one arena in which a hard-hitting Selma expressed definite opinions.

In a court of law.

Now, however, she was in full flow in Jan Morell's living room.

'Football's all about winning,' she went on. 'Fundamentally it's a dreadfully boring sport for eighty-five of the ninety minutes. It matters not a jot whether the players are yellow, brown or white as far as the vast majority is concerned, as long as their shirts have the Norwegian flag on their chests. And they win. Football has a long tradition of multi-ethnicity. Cross-country skiing hasn't, as you well know. Until yesterday I was reasonably sure that Hege was sabotaged because she's different. Some madman or other who ...'

The spaceship doors opened. Maggi moved towards the coffee table.

'Have you had enough?'

Jan glanced again at the time.

'Yes. I fancy a dram. The usual. What about you?'

He shot a look at Selma, who had finally sat down again.

'If you have a Pepsi Max, I'd like one of those. If not, nothing. Thanks.'

'Unfortunately we don't have any soft drinks at all.'

Without another word, Maggi cleared the table.

Jan Morell liked having Maggi around. He didn't really know what he thought of her, apart from that she was good at what she was employed to do. A woman of few words, simply, who had come into the family at a time when he couldn't even manage to speak to his own child. Magdalena Wajda arrived with excellent references into a house that had come to a standstill because of grief. He gave her short, sharp orders in the first few days. Later she found things out on her own initiative. There was nothing to be said about her efforts, though the food she had prepared in the first six months had been tasteless and bland. For her first Christmas she had received three cookery books from Hege and him in a present she had taken with her to Poland. The books returned with her to Vettakollen, and everything improved after that.

He didn't know her. It had never been necessary.

Now, however, something unfamiliar had come over her, he realized. Usually she moved in a light, determined manner – Maggi was an efficient woman who had never broken a single object in all of her thirteen years as housekeeper. Now she knocked over Selma's coffee cup. It was half full, and a Polish curse slipped from Maggi's lips before she dashed to the kitchen for a cloth.

Jan had never seen her run before.

'There you are,' Selma said, having gathered up the dishes by the time Maggi had come back. 'I'll carry them out.'

Despite Maggi's protests, she was as good as her word. Maggi wiped up the spillage, brought Jan a tumbler of whisky with ice cubes and made herself scarce again.

'You don't drink,' he said, raising his glass in a toast. 'I've read that. Sensible of you.'

Selma scratched just above her eyebrow and asked: 'Where's Hege?'

'Out running. Up the Korketrekkeren track.'

'So late?'

'She can't settle.'

'No. Who can?'

Yet again she stood up and crossed to the window.

'Who in heaven's name could possibly be behind all this?' Jan ventured again.

'I don't know, as I've said. Repeatedly.'

'No, but can't you think of anyone? What could be the purpose of it? Who could be interested in harming both Hege and Haakon? And maybe Hedda?'

'Stian Bach comes to mind as far as the last-mentioned is concerned,' Selma said, as she put more wood on the fire. 'But we know for certain that he hasn't been anywhere near Hege since then. She said so herself.'

'And how on earth would Hege and Haakon ingest such a thing? Neither of them suffers from herpes, and ...'

'The ointment could quite simply be applied to the skin.'

'To the skin?'

'Yes. If the skin is grazed, the uptake would be more effective, of course. But that's not strictly necessary. Lots of medications are intended to be absorbed through intact skin. Nicotine patches, for example. Voltaren in gel form. Quite normal. As far as I've understood, it's not a matter of whether or not the skin is broken, but of the properties of the medication.'

She drew back her sleeve and rubbed her lower arm. She had freckles, he saw, pale freckles scattered all over her skin, even at this time of year.

'An ointment,' she ploughed on, 'will have active ingredients intended to be absorbed through the skin. A pill is designed to be absorbed through the gut. Or the stomach. With broken skin, the ingestion process is faster, but as far as I could discover, not crucial. Besides ...'

She examined her arm, found a little scratch, and pointed: 'Most of us have cuts and scrapes on our skin at any particular time. Our skin is extensive. Our largest organ, in fact.'

'So anyone could just ... shake our hand, for instance?'

'That would be some handshake,' she said. 'A bit sticky, I would think.'

'But you know what I mean, don't you?'

'Yes.'

'This means that anyone at all could have done this. We're not any further forward.'

'No. We have ...'

She wandered around the room, coming to a halt at a dark-oak sideboard just beside the kitchen door.

'Someone in the NCCSF knows the story from Italy. There can't be many, otherwise the story would have leaked out. I'm actually surprised it wasn't publicized long ago. And even more surprised that Stian Bach is still in post.'

Jan put down his glass.

'That's the big problem with the NCCSF,' he said, sighing.

'What is?'

'Jobs for the boys. Lack of transparency. It's the same old gang that tramped around down there at Ullevål who now hold sway in the crystal palace they've built on the hill up here. Friendship cuts across everything. Vacancies are filled without being advertised.

In the best-case scenario, they advertise them for the sake of appearances, but employ someone they already know anyway. A brother-in-law. A pal from student days. Someone they're certain will sit completely still, without rocking the boat, and not insist on any changes.'

'*Dagens Gang* has pressed them pretty hard for a long time, though.'

'Yes, indeed. But it doesn't seem to have helped any. You know ...'

He clasped both hands to his face and rubbed until the skin was red. Shook his head, took another mouthful from the glass and inhaled deeply.

'They let themselves be measured only by results,' he said. 'And as long as we're the world's top cross-country skiing nation, the rest of us will let them do it. Just wait. If we do as well in PyeongChang as everybody predicts, we'll once again see a nation intoxicated by medals without any thought of accounts, organization or efficiency. The system is absolutely ... wrong. It was a system error that led to Martin making a fool of himself over that asthma medication last year, and that's *definitely* ...'

He stopped of his own volition. Held the glass up to the light. The flames from the fire made it sparkle with glints of amber, and he drained the glass in a final gulp.

'It was definitely a system error that meant Stian Bach could make such a catastrophic blunder as what happened in Italy. And not least that he got away with it. If the story had become common knowledge, the boys would have persuaded the guy to quit, and then blamed it on human error. Human error! It's to protect ourselves from bloody human error that we have systems! And Hedda, she'd have been the one who'd have had to give up all hopes for the Winter Olympics and probably the whole of season eighteen/nineteen into the bargain.'

He stared into his empty glass.

'Dilettantes, the lot of them. To some extent they let me take part as well. I've personally picked out at least three of the employees over there. The Finance Director, for example. Arnulf Selhus. He worked for me earlier. And I don't even have any formal connection to the Federation any longer. Christ ...'

He gave a lopsided smile. Actually longed for another drink.

'MCV would have gone down the tubes if I'd run the company the same way,' he muttered.

'Could you find out who knew about what happened in Italy?'

'Why should I ... yes! Exactly. Those who knew about that near-catastrophe ... They also know you can walk right into a pharmacy in Italy and buy an ointment containing Clostebol. After all, getting hold of the stuff is the first thing you have to do if you're out to sabotage anyone.'

Selma nodded.

'That would be a start at least. A start is more than we had this morning.'

'Here,' Jan said, handing her his mobile phone. 'I've had this list since Hege told me about that episode down there.'

Selma read the note.

'Stian Bach,' she murmured. 'We knew that. The president, Bottolf Odda. One, two, three, four, five coaches. Arnulf Selhus. Astrid Beita. Who's that?'

'The cook.'

'Physiotherapist. Only one. Knut Nilssen. Don't they usually have more?'

'It varies. The skiers themselves would rather have more physios at the expense of having a doctor, but it's all a question of cost, you see. But before the start of the season, there's always a doctor with them. And then as a rule it's only Knut who travels. Go ahead and send that list to yourself.'

'I'll probably remember it,' she mumbled.

All the same, Selma's fingers followed his instructions, and she gave him back the phone.

'Journalists,' Jan added. 'There was a group of journalists there for two days. I'll rustle up their names and send them to you.'

'Fine. Thanks. I have to go now.'

Once again she rose to her feet. Jan followed her out into the hallway. She pulled on a dark-green quilted jacket and thrust her hands into a pair of gloves.

'Tomorrow by five,' he reminded her softly. 'A certificate. From a psychiatrist or a psychologist. Last chance, Selma.'

'Understood,' she answered, with a faint smile, as she opened the door. 'By five.'

'And no more gambling?'

She looked him straight in the eye.

'No. That would break our agreement. Besides, I don't have any money.'

Her gaze was steady. Open, but not strained.

'Fine,' he said tersely, and closed the door behind her.

His phone gave a peep. He took it from his trouser pocket and tapped his way into his mailbox.

Hi Jan. Have you seen Klaus lately? Have tried to contact him for past few days, but no one knows where he is. Want to get some good photos of the old girl before she finally pops her clogs. Let me know if you hear anything. Goggen.

Jan Morell hadn't seen Klaus for at least six months. They had become increasingly rare, these get-togethers with the boys from Kjelsås. Klaus could be anywhere at all. He was still a bachelor, had no children, and had finally become a world-renowned nature photographer. Last year he'd been in the Caucasus, off the beaten track and with no internet access, for six weeks at a stretch. The results had been published in *National Geographic*. Now and then he took portraits, but only as a favour to friends.

Klaus had been given a bottle of malt whisky in return for the big picture of Katinka and Hege on his office wall.

He was his own man, Klaus, an old-fashioned free spirit, and he was often difficult to pin down. Jan Morell, with far greater problems to contend with, didn't even bother to answer.

THE DILEMMA

Maggi was so perturbed she couldn't sleep.

She couldn't just pretend nothing had happened, that much she knew. Sooner or later Hege would discover that the tube of ointment was no longer in the air vent. If she had been the one who had put it there. It could scarcely have been anyone else – with the best will in the world, Maggi could not imagine that Jan Morell would have any reason to conceal something inside a bathroom he barely ever visited except for the odd time when he changed a light bulb.

It must have been Hege who had tried to stash the tube in there.

It was empty, all used up.

Maybe she was guilty after all.

An accident, surely. A dreadful misunderstanding.

Maggi considered returning the tube and forgetting the whole thing. Attempting to do so, at least. No one apart from Hege and Maggi had any reason at all to open the faulty grate, and what the world didn't know, certainly couldn't harm it.

The tube could stay there till the end of time.

On the other hand, it was possible that the ointment could get Hege off the hook. Maggi knew a fair amount about skiing after all these years in the timber house in Vettakollen. She was less certain about the anti-doping regulations. They couldn't possibly be downright unfair. Regulations usually weren't. If it turned out that Hege had ingested that blasted substance by some demonstrable accident, then the punishment would surely be reduced. Maggi had Googled the difficult name of the cream, Trofodermin.

It was quite simply an ointment for cold sores.

No one would improve at skiing through using a cold sore ointment.

Everyone would understand that.

She tossed and turned fitfully in the bed. It was nearly midnight, and Jan had, as usual, asked for a very early breakfast. The room was too warm, she felt, and got up to open the window.

She could tell Hege what she had found. Convince her to talk to Jan. Get Jan to sort it all out, the way he always sorted everything out. Except for now, as he didn't know about the ointment. And therefore didn't understand any of it. He was even more silent than usual. When she observed him without his knowledge, he had an expression in his eyes that she couldn't recall ever seeing since she had first moved in and everything had been impacted by the death in the family.

Maggi opened the window slightly and switched on the bedside lamp before moving the pillows and sitting up in bed. She took out a book and reading glasses, but her brain refused to cooperate. The letters turned into meaningless codes she couldn't crack. It was as if the tube of ointment, which now lay in a plastic bag at the bottom of her underwear drawer, was sending out an annoying, high frequency sound that only she could hear.

It would be difficult to talk to Hege.

Years ago, when her diary used to be hidden in there, Maggi realized that Hege had no idea that the cleaning routines also included the air vent. There was no reason to enlighten her. Young girls often wrote diaries, and Maggi had never succumbed to the temptation to read it. From that point of view, the air vent was a good hiding place. The book was allowed to rest in peace.

Nevertheless, Hege would have been terribly embarrassed.

On the other hand ...

Maggi put aside her book, but left the light on. All this nonsense about drugs, suspension, punishment and the secret ointment was far worse than an old diary written by a teenager who, strictly speaking, had never done anything wrong. Hege was sensible.

But maybe she wanted to back off, anyway. To start with, Hege had hidden this ointment. That must mean she had done something she didn't want other people to know about. A slip-up, certainly a mistake, an easily explained misunderstanding that could possibly get the punishment reduced, but which in a panic she had chosen to keep hidden.

Maybe Maggi ought to go straight to Jan.

But on second thoughts, that wasn't an especially good solution. Bypassing Hege like that would make her look small. Her relationship with Hege was the most important thing in Maggi's life, and she had never told tales to Jan about anything whatsoever. Not that there had been very much wrongdoing to tell him about, but on an odd occasion during all these years she had certainly kept one or two things from the strict, but loving, father of Hege Chin.

She needed to go to the toilet.

She had diarrhoea, felt unwell and was so beyond all hope of sleeping that after her visit to the toilet she switched on the TV. The volume low, almost mute, so that no one else could hear. At this time of night only *Animal Planet* had anything to offer. Maggi sat in her winged armchair, watching a programme about spotted hyenas in Tanzania. She had rarely seen such ugly animals and this gave her respite from her thoughts.

But only for a few minutes.

Maggi really yearned for someone to give her some advice. She had so few people in her life. Her sister, of course, in Wroclaw, but what would she know about such things. Maggi still kept in touch with Agnieszka, a woman whose acquaintance she had made when she first came to Norway. At that time they both planned to stay for a year or so, and then return to Poland to find their own apartment. A life of their own. They were both still in Norway.

Agnieszka was kind and generous, but wouldn't be able to tell Maggi what she should do. Of course she couldn't.

All of a sudden Maggi had a brainwave.

Sølve Bang!

He had been a dinner guest at Vettakollen a number of times. Praised the food and engaged Maggi in pleasantries spoken in fairly good Polish. He had studied in Warsaw for two years and was a Catholic. A good Catholic, just like Maggi; she had seen him several times at mass and on other occasions in the congregation at St. Olav's Cathedral. Another time he had also spotted her and approached for a friendly chat. He knew a lot about skiing as well, since he was a VIP in the Cross-Country Skiing Federation. Maggi didn't entirely know what he did there, but the fact that he had been Jan's invited guest three times in the past few years indicated that they were friends. Good friends, she would certainly imagine.

Friends wished each other well, and Sølve Bang would be able to tell her what to do. The idea seemed reassuring, almost magical. She switched off the TV, went to bed and fell asleep almost at once.

THE CERTIFICATE

Selma wanted more than anything to log on to gambling sites, but contented herself with emptying Darius's sandbox of cat dirt.

There were many internet sites she often visited, but she mainly restricted herself to currency, shares, British betting and online poker. If she had understood Jan Morell correctly, he was still monitoring her data use. If he wouldn't exactly do anything illegal, such as getting someone to hack into her computer, he might turn up at any point and demand to check her data log. Even though she could delete it on an ongoing basis, he might well bring a computer expert with him who would take only two minutes to reveal which websites she had visited.

Jan Morell was the one who sat with all the cards.

She should really go to bed. It was almost midnight, and she was exhausted by her uneven sleeping pattern in the past few days. The agitation in her body, the little tics along her neck and in her right arm – she knew they would only worsen in the days ahead.

Selma was far from being a compulsive gambler, as Jan claimed. She just liked to gamble, and had always kept everything under control. For a very long time, at least for many years, she had been able to live a successful life in every respect without anyone discovering what she was up to when no one was looking. She was skilful, but also careful, in her opinion. That was the key to success, and she had made a profit in most years. Or at least broken even. More or less, she didn't calculate down to the nth degree. On Ormøya she had her own computer for that sort of purpose, concealed in the basement amongst old sports equipment no one used, but which Jesso nonetheless was too mean to give away to a jumble sale. Days could pass between the times she unearthed it, sometimes even weeks.

She couldn't possibly be a gambling addict.

In the first week after Jan Morell had exposed the discrepancy, after Jesso got to know and she really didn't have anywhere to live, she had checked health service websites. Sitting in her office after everyone else had gone for the evening, she had quickly concluded that the diagnosis couldn't apply to her.

For instance, she certainly didn't isolate herself. On the contrary, she lived an outgoing life and very rarely turned down an invitation. During the filming of the many TV programmes she had participated in, she never once went near a gambling site. The competition was enough in itself. It gave her a thrill while it was on the go, and the peace and quiet she needed when it was over.

The peace and quiet only lasted so long.

Darius had caught yet another mouse.

This time he had at least killed it. And then dropped it on the doormat. Selma fetched a carrier bag, twisted it inside out with her hand inside, picked up the mouse and buried it at the bottom of the rubbish bin.

The worst thing had been quitting her job.

She had been within six months of becoming a qualified lawyer when, for the first time in six years, she had not been selected for the national team. Since she felt this was a dreadful oversight, she had suddenly packed it in, though she had kept her rage hidden from everyone except Jesso. She had won a randomly placed bet in London, something that gave her a more intense pleasure than she ever confessed to anyone. She went on to take her final exams with brilliant results and was immediately offered a job working with Nils Holm, Kristina's older brother. He had a major law firm in Aker Brygge, the most prestigious part of Oslo at that time. Fifteen partners and a multitude of intermediaries. The work was challenging enough, but she missed competing so much that in the end she had screwed up.

Nils and the other named partners were unable to prove anything illegal, so the case had not ended up with Økokrim, the police branch dealing with economic crimes. Selma had made almost a million kroner from a tip-off she had picked up when passing an office with the door slightly ajar. Buying stocks and shares was an advanced form of gambling that apparently brought her the same satisfaction as playing important games. She never admitted to the business with the open door, and in order to avoid damaging the firm she was allowed to leave quietly and find her own explanation for going.

She wanted to set up on her own, the best reason of all.

The new firm, her own, grew rapidly. Selma continued to invest in stocks and shares with the sum of money she had won when she had worked for Holm, Hansen & Herøen. An excellent portfolio with conservative, low-risk investments, mainly to have something to show for it. It gave her a tidy little profit, but nothing more.

She found her thrills in far more risky purchases and sales. Smart and fairly complicated ones. For a period she had gone for contracts for difference, and found she was proficient. After a minor operation for a painful toe in 2008 she was confined to bed for a week. That was when she tried her hand at day trading. She quickly got the hang of that too.

Then internet gambling came on the scene in earnest, and the opportunities mushroomed.

It had all gone really well. For a very long time.

Six months ago she had suffered a greater setback than she was used to. A predicament the previous month had made it necessary for her to borrow from Jan Morell's account. One false step followed another until an overconfident stake had upset the applecart. It could have saved her, the whole amount all at once. When one late night after five terrible months of losses, she finally dared to check how much Jan's account was in debit, she had decided to make one last effort to regain the money. She had read, speculated and reasoned her way into a shorting chance on the New York stock exchange that had huge potential.

She didn't make it. The next morning Jan had asked to transfer money that no longer existed.

Computer games, the kind that teenagers get hooked on and shut themselves indoors to play, had never interested her. She was expert at leaving a poker table in time. Right up until the last six months she had been in complete control. Marriage and children, friends and a demanding job: she had coped with it all, no problem, for years, and it was only circumstances and sheer bad luck that had turned everything on its head in the end.

She was not addicted to gambling, and never had been.

So, logically enough, she did not need any treatment either. All the same, she would have to produce a certificate stating that she was receiving help. By five p.m. tomorrow.

There was only one way out.

It took Selma an hour and a half to fashion a certificate. She chose the most famous specialist in Norway. Bjørn Kragh, clinical psychologist with an office in Akersgata and frequently used commentator every time some sports star allowed himself to be recruited as an ambassador for foreign gambling companies and NRK, the state broadcaster, felt responsible for sounding the alarm.

Bjørn Kragh was professional enough to comply with his duty of confidentiality. If Jan took it into his head to phone to check the authenticity of the document, the psychology specialist would neither confirm nor deny Selma's status as a patient.

The clinic's logo comprised three consecutive circles in shades of dirty yellow. The last and lightest of these dissolved obliquely on the right, with dwindling pixels. Selma managed to make a perfect copy at the top of the sheet of paper. She signed with what she felt was an acceptable signature for a man in his late sixties.

Perfect.

A rush of adrenaline made her breathe faster.

She simply couldn't do this.

She stood up from the settee and stood with the paper in her hand for what felt like an eternity. Suddenly she went out to the kitchen and put the forged document down on the top of the kitchen cupboard. She changed the water in Darius's bowl and dashed to the door. In her hurry she snatched up the blonde wig and glasses, both of which were in the hallway in an unopened box.

In the basement in Ensjø she was at least beyond Jan Morell's control. The game at the Poker Turk's place would be well under-way, but she would undoubtedly be able to charm her way to the table.

THE MANUSCRIPT

401 OUTSIDE, OSLO CITY CENTRE, EVENING

The MAN is waiting in a city park. Early autumn, leaves and wet grass. Still fairly light in the evening. The MAN glances impatiently at the building on the opposite side of the street. The WOMAN comes walking along the pavement, on her way to the apartment block. The MAN crosses the street, jogging.

MAN: Hey! Vanja!

VANJA (turns around): Oh. You. I've sent you a message.

402 OUTSIDE, IN FRONT OF APARTMENT BLOCK, OSLO, EVENING

VANJA walks quickly towards the entrance door with a bunch of keys ready in her hand. The MAN follows her. As they reach the door, he puts a hand around her lower arm. She pulls it away.

VANJA: Let go!
MAN: OK, but stop for a minute! You have to explain why I can't come to you any more. I have …
VANJA (calmer now): I've explained everything in my letter. There's no point in continuing. I haven't anything more to offer you.

MAN: Yes, you do! Now is when it all begins, Vanja. Now is when I need someone to talk to. I've been in limbo all these years, but now, since I saw that picture from the Ski Museum, I'm where I want to be. Now's the time for me to put right everything that's happened.

The MAN is agitated and tries to touch her again. VANJA, seeming somewhat anxious, pulls away.

VANJA: Nothing can put right what happened. It's far too long ago. You were children, all of you. If you still want help, I can give you a couple of recommendations. For good colleagues of mine.
MAN: I don't want recommendations. I received a recommendation. From your son. For you. I want to have you.

The MAN is increasingly agitated. VANJA inserts the key in the lock. Fumbling, clearly nervous now.

MAN (cont.): This is unprofessional. Fucking ignorant. You can't just get rid of me like this. I'm not finished yet.

VANJA finally manages to turn the key. Opens the heavy door into the apartment block sufficiently for her to slip inside. The MAN shoves his foot into the gap between the door and the frame.

MAN: I'm going to send in a complaint! I'll get you struck off, Vanja. You can't do this. I'm in the midst of a process and you have to take some responsibility! We've loads still to do.

VANJA hesitates on the other side of the door. Opens it a touch wider.

VANJA (feigning calm and speaking slowly): You have to listen to me now. I'm downright uncomfortable about the interaction between us. I'm the one who has fallen short. Not you. I can no longer understand you. I can't have patients I simply can't understand. You have changed. I'm absolutely incapable of helping you, because I don't know how.

VANJA opens the door slightly wider. The MAN withdraws his foot.

VANJA (cont.): Of course, it was the intention that you should change. That you should feel better, I mean. We had actually made good progress. But after ...
MAN (making a desperate appeal): Please! Please, Vanja! I need someone to talk to. I've got plans!
VANJA: You scare me.
MAN: Me? Now?
VANJA: Yes. No, not right now. But at other times. We can't discuss this here and now. You must ...

VANJA slams the door shut. Hurried footsteps are heard ascending the stone steps inside. The MAN hovers at the door, watching her through the leaded glass. For a long time.

THE CEREMONY

Haakon Holm-Vegge would certainly not be forgotten any time soon. A viewing yesterday, and today a ceremony with the lighting of candles and laying of floral wreaths beside the ditch where he had lost his life.

It was bitterly cold.

The previous evening had brought freezing rain, with a sudden drop in temperature after midnight. In the morning, Maridalsveien wound its way like a glassy, dark canal from the city up the hillside to the accident site. At the last moment someone had organized a bus equipped with tyre chains. Everyone who wanted to be included in the event was ferried from the large car park just beside Skjerven Farm. Most of them had driven there in their own cars, two of which had already come to grief on the ice at Brekke. Selma had travelled from Grünerløkka, with studded shoes on her feet and elegant boots in her bag, and she could swear that the three roses she carried would be crushed to dust at the slightest touch. The frost had already tinged the tips of the petals icing-sugar-white.

She was nearly 16,000 kroner richer than yesterday evening and felt light-hearted. Despite her lack of sleep.

There were so many people that the bus had to make two journeys. Selma arrived with the first load and unfortunately had to sit beside Sølve Bang. He was unusually quiet, which suited both

Selma and the occasion. She had tried to avoid the crowd waiting at Skjerven by standing at the roadside, engrossed in her mobile phone. Her fingers grew numb, and once on board the bus she regretted having worn chic gloves instead of warm mittens.

When the second bus had emptied, she thought there must be more than a hundred people present.

Selma recognized some of Vanja and Kristina's friends from the previous day. There were also many skiers here, and as far as she could see, significant numbers of staff from the Cross-Country Skiing Federation. Arnulf Selhus, the Finance Director, looked as if it was his own son who had died. Tears flowed in silent weeping, and he was pale as a corpse. Stian Bach, the national team doctor who had almost cost Hedda Bruun a conviction for doping, looked livelier, in an inappropriate red anorak and clumpy boots. Selma also recognized Knut Nilssen. He was the oldest and best of the national team's physiotherapists, a taciturn loner with a taste for Eastern philosophy. He stood on the outside edge of the large group, diffident and unassuming, in company with a couple of younger colleagues who just seemed ill at ease. Bottolf Odda was also in attendance, with his burly figure and ever-prominent chin. He looked better than he had on Monday, Selma thought, and in contrast with the physiotherapists, he was making a great display of his own presence. Elise, a slight figure in floods of tears, stood with her parents and parents-in-law in the centre of the huge semicircle of people now blocking Oslo's longest road. Vanja had her arm around her daughter-in-law, while William had apparently been safely deposited elsewhere for the occasion.

One or two journalists had also been sent out at the crack of dawn. Selma could count at least four photographers, all keeping a suitable distance from the most distressed of the mourners.

It was ten past eight in the morning, and people had started to light candles.

She noticed at once that Jan Morell was standing in the innermost circle, wearing a dark coat and engaged in hushed conversation with Bottolf Odda. The information about Haakon's drugs test had obviously not broken. The media was still overflowing with discussion of Hege Chin's positive result, but Haakon's tragedy had put a certain damper on the most outrageous coverage.

It was significant that no one approached Selma. She had been tempted not to come, but this would have been so obvious it would have given people even more to talk about.

Selma certainly didn't want to be a subject of speculation any longer.

Gracefully manoeuvring herself into the crowd, she carefully laid down her roses and gave Vanja and Kristina each a hug. Elise seemed preoccupied by lighting a candle, and Selma nodded to her parents with as much sympathy as she could muster, before withdrawing just as quickly back into the throng.

The number 51 bus approached from the north. It reduced its speed, which already could scarcely be in excess of twenty kilometres per hour. The driver must have had prior information about the melancholy gathering, because he stopped at a respectful distance. Selma retreated even further from the semicircle of people. Now she was standing on the side opposite the spot where Haakon had somehow plunged into the bushes, down into the stream, struck his head and apparently drowned. She turned and peered down into the ditch. In the stream, which on this side disappeared into a concrete pipe beneath the road, ice had formed in several places like a crystal-clear lid above the still-trickling water. The slope up into the forest was steeper on this side.

Selma spotted something attached to a tree up there. Smaller than a bird box, larger than a box of long matches. A sudden thought made her curious to take a closer look at the device. She regretted having changed on the bus from her studded shoes to her leather boots. Nonetheless she carefully put down her shoulder bag and took a step down into the ditch. With an energetic leap she reached the other side. She turned around for a second. No one had noticed her: everyone's attention was focused on the ceremony on the other side, where a man's voice had started to speak. Shout, almost, though because of that she could not recognize the voice.

She sprinted the thirty metres or so to the device on the tree trunk. It was exactly what she had hoped for.

A wildlife camera.

Not of the modern type, with remote control, GPS and software that meant the owner could sit anywhere in the world watching what was going on. This edition was simple, she saw, and was stamped with the Public Roads Administration logo. She supposed it had been set up with a view to tracking the movement of wild animals across the road that bisected the Maridalen valley, with abundant wildlife on both sides. The red and yellow logo was almost worn away. The cable ties holding the camera fastened to the spruce trunk, on the other hand, looked new.

Selma glanced yet again towards the road.

Someone had started singing. More and more people joined in. A psalm, she presumed, at least it was slow and sombre enough. It didn't look as if anyone had noticed her little detour. She was clearly visible from the gathering down there. So she moved behind the tree to avoid being so easily discovered. After fishing out a bunch of keys from her pocket, she began to saw through the plastic ties.

The camera was state property.

A couple of minutes later, it was lying on the ground.

Now, in other words, it was abandoned goods. A camera on a frozen forest floor: she should take it with her and deliver it to its rightful owner. She would most certainly do that. After having a closer look at it, admittedly. She put the camera in her pocket. There was just enough space. Almost silently, she descended to the road again, crossed the ditch in a single bound and then sneaked the camera out of her pocket and into her bag.

Bottolf Odda had started speaking on the other side of the crowd.

'If we could all just let the service bus pass,' he said in a loud voice, 'then our bus will come down from Skar shortly to pick us up. In the same groups as we arrived, please. We thank you all for coming, and wish to announce that the funeral will take place on Friday at 11 a.m. in the Trefoldighets Church.'

In silence, people began to follow his instruction. The fittest moved beyond the ditch on the lower side. The rest spread out along the edge of the road, and it took only a couple of minutes for the number 51 bus to set off again. Conspicuously slowly, as if the driver wanted to pay his last respects.

Selma jogged northwards and knocked on the bus door. The driver hesitated. Staring at her with scepticism that a moment later dissolved into a smile of recognition. With a low sigh, the bus door opened.

'Thanks.' Selma gave a sad smile as she clambered aboard. 'There were so many of us.'

'No problem. Is he with you?'

Selma didn't have a chance to answer before a man's voice behind her said: 'Yes, I'm with her.'

The door slid shut. Selma sat down in the middle of the almost-empty bus. A tall, slim man collapsed into the seat beside her, smiling as he touched his forehead with two fingers.

'Lars Winther here. Journalist with *DG Sports*. What are you actually planning to do with that wildlife camera you just stole?'

THE REALIZATION

O nce again he attempted to concentrate on the motive.
Why he was sitting there.

Was standing there. Why he was lying there, on this hard bunk, or why he had been left to go to the toilet over a grate that was now stinking out the whole cell. He jogged occasionally. Along the walls, around in a small circle, his feet were sore from the rough underlay, and he could not for the life of him understand what he had done wrong. His balls were smarting: they were damp and had broken out in a red rash.

It was a long time now since he had received any food. Bizarrely enough he was hungry, though he had never felt the need for food in here. He had eaten just because he knew that he must. Thirst was never a problem. Although the trickling hole was ever so disgusting, the water that came out of it was fresh and cold. Food was delivered so seldom that he had actually managed to swallow down most of it. A few hours ago he had gobbled down a slice of bread from yesterday, with liver paté that had hardened at the edges and tasted of cod liver oil. Now there was nothing left.

The consolation was that it was just as long since the machine had been switched on.

The room was still square.

He thought about women. There had been many of them. They never stayed long. Once or twice they had been the ones to leave, but as a rule he had been the one to become bored. Not all the break-ups had been particularly dignified. A couple of them had been downright brutal, on reflection. To the best of his knowledge, however, he could not imagine having done anything to deserve a punishment like this.

A wicked hellhole such as this cell. At his age it was impossible not to have fallen out with anyone in the course of his life. A couple of colleagues, maybe, but never any really serious rift. A neighbour, he remembered now, involved in a furious row about the siting of a garage. The conflict had nearly landed up in court, but he had chosen to sell his childhood home and move to an apartment before it reached that stage.

The person who had put him in here knew of his worst nightmare.

Even though he had mentioned his phobia to the *New York Times*, he had refused to talk about it here at home.

He had been naïve.

The person who had kidnapped him must hate him.

After perhaps forty rounds of the little room – he had to change direction every other time to avoid becoming dizzy – he lay down on the bunk. Closed his eyes.

That was when it dawned on him.

The incident he had tried to forget for so long. He *had* forgotten.

Everyone had forgotten what had happened.

The fear that raced through him was so intense that he fainted. When he woke, he realized he was going to die.

THE WILDLIFE CAMERA

S elma Falck really had no choice.

Lars Winther had agreed to postpone discussion of the wild-life camera's fate until the bus trip was over, but only if they could then find a coffee bar where they could sit down and talk. Of course she could ignore him, go home and lock her door, but in that case he would alert the police. At least that was what he threatened to do.

Selma considered taking a chance. She could easily come up with a credible story about why she had taken the camera. She was on a good footing with the police, and they would have more faith in her than a sports journalist. The downside of such a solution was however obvious: Lars Winther would know that she was lying. He had by all accounts seen her cut down the apparatus. No journalist should have such a hold on her. So she had given her mumbled consent and then spent the precisely twenty minutes of silence on the bus trying to formulate a plan.

When at last they were sitting in Starbucks in Nydalen, each with a big cup of black coffee, she still hadn't come up with anything.

'We can watch it together,' Lars suggested.

'Here? Now?'

Selma took a sip of her coffee.

'I suppose so, or we could go somewhere else.'

He scanned the room. The place was almost deserted. The barista was bored to death, and an old woman with a trolley bag was struggling to make up her mind about something to eat.

That took some time.

'What would we actually be looking for?' Selma asked.

The journalist raised his eyebrows in a condescending grimace.

'Seriously? Shall we start with that, then?'

'The camera was more than thirty metres away from the spot where Haakon had his accident. The filming won't be activated by movement at such a far distance.'

'That depends how it's set up. Let me have a look at it.'

He held out an open hand.

'No. And it's a basic camera. Belonging to the roads authority. Believe me, it's triggered by movement within ten metres. Maximum. Five, maybe.'

Lars Winther kept his hand held out. Impatiently.

'So? Don't fool around. Let's look at it. How can you know what kind of wildlife camera this one is?'

'I'm a hunter. Are you?'

He smiled for the first time since, uninvited, he had sat down beside her on the bus.

'That too, I see. What do you hunt?'

'Hunted, past tense. Big game. For years and years. Gave up eight to ten years ago.'

'Why?'

'I no longer found it exciting.'

At last he withdrew his hand. Drank some coffee, wriggling restlessly in his chair.

'This is getting too silly,' he said. 'We're both after the same thing.'

'Are we?'

'Yes. We both find it pretty astonishing that the world's best athlete on skis should die in this way. How many hundreds of kilometres had this guy put behind him on roller skis?'

'Many,' Selma replied. 'And he fell a few times, too.'

'Exactly! They sometimes fall. They hurt themselves. Get a few scratches here and there. Dislocate a shoulder, maybe. But die from their injuries? Come off it.'

He held out his hand again.

'It hasn't got a screen,' Selma told him, as she picked up a stick sachet of sugar, tore it open and let the sugar drizzle into her coffee cup.

'It has to be connected to a computer,' she added. 'It might even be password protected.'

'Let's try it, then.'

Lars Winther grabbed his shoulder bag, placed it on his knee, opened the catch and took out a small laptop. From a side pocket he produced a cable.

'Shall we?'

Selma stirred her coffee, following the swirling black liquid with her gaze, all the while wondering what choices she had. They were getting fewer by the minute. Without a word, she suddenly put her hand into her own bag.

'Here,' she said, placing the wildlife camera on the table without letting go of it. 'We'll check. With one clear proviso.'

'Which is?'

'If there's anything here with any significance for Haakon's death, then I'm the one to decide what we do.'

'I'm a journalist and it's obvious I can't enter into any agreement of that kind.'

Selma gave a broad smile.

'You journalists enter into agreements all the time, Lars. You twist and turn whatever way suits you, piling on pressure, making threats and pulling the wool over people's eyes. Don't try that on me.'

'Well, we don't ...'

Suddenly he checked himself and raised his hands in surrender.

'OK. You decide. Within reasonable limits.'

She hesitated for a moment before nodding, still gripping the camera.

'Do you know how it works?'

'Er ... yes, in principle.'

'Passive infrared detection,' she elaborated all the same. 'PIR. The principle of wildlife cameras is based on the fact that all objects have a temperature that generates infrared radiation. That's a kind of invisible light, you might say. A spruce tree normally has a lower temperature than, for example, a bear. Are you with me?'

He nodded impatiently.

'A PIR consists principally of a sensor, a special lens called a Fresnel, and a circuit board with a relay to activate the camera. When something that is warmer than its surroundings is detected, then it switches ...'

'I get that. When an animal passes within a certain distance, the camera switches on.'

'Yes. An animal. Or a human. Close up. I can guarantee it won't start filming because a roller skier whizzes past thirty metres away.'

'I understand that,' Lars said, increasingly impatient. 'Then it would whir and buzz all the time, triggered by cars and buses and cyclists and ... Shall we link it up?'

'We don't even know if the battery's working. And if there are videos or images here at all.'

Selma was still holding her hand protectively over the camera. She studied Lars Winther as he fired up his laptop. He was tall and muscular and his long legs barely fitted underneath the table. His skin was taut over his cheekbones, and his eyes were uncannily blue. When he was ready, he asked yet again for the wildlife camera.

This time he got it.

With accustomed movements he connected it to the laptop.

'Hah!' he said, raising two fingers in a V. 'No password, great.'

It took him three minutes to gain entry to the camera. Selma pushed her chair closer to him. A gang of boisterous school pupils entered the café. Ostensibly from senior high school, but they could well have been in the final year of junior high. All girls. Blonde, and every one of them with a ponytail. Their clothes were all identical, and at least five had light-coloured Timberland boots on their feet.

They could have been octuplets.

'The images are date stamped,' Lars said.

'Of course they are. They're of little value otherwise.'

The chair scraped on the floor as Selma moved even closer.

'Friday 8 December,' Lars murmured. 'In the evening.'

His fingers pecked at the keyboard.

'Here!'

A picture flickered. First in black, then grey. After a few seconds the wet, ashen landscape emerged more clearly.

'A ...'

Lars leaned nearer to the screen and lowered his voice.

'A lynx? Bloody hell, that's a lynx. Do they come so close to the city?'

'Yes. A couple of years ago I read about someone in Bøler who had a visit from one on their verandah.'

'The time is 20.27,' Lars read, pointing at the clock.

The lynx moved gingerly, slowly. It came from above, obliquely from the right in the image. Approximately halfway, it stopped. Looked straight at the camera. It approached, sniffing so close to the lens that the picture grew foggy for a moment. It came closer and lingered at the left, lower corner of the picture. The camera was directed down along the course of the stream, where no trees hindered the view of the road.

The lynx was still sharply delineated, maybe five or six metres away. The road down there was, however, out of focus. It was dark, and only a streetlight made it possible to see anything at all.

A figure emerged from the north on roller skis.

A car emerged from the same direction.

When the car passed, the man was gone.

'Stop,' Selma said, so loudly that all the teenagers spun around to look at them.

Some of them sniggered. They had ordered plain mocha coffees and had chosen to sit at the table furthest away from them in badly concealed antipathy. None of them had recognized Selma, which despite her shock at what she had just seen, she didn't entirely appreciate.

'What the hell ...'

Lars wound back. His fingers raced over the keyboard now, and after a couple of minutes he had discovered how they could view the film frame by frame.

His forefinger moved the cursor.

A shapeless figure entered the field of vision. The speed and the lack of depth of focus in the picture would have made it difficult to guess what it was, if they hadn't already known.

Lars pressed again. The vague shape was now completely within the frame.

Yet another frame. And another. Three more.

He pressed once per second. Tap. Tap.

There.

A car moved in towards the man from behind. The type and colour were impossible to identify, but it didn't look terribly large. They sat watching the same image, in silence. For a long time.

'Click,' Selma said tersely.

The car was on its way up beside Haakon. It looked as if it swerved to overtake him.

'Haakon is skating,' Lars said softly. 'So he's using the larger part of the road.'

Selma had experienced that many times herself, on her way in her car up towards the car park at Skar. The diagonal striders were easy to pass, the skaters were provocative wide boys. In both meanings of the word.

'The car should have braked,' Selma said, leaning even closer to the screen. 'Go back. All the way to the frame where the car comes into sight.'

Lars Winther complied.

'Start,' Selma commanded. 'Frame by frame.'

They both saw it in the same split second.

By moving the image forward slightly faster than last time, it became an almost continuous movement of the car's trajectory.

It accelerated towards Haakon.

When the car first entered the picture, it braked. Before it reached the man on the roller skis, the driver increased his speed.

'It accelerates too early,' Lars whispered. 'In a situation like that you have to brake first, and then wait for the skier to stop skating and move to the side, The road is quite simply not wide enough for two in that particular stretch.'

'No. That applies in almost all of Maridalen. Click.'

Another image. Then more. Six more.

Lars pointed: 'Haakon swings his pole at the car. Before it comes all the way up alongside him. He's annoyed.'

Yet another image. Seven more.

'He's furious,' Selma said. 'He's hitting out as hard as he can.'

Lars Winther clicked his way onwards. The car disappeared out the left-hand corner of the picture. Haakon was no longer anywhere to be seen.

The lynx lingered for a while, watching. It seemed as if it sniffed the air, even though it was difficult to tell. It stood with its short tail facing the wildlife camera. A few minutes later, it began to move towards the road.

The picture went black. There was no longer any heat in the camera's search field.

The video was over.

'Bloody hell.'

Lars Winther stared at her open-mouthed.

'He was killed,' he snarled angrily, as if Selma were to blame.

'Maybe just the victim of an accident.'

'Accident? That car speeded up! And if it was an accident, why didn't he stop? He must have noticed that ... Were there ... Were there bite marks on the corpse? Was he gnawed at? By the lynx?'

Selma placed a reassuring hand on his arm.

'No. Definitely not. And the police need to have this camera. As fast as possible. The question is how.'

'How? It's just a matter of handing it in!'

Smiling, Selma canted her head. Looked him straight in the eye. They were really amazingly blue, with long, dark lashes.

'This is a joint effort, isn't it? Between the two of us?'

She nodded at the laptop and camera on the table.

'Er ... yes, I suppose so. You could say that.'

'So if I give the camera to you to take to the police, I'm a source, right?'

'You haven't given me information.'

'Yes. I've given you the camera, which contains information. So that makes me a source, and I want you to describe me as such. And give me the right of confidentiality.'

All of a sudden she grabbed the camera and pulled out the cable.

'If I give you this, I'm a source who demands protection. Is that acceptable to you?'

His eyes sized her up.

'I don't entirely understand your role in this,' he said, running his hand through his thick blond hair.

'Fine,' Selma said. 'You don't need to know.'

'They say you're no longer a lawyer. And that you're ill.'

'Both are wrong.'

'But you've sold your law firm?'

'Yes.'

'Who are you actually representing, then? Haakon? His mothers?'

'None of them. Send a copy of the video to me, please.'

'Copy? I haven't …'

'Don't give me that. You'd be an idiot if you hadn't downloaded it while we were at it. selmaf@hotmail.com. No full stop between Selma and the f. All lower case.'

He hesitated for a second or two before acceding. Selma checked her email on her mobile. The extract dropped into her mailbox with a ping.

'There you go,' Lars Winther said. 'Do I get the camera now?'

'Yes. And you have to take it to the police right now. Without saying who you got it from.'

'You're aware that I'm going to write about this? That in a few hours it'll be public knowledge that Haakon Holm-Vegge didn't die in an accident all on his own, but was killed?'

Selma nodded. Smiled.

'Of course. You're a journalist. You can write whatever you like, but deliver the camera to the police. Just keep me out of it, OK?'

Once again he hesitated. Leaning back in his chair, he clasped his hands at the back of his head.

'You're different from how I'd imagined,' he said coolly.

'Aren't we all? Do we have a deal?'

He nodded, almost imperceptibly.

Selma shrugged on her coat and slung her bulky bag over her shoulder. Then she placed the wildlife camera on the table with a thud, smiled even more broadly, and departed.

Leaving a half-full cup of coffee.

THE ACCOUNTS

F or once Arnulf Selhus hadn't only closed his office door, but had also locked it.

He was shaking. In the past few weeks he had hardly slept more than two or three hours a night and he was really beginning to feel the effects. Not only mentally, but also physically. His clothes had become baggy. His ears were ringing, and he had great difficulty concentrating.

Concentration was essential.

Everything had been put straight, but there were still mistakes to be made.

The money was no longer hanging in the balance. The necessary receipts, once the auditor had been made aware of the incorrect entries, had been inserted in the right files. If the angels were on his side, everything would proceed smoothly.

He hadn't done anything wrong with the accounts. Quite the opposite: for the nearly ten years he had been the Director of Finance in Norway's Cross-Country Skiing Federation, he had been more pedantic than was good for him. At least that was the opinion of his subordinates. He knew he couldn't be called a popular boss. That didn't matter. The most important thing was to be correct. Painfully exact.

A long time ago, in a different life, he had made a faux pas. Under pressure, during a difficult period, he was getting divorced, his son was sick, and the new summer cottage had turned out to be more expensive than anyone had anticipated. Arnulf Selhus knew there were no excuses, only explanations, and that he was the luckiest man alive when he got away with having to explain himself to only one person.

He had been given another chance, an undeserved clean sheet, and he had been grateful ever since. So grateful that he was totally exhausted.

These mistakes were not his.

The copy invoices lay in front of him.

They looked trustworthy. Relevant. Two of them concerned renovation of the garage at headquarters. One of them was from a hotel in Lillehammer – the wax technicians had held an autumn seminar there at the end of September.

They all looked genuine, but they were not.

The accounts they should be paid into were different. The amounts varied. Altogether they came to a total of less than 250,000 kroner. Not a huge sum. Maybe that was the problem. It had all slipped under the radar for Arnulf.

And he thought he took note of everything.

120,239 kroner had been paid into the bank account of Arnulf Selhus's son. The boy was nineteen, in his final year at senior high school, and earned pocket money doing odd jobs on top of his schoolwork. None of these had been in the Federation's garage. Exactly 75,000 kroner had been paid into one of Arnulf's own savings accounts. That must be why he hadn't noticed the error: he knew only his current account number by heart.

He had authorized them without any fuss.

Including the invoice from Lillehammer, which had sent 53,566 kroner into Haakon Holm-Vegge's bank account.

Of all the skiers in the entire world, the money had been credited by mistake to the best athlete in the world, and to make matters worse, one who had taken a degree in business administration.

And it was all Arnulf's mistake. Normal authorization powers in the Federation were limited to 50,000 kroner. All claims for higher sums than this had to be cleared by him as the senior person responsible for finance.

Which he had done, and by doing so had made it look as if he was stealing from the Federation.

Haakon hadn't been merely annoyed about the erroneous transfer of money. He had been furious. Called it careless. Unforgivably slipshod. A gaffe that could have cost him dear. *Dagens Gang* was all over the place these days, rooting around in accounts and minutes and everything that might resemble shady business. Having large sums of money paid from the Federation for absolutely no reason, camouflaged as an invoice from a wax technicians' seminar in Lillehammer, could have landed him in one hell of a predicament.

That was how he had put it: one hell of a predicament.

And he had said more.

If only he hadn't said more.

Now he was dead. All Arnulf Selhus's efforts to make Haakon change focus had been in vain. The plan had always been idiotic. Wouldn't guarantee anything whatsoever.

But now it was over.

Arnulf Selhus rose from his office chair. He remained on his feet beside the desk. Staring at the three invoices. He loosened his tie, feeling hot under the collar. If no one started to dig around in this, everything would be fine. If no one began to delve into his trip to Milan almost a fortnight ago, it would all blow over. The money was back with its rightful owner. Arnulf had sorted it all out. No reason for anyone to know anything. Discover any of it. He had made sure of the most important thing the night Haakon died and hardly anyone had any idea yet about what had happened.

Just one thing remained. The easiest of all.

'Then everything will be shipshape,' he murmured.

Nothing was shipshape, and he thought he was about to have a heart attack.

ELISE

The apartment looked like something from a Skeidar catalogue: white walls and a living room dominated by a comfortable, pale-grey corner settee covered in washed-out-pink scatter cushions. Fairly trendy, but also insipid.

A wooden tray with raised edges, straight out of *Home & Cottage*, was perched on an enormous footstool, on which three perfumed candles were burning beside a stack of interiors magazines and a bottle of Farris mineral water. The curtains were pale pink, almost white, and a colossal photograph of William had pride of place on the opposite wall. He must have been around six months old in the picture, Selma reckoned. Oddly enough, he was placed in an old porridge trough, and was wearing nothing but a cap knitted in the traditional Marius pattern. The background was as white as the walls.

No trace of Haakon was evident here, Selma noted. Other than what at first glance appeared to be a wedding photograph. Since Haakon and Elise were not married, it must have been taken on another occasion. By the photographer with the porridge trough, in all likelihood; the couple were posing in front of an old stabbur, a timber storehouse on stone pillars. Both Elise and Haakon were dressed in national costume. Four pairs of skis were propped up against the wooden walls. Ancient ones, big and broad, with wicker bindings and tarred bases.

Family photographs and an enormous full-face portrait of an angry African elephant were all that adorned the walls.

There was not a trophy to be seen.

Not a single medal, not even in the hallway.

Jesso hadn't liked Selma's collection of prizes either. In the beginning, when they lived in two rooms and a kitchen in Løkka, he had been sufficiently in love to let her display her finest prizes in a cabinet in the living room. Once they had children and eventually moved to Ormøya island, the cabinet was relegated to a storage cupboard in the basement. Along with signed balls, old kit and her very first pair of Adidas trainers. Selma had bought them with her own money at the age of ten, scarcely dared to wear them, and since then had kept them in the original box. They were of sky-blue dressed leather and had contained so many of her dreams that she would really have liked to frame them.

A few decades had now passed since Selma hung up her boots.

Haakon had been in the middle of his career, but all the same there was no sign that this apartment in Tåsen had, until three days ago, been the residence of a three-times World Cup winner on skis.

Elise had welcomed her without demur.

Perhaps it seemed natural for Selma to visit. She was one of the best friends of Haakon's parents, and she was his godmother too. Anyway, the apartment showed evidence of people coming and going in recent days. Selma caught a glimpse of the kitchen on her way in, and it was overflowing with coffee cups.

The floor could also have benefited from a run round with the vacuum cleaner.

And Elise could have benefited from some sleep.

The far-too-young widow had no make-up on. Her eyes were ringed with red, and her bleached hair looked as if it was in mourning too, entirely of its own volition. Elise had changed clothes since the ceremony that morning in Maridalen. Now she was padding around in a beige knitted sweater and jeans with holes on both knees, a style she was a bit too old for, in Selma's humble opinion.

Elise Grønn was colourless, almost transparent.

'I'm really so very sorry,' Selma said gently once she sat down. 'There just aren't the words, but I expect you've heard far too many of them lately all the same.'

Elise nodded.

'Coffee?' she asked, indifferently.

'No, thanks.'

'Pepsi Max?'

'No, I don't want anything, thanks. I really just came to ...'

Essentially Selma had come to pose a question. In addition, she had thought to warn Elise, to alert her to the fact that Haakon's death might be more than a self-inflicted accident. Selma wanted to shield her from having to read about it in *Dagens Gang* in the course of the afternoon, as it was doubtful whether the police would have time to let the relatives know before the story hit the headlines.

On the other hand, Elise was probably not particularly interested in the media right now.

'... say I'm so sorry for your sake,' she said, changing her mind. 'For my own, too, of course, but I just wanted to say that I'd like to help you. If there's anything you need. Maybe by dealing with the insurance. That sort of thing. I assume you had ...'

'Dad's taking care of that. But thanks anyway.'

Elise tucked her legs beneath her on the settee. She opened her eyes wide and used a slender thumb to rub underneath each of them, as if she had forgotten she was not wearing any mascara.

'Where's William?'

'At nursery. He doesn't understand any of this, anyway. He's so little. And he's used to Haakon being away. To put it mildly.'

She put some force into her final words.

'That's how it is,' Selma said. 'Elite sports demand sacrifice.'

It crossed her mind – too late – that she might have been too literal in her choice of words.

'Such as absence,' she added. 'Being married to a top athlete means having to manage on your own.'

'I'm sure I will.'

The sharp edge in her voice was even clearer now.

'Yes, from that point of view I suppose, in practical terms at least, the change won't make too much difference.'

Selma could have bitten off her tongue.

Fortunately it looked as if Elise wasn't really listening. She was staring at a point far above Selma's head before she suddenly covered her face with her hands and dissolved into tears. Almost soundlessly, and only the slight tremor in her shoulders betrayed her.

Selma knew why she had come, but she had begun to doubt whether there was any point in asking. Elise had enough on her plate. To be honest, she should really not be left alone, and from that point of view it was a good idea to have come, but on the other hand there were a lot of people who were closer to Elise than Selma. She knew that Vanja and Kristina's apartment had been packed with visitors since she had left it on Saturday morning, and she was pretty sure that a whole battalion of them must have gone home with them to Pilestredet following the morning's excursion to Maridalen. To put it bluntly, Haakon's parents had not been left to their own devices for four days.

'I see you've had lots of visitors,' Selma said quietly. 'To judge by the coffee cups. Being on your own just now ...'

She leaned forward. Elise let her hands fall as she looked straight at her.

'... is that through your own choice? Being by yourself?'

Elise nodded, almost imperceptibly.

'Then of course I'll leave,' Selma said, standing up.

'No. Please stay.'

Selma hesitated but then sat down again.

'Would you like anything?' she asked. 'I can pop out and buy something for you if you ...'

Elise sat up so abruptly that Selma stopped speaking.

'Haakon was unfaithful!' she blurted out. 'He was doing something he shouldn't have been doing, and he was unfaithful to me too!'

Selma caught herself staring with her mouth open. She closed her mouth with a snap, moved towards Elise and put her hand gingerly over hers.

'Tell me about it,' she said softly.

There was no reason to regret this visit after all, she thought with elation. This might be far simpler than she had feared.

'Tell me all about it,' she repeated, diffidently squeezing Elise's hand.

THE CONFIDENCE

Sølve Bang had been so friendly on the phone.

Of course he could tear himself away from everything he had to do in order to have a chat with Magdalena Wajda. They could, for example, meet up for a cup of coffee, he had suggested. At the Åpent Bakeri in Damplassen, since he had some business to attend to at the university anyway, not far from there. That suited Maggi very well – she took the subway to Majorstua, changed line for Ullevål Stadium and walked down from there to the café. Although it was both cold and slippery, at least the wind had died down.

She had arrived early and had to wait for nearly quarter of an hour until he arrived. Without looking out for her, he had headed straight to the counter. The café was almost full to capacity and there was a considerable queue, but somehow as if by magic he had sneaked his way to the front without anyone protesting. He looked around, smiled broadly at Maggi, approached her and put down his cup of tea. He greeted her in man-of-the-world fashion, with a kiss on both cheeks, before sitting down in the chair immediately opposite her.

'You already have coffee,' he noted casually. 'Then we can get straight to the point?'

Maggi was nonplussed. She had expected him to ask how Hege was. How things were with Jan Morell, Sølve Bang's good friend, who was now enmeshed in such a serious crisis. Maggi had perhaps expected some conversation about the church. She had thought of asking him whether he intended going to the Polish morning mass at eight o'clock on Christmas Eve, and whether he might possibly consider accompanying her.

Sølve Bang did not invite that type of question. On the contrary, twice now he had ostentatiously checked the time on his heavy wristwatch.

Maggi was having second thoughts.

'*Powiedziec*,' Sølve Bang said with a smile. '*Powiedz teraz.*'

Tell. Tell now.

And Maggi spilled the beans.

About Hege's despair. Jan's obstinate, frenetic silence. About the bathroom, with its memories of Hege's mother, and about how important it was to retain the nail varnish heart and the door trim with the growth chart marked on it. She told him about how she had put down roots in the house at the edge of the forest, how she dreaded the question of what would happen when old age caught up with her. Magdalena Wajda bared her soul in a way she couldn't remember having done for a long time.

For an entire eleven minutes.

Then the man on the other side of the table looked at his watch yet again.

'I found something,' Maggi rushed to say. 'In the air vent in the bathroom.'

'Oh?'

His eyes brightened. They somehow opened wider, slightly surprised and mostly curious.

'What was that?'

Maggi squirmed in her chair. Took hold of her coffee cup and hid her face in the bowl while she pondered.

'I don't know if I should tell you this,' she mumbled in the end as she put her cup back on the saucer. 'But I'm so confused. Maybe

'I should just do nothing. Or maybe I should take it up with Jan. Or Hege. One of them. I don't really know.'

Sølve Bang leaned closer. He placed his hand over hers. It was narrow, and the nails looked manicured. Elegant, clean and flesh-coloured. Maggi's hands were rough and dry, marked by years of dishwater and bleach. She wanted to pull her hand away, but didn't dare.

'Zaufai mi,' Sølve whispered. Trust me.

He became almost like a fellow countryman. And he was a friend of the family, after all. Nevertheless the words stuck in her throat.

'Does it have anything to do with the drug-taking?' he whispered.

She did not answer. Merely stared at him, before looking down into her cup.

'What?' he insisted, and his grip on her hand grew stronger.

She nodded. One nod.

'Did you find the offending substance?'

'Yes,' she whispered. 'A tube of ointment. In the air vent in Hege's bathroom.'

This was crazy, she realized. A betrayal. Of Hege, but also of Jan Morell, who despite often using an unfriendly tone had never done her any harm. Quite the opposite: he had given her a home. A sense of belonging, a kind of family, the three of them, Hege, Jan and Maggi: a trinity that should never be broken by her seeking advice and help from a stranger. She was not a real family member, she was well aware of that, she was an employee, a paid help with her own quarters in the basement, but she was important all the same. At least to Hege.

The house in Vettakollen was her home, and the people there were her family.

This was insane.

'I have to go,' she said in a low voice, as she got to her feet. 'Sorry.'

'No,' Sølve said, reluctant to release her hand. 'You've done the right thing by telling me this. You know that I wish Jan and Hege nothing but well. They've got so much to cope with right now. Far too much. Let me help, Magdalena. *Pozwól mi pomoc!*'

She tore her hand free. Wrapping her scarf around her neck, she hoisted the strap of her bag over her shoulder. Without saying another word, she walked out of the café, turned right, and strode towards the subway station at Ullevål.

As fast as she could on the icy pavement.

THE MONEY

'**I**n the first place,' Selma said, 'Haakon can't have been unfaithful.'

Elise wiped her nose with her sleeve.

'Yes, he was,' she said angrily. 'He must have been.'

'Now you're going to listen to me.'

Selma stood up. There were limits to how long she could bear to sit so close to another human being. She pretended she had to stretch her back. Placing two hands flat on her tailbone, she gently swayed from side to side.

'He simply wouldn't have had the time,' she insisted.

'What?'

The elephant on the poster looked really enraged. Its ears were flared, and the frighteningly human gaze seemed full of hate and wisdom at one and the same time.

A remarkable image to have on the wall.

'I know most things worth knowing about infidelity,' Selma said. 'So many variables can be the background to it. The thrill. Self-affirmation. Vanity. Diversion. Falling head over heels. And true love, which of course are the worst cases. Common to them all, however ...'

She turned away from the elephant and looked straight at Elise.

'Infidelity takes time. A horrendous amount of time. And energy.'

'Exactly. He was never at home. Who knows what he might have been up to out there, after all he was away for two hundred and forty days a year! And when he was at home, he was hardly in the door before he was rushing out to training or some sponsorship event or TV or ... He even took his degree exams last year!'

Elise exhaled with a slow, hissing noise, as if all the air inside her was being expelled.

'That's the whole point,' Selma said. 'He can't possibly have had time for another woman. He kept a training diary. Haakon trained more than anyone else. Last year he reached almost eleven hundred hours of training. That's sheer madness. And as we both know, so many hours of exertion have to be followed with an equivalent amount of rest. Sleep. Food intake. Otherwise there's no point. Besides ...'

Selma perched on the edge of the settee.

'The requirement to give notification,' she said, shaking her head. 'In principle, Anti-Doping Norway wants to know where he is at any particular time. At the very least where he spends the night. Where he trains. When he trains. He must be accessible to the anti-doping inspectors at all times of the day and night. Sneaking a relationship on the side in between a family and elite sports at this level would be really tricky. You know that, Elise.'

Her disheartened eyes finally managed to make contact with Selma's.

'He had changed so much,' Elise whispered. 'The last couple of weeks. He was irritable and impatient. Even with William. He never had been before, no matter how exhausted he was. The opposite, in fact ...'

She sobbed and picked up the bottle of water from the tray. Took a long swig, paused to think and then continued: 'He was always so pleased to see us. So warmhearted. Haakon always felt guilty about us coming second. William and I. Haakon's favourite pastime was to plan everything that was going to happen when his career was over. But in the past couple of weeks he was so ... short with us. Abrupt, really. He raised his voice to William just because he knocked over a tumbler of milk. A tumbler of milk! He's fifteen months old and has only just learned to drink out of a tumbler!'

'A fortnight, you said? Since the change started?'

'Yes, something like that.'

'But why did you think of infidelity? I mean, it could have been about something totally different? His sore shoulder, for instance. Worse test results than expected. Disagreements in the team. Squabbles with the coaches, or ...'

'He talked to me about those things. Always.'

A blush suffused her neck, bringing unexpected colour to her pale figure.

'We've been together since I was nineteen and he was twenty,' she said so softly that Selma unconsciously leaned forward. 'And he has never, not a single time ...'

The blush spread to her cheeks.

'... given me a brush-off. Not once. The very opposite, with so many days spent travelling, it was ...'

She ran both hands through her hair and inhaled with a sudden sob.

'Now he turned his back on me as soon as we went to bed. Because of his shoulder injury, he'd been at home for the past little while. But he'd been training, of course. If he'd just been so worn out that he fell asleep at once, I would have understood that. That happened loads of times – he could fall asleep before his head hit the pillow. But I could hear it from his breathing. He was just lying there. Awake, with his back turned.'

Selma leaned back on the settee. She was thirsty and would have been glad of a Pepsi Max. Maybe she could go and get a bottle herself.

'Can you tell me more about what had changed?' she said instead. 'Did he alter his routines, for example?'

'No, not that I noticed. But one evening ...'

Elise was no longer weeping. On the contrary – she suddenly looked alert. She tilted her head and stared intently into space as she tugged at the holes on the knees of her jeans.

'There was that first evening, of course,' she said, sounding almost surprised.

'Of what? The first evening of what?'

'Of the change. He sat up unusually late. With his laptop on his knee. Right here.'

She gingerly smacked the settee. Selma rushed to ask another question before the girl was overcome by sobs again: 'Do you know what he was looking at?'

'Yes.'

'What, then?'

'The bank statement. He was looking at his online account. He doesn't often do that.'

'What?'

'His internet bank. So ...'

For some reason she was drumming her fingers as if typing on an invisible keyboard.

'I see,' Selma said quickly, though she didn't understand at all. 'Do you know why?'

'No. I'm the one who's always dealt with our finances. That is to say ...'

The shadow of a smile crept over her face and then vanished.

'Haakon was the one who earned the money, of course. I just managed it. Loans, insurance, nursery fees. That sort of thing. Plus I always made sure there was money in his current account. He spends next to nothing, but he does need some, you see. I organize it all. We decided that I should stay at home for as long as his career lasted. To take care of everything, sort of thing. We planned to have more children eventually, and ...'

'Do you know if there was anything in particular he was looking at?'

'No. Not really. He logged out and closed the laptop as soon as I came in to ask if he wasn't coming to bed soon.'

'Did you check later? Since you were the one to take care of the finances, did you later notice anything irregular?'

'Nothing that had to do with infidelity, at least.'

Selma smiled sympathetically to hide her own impatience.

'He wasn't unfaithful,' she said slowly. 'But did you find anything else there? Anything out of the ordinary?'

'Nothing of any significance.'

Selma struggled to keep smiling. It was becoming difficult.

'Anything at all? Something that might have explained why he was on the bank's web pages, something you say was out of character, so late one night?'

'N... yes ...'

Elise hesitated. She picked up the bottle of Farris, but left the lid on.

'Just an incorrect entry.'

'Oh? What kind of incorrect?'

'They had transferred a large sum of money to him. Over fifty thousand kroner.'

'Who do you mean by "they"?'

'The Cross-Country Skiing Federation.'

'A payment that was ... incorrect?'

Elise nodded.

'At any rate, it was paid back a few days later. A week or so, as far as I recall. Exactly the same sum. Into exactly the same account that it had come from. So, yes ...'

Her narrow shoulders heaved.

'So I assume it was just an incorrect entry.'

'Has it ever happened before?'

Elise stood up.

'No. And I feel terribly tired now. Do you really not believe that Haakon was unfaithful?'

'I'm completely convinced. Both because I've known him since the day he was born, and because I can't fathom how he would have managed to insert a secret like that into such a transparent and chock-full life. Besides, he loved you.'

'Are you sure? You can't really be sure of that. No one can be sure of that kind of thing.'

Her voice grew increasingly weak. Her shoulders were as angular as clothes hangers beneath her chunky-knit sweater. The skin on her knees was dry, Selma saw; the holes in her jeans had enlarged in the past half-hour.

'Absolutely sure. And Elise ...'

She ought to tell her about the drugs test.

When Bottolf Odda had given her the warning during yesterday's viewing, it was on the cards that she would pass on the information to Vanja and Kristina about the positive result from the post-mortem sample. She hadn't done so. Selma still couldn't understand why she had left Pilestredet immediately after the visit by the Federation's president, without saying a word to anyone. It had something to do with restlessness, she thought. With a picture, the contours of which she was beginning to make out, but the meaning of which she still did not comprehend. When she was visited by Jan Morell on Thursday evening, and offered a wager she could not refuse, she had accepted the craziest odds she had ever bet on. And it was Hege Chin's life she was supposed to investigate. Hege was the one she was meant to exonerate, and Selma didn't have any idea where to begin.

This picture was bigger.

Far bigger and far more indistinct.

In a flash she felt a kind of fear, a shot of adrenaline that made her suddenly get to her feet and head out into the hallway.

Elise deserved a warning.

She deserved two, in fact. Both that Haakon had apparently been knocked down on Friday, and that he had died with illegal substances in his bloodstream. Both of these would soon become public knowledge – it could be a matter of merely hours, and it would create an incredible rumpus.

Elise ought to be warned, but in that case Selma would have to stay.

'Thanks for your hospitality,' she said, pulling on her coat. 'We'll talk again soon, OK?'

A hug, a caress of Elise's straggly hair, and yet another promise to see her again soon, on Friday at the funeral at the very latest.

And Selma dashed out the door.

THE CERTIFICATE

It was one fifteen p.m.

As usual in Advent, the cold had relented after only a few hours of battle. The world was once again sodden and grey. The clouds were so low above the city that the spire of the Kulturkirken Jacob church had disappeared. Selma stood outside a nine-storey building at Storgata 38.

An exercise studio occupied the whole of the ground floor, but that was not where she was headed.

At home she had a completed certificate stating that she was attending a course of treatment for compulsive gambling. She could give it to Jan Morell and in all likelihood get away with it.

'In all likelihood' was far from being a sure thing.

'One chance' was what Jan had said. He gave people a second chance.

Selma took a deep breath and closed her eyes as she let the air exhale slowly out of her nose. With a shrug, she decided to go in.

The Blue Cross, a well-respected interdenominational organization, offered a number of options.

Selma did not intend to avail herself of any of them. A certificate was all she needed. Proof of some kind, that she was taking her compulsive gambling seriously. With a certificate in the bag her agreement with Jan had been fulfilled, and no one could force her to go through with it.

All she needed was a wretched certificate.

She opened the door and stepped inside.

THE TRAIN JOURNEY

H ege Chin Morell ran faster than she had ever done before. She had trainers on her feet, but sprinted without hesitation over ice and slush, on muddy paths and roads, traversing gardens where she had to jump over fences in order to pass through. She had leapt off the tram as soon as it reached Gulleråsen, one stop earlier than her usual.

It was almost time for dinner, and she was running for her life. She had been awake since four a.m. When she couldn't fall asleep again, she had got up. With not a single plan for the day, she had crept into the kitchen and taken bacon and eggs out of the fridge.

Admittedly she normally had to consume more than five thousand calories per day, at least during the periods of toughest training, but pork fat did not feature on the list of acceptable food. This morning she had fried a whole packet.

Three eggs. An enormous glass of milk, and for dessert she had helped herself to one of Maggi's coconut buns from a box in the dried foods larder. Before she was finished, it was nearly five o'clock. Everything was still quiet. She had wrapped up warmly, pulled a cap down over her forehead and gone out. In plain clothes, hat and scarf, she was seldom recognized. Whereas the other girls in the national team quickly gathered a gaggle of autograph hunters wherever they went, Hege was just an ordinary skier.

The best cross-country skier in the world when dressed in national team colours.

But someone scarcely anyone recognized without them.

That's how it had always been, and anyway, she was all alone in the world when she left the timber house in Vettakollen.

No animals by the apple tree. No journalists down on the road. Not even a stray dog to be seen, and the houses were shuttered all the way down to Smestad.

The subway began to run around half past five, and she had jumped on the first and best of these.

Hege could barely recollect the last time she had taken the subway.

Her mother had often taken her out in Oslo. Usually on Saturdays, from the moment Hege could walk independently. Mother and daughter packed a knapsack with sandwiches and a thermos and ambled hand in hand down to the station, setting off aimlessly. They had criss-crossed the city for hours on end, Hege with her nose pressed so close to the window that she could draw hearts in the condensation from her own hot breath. Only rarely did anyone see them out there, and smile back.

Her mother had stories from all over the place. Fairy tales, fables, stories and anecdotes from the war, when Hege's great-grandfather had been a saboteur and awarded a medal by King Haakon when all the vileness was over. They travelled eastwards and southwards, Hege and her mum, then west and finally to the north, to Vettakollen and rice pudding and marking on the map where they had travelled that day.

Mum had called their journeys 'odysseys'.

It wasn't the same without her.

Hege Chin had been to Bergkrystallen and Vestli, to Tøyen and Lambertseter. To Brynseng and Hasle and Furuset. For nine hours she had followed the daily rhythms of the city. Almost on her own for the first half-hour, crowded carriages during rush hour, cold in the early morning, sleet dispersed by rain in the course of the late morning hours. She had seen grey blocks in Groruddalen and detached houses on the hillside. People rushing here and there, grumpy children in the morning being pushed into nurseries. Stressed teenagers making their way to and from school, while beggars were the only people who sat still. A sudden impulse made Hege hop on to a train to Drammen around noon, but she had got off in Asker and turned back. She had travelled home in the dark, having watched a grey, short pre-Christmas day come and go.

No one had spoken to her.

For long stretches of the day she had stared straight at a picture of herself. The *Aftenposten* newspaper carried an interview with a Swedish doping expert who found it unbelievable that Hege had somehow ingested Clostebol without her knowledge. He asserted that Norwegian cross-country skiing had a serious credibility problem, and demanded an uncompromising reaction. A photograph of Hege, taken during the press conference on Thursday, was used to illustrate the misery. Splashed on the front page. She looked sombre, but sat with her head held high.

With no tears, which for her was the most important thing.

She graced the front page of every other passenger's newspaper, and was named in one conversation after another. Nevertheless, she had been left completely in peace. When anyone gave her a second glance over the top of a newspaper, she hid her chin in her scarf, tugged her hat even further down her forehead and looked out of the window.

The journey had finally neared its end. She hadn't eaten since her extravagant breakfast, and felt tired. Her mobile had vibrated only once. It was Maggi, but Hege could not bring herself to talk, so she had sent a reassuring text instead.

She wanted to quit, she thought, as the subway train ascended the hill.

Everything would ease off if she just stopped skiing. The story would be forgotten in a couple of months, maybe before that, at least until the Winter Olympics started, and Hege had really always wanted to study. Maybe medicine. Or pharmacy, since chemistry had been her favourite subject at high school.

Mum would have listened and let her give up.

Dad would never go along with it.

Her phone had vibrated again.

Hege did not recognize the number. A journalist, probably, even though approaches from them had diminished drastically in the course of the past few days. They had begun to learn that she wouldn't answer.

Not now either.

It took only a few seconds from the call ending before a text message illuminated the screen.

This is Sølve Bang calling. I realize that these days you need to know who it is. I have something urgent I need to speak to you about. Can you phone me back?

Hege had never been particularly keen on Sølve Bang. She didn't really know why. She had read all his books and liked them. Particularly *Forgotten Tracks*, his first novel. All the same, there was something sleazy about him, especially the way he spoke to Maggi. He was so exclusively friendly to the almost invisible home help, but Hege was convinced this was mainly an opportunity to impress the other guests by speaking Polish. There was something servile and at the same time exaggeratedly self-assured about the man, and she had always felt slightly ill at ease in his company.

Dad liked Sølve Bang. Called him a colourful character. A renaissance man. Well versed in languages, knowledgeable and an important writer. As if Dad had any idea about that, as he never read anything other than business documents and newspapers.

Hege could not fathom what he wanted with her.

However, she called him back. He was a friend of her father's and had delivered a beautiful speech at her mother's funeral. Hege did not remember much about that day, but she had never forgotten that. Sølve had called her mother 'a fairy straight from the pages of Tolkien, a gracious bearer of light and goodness'.

Hege had read the whole of the *Lord of the Rings* trilogy in the following six months, even though she was only eleven years old and her mother had thought she ought to wait.

She phoned Sølve Bang and heard what he had to say. Gave him a blunt response, broke off the conversation and then took off at top speed. She had never run so far and so fast, and when she reached her destination, her head was in a spin.

THE CAR

Standing in Ormsundveien, Selma Falck stared up at a house that was no longer hers. It was close to eleven o'clock at night.

As usual it had grown colder again in the afternoon and at eight p.m. it had started to snow once more. Wet, massive blobs of snow that eventually lay everywhere as slush before finally freezing to ice. She had run from Grünerløkka and was drenched. She quickly tore off her orange reflective waistcoat, rolled it up to next to nothing and stuffed it into her Camelbak rucksack after rummaging to find her car keys.

The house, which in Selma's opinion was the most hideous in all of Norway, was shrouded in darkness. Only the lamps around the swimming pool, covered over for winter, were lit; the bulbs in the wrought-iron lamps flanking the steep driveway up to the main garage had not been replaced when they had all gone at the one time due to a short circuit earlier that autumn.

Selma stood gazing at the house.

She wished him all the best in owning it. He loved every bay window and pillar of it. He was the one who had insisted on glazed roof tiles when they had to renew them in 2010, at least twenty years after the shiny roofs had gone out of fashion. Jesso had laid out most of the garden. He had taken a stand about the swimming pool as well, even though environmental concerns meant it was unheated and so served the same purpose as the fjord directly across the road.

And which was free of charge into the bargain.

Selma had put her foot down when it came to the interior, but the house in Ormsundveien had always been mostly his, in actual fact.

And now his mother was living there too.

As an MP, Jesso earned around a million kroner a year. He had not been able to buy out Selma's half-share in the house. The valuation was set at 26 million, the mortgage had been paid off two years ago, and Selma had asked for her rightful 13 million virtually overnight.

But he was the only son of a mother aged eighty-four, a widow living in a huge villa in Nordberg. Her house had barely seen a tradesman's work since the sixties, and some of the land had been parcelled out and sold by Jesso's father after a bankruptcy. Nordberg was still Nordberg, however, and on a promise of being allowed to live in a basement apartment in Ormundsundveien for the rest of her natural life, his mother had allowed Jesso to sell his childhood home and use the money to become sole owner of what had once also been Selma's residence.

Her mother-in-law was allergic to cats, so Darius had been included in the arrangement. Selma had to take the cat with her and renounce all claim on the house and its contents, in exchange for 10 million kroner and a mortgage credit bond on Ormsundveien as security for the remainder of the sum owing.

That could not be called in for at least ten years.

It crossed her mind that it did not matter as she stood there looking up at the building. It seemed like a lifetime ago that she had left. The only sound to be heard was the constant hum of traffic from Mosseveien on the other side of the water and the lazy lapping of the waves on the foundations of the boathouse behind her. The air was filled with the tang of the sea, wood smoke and a faint hint of engine oil.

For eighteen years she had called this place home. She knew the sounds and the smells, the plants and trees and every stone on the solid perimeter wall on the western side that she and Jesso had built the summer Johannes turned four.

It was good to be rid of it all.

Liberating, Selma realized: this was not her life. She did not know where her life truly lay. Not yet, but the sight of the ridiculously expensive villa by the fjord, with its projections, mullioned and dormer windows, and eaves that were far too deep, made her suddenly appreciate it was not just her marriage that, deep down, she was glad to be finished with.

They were all asleep.

Selma did not need to go up to the house. At the bottom of the property, right beside the road, there was an ancient garage that should have been demolished a decade ago. They had let it remain because they probably didn't want to build a replacement so close to the fjord. Only the most necessary maintenance was carried out on the sagging, red-painted building, and the door springs were so stiff that Selma was afraid it would be difficult to open.

Up in the double main garage, flush with the house, was a Volvo XC90 T8, 2017 model. Jesso had been allowed to keep that, in accordance with an agreement with a list no lawyer in the world would have advised Selma to sign. As far as she was concerned, the car she had bought in January for almost 1.3 million kroner was of absolutely no interest, as long as she was allowed to keep the vehicle that came into sight as soon as she, with surprising ease, opened the manual garage door.

A Volvo Amazon 123 GT from 1966.

The year of her birth.

Even in the sparse light from the street lamp, the red paintwork shone with an intensity that made her shudder. The roof was covered in a thin layer of dust, she noticed as she ran her fingers over the dull, black material that looked like leather and was actually synthetic fabric.

'Are you taking out your swanky car in this weather?'

Selma bumped her head on an old bicycle hanging on the wall.

An ugly dog wagged its tail and pulled on the lead, anxious to make friends.

'Do you have winter tyres on it, then?'

'Yes, of course,' Selma said, smiling: she hoped the darkness would prevent her neighbour from seeing that she was bluffing. 'It's to go for a service. Needs a complete overhaul every year, you know.'

'So late? It's nearly midnight. And wouldn't it be wiser to wait until spring?'

The man smiled as he came closer. He lived in the house to the north-east. Notoriously argumentative, but of the kind who prefaced every criticism with a broad smile. Nasty comments presented as jokes. Protests as apparently pleasant, incontestable suggestions.

Selma grew increasingly relieved not to live here any longer.

'Of course not now,' Selma said, as she exited the garage. 'Early tomorrow morning. Just wanted to check that everything was OK.'

She closed the door without too much exertion.

'Good night, then,' she said pleasantly and set off towards the driveway.

'Have you been away somewhere?' he virtually shouted after her. 'I've not seen you for a while! By the way, I read in the newspaper that you had sold ...'

Selma did not reply, but simply picked up speed.

Without really doing so.

She was walking with tiny steps, but extremely fast, to create the illusion that she was in a hurry. It worked. She had barely gone more than six or seven metres up the driveway before the man and his dog disappeared.

She stopped. Waited for a minute or two. She was about to go back down again when she noticed another set of footprints in the frozen slush on the new asphalt they had laid last year.

There was nothing strange at all about footsteps leading up to the house. They could belong to Jesso. Or Johannes. Since the footsteps did not go back down again, they must necessarily belong to someone who was still in the house, she concluded, and almost calmed down at that thought.

But not entirely.

There was something familiar about the footprints.

The pattern was distinctive, and the frozen slush sufficiently deep to see very clearly the impression of the steel rod across the sole.

Ski fastenings.

Someone had walked here in ski boots.

Recognizing the model, Selma was able to confirm it as soon as she had compared it with the photos she had taken in Jan Morell's garden. They seemed identical. She carefully dangled her keys beside the clearest footprint.

Snap, said her iPhone, and Selma could understand precious little.

She tucked her mobile into her bag and continued on up. Fairly slowly and close to the cedar hedge, towards the swimming pool area. It was so high and dense that the house did not become visible until the driveway ended in a large, paved courtyard. The garage was right in front of her, the entrance to the house on the left-hand side. Even at a distance of so many metres, she could see that Jesso had changed the nameplate. The plastic-laminated, faded drawing of the whole family that Anine had produced as an eight-year-old had been replaced by an enormous brass plate.

'Mork' was all it said, as if Jesso and his mother already lived there on their own.

Things were really done and dusted here.

Selma realized she was breathing with her mouth open, slightly too fast, because she was so disconcerted by observing that the footsteps undoubtedly crossed the courtyard, but did not reach as far as the door. Instead they continued towards the north-west and past the corner of the house. Selma let her eyes scan the building again. Everything was in darkness. Silent. She followed the footsteps.

At the rear of the house it was difficult to see anything at all. For a moment she considered using the flashlight function on her mobile, but dropped the idea. Now she was standing only a metre away from Johannes's bedroom window. It was slightly open, despite the weather, and Selma held her breath in the forlorn hope of hearing his.

Don't think of the children. Don't.

Her eyes began to adjust to the darkness. The prints moved out on to the lawn, she could now see, all the way to the spot where Jesso had built a carp pond a few years ago. Four fish had to suffer an apparently painful death before Jesso accepted that he did not have a clue about aquaculture. The pit had become a birdbath instead, and was usually covered in green slime for the summer half of the year.

At the edge, constructed from small pebbles the children had been well paid to collect, the man in ski boots had come to a halt.

It looked as if he had stood there for a while, then trudged around a little, but always with his face turned to the house. Selma tried to get closer to the clump of footprints, but the frozen ground crunched so loudly beneath her shoes that she stopped. If Johannes turned on his light and looked out at that moment, she would be the first thing he saw. Her pulse accelerated at the very thought, and she suddenly grew angry.

Selma Falck was very rarely angry.

She showed it even more rarely.

This was her house. At least until a short time ago. It was her own almost-grown son who was behind those drawn curtains on the first floor, and naturally it did not matter if he discovered her. The truth was on her side. She merely wanted to collect her car, and had taken a walk up to the house to investigate some suspicious footprints.

'Fuck,' she said under her breath, switching on her mobile and walking diagonally across the grass, parallel with the footprints.

Quite right, beside the birdbath that was now empty of anything other than decaying leaves and dirty ice crystals, the man had lingered for a spell. Then he had taken a short cut towards the most northerly corner of the house. Selma followed and discovered that he had not moved on to the front of the house. That would have been risky. The living room window was massive, and the lights from the swimming pool area would make him easy to spot.

He had also lingered at this corner of the house. Not for quite such a long time, apparently. Then the footprints showed that he had walked towards the stone wall, climbed over and disappeared through the neighbour's garden.

Selma was tempted to follow, but ditched the idea. She could always get away with prowling around in her own former property. A nocturnal visit to her neighbour would be more difficult to explain, and after a moment's hesitation she therefore returned the same way she had come.

No one woke. No light was switched on. As quietly as Selma could manage, she again opened the garage door down by the road, clambered into the Amazon and turned on the ignition while murmuring a prayer. Two further attempts, two more prayers, and the engine started.

She slipped out on to the narrow road and drove towards the city. To Ensjø, where the Poker Turk had offered her garage space in exchange for help with his tax return in a few months' time. She did not dare to leave the Amazon parked in the street in Grünerløkka, so she had accepted with alacrity. It would at least be more accessible to her in Ensjø than out on Ormøya.

The footprints in the garden had made her feel uneasy.

She drove slowly. If she were stopped with summer tyres on these slippery roads, her driving licence would be at stake. It would be easier as soon as she emerged on to Mosseveien, where the traffic kept the asphalt perpetually clear. From there it would only take minutes to reach Ensjø.

It could all be coincidence. Most things happened by chance, as Selma was well aware. She seldom searched for connections when there was no necessity to do so, and no harm had been done either in Vettakollen or on Ormøya. Besides, there might well be credible explanations for someone having wandered through the garden in the same type of ski boots in the north and south of Oslo.

Within the space of a few days.

Despite both places being some distance from snow at this present time.

And the expensive boots were scarcely something anyone would roam around in without skis on their feet. It was entirely possible to use winter shoes on roller skis, Selma knew, but most people who trained so rigorously that they would be out on days like this would be wearing special boots.

At least she thought so.

As she drove along Ormsundveien, she tried to tear herself away from thoughts of the boots and instead imagine what the person in question had been after.

Supposing it had been the same person.

Supposing it had been a man, something the shoe size at least indicated.

A housebreaker might well do a recce before breaking in, but would also have checked doors and windows. Alarm installations. The residents' sleeping patterns could be partially discerned through surveillance, but not on only one visit.

It was all quite simply incomprehensible.

Unless skiers had taken to trudging through all of Oslo's gardens for the time being, it was also impossible to understand the link between the footprints in Vettakollen and the ones in Ormsundveien. As far as Selma knew, no one apart from Jan Morell, Hege, the home help up there and herself had any notion of the assignment she had been given. Other than Einar Falsen, of course, but he never spoke to anyone except her. Quite literally.

Selma was the only link between the two properties. One was owned by her client, and the other had belonged to her until very recently.

Practically no one knew she had moved out less than a week ago. Next to no one.

The car rolled quietly over the bridge to the mainland. The traffic was sparse, and when she reached Mosseveien a couple of minutes later, the lights flashed yellow and let her swing towards the city centre without stopping.

She should speak to Jan Morell. Find out if he had told anyone about their unusual wager. It was close to midnight, so she dropped the idea of ringing him now.

She would contact him tomorrow. As early as possible, she decided, as she speeded up across the Ekeberg hillside. In the middle of the bend leading to Gamlebyen, a thought struck her so suddenly that she forgot to check in her mirror before changing lane. A collision with a German camper van was avoided only by the skin of her teeth, and she saw the driver give her the finger.

The tracks in the two gardens had been left deliberately, Selma realized.

There had been no attempt to hide them.

On the contrary.

Every single day in the past ten-to-twelve days had featured the same, bleak weather alternating between rain and frost, between wet snow and sheet ice. The media reported that the orthopaedic department at Ullevål hospital was catastrophically overcrowded, and the newspapers were filled with daily moans about the council's failure to spread grit on streets and pavements.

The man in the ski boots had left clear footprints. He had chosen to wear distinctive boots: an ordinary bootprint would not have identified him so emphatically in both places. In Vettakollen and Ormsundveien, he had chosen to turn up while the slush was still thick enough to leave a trail, but late enough so that they would freeze fairly rapidly to leave identifiable prints. They were placed in the middle of the driveway in both places as well as distinctly across the lawn.

There had been no intention to stake out the place or steal anything, Selma realized, tenaciously struggling to focus on her driving.

The man in the ski boots wanted to cause fear and alarm.

He was determined to frighten someone, and that someone could not be anyone other than Selma.

To be honest, he had succeeded.

THE BONFIRE

'To think it's possible. To think it's at all possible, Hege. Bloody hell.'

Jan Morell sat on his dark leather settee, squeezing a tennis ball in each hand. He was speaking more quietly than his words might suggest.

'To tell the truth, this is the most idiotic thing you've done in the whole of your twenty-four-year-old life. Why ... why didn't you come ...'

His jaw muscles were bulging under his day-old beard, his knuckles white around the dirty yellow balls. The sweat rings in the armpits of his tennis shirt, pale pink with a white stripe across the chest, had dried into dull stains rimmed with salt.

'Why didn't you come to me?' he asked. 'Haven't I said that you must always, always, come to me when you're faced with a problem?'

Hege did not answer. There was nothing more to say. She sat on the settee directly opposite him and had been in endless floods of tears since she'd come running in from the evening darkness to discover that the tube of Trofodermin was no longer where she had left it, tucked away inside the air vent in the bathroom, hidden behind the broken grate, and forgotten to the best of her ability.

'I'm so worn out, Dad.'

'We both are. Even so, that's of no importance. We have to sort this out, we have to ...'

He stood up. Lobbed one of the tennis balls into a corner. Both Maggi and Hege jumped and followed the ball with their eyes as it bounced off the wall and rolled back, to disappear under the nearest settee.

Jan stuffed the other ball in the pocket of his pull-on trousers as he crossed to the fireplace. An overly large fire that filled nearly the entire hearth was burning furiously. The fireguard was not high enough to stop the glowing red flakes that sparked out into the room, and Jan grabbed a Farris bottle he had left on the mantelpiece. Shaking it energetically, he unscrewed the lid and placed his thumb over the spout, before showering a fine spray on the floor beyond the wrought-iron floor panel and then directing a couple of forceful jets on the fire itself.

'That's it, then,' he murmured almost inaudibly, holding out his hand and issuing an order: 'The tube. Now.'

Maggi had stood upright for more than two hours, halfway between the living room and the kitchen, as she was afraid it would become necessary for her to flee. She approached him. Obviously anxious, Hege saw; every step was hesitant. Finally she withdrew the empty, dented tube of ointment from her apron pocket. Jan had looked at it several times in the course of the evening, but hadn't wanted to touch it until now. Snatching it from her, he pushed it so far into the flames that he had burned his fingers before he let it go.

'There,' he said resolutely, waving Maggi away. 'In a few minutes it'll be gone. Completely gone. And we've never set eyes on it. Understood?'

The home help nodded energetically, already almost at the kitchen door.

'And you?'

He looked at his daughter.

She did not bat an eyelid. Her weeping had subsided at last and her eyes stared into space. She was trying to picture her mother.

Hege struggled to catch the scent of her mother, at night, when she came in with water and sat on the edge of her bed until sleep overtook her again.

It was impossible.

'What did Sølve say?' Jan Morell demanded.

'I've already told you. At least five times.'

'And now I want to hear it again.'

Hege reached out for the glass of water on the polished concrete table. Took a sip and then sat twirling the glass in her hand.

'He asked about what I had hidden in the air vent in my bathroom.'

'And you said?'

'Nothing.'

'Did you say "Nothing," or did you say nothing?'

'I said nothing. Didn't answer him at all.'

'Why didn't you deny it? Why didn't you say that ...'

'Dad!'

The exclamation turned into a screech. She slammed the glass of water on the table and covered her face with her hands.

'Can't we stop this? How long do we have to sit here and ...'

'Just as long as I say so.'

Her father was unrecognizable.

Jan Morell could be excessively inflexible. Abrupt and impatient. All the same, there was always something restrained about him, something that held him back when he was close to breaking point. Hege had never experienced her father losing his cool, even though he had become considerably more authoritarian since her mother's death. She imagined it must be impossible to build up a million-kroner business without having control over the last, dangerous button on his temperament. Now his face was deep red. He slammed the other tennis ball on the floor.

'And you!'

His trembling forefinger was pointed in Maggi's direction.

'I've given you house room here for more than twelve years,' he spluttered. 'You've had a better life than you could ever have dreamed of. Under my roof. With a generous, legal wage. And you repay me by being so disloyal as to run to *Sølve Bang ...*'

He spat the name out into the room as he made for the sideboard along the windowless main wall.

'Of all the windbags in the whole universe you had to go to Sølve Bang, no less. In order to ... *ask for advice!*'

His voice distorted into an imitation of Maggi's.

'You have to come to me if you're in doubt about anything!'

Throughout the evening, Maggi had been virtually silent. She had given short, succinct answers to all of Jan's questions, that was all; she was still in shock over the initial, blazing dressing-down she had received when he had arrived home around half past nine and got to hear of what had happened. Otherwise, she had not even attempted to console Hege each time she had burst into another wild paroxysm of weeping.

'What did he do when you didn't answer?'

It was Hege he was looking at now, before opening a drawer and extracting an unopened pack of Marlboro cigarettes.

'He asked again,' she said. 'I still didn't reply. Then he claimed to have information from a reliable source that I had used a banned medication containing Clostebol. And that I had hidden it in the air vent. In the bathroom. My bathroom.'

'And then?'

He fumbled in annoyance with the cellophane.

'I ...'

She took a deep breath and leaned back in the settee with her shoulders drooping. On the back of her left hand, a vein was throbbing just beneath the skin. Dark-blue and frighteningly distinct.

'I said I didn't want to talk to him. That he should get in touch with you. Idiotic of me, of course, because you didn't know any-thing about this, but I couldn't think of anything else. Then he said he was obliged to take the matter further. That it was his moral duty. That his loyalty was to the system. To the Federation. Always. He continued with a whole lot of …'

Suddenly she turned around on the settee and looked her father straight in the eye.

'He came out with a lot of high-flown drivel. About truth. Integrity. Clean sports. That sort of stuff.'

'But you didn't confirm anything, then?'

He took a cigarette from the pack and headed back to the fire-place.

'No. I hung up. And jumped off the tram one station early. Ran home. Checked the air vent. The tube was gone. And then …'

She looked at Maggi.

'… Maggi came in and asked what was wrong. I told her, and she admitted that she had taken the tube. And spoken to Sølve. In good faith, Dad. In good faith.'

Jan Morell lit the cigarette. Took a deep drag, and coughed a little. He was holding the cigarette as if it was the first time he had ever smoked, at the very end between the forefinger and middle finger of his right hand. He was staring intently at the embers glowing amongst all the grey ash.

Silence descended on the room, a protracted silence.

Hege had never seen her father smoke. She knew he had been a heavy smoker from his youth, despite his interest in skiing, but that he had stopped all of a sudden when her mother had asked him to. Hege had also noticed that there was always an unopened pack in the sideboard, among the napkins and candles. A long time ago, when she was a child, she had asked him why. The answer was that it was to remind him of how stupid he had once been. This couldn't be entirely true, since it wasn't an ancient pack he had just opened.

'This simply never happened,' he finally declared. 'There has never been some strange ointment in your sponge bag, Hege. You never emptied it out into the toilet. You never hid it in the air vent, and Maggie never found it. It's not been burned in the fire, because it has never existed. Sølve can claim whatever he likes, but he'll be left looking like an idiot if he divulges it without any proof.'

He wheeled around to face the two women, one standing pitifully at the kitchen door, the younger one completely deflated on the settee.

'We deny it. Understood?'

'No.'

'What?'

'Dad ...'

Hege got to her feet.

'I can't bring myself to lie, Dad. I'm no good at it, anyway. We should instead find out who put that tube in my luggage. If we find the person concerned, then we find the saboteur. He or she has somehow ...'

'You let me take care of all this. As far as you're concerned, none of this ever happened.'

'No. I refuse to lie. The girls in the team will believe me. They know I'm not guilty. They've been sending me text messages. Hedda phoned me today. They're supporting me, Dad, they ...'

'The girls in the team? *The girls in the team*?'

Again that darkness in his eyes.

'Do you think it's the girls in the team who'll decide this case? Do you think Hedda Bruun has anything whatsoever to say about it? That she can do anything about the tribunal's handling of the case? Does Hedda sit on the panel of judges? Or on the CAS, if it should go that far?'

He was quite literally tearing out his hair.

'Athletes should just perform, Hege. You know that. The system only functions if you fall into line, do as expected and win medals. You get drummed into you words such as 'winner culture', 'solidarity' and 'community solutions', to prevent the most precious of you from stealing most of the cake for yourselves. But those thoughts go only one way, Hege. They should go both ways. Because where are those boys now? Where are Bottolf and his gang now that you've been hung out to dry? Where's their solidarity now? If it gets out that you've been walking around with a tube ...'

'I'm not going to lie,' Hege broke in.

She padded towards the kitchen. She took hold of Maggi's hand on the way and pulled her along. The door slid open.

'Then Maggi's days here with us are numbered,' she heard behind her.

Sudden stop.

'Maggi is fired,' Jan Morell said. 'Now. As of today.'

'You don't mean that, Dad. You just can't do that.'

'Yes, I can. I want both your and Maggi's word that you'll forget this whole thing. That bloody tube has never existed. If you don't go along with that, then Maggi can start packing.'

Hege still stood with her back to her father. Maggi's hand, frail and warm, was held in hers.

'Dad ...'

'Yes or no?'

Maggi released her hand. Tenderly caressed Hege's cheek. She smiled, as if everything was fine and nothing terrible had happened.

'I can go,' she whispered. 'I'll manage. I've saved up ...'

'OK,' Hege said in a loud voice. 'Maggi stays. You have my word of honour.'

She turned around abruptly and took three steps towards her father.

'But soon that's all you'll have.'

THE MANUSCRIPT

501 INTERIOR, TOILET CUBICLE, DAYTIME

The MAN sitting crouched on a toilet seat with the lid down. The cubicle door is unlocked, but almost closed. The MAN is dressed in jeans and a college sweater. VOICES can be heard.

INTERIOR, COMMUNAL WORKS TOILETS

VANJA and a female COLLEAGUE are standing by an open window. They are both smoking cigarettes, and making sure that the smoke is blown outside, where gusts of wind are fluttering yellow and red leaves on a tree in the back yard.

VANJA: I'm not exactly afraid. But I feel a certain distaste. No, a strong distaste. Enough to tell me it's time to stop.
COLLEAGUE: But is it advisable? I mean … for him? How long has he actually been coming to you?
VANJA: Six months or so. I thought it had been going well so far.
COLLEAGUE: What happened, exactly?
VANJA: He identified one of them. In a newspaper photograph from the Ski Museum last spring. The opening of an exhibition. 'Skiing in Norway through Four Thousand Years'. Or something like that.
COLLEAGUE: He surely can't be sure. Wasn't he just a young child when it all happened?

VANJA: Yes. Seven years old. Of course he can't be certain, even though he himself is convinced. He says it had something to do with a pair of skis. Very special, the very first fibreglass skis he had. Or rather, his brother's skis.

VANJA taps ash out of the window. Her COLLEAGUE inhales and then drinks from a mug of coffee she has placed on the window ledge.

VANJA (cont.): It could well be that a particular event could trigger the memory. In this case it was a connection between a pair of black Madshus skis and something that was said.

COLLEAGUE: Was the actual incident initially suppressed? Are we dealing with a dissociative disorder?

VANJA: No. Definitely not, as I see it. He remembers everything that happened at that time. In detail, in fact. We've gone through it many times. My aim has been to get him to realize that he can't go on carrying around the guilt. That in actual fact it's irrelevant to talk about guilt, since he was only a little child. And that, regardless of what happened to his parents afterwards, it's certainly not his responsibility.

COLLEAGUE: So the incident at the Ski Museum was simply a matter of ... identification?

VANJA: Yes. Fairly straightforward. He was too young when it all took place to know for certain who they were. Besides, he moved away not long afterwards to another part of the country. With his father.

COLLEAGUE: At that time? In the seventies? Surely it wasn't usual to stay with the father in those days?

VANJA: No. And the accident, the divorce and a difficult upbringing from then on affected him. But being affected is not the same as being ill. A couple of times I've considered the idea of a bipolar disorder. Until the moment he saw the photo from the Ski Museum, he seemed quite depressed. Since then, he's been more … aggressive. Almost manic. But we're not talking about mood swings. Just … a change. He's definitely excessively preoccupied with symmetry. Purely physically, I mean – he wants to place chairs and cups and God knows what in perfect balance. But it's more a kind of … hang-up rather than a real compulsion. I'm sure of that. My conclusion was that he would benefit from CBT.

VANJA takes one last puff, stubs out her cigarette on the brick wall outside the window and pinches the butt.

VANJA (cont.): The photo from the Ski Museum was sheer association. The sight of the skis unlocked his recognition of the man. Almost as if you had met Solveig Gulbrandsen in the street in ordinary clothes and had no idea who she was. But if you spotted her with a football under her arm …
COLLEAGUE: Who is Solveig Gulbrandsen?
VANJA: Forget it. Shall we go?

Her COLLEAGUE turns on the tap at the basin and lets the water run over her cigarette butt. She throws it into the rubbish bin. Turns on the hot water and starts to wash her hands.

COLLEAGUE: I still don't know what you're scared of.
VANJA: Me neither. It's just …

VANJA heads for the door, stops and stares thoughtfully into the distance.

VANJA (cont.): Something's come over him that I can't understand. He's changed. He's far more intense. Persistent. The other day he was waiting for me at my home! Outside, in the street. I mean, if it had been a crisis, or a serious illness, then there are no limits to what I would accept. But as I said, he's not ill. Not by my reckoning. Some of his problems for all these years have mainly centred on a lack of social skills. Difficulty in being accepted by people. In letting them get close to him. He's not married, and he's scarcely ever come near a female, I think. He probably has a slightly difficult, not to say repressed, relationship with women. Often feels rejected. It was possibly quite traumatic for him not to be allowed to stay with his mother after the accident. Understandable. But now he seems almost …

VANJA shakes her head and walks towards the door.

VANJA (cont.): … obsessed. About everything that is going to change. That the tables are turned, as he puts it. Everything is going to come into balance, he says, though I can't quite grasp what he means by that. It's frightening. I can't have patients that make me feel afraid. That I quite simply can't understand. Then I'm not doing a good job. I've offered to find someone else for him.

Her COLLEAGUE turns off the water, dries her hands and follows.

COLLEAGUE: Is he dangerous, do you think? Are you afraid he'll do something to them? That he might …

Their voices grow fainter, inaudible and finally disappear, as the door slides slowly shut. The MAN emerges from the cubicle. He crosses to the window, carefully climbs out and vanishes.

The world had exploded.

At least Norway had. At exactly seven a.m., the news cycle kicked off. It snowballed once *DG*'s original headline story had been quoted and dissected, and attempts made to follow it up by all the other Norwegian and several foreign media outlets. Radio, TV, internet. Every channel. Even the alt-right forums and 'newspapers' that really were nothing other than blogs by conspiracy theorists, cleared space for the stories pouring out of the *DG* building in the early hours of this thirteenth day of Advent. In nurseries, parents sat engrossed in their mobiles without even trying to hide it, to the annual soundtrack of overexcited youngsters with candle crowns and glitter in their hair. There was hardly a newspaper to be seen on trams and subway trains: everyone sat hunched over iPads and telephones without noticing that the weather promised to be unusually, and very surprisingly, fine. The day had announced its arrival in the east as a narrow strip of ice-blue sky around eight o'clock, and by half past nine it was brighter than it had been for three whole weeks.

'They're only good if they have saffron in them,' Selma Falck said after tasting the St Lucia bun. 'This one definitely has turmeric.'

The first news that had broken was that Haakon Holm-Vegge had drugs in his system when he died.

'Drugged?' Selma said, holding the phone display reproachfully up to the man on the other side of the table at the Åpent Bakeri café in Åsengata. 'A bold statement, if I may say so.'

Lars Winther shrugged.

'Rules are rules. You and I can probably agree that they're too strict, but if any trace of banned substances are found in your urine sample, then you're ...'

He cocked his head and gave a lopsided smile.

'... drugged. That's the way it goes.'

'We're talking about really microscopic amounts. How did you find out about it?'

Lars Winther laughed.

'Yesterday you were after confidentiality for yourself, and today you want me not to give a damn about someone else's? Nice try. Not.'

Selma took another bite of the bun, chewed slowly and pushed away the plate with the leftovers.

'You've got time for this, then. Meeting me.'

'I'm on an all-nighter. Should really grab a few hours' kip now, but of course ...'

He gallantly flung out his hand and bowed his head.

'When Selma Falck, no less, wants to talk to me, I'll certainly come running. What did you want?'

The other snippet of news *DG* had released, exactly an hour after the first, was that Haakon Holm-Vegge had been involved in a road traffic incident with a passing vehicle when he had his accident. Selma had read both the main report and the brief interview with a police inspector three times over, and was impressed. Nowhere was it mentioned directly that this might be a case of an actual collision. Nevertheless it was impossible not to be left with the impression that this was precisely what had happened.

And that it might have been done deliberately.

A homicide, was the suggestion, so subtle that most likely it fell entirely within press ethics.

'What did you say to the police when you delivered the film?' Selma asked.

'Isn't it more interesting to hear what the police said to me?'

Selma did not answer.

Lars Winther lifted his cup and drank. Setting it down again, he bit the top of a paper tube and emptied the sugar into his coffee.

'In response to your question,' he said, stirring the liquid, 'I said exactly what I had to. That the wildlife camera had come into my hands from a source whose name I could not give them. From experience, the police accept that. At least in the first instance. I explained to them where the gizmo had been hanging. As far as I know, they've already had people up there, so for your sake we'll have to hope that you didn't leave all kinds of clues behind.'

Selma stared expressionlessly at him.

The forces of law and order faced far more pressing issues, she knew, than trying to discover who had taken down a wildlife camera that had been handed nicely to the police the very same day. Besides, she'd already thought up a good explanation for everything that had happened.

'And to your question?' she said. 'What did the police say to you?'

'First of all I need to know something.'

He tapped the teaspoon on the rim of the cup and wiped it fastidiously with a paper napkin.

'What's your role in all this? Who do you represent? We've received confirmation of *Dagbladet*'s report that you've sold yourself out of your own practice. As far as I know, you don't have a job right now. You've moved away from home. I haven't found out where you're living, which means that you haven't yet registered the move with the Population Register. That's mandatory, you know. Within eight days.'

The sudden surge of adrenaline forced her to swallow.

The adrenal medulla, she thought, as she bought some time by lifting her mug of tea. She did not relinquish eye contact with him over the rim of the mug. Did not blink. *Adrenaline is formed in the adrenal medulla from amino acids.* Still did not blink. *Pure biology. Relax. The veins in your skin are contracting. You're going pale. The steam is saving you.*

'I haven't moved,' she said, unruffled.

Blinked. At last, controlled and natural. Her pulse rate was over one hundred, she noted, and put the mug down before the unavoidable shaking of her hands began.

She folded them and placed them on her lap.

'No?'

Lars Winther smiled, the same crooked smile, half boyish, half ironic.

'No. We're just going through a bad patch in our marriage, that's all.'

She thought the new deeds for the property in Ormsundveien couldn't possibly have been registered yet.

It was out of the question.

'These things happen,' she said, returning his smile. 'Sometimes it passes. Sometimes not. Are you married?'

'Yes.'

'If it's lasted a while, then you'll know what I mean. And instead of talking about my personal ... challenges at the moment, I'm really interested in hearing what the police had to say.'

'And as I said, I'd like to know what role you have in this case.'

The situation was at an impasse, she realized. Deadlock. She ought to get up. Leave. She ought to forget all about Lars Winther. He was dangerous, despite his blond Tintin quiff and blue eyes.

At least to Selma.

'My role is really modest,' she said after a pause for thought that was exactly one second too long. 'Just a friend of the Morell family. And for that matter, a good friend of Haakon's parents. He was my godson. From that point of view, I know too many people in this … in these cases to control my own curiosity. But I don't have an official role.'

He nodded.

'Jan Morell was a client of yours, I know that.'

'Was?'

'Yes, you've sold your practice, haven't you?'

'Yes, you're right. He was my client. For many years. It happens that you become friends. Not the best of friends, but in this case …'

She broke off to look at her Rolex.

'I don't think we're going to gain much from this little meeting,' she said, smiling as she picked up her phone from the table. 'Thanks for coming, and sorry for wasting your time. Really.'

She put her mobile in her handbag. She pushed the chair back and made to stand up. With a hand gesture and something that might resemble an apologetic expression, he persuaded her to remain seated all the same.

'It wasn't a new theory for the police,' he said softly. 'That there had been a vehicle in the picture, I mean.'

Selma drew her chair a little closer to the table again and leaned forward.

'No?'

'They weren't exactly communicative, you might say. But thanks to me giving them the wildlife camera, I did at least get to know that. They probably thought, like all the rest of us, it seemed strange that things could go so wrong for a really well trained athlete. He's fallen before, and the worst thing that happened was a serious abrasion.'

243

Selma made no sign of filling the ensuing pause.

'However, they hadn't found any evidence of a collision,' he continued at last. 'Not until now, at least. After all, he was pretty battered and bruised, but all his injuries were consistent with the actual fall.'

Selma maintained eye contact, and remained silent.

'I don't know, but I assume they're having his clothes examined now,' he said, as if her silence was making him feel self-conscious. 'For traces of car paint and so forth.'

'The clothes were sent for examination by Saturday morning,' Selma said. 'Together with his roller skis, poles and ski helmet. But what did they say about the film clip?'

'Nothing. Of course they didn't.'

'Excuse me,' a ponytailed girl of twelve or thirteen in a dark-blue Svea jacket interrupted them. 'Could I have your autograph, please?'

Selma gave her a friendly smile and took the receipt for three buns, a cola and two mocha coffees. Turning over the paper, she accepted the pen she was offered and asked the girl her name.

'Marthe. With TH. I play handball.'

'What about school, then? Do you have time off?'

'I'm ... sick.'

'I see.'

The pen scraped across the paper as Selma dictated the message to herself.

'To Marthe, handball player, with best wishes from ...'

The signature was illegible.

'Here you go!' she said, returning the note. 'Good luck with everything! Especially school.'

The young girl disappeared.

'Must be a nuisance,' Lars said sotto voce. 'As things are.'

'No, not at all. Do you think there's a connection?'

'Between what?'

Two other truants had got up from their table at the other end of the premises as the first girl returned, triumphantly waving her receipt. They glanced hesitantly across at Selma, who quickly pulled her cap down over her ears and donned a pair of reading glasses from a case in her coat pocket.

'We can change places,' she said, getting to her feet.

The other girls were not as dauntless as their friend. Or perhaps they were just good at reading body language. Selma sat with her back turned to them, something she would have done from the beginning, if it hadn't been for Lars Winther already being seated when she arrived.

'Connection,' she reminded him. 'Between the cases of Haakon and Hege. Do you think so?'

His eyes narrowed a touch. He grabbed his cup, which was now in front of her, and drew it to him.

'I'm not here to help you,' he said. 'At least not when you insist on keeping your assignment secret. Since you're hardly working in competition with me and *DG* ...'

He stopped and raised his eyebrows a little.

'Or are you? Are you writing something? For a newspaper? NRK? A book? After all, every celebrity is writing a book these days. I was wondering when your turn would come round.'

Selma's laughter was genuine. He noticed that, she saw. He smiled back, with no trace of sarcasm at the corners of his mouth.

'No,' she said. 'I'm not writing anything. Although there have been loads of offers.'

'I can believe it.'

'Believe this too: I've got time to spare. Quite simply time to spare, Lars.'

She touched his arm with her hand. Just for a second, just long enough for her to notice that he felt uncomfortable. She pulled her hand away and straightened her back. He squeezed his eyes shut and then opened them, wide open, twice over, as if they had suddenly become dry.

'Call it a midlife crisis,' she went on in an undertone. 'I've worked far too much for all my life. Far too hard. I haven't exactly hit the wall, but I want to try to take better care of myself for a spell. Have more time. Help people without submitting a bill for it. Without being a participant in some TV programme or other.'

He nodded.

'Let's be open with each other,' she added. 'I'm curious and keen to help my friends. You probably appreciate that Jan Morell is convinced of his daughter's innocence. The same applies to Haakon's parents.'

Her phone vibrated quietly and she glanced at the display before tucking it back into her bag.

'You're a journalist. You're looking for the facts. Just the same as me. And I'll give you one. A sign of good faith, you might say.'

'Can I use it?' he asked, tapping his way into the recorder function on his phone.

'No. But go ahead and take notes.'

Selma glanced over her shoulder. The café was almost deserted. Breakfast time was over, and there was still a while until lunch started. An elderly woman sat on her own at a table a few metres away from them, reading a book while her tea grew cold. She had been sitting there before Selma arrived, and seemed totally engrossed. Also, she had a hearing aid, Selma noticed. The school pupils had disappeared. Away on the other side of the café, nearest to the window overlooking Åsengata, sat a postnatal group of five women. Two of their babies were screaming as if possessed.

Lars Winther had taken out an iPad and found his way to the notepad app. His fingers hovered only millimetres above the display.

'Haakon was given a drugs test last Monday,' Selma said, so softly she was almost whispering. 'And the results are already available. The test was negative.'

The journalist did not start writing. His fingers still hung like claws above the keypad.

'What?'

'You heard what I said.'

'Last Monday? He was clean last Monday? Then that means ...'

It was obviously necessary to give this some thought before drawing a conclusion.

'That means at some time between last Monday and last Friday he somehow ingested Clostebol,' Selma said to help him out. 'And in such tiny quantities that it definitely can't have been in order to obtain any performance-enhancing effect. The time window is only four days.'

'But ... what would be the point of that?'

Selma stared at him. Did not answer. When he hadn't spoken in almost half a minute, she gave him a condescending smile.

'There's no point in that kind of use of Clostebol,' she said. 'None whatsoever. So either it's happened by accident, or else he's been sabotaged.'

'Sabotaged? *Sabotaged?*'

His whisper morphed into a hiss.

'Are you telling me that someone intended to ... *harm* Haakon Holm-Vegge? Intentionally?'

Selma fixed her gaze on his. Shrugged imperceptibly. Tasted her tea. It was almost cold, and the skin that had formed on top attached itself to her upper lip. She licked it away slowly and said: 'Think about it. Clostebol, Lars. An active ingredient used by no one except suspect athletes in heavy sports beyond the control of the official organizations. A substance that demanded a regime such as the East German one to achieve maximum efficacy.

Closed, uninhibited, and with no thought for the long-term effects it must have on the athletes. They made women into men. With an anabolic-androgenic steroid we've scarcely heard of since the Berlin Wall came down, despite an increased focus on cheating in sports. And then, in the course of only a few days, we get two cases in the same environment, with the same obscure active ingredient. Coincidence? Well, I ask you. It does at least provide a basis for further thought in the direction of ... system error? Isn't that what you call it in *DG*? Or maybe it centres on something entirely different. Sabotage isn't inconceivable, is it? Many envy us our medals. It's only two months until the Winter Olympics. The way things look now ...'

She lifted a finger to correct herself.

'The way things looked a week ago, we were ready to make a clean sweep. In cross-country, at least.'

Lars Winther still hadn't written anything. He still sat with his fingers poised.

'You're a damn slippery customer,' he said.

'What do you mean?'

'You didn't ask for this meeting to obtain information.'

'Well, I ...'

'You wanted to give me some information.'

'That too. Both, in fact. In the hope that this might be the start of a beautiful friendship.'

Selma peered at him over the rim of her glasses before taking them off with one hand and leaning forward.

'You're not the first journalist I've spoken to in my life,' she said without taking her eyes off his. 'And you're not the only one who builds networks. Swaps info. We're after the same thing, you and I.'

'Which is?'

'The truth,' she answered, with a smile.

He folded the cover of his iPad without having made a single note. He shoved it into his shoulder bag and wrapped a long, thin scarf several times around his neck.

'Who knew about the first drugs test?' he asked as he stood up. 'The negative one?'

'The top brass in the Federation, at any rate. Me. And now you. Are you going home to catch some sleep?'

'After learning of this? No. I need to get back to work.'

He was so tall that Selma inevitably had to lean back when she looked up at him. A certain reluctance had come over his whole demeanour. His jacket was still halfway on, hanging over one shoulder with the collar partly turned.

'See you again,' Selma said cheerfully.

His phone gave a short, shrill ring. He pulled it out of his pocket, glanced at it and held it up to Selma.

'There it is,' he said, not entirely able to conceal how elated he was. '*DG Sport*'s third headline story of the day.'

Selma read it.

'Good God,' she said slowly. 'Norway's at risk of being excluded from the Winter Olympics.'

'Yep. Both Sweden and Finland are rattling their sabres. If the Germans jump in, things could turn nasty. The IOC are to deal with the case before the end of the week.'

'About us ... possibly not being permitted to participate at all?'

Lars spread out his arms.

'It's too early to say. The IOC has just decided that clean Russians will be allowed to take part, if such a thing actually exists. But not under their own flag or with their own colours. There's been far too systematic a doping regime in that camp. How things will end in Norway's case, it's too early to tell. But as I said, it doesn't look good.'

The shrieking babies had wakened the sleeping one over by

the window. Lars flashed a look at the mothers who sat in a circle around the table in a strange, swinging dance, each with a howling baby at the breast. He was still slightly hesitant about leaving. He finally took his leave by putting a finger to his forehead and saying, '*See you soon, just give me a call*,' before taking a few steps towards the exit. Stopped, turned and came back. He leaned down towards Selma from behind. His mouth was only five centimetres from her ear when he whispered: 'You need to take better care, Selma. A better disguise, at least.'

'What?'

'A wig and sunglasses, Selma? Seriously?'

She froze.

'I was out to expose a well-known footballer in the national team. Illegal poker's not a good idea for that sort of guy. It wasn't difficult to recognize you, Selma.'

He held out his phone, only thirty centimetres from her eyes.

'The Poker Turk,' he said. 'This is you on your way into the Poker Turk's place. Four weeks ago. Blonde and with a cap, but unmistakably you all the same.'

His mouth was so close to her ear that it tickled when he spoke. The photo had been taken in darkness: it was grainy and slightly out of focus.

She could deny it. She could pretend not to have a clue about what he was alleging. She could stand up and give a discouraged smile. Indulgent. Or get angry. Burst out laughing.

Selma did nothing.

She concentrated on breathing. Lars continued to whisper: 'If you'd still been a high-profile lawyer, I'd have given this photo to my wife. She works in the news section. But you're no longer a lawyer. As far as I understand, you're nothing. So I'll let the story lie. *DG* has no interest in hanging out people who're nothing. I'll give you a good piece of advice all the same, since you think we're on the way to becoming friends: give it up. Or find yourself a new, improved disguise. You're far too well known, Selma, to have a skeleton like that in your cupboard. See you later.'

He pulled back his arm, straightened up, pulled the strap of his shoulder bag over his head and left the café. One of the mothers had started to sing the 'Lucia' song to her infant. That helped. The other mothers joined in quietly. The elderly woman still sat silently, keeping company with her novel.

Only Selma was all alone.

She was, as Lars Winther had said, nothing.

That was exactly how she felt too.

Like a nothing, and she had never felt like that before.

THE DOUGH

The wall had moved closer.

For the second time in the course of what he reckoned to be only a couple of hours, the motor out there had started to thrum. As before, the hatch was first opened, and something edible thrown inside. He hadn't even begun his earlier meal yet, and now unwrapped potato crisps started to drop through. The flakes lay like dead leaves just inside the door before the machine was set in motion.

He could no longer bear this.

Battering his head against the wall did not work.

He couldn't manage to do it hard enough to die. The result of his many attempts was merely a perpetual headache and bloody tangles in his hair.

In a TV series, he could not remember which one, a life prisoner in the same situation as he was had gnawed through to the main artery of the wrist. She, for it had been a woman, imprisoned without charge or trial in a system beyond the system, condemned to eternal darkness without any hope of ever being set free, had overcome her most basic instincts by biting herself in order to die. He had been disgusted when he had watched the episode. Thought that such a suicide was completely lacking in credibility. Admittedly, he knew that an animal caught in a trap could chew off its own leg in order to free itself, but that the wolf fought for its life. A fox wanted to live and was willing to sacrifice everything to avoid death. The woman in the under-ground dungeon had spent ages inflicting more and more pain on herself, not in order to survive, but to bleed to death.

Now he understood why.

He was going out of his mind. He no longer slept. Neither was he ever completely awake: his condition had become a state of angst-filled apathy. A steady, dull fear. Literally scared stiff, he could barely bend his legs any longer. It was impossible to fully flex his fingers: he wanted to smash them on the wall until they bled the last time it moved closer, but couldn't clench his fists. When he first ended up in here and understood how the mechanism functioned, he had alternated between panic and frenetic mental activity. Terrified of the wall, but fairly clear and alert during the many hours he had spent struggling to find a way out. A solution. A life.

Now it was over.

The cell was only three times four paces in size now. He real-ized that the room would never disappear entirely. The narrow bed along one of the short walls was moulded concrete, and he doubted whether the motorized wall would be powerful enough to crush it. At least he had doubted that when he was still capable of rational thought.

By the time it came so far, he would be without both water and food. The door would disappear first, then the water pipe. In the end he would be left sitting on the concrete bed, enclosed by walls on all sides, with the ceiling above him. Like in a coffin.

In the end the room would become a coffin.

He could not wait so long.

He would never manage to gnaw his way out of life.

There must be another way.

In a flash of clarity, forced out by a desperation he had never believed possible, he understood what he had to do. For a while he sat on the edge of the bed, quietly, his breathing regular and his eyes closed. He envisaged what he would have to do. How it would have to be done. Bit by bit he went through his plan. Correcting it a little, thinking again. Understood what would be the critical phases, and what would come easily to him. Finally he stood up on his stiff legs and stretched his arms up as high as he could manage. His fingers nearly reached the ceiling. He raised his legs one by one to let air circulate around his balls – one of them was so painful that he was almost unable to walk.

All the same he dragged himself the couple of paces across to the plaster he had torn off the movable wall. Grabbing two pieces, he sat down again on the bunk and began to crush them. Once he had a pile consisting of a mixture of tiny fragments and plaster dust, he picked up the potato crisps from just beside the door. He pulverized them too, and placed them in the pile of plaster. Then it was the turn of the bread roll he'd received from the man out there. He picked at it to make crumbs, and then ripped the cheese to pieces and mixed it into the by now fairly large heap of powder and scraps. To finish off he stirred in some of the filthy straw.

Holding the pulp under the water pipe proved tricky. He needed to make a bulky dough, but his hands were too small and the water trickled out so slowly. Instead he put the mixture on the floor in front of the pipe in the wall, collected the water in his cupped hands and poured it over what had now begun to resemble dough. He had fashioned a hollow at the top of the little mound, as if he were making pasta.

It took time. Drop by drop his plan was implemented.

And he was ready.

The sticky mass began to dry out almost immediately in the overheated room. He made it extra wet, as syrupy as possible. He brought the dough with him and sat down on the bunk bed.

His nose must be closed first. That was easy. He stuffed the plaster mixture as far up each nostril as he could manage while breathing through his mouth. He retched a couple of times; the dough was pushed so far up his nose that he began to taste it, but that didn't matter. In the end, when his nose was so full on both sides that it ached, he plugged the holes again with two whole fragments of plaster he had measured for that specific purpose before he embarked on making the dough. An intense pain spread through his face, his entire head, and he began to bleed. Not only inside his nose, but so far back that he could feel a distinct, warm taste of iron on his tongue.

Gingerly, he tried to blow out through his nose.

The block held firm.

He took a deep breath through his mouth, closed it, and forced the air even harder against the doughy obstruction. It had to withstand a lot; he would fight against death, he knew that – nearly three million years of evolution would make him struggle for survival. Before he began to stuff the rest of the repulsive pulp down his throat, he had to be sure that his nose would not let him down. Not let him breathe.

It held.

But not the third time. The plugs shattered when he took a really deep breath.

Snotters and blood, plaster and crumbs all gushed out. A reflex made him take a sudden breath, and the rest of the dough went the wrong way down his throat. He coughed and spluttered. Crying and screaming, he took hold of the heap of dough with both hands, crammed it into his mouth, pushed in the pile of plaster, furiously, using all his fingers, up into his nostrils and down into his throat, gasping for breath and getting even more dough in his lungs, sobbing and weeping and swallowing and stopping up all the possible breathing routes.

But he went on breathing.

He coughed, spat and breathed.

Life refused to let go of him.

A sudden, lightning flash of pain shot through his left neck and shoulder. He froze. Touched his upper arm. His jaw. His heart, which was about to stop. He knew it, it was as if the very air in this appalling room had become heavy as lead, it was pressing him down, he turned over on his side with both hands clutching his chest, he wept, in delight now, that it would all soon be over.

He saw colours. Red and blue. Yellow and a beautiful green. Indigo. A rainbow, the most exquisite one he had ever seen; he lay quite still on the bed with his eyes open, ever so quiet, and did not blink.

It was no longer necessary to take a breath.

THE MACBOOK

'I'm really sorry for your sake.'

Bottolf Odda looked as if he meant it. He stood in the doorway and had just put a huge cardboard box down on the floor beneath the row of coat pegs. His complexion was ashen, and his chin far from being as outward thrusting as usual. The bags under his eyes were growing bigger day by day.

He had no desire to enter. Elise, Haakon's grieving partner, had made an apathetic and rather grudging offer of coffee. Fortunately he had turned it down. She wanted to be alone. Didn't even want to see William, who had been handed over to her sister for a few days. At least until the funeral.

'You could have warned me,' she said softly.

'I did. I told Selma Falck about the drugs test on Monday, and she promised to let the relatives know. I had no idea about this business with the car until I read it this morning.'

Monday, Elise thought dully. Meaning that Selma could have told her about the positive drugs test yesterday. Which she definitely hadn't done. For some reason or other.

Elise couldn't care less. Yesterday, today, tomorrow. It didn't matter at all. Her existence was going up in smoke, regardless. When her father had turned up unexpectedly at half past seven that same morning to let her know about the latest news, she had scarcely had the strength to listen. The police had contacted him at six a.m. This was of no interest to her, Elise realized. Neither the doping charges nor the possibility that a car had been involved in Haakon's accident.

He was dead and gone, and nothing could change that.

At length Elise had sent her father away and taken an Imovane tablet. It had knocked her out for nearly six hours, totally exhausted as she was after far too many sleepless nights. She had still felt groggy when she dragged herself out of the coma when the doorbell rang a few minutes ago.

She sighed almost inaudibly and used her small, pale hand to push her hair back from her face. Peering down at the box, she gave Bottolf a quizzical look.

'Haakon's belongings,' he said. 'He'd been up at the Federation before he went out training. Obviously planned to come back again before he went home, because he had changed clothes there. His car ... your car was, as you know, found at Tåsen – the police assume he had set off from there on his training session. I've emptied his locker.'

'Thanks,' she said, opening the box.

The red all-weather jacket with the Olympiatoppen Sportshotel logo lay on top. She lifted it up and held it to her face. It smelled a bit off, a hint of sweat, and not at all of Haakon.

'Are there only clothes in here?' she asked, hanging the jacket on a peg.

'More or less. Most of them are dirty. I thought ...'

His hand made a helpless gesture.

'Fine,' Elise said.

'Two pairs of trainers. Four pairs of ski boots. And then there are three pictures in there. Of you and William. Laminated. He had them on the inside of his locker.'

'Thanks.'

'Then I hope you'll be as well as can be expected. See you on Friday.'

Elise forced a smile and moved to close the door behind him.

'By the way,' she said, changing her mind: he was already making his way down the stairs. 'Was his laptop there? Or his mobile?'

Bottolf Odda turned around, plainly disconcerted.

'No. Didn't he have his phone with him in Maridalen? While training?'

'No. He had a fitness watch with all kinds of doodahs, but rarely wanted to have his phone with him. Especially not in rainy weather. Usually he used ...'

She put a thumb and forefinger on her eye sockets and pressed hard. It felt as if her head was full of treacle.

'Haakon had an old iPhone 4, which didn't matter too much. It was in his car, I think the police have it now. That was the one he used most. But he had just got himself a ten.'

'A ten?'

'An iPhone X. Two or three weeks ago. It's not here, so I thought ...'

'Maybe at the Olympiatoppen? Have you asked them?'

'Yes, Dad was in touch with them. They had nothing there belonging to Haakon. Are you sure?'

'Yes, no laptop, no phone. Just clothes, footwear and photos.'

As if to emphasize how certain he was, he came back and lifted the things in the box.

'This is all that was there. Nothing else. Is it ... does it mean anything?'

'Probably not. It's not so important. Forget it.'

He hesitated for a moment, but then obviously made up his mind to drop it.

'Look after yourself, then.'

'Thanks. You too.'

She closed the door behind him. Tried to think. It was difficult through the grey fog of sleeping medication and she went to the kitchen to make a cup of coffee.

Two phones. Two laptops.

A couple of weeks ago, he suddenly had two of each.

If Haakon couldn't be called stingy, he was at least thrifty. Good with money was how he put it himself, every time Elise became ever so slightly annoyed that he had bought the cheap make of mackerel in tomato sauce, First Price, instead of the proprietary brand, Stabburet. While his mates were obsessed with the very latest in mobile phones, games consoles, flat screens and hifi, Haakon searched items on sale only when the old ones were so worn out that they could no longer be repaired. Only with sports equipment did he know no limits, but usually he received those free of charge. Either from the NCCSF, the manufacturer, sponsors or quite simply from shops that generally foisted a new pair of trainers on him if he dropped by.

Elise filled the kettle and pressed the button on the coffee grinder.

The grating noise irritated her, and she stopped the machine before it was completely finished. Enough for half a cafetiere, she thought, as she poured the ground coffee into the jug and placed it on the kitchen table to wait until the kettle boiled.

It was so beautiful outside, she noticed as her gaze strayed out of the window. The view faced west. The sky was collapsing into bright colours, orange and pink, pale-blue and almost lilac. In the little grove of birch trees on the other side of the lawn, the bare branches stretched out in a coal-black pattern towards the horizon. It had grown cold, according to the thermometer at the window. Minus six degrees Celsius.

She hadn't thought too closely about either the phone or the extra MacBook. Mainly because Haakon had grown so distant recently. And maybe because she had simply assumed he had received them as gifts. There were strict rules about what he was permitted to accept, not to mention use. The sponsorship agreements were almost as much a straitjacket as an important source of revenue. Nevertheless Haakon continually arrived home with various things, small and large, that he didn't think mattered too much. The point was that they mustn't be competitors' merchandise, as he had explained to her a couple of years ago. No products that competed with those of the sponsors, belonging to neither the Federation nor himself.

Elise hadn't thought too deeply about the fact that Haakon was suddenly walking around with a double set of both one thing and another.

It dawned on her that she should have done. Especially because he had tried to hide the new phone from her. She had come across him when he was opening the package, and he had jumped out of his skin. Pushed the whole shebang under a settee cushion.

The kettle whistled loudly. She took it off the hotplate and half-filled the cafetiere. She stirred the mixture with a spoon and replaced the lid.

The strangest thing, and the one that should have made her react, was that he had never switched over from the old to the new device. She herself could hardly wait each time she had a new phone. It could take more than an hour to transfer all the data, apps and games, but she always did it at the first opportunity.

And then laid aside the old phone, usually never more to use it.

They had a whole drawer full of them.

Haakon continued to use everything. Both mobiles, and both laptops. The older phone had been lying in his car and was now with the police. She hadn't even given a thought to the latest acquisitions until last night, for want of something to do and refusing to take the damned sleeping pills, she had started to tidy up. Clean. Vacuum. Sort out Haakon's things. No iPhone X or brand new MacBook had turned up anywhere.

Only the old laptop, which was in a drawer in the guest bedroom.

He had reset the machine. To the factory settings. It was empty. No notes, no mailboxes. No photographs, just as she had taught him to do when you no longer intended to use a device.

Maybe the new one was for himself after all. Elise felt a trace of relief, a sensation that left her as quickly as it had come. Something might have been wrong with it. That had happened before, when he had acquired an obstinate virus, and Elise had shown him how thoroughly he had to proceed in order to get rid of the atrocity.

She pressed down the plunger in the jug and poured some coffee into a Liverpool FC mug. Grasping it with her hand through the handle, she shuffled out into the living room. She sat down on the settee, so listlessly that she spilled some coffee. Without bothering about it at all.

And then the iPad occurred to her.

That wasn't new either. Probably five years old. Haakon used it mainly to watch films when he was travelling. Sluggishly, as he had reluctantly admitted earlier that autumn, and Elise had already bought him a 12.9-inch Pro edition that he was due to receive as a Christmas present from William. The thought made her eyes well up with tears again, but she straightened her neck, gritted her teeth and refused to cry.

Haakon was dreadful with IT. He didn't even have a mailbox on his phone. Not on his iPad either – in his opinion the world contained enough intrusions and he didn't want to have to answer emails from all over the place. Of course he could have used a computer, and he was a whizz at Excel. He used the program for his training diary. When it came to setting up the machines, on the other hand, she had to help him sometimes, and always make a fuss about passwords and security. It was as if he didn't quite understand the potential consequences of being lazy about safeguarding data. He had no secrets, he usually declared when she nagged at him, and then shrugged his shoulders.

However, Haakon was well versed in the *Find My iPhone* function. With so much time on the move, constantly changing hotel rooms and trips in other people's cars, he often had to use it.

Elise put down her mug of coffee and fetched the iPad from his bedside table.

Selma Falck had thought Haakon couldn't possibly be unfaithful, that the life of a national team skier was too transparent. But what did Selma know about it? His existence had not been more open to others than that he had been able to do some double-entry book-keeping on the tech front for days on end without Elise giving it a second thought.

Selma might be wrong.

Not knowing was intolerable.

She stared at the black display, covered in fingermarks and stains of something that might be William's breakfast porridge. It was difficult to imagine that Haakon had bought new equipment without registering it. And initiating the 'find' function, which he had previously needed to use on several occasions. A couple of keystrokes on Haakon's iPad might well tell her what had happened to the two vanished machines.

Whether she really wanted to know was a different question altogether.

She had sometimes used his iPad. She used the tablet primarily to keep William amused. Haakon had downloaded a number of games for young children. William especially liked an aquarium with colourful fish. He could feed them until they burst and turned into angels with fins and gills. Haakon had never objected or expressed any form of disgruntlement when she had openly picked up his iPad.

He had always, until the last few days of his life, shown her limitless trust. All the same, or maybe precisely because of this, it felt slightly criminal when she grabbed the iPad, switched it on and opened Safari. Only a few seconds later she had gained access to *Find My iPhone*.

Haakon used the most ridiculous codes, and she often had to nag at him for weeks on end before he locked his devices. This past year he had used the password OL2018.

She keyed in the code.

A map of Oslo appeared in the top half of the display. The lower half comprised a list of Haakon's devices. The machine in the guest room was gone. The iPhone X was on the list, simply entered as *iPhone X*, but it wasn't visible on the map. The list also included several names, but they were both disconnected and invisible on the map. Probably these were old devices that had died a long time ago and were now lying in the drawer in the storeroom.

Haakon4's iPhone was situated in Grønlandsleiret 44, the display told her.

At the police station. He wasn't betraying delusions of royalty by attaching the number 4 to his name, but had included the model number.

That this phone was shown on the map meant that it was switched on and in contact with a network.

The police were examining Haakon's phone at this very moment.

Tears filled her eyes again.

Haakon's iPad was the one she was holding in her hand. On the map it was shown as a pulsing, pale-blue circle.

The new laptop also appeared on the map. She did not recognize the address, somewhere in the north-east of the city. She used two thumbs to zoom right in.

Stølsvegen. Årvoll.

She made the map move even closer. Registered the street number. Grabbing her own phone, she located the phone directory, and tapped in the address she had just found.

It took a few seconds before she understood it all.

Selma had been mistaken.

Elise was the one who was right.

Time stood still when she saw who lived in Stølsvegen. She knew the man well. She knew his daughter even better. Sophie was twenty-two years of age, danced in the youth wing of the National Ballet, and was the most beautiful woman Haakon knew. He had admitted as much one evening in April, at the close of the season, but before summer training had started in earnest.

They had been at a barbecue at a friend's house, and Haakon had drunk a couple of beers too many. He wasn't used to drinking. For eleven months of the year he didn't touch alcohol at all, and when the boys had embarked on a silly party game, she and the other women had finally made themselves scarce. William hadn't yet turned one. Elise's mother had phoned about eleven p.m. to say that the little boy had a temperature. Elise had gone searching for Haakon to tell him she was going home. As she approached the group of lads at the bottom of the garden, beside a trampoline on which they had just tried to outdo one another, she had heard it. Haakon was standing with his back to her and his words were slurred. He was waving a beer can, holding on to the trampoline, as he loudly declared that Sophie Selhus was the most attractive woman in the whole of Norway, and that he would cut off his right hand for a night with her.

His pals had laughed and shrieked, and none of them had noticed Elise. She turned on her heel and went home to a baby who developed terrible feverish convulsions in the course of the night. Elise had never been so scared before, and took him to A&E

with her mother. William was cooled down, given diazepam, and the convulsions disappeared. When Haakon, pale and hungover, woke the next day just as Elise and their son returned from the hospital, he obviously remembered none of it.

Elise had also made up her mind to forget it.

Sophie Selhus, the graceful, brown-eyed daughter of the NCCSF's Finance Director, had been given a brand new MacBook as a present from Haakon. He had even set it up for her. Elise could not think of any other explanation for him having unpacked it and kept it here at home for a few days.

She had not lost her man in an accident last Friday. She had lost him to a dark-haired ballet dancer from Årvoll, God only knew how long ago.

The thought was unbearable.

REPORTED MISSING

I t was as if the apartment in Pilestredet had faded.

A fine layer of dust covered everything. Vanja normally complained about it: the only disadvantage of living in such a central location, just beside the roundabout in Bislett, was all the dust. Since Kristina had allergies, they allowed themselves the luxury of having a cleaner in twice a week. The woman had now been laid off for an indeterminate period.

Scattered here and there were empty bottles no one had gone to the bother of removing. Coffee cups. Two stemmed glasses adorned the window ledge, with dried red wine dregs at the bottom. Beside the front door lay a pile of newspapers that seemed unread. Selma could hear P2 playing on a radio in an antique corner cupboard. A documentary about the significance of the placenta, as far as she could make out.

However, she didn't have enough energy to feel inquisitive.

If the countless bouquets of flowers hadn't really started to fade, their scent had become so cloying that Selma felt slightly nauseous.

'Kristina's sleeping,' Vanja said in a monotone, pointing at the purple velour settee.

Selma had already been here for a few minutes without them having exchanged a single word. She sat down. Opened the bottle of Pepsi Max she had brought with her and drank one-third of the contents.

'Good for her,' she said.

'She can't sleep at night. Collapses in the middle of the day. Then evening comes, and we're no further forward.'

'You just have to give it time.'

'Time? Honestly, Selma. If you've come here to throw around some clichés, then you might as well go again.'

Selma raised her palms in a placatory gesture and lowered her head.

'Just wanted to see how things were going,' she said quietly. 'Today's news can't have been much fun for either of you.'

Vanja hadn't taken a seat. Until now she'd been moving haphazardly here and there, stopping to touch something or other, before listlessly meandering onwards. Now she came to a sudden halt. Fixing her eyes on Selma, she said: 'Bottolf says he gave notification of the drugs test on Monday. To you. That he came here during the viewing, and you promised to let us know. What happened?'

Selma put the bottle down on the coffee table, placed her hands on her lap and looked up.

'What would have been the point of that? Spoiling the wake? You had a beautiful moment here, Vanja. A quiet, respectful occasion in the company of good friends. And if life has taught me anything, it's not to inflict unnecessary problems and worries on other people. You would get to know about it soon enough all the same. I had hoped that the drugs test wouldn't become public knowledge before the funeral, so that it would be over and done with without too much unnecessary fuss. It didn't turn out that way.'

She used her hand to rub her nose and then tuck her hair behind her ear.

'What you don't know can't harm you. And you were already suffering enough.'

Vanja did not answer.

'Do you understand?' Selma asked.

'Haakon was killed,' Vanja said.

'We don't know that for sure.'

'Yes, he was. I can feel it in my bones. I've felt it ever since Friday night, when the police and that dreadful clergyman turned up here, I've felt it deep within my mother's soul. It wasn't like Haakon to be so careless, it was ...'

She supported herself on a capacious winged armchair. All of a sudden, she covered her mouth and nose with her hand and sobbed.

'He was murdered. I just know he was.'

Selma was at a loss for anything to say. Of course there was every reason to take a closer look at the images on the wild-life camera, something the police had initiated some time ago. However, she had watched the film clip over and over again, most recently this morning on her own mobile phone, and there was absolutely no basis for claiming that any collision had actually occurred. *DG* had not published the live images on the internet, as that would probably antagonize the police too much. All the same, they had taken the risk of issuing a still image. It showed so little that their only intention must have been to demonstrate that *DG* was in possession of better material than any of the others. The car was just a dark, maybe reddish, shadow, and the skier could be anyone at all.

'It could of course have been an accident,' Selma finally said. 'But right now it might be better to concentrate on ...'

She looked around. It could really do with a spring clean in here.

'... the funeral,' she concluded.

'He was deliberately knocked down,' Vanja said defiantly. 'Haakon was born with a phenomenal sense of balance. Which was subsequently honed to perfection. He would never have been run into the ditch just by a passing car.'

Selma tried to bite her tongue. She was here simply out of duty. She could leave now, since she had already shown a commensurate amount of sympathy.

'Who would be interested in killing Haakon?' she asked instead, with a touch of resignation.

'A Swede, for example. Sven Feldin. He's always been critical of Haakon. Jealous. The year before last, when Haakon published his entire training diary online, he claimed it was a fake. That it was impossible to train so much without doing yourself any damage. That it wouldn't improve your performance.'

'Sven Feldin was in Davos last Friday,' Selma said, with a loud sigh. 'He took part in a World Cup race on Saturday.'

'He could have got someone to do it for him.'

Getting to her feet, Selma grabbed the bottle of Pepsi Max and stood twisting it round and round in her hands.

'So Sven Feldin, Sweden's best cross-country skier, paid a hired killer who drove up to Maridalen in a car one chilly Friday night in December, just four days after it emerged that Haakon wasn't able to travel to Davos because of a minor shoulder injury, and ...'

She paused and glanced up. Vanja was sobbing silently.

'... and knocked Haakon down and killed him?' she said in conclusion.

'If not him, then it could have been someone else. A Russian. Or a German.'

Now she was in floods of tears. Her head was bowed, her shoulders hunched. Her hair was greasy, Selma noticed, and was hanging lank on her shoulders. The lilac-coloured garments, layer upon layer to hide the fact that Vanja had steadily put on weight after her career as a handball player was over, made her resemble a withered hydrangea.

Selma approached her. Vanja willingly accepted her embrace: she put her hands around the small of Selma's back and hugged her as she pushed her face into the crook of her neck.

'He's dead,' she sobbed. 'I don't know how I'll ever get over this.'

Selma did not reply. Just held her tight. Let herself be hugged, listened to Vanja's weeping mixed with the occasional word she could not make out. The tram jangled at the roundabout. A driver blasted his horn. The placenta programme on the radio was finished, and Selma still stood there, holding her old friend, someone she had known since primary school.

'I have to go now,' she whispered, gingerly trying to loosen her grip.

'No. No! Please. Stay until Kristina wakes up.'

Selma grew dizzy. From the unaccustomed physical touch. From the smells, both the scent of the flowers and the slightly rancid odour of greasy hair and stale perfume. She planted her feet further apart.

The news roundup came on the radio over in the corner.

#MeToo was the top story. Several complaints had been made about the behaviour of the Labour Party's Deputy Leader. In addition, a Conservative Party MP was on the offensive about public money being spent on attendance allowance for the parents of gravely ill children. In the north of Norway, the Chair of Helse Nord, the health board, felt personally threatened in a conflict about the location of a new cardio-clinic.

The world-famous photographer, Norwegian Morten Karlshaug, has been reported missing.

Selma now tried in earnest to release herself from Vanja's embrace.

Vanja was reluctant to let go. Selma tilted her head to hear the radio more clearly.

He was last seen in his home on 2 December this year. The

following day, he intended to travel to a photo assignment in Mongolia, which is, according to the police, the probable reason for him not being reported missing until now. Karlshaug is mainly known for his landscape photography and he has had a number of photo reportages published in the well-respected National Geographic *journal. Information about the case should be reported to the nearest police station.*

'I have to go now,' Selma said softly but firmly.

She released Vanja's grip and took a step back.

'Phone me if you need me to come over.'

'I need you to be here now.'

'I can't, Vanja. But I could come tomorrow. I'll try. I promise. Now I have to go.'

She grabbed the bottle of sugar-free cola, snatched her coat from the peg in the hallway as she went past, and dashed for the door.

Fortunately she hadn't taken off her high-heeled boots.

THE PRISONER

It was time to set him free.

It wouldn't be easy, thought the man with the silver-grey hair. The actual abduction had gone surprisingly well. Inside the underground car park, there had been no CCTV cameras. It had been easy for him to disable the one mounted on the massive garage doors by cutting a cable ridiculously far down on the wall. His victim had been lost in his own thoughts as he strolled towards his car and hadn't noticed a thing until he woke in the cell.

The greatest problem had been that he was heavy.

At least fourteen stone. Maybe a bit less now, since it seemed that he didn't have much of an appetite. It was difficult to say, really: the view was restricted into the cell through the little hatch on the door.

The guy was tall and stout, at any rate.

Since he needed to be completely unconscious during the journey, it was no use depending on the scumbag's own strength. He had to be knocked to the ground.

Not quite literally, of course. When he had picked the man up, he had used chloroform on a cloth. Like in a film from the fifties. Easy to procure, easy to use. And particularly effective, as he had discovered.

He had become giddy himself from the smell.

Now he would use GHB. Gamma-Hydroxybutyric acid.

While the chloroform had been stored in a jar in the basement from the time when he had tried to suppress his uneasiness, anxiety and loneliness through an interest in entomology, the GHB was a bit more difficult to get hold of. But not as difficult as he had feared. The police were absolutely right.

There was a lot of GHB going the rounds.

A hosepipe was attached to the tap above the utility sink and led across the wall, fastened with staples all the way to the hole. It was exactly large enough, and snug enough to hold the end of the hose in its grip. He had turned on the tap once he had rolled the unconscious man on to the bunk ten days ago. Only a trickle. All he had now needed to do was to exchange the hosepipe for a different spout, a five-litre petrol can that now contained two litres of water. The GHB was still in the bottle he had put down on the sink yesterday. It had been tricky to calculate how much he should use, and he still wasn't entirely sure. An addict's dose was about the size of a screw cap. Two or three grams. The problem was getting the liquid into the prisoner. A dose sufficient to knock him out, but at the same time not large enough to kill him.

The man with the mop of silver hair hesitated.

He had been concerned for a few days now. Worried, and with the occasional hint of genuine anxiety. His excitement, the euphoric self-assurance he had started to get accustomed to, had evaporated.

Selma Falck was not included in the scenario. Nothing had been quite right since she had entered the picture.

It hadn't been intended that anyone else would put an oar in. It should all have been straightforward, the way he had planned everything so carefully, and the way he had been so certain in advance that it would proceed. Nothing should be investigated. There shouldn't be anything to uncover. No nosy lawyers should start poking around in anything whatsoever.

It dawned on him that it was very quiet in there.

There was usually a terrible racket each time he approached. Wailing and weeping and gnashing of teeth. He had never answered any of the screams. Just opened the hatch, tossed in something edible, assured himself that the trickling water was still accessible to the prisoner, and then fired up the motor that pushed the wall in and made the room smaller.

He had never spoken a word in all the time he was down here.

'Go away,' he said suddenly, in a low growl, and gave himself a slap on the ear. 'No. No. No.'

The guy in there was still very quiet. He must sleep from time to time, but he always made such a hullabaloo. It could be the stairs, the creaking stairs, or the sound of his footsteps on the bare concrete that woke him up. Every time.

Except for now.

He had an idea.

Forcing the GHB into him through the water hole was such a waste. After all, it would run continuously, and in the worst-case scenario the prisoner wouldn't ingest any of it. Or maybe only enough for a pleasant high.

He shook his head.

A hole in the plan. A hole in the head.

He smacked himself on the forehead.

'Idiot,' he snarled resolutely.

Single-minded, he moved towards the sink. Turned off the water supply.

He would have to make the guy in there thirsty. Totally crazy and mad with thirst. Then he would come and offer him a glass through the hatch in the door. A carefully measured dose, not too diluted. Just a little glass of water, so that it was certain that he would pour it all down his throat. It would taste odd, but he would have no other option.

Satisfied with his decision, he put down the can.

He ascended the stairs and bolted the door behind him at the top.

In twenty-four hours the man in the impregnable cell would be dying of thirst. Then he himself would return and get ready to set him free.

After all, there was no intention for anyone to die.

THE NICKNAME

'In any case, this ointment is the final proof,' Jan Morell said sharply as he opened the elegant, illuminated drinks cabinet, beautifully integrated into the wall unit.

'Of what?' Selma asked, as she stood gazing out of the enormous window on the top floor of the Fornebuporten building.

'That we're dealing with a case of pure sabotage. A tube of Trofodermin was left in Hege's sponge bag. It wasn't placed in there by her. Ergo someone else must have done it. It can't have been for any other reason than to compromise her.'

'Stupid, then ...'

Out on the fjord she spotted the lights of a cargo ship en route to Oslo harbour. The weather was still clear and cold. Since she could not afford to buy winter tyres for the Amazon, and also felt it would be sensible to stay away from the Poker Turk and his garage for as long as she could, she had taken a taxi out to MCV's premises in the fabulous building beside the Telenor Arena.

She was keeping tabs now and would soon have to ask for payment of expenses.

'Stupid, then,' she repeated, 'that Hege has no idea when it was put there. That we can't confine ourselves to Lillehammer and the weekend before she came across it, since she can't remember the last time she delved right down to the bottom of the bag. Stupid too that your *proof* has also gone right down the toilet. Quite literally. And that the tube has been burned to oblivion.'

'What was I to do?' he said in a voice that was far too high-pitched. 'That fucking tube could have destroyed everything! Even though I know that Hege never tells a lie, we can see now, clear as crystal, that many other people do believe she's a liar!'

'And Sølve Bang knows about the tube, then?'

'Yes. Because of that ... *muttonhead* who keeps our house clean.'

He poured a solid swig of whisky into an engraved crystal glass.

'It's past eight o'clock,' he muttered. 'There's some Pepsi Max in the fridge over there.'

He used his glass as a pointer.

'No, thanks,' she said. 'And now he's been in touch with you, is that right?'

'Yes. He threatened me, Selma. He actually threatened me.'

'I would take that with complete composure.'

She still stood by the window. She felt old. Her body felt heavy and lethargic and unfamiliar. Tired, she thought. Fed up.

Still quite scared, she noted, and gave a smile.

'With complete composure?' Jan Morell repeated scornfully. '*Composure?* You don't know what that man's capable of.'

'No. I don't. I actually find it more difficult working out what his role is in all this. Admittedly, he has one or two duties to perform in the organization, but how he can just ...'

She placed her hand on her neck and massaged it slowly before letting go, crossing over to the fridge, opening it up and taking out a bottle of cola after all.

'At that press conference,' she said. 'Or rather that little ceremony to honour Haakon's memory. On Saturday up there in Holmenkollen. A journalist suddenly raised the question of whether a drugs test would be conducted post-mortem. Everyone was totally taken aback. Sølve simply ...'

As she opened the bottle, it erupted with fizz.

'... leapt up on the rostrum. As if he were the host or something. Why did he do that? Why is he allowed to do that?'

Jan Morell sat down on one of the dark leather chairs in the seating area by the window.

'To tell the truth, I don't really know,' he said, surprisingly submissive. 'I've wondered the same thing myself. For years. I ...'

He had ice cubes in his whisky. They rattled noisily as he drank. He rolled the liquid in his mouth before swallowing, and then went on: 'In actual fact, Sølve cuts a pretty ridiculous figure. He's a peacock. But charming. Bright bastard. Knowledgeable and good on TV. He's taken part in some debates on behalf of the Federation, in connection with these ...'

The ice clinked even louder as he waved his glass distractedly.

'... this hassle from *DG*. About accountancy shambles and systems failures and all that jazz. He's capable. A bit short-tempered, perhaps, but he knows an amazing amount. He just shouldn't take a drink. At least not so much. In the course of a whole night there's no limit to what he can bring himself to boast about. Not that I've ever spent a whole night drinking with Sølve Bang, but he apparently starts screeching about becoming the Minister of Culture around two in the morning. Always. Now that the government is wearing green socks to keep in with the left wingers, it wouldn't surprise me if he joined the party just to show ready and willing.'

His laughter was dry and humourless.

'If anyone's still standing by the time the sun comes up, they get to hear that he's going to win the Nobel Prize for Literature.'

'Maybe he will. What did he threaten you with?'

'To make it public. Go to the press.'

'About what exactly? After all, he has no proof?'

'No. I think I eventually persuaded him to realize that. So I threatened him back, of course. With a juicy lawsuit. It made some kind of impression, I think, since he's afraid for his money. And obviously too smart to come out with allegations of tubes of banned creams hidden in Hege's bathroom without having any evidence for it other than a hint from a Polish home help. But it's ...'

He raised his eyes and looked at her.

'Sit down,' he said.

'I prefer to stand.'

A ship sounded its horn as it passed a marker buoy. It was now ten to nine and the traffic around the iconic building in Fornebu had eased off. The vast construction sites between MCV's offices and the sea lay deserted and dark. Jan's secretary had left before Selma had arrived. The entire building had gone to sleep.

'Where do we stand, Selma.'

It lacked a question mark. His voice sounded resigned and low. The way he sat there, slumped in the chair, with his tie loosened and his jacket open, he looked as if he had woken after a drinking binge.

Selma sat down.

'Yes, where do we stand.'

'Not a single millimetre closer to an explanation of what has happened, I'm afraid.'

'Maybe not. But we have a good deal of information. We have to start putting our facts in order.'

Leaning forward in the chair, Selma sat with her elbow leaning on her knee. She tried to catch his eye, but it was trained on something on the dark horizon to the south-west.

'Have you anything as archaic as a flipchart in this hi-tech palace?' she queried.

He looked as if she had asked for a weaving loom.

'A flipchart?' he repeated. 'Er ... no. But we have ... do you want something to write on?'

'Yes. Something big. A board, maybe? A whiteboard?'

'No. But we have this.'

He got up stiffly.

'I played tennis yesterday,' he mumbled as he rubbed his thigh. 'Just had to fill my mind with something else for a couple of hours. And arrived home to hell on earth. Look at this.'

In the middle of the pale unit that stretched along the entire inner wall of the office was a cupboard. Almost two metres wide and one metre high, Selma estimated. Jan picked up a remote control. The double doors slid to either side with a humming sound. An enormous flat screen appeared. One more touch of the keypad and a glass surface lit up in an attractive shade of egg-white.

'You can use this,' Jan told Selma, handing her a little metal rod. 'Use this as you would a marker pen.'

Selma tentatively wrote *Hege* on the left of the screen.

'My goodness. I've never seen one of these before.'

'There's a button in the middle of the pen. It lets you change colour.'

Haakon, Selma wrote on the other side of the screen, and drew a blue circle around both names.

'Sit down, Jan.'

He turned his chair to face the electronic board. Replenished his whisky glass and sat down obediently.

'The biggest change since last Thursday is obvious,' she began firmly. 'There's been another doping case. We really can't ignore that. But what is actually the similarity between Hege and Haakon?'

Such a deep frown appeared on Jan's forehead it looked as if his eyebrows had merged.

'They are the two best cross-country skiers in the world,' he said tersely. 'They are both Norwegian, they would both have won more medals if they went to PyeongChang. They are both in their twenties, they were both already good as juniors. Shall I go on?'

Selma drew a line between the two circled names.

'No, thanks. Two cross-country skiers. Damn good ones. Norwegian. Medal candidates at the Winter Olympics. Of course, it could be that someone is out to attack them for that very reason. Either as individuals or as representatives of Norway.'

NORWAY, she wrote in big, red letters at the top of the screen.

'But anyway, you can scarcely think of two such different people as Hege and Haakon,' she said. 'Haakon was the leading light of the men. Outspoken. Politically engaged, at least in the politics of sport. He has taken a forceful and distinct stand against doping. On more than one occasion, he has criticized the Norwegian Skiing Federation, the Norwegian Confederation of Sports, the International Ski Federation and the International Olympic Committee. For everything from nepotism to stupid technical requirements, via economic foul-ups. Haakon was a man of strong opinions. With a family. A partner and child. Open with the public to an almost comic extent, such as when for example he chose to publish his training diary in detail.'

The metal pen soundlessly drew three lines down from Haakon's circle.

The public, she wrote in blue.

'Hege is Haakon's total opposite. Unassuming, almost mysterious. Little involvement in events beyond sports activities.'

'If you had any idea what both she and I do for UNICEF and Médecins Sans Frontières then ...'

'Exactly. We're left without any idea. We see it so seldom. Hege is a quiet, almost taciturn young woman. Lives with you. Her father. A widower. Almost certainly has had a boyfriend or two, that's none of my business, but nothing serious. Hege can seem ...'

Selma restrained herself. In distraction, she nibbled the metal stick.

'You'll break it.'

'Sorry. To outsiders, Hege can seem a bit ... immature?'

Jan Morell did not bat an eyelid. He had put his glass down on the floor and, elbows leaning on the armrests, he pushed the fingertips of both hands together to form a tent.

'Immature,' Selma reiterated, nodding. 'From the outside, she seems immature. Following the conversations I've had with her, I see that this might be wrong. Quite the opposite, in fact, she gives the impression of being thoughtful, but all the same there's something ...'

She smacked her lips, searching for the word she was after.

'... *naïve* about Hege. I think for example that she's very bad at the art of lying. Before I met her for the first time, at your house on Thursday evening, I was far from convinced of her innocence. I am now. At least from a moral standpoint, I'm pretty sure that your daughter is a young woman who sticks to the truth. There still remains the possibility that she ingested Clostebol through some accident she knows nothing about. But with the discovery of the tube of Trofodermin in her luggage, I agree with you: someone has done this to her. She's most certainly not lying. I don't think she's capable of it.'

'As opposed to you and me,' Jan said, barely audibly.

'True enough. The ability to lie when necessary is an adult's painful duty and burden.'

She smiled at him, almost teasing. He still did not bat an eyelid.

'Where are you going?' he asked brusquely. 'What's the point of all this?'

'What if we're not dealing with one case?'

'What?'

'What if Haakon and Hege have both been the victims of

sabotage, but by different perpetrators? And therefore for different reasons? Quite apart from the fact that they both move incredibly fast on skis, they have lived very different lives.'

The metal pen drew an angry zigzag between the two names on the board.

'Everything isn't always connected to everything else,' Selma said. 'Not all the time.'

'To tell the truth, that's the stupidest thing I've heard.'

Jan bent down to pick up the glass. Raising it to his mouth, he hesitated for a second, shook his head and drank it down.

'Wait a minute now,' Selma said.

'No,' Jan Morell retorted as he got to his feet.

He grabbed the remote control from the wall unit. Pressed a button. The screen suddenly turned white again.

'But listen to me,' Selma insisted. 'Listen to me now.'

He was becoming enraged, she saw. The hand holding the glass was trembling a little, and narrow, white stripes were etched at each side of his nose. She smiled as warmly as she could, turned the two chairs to face each other, and sat down in one of them. Crossing her legs, she tucked her hair behind her ear. And folded her arms.

'I've defended clients who have looked guilty solely because the circumstances were simply unbelievable,' she said calmly. 'Logical links to events that, taken together, build into weighty circum-stantial evidence. So convincing that the person in question is convicted. Or acquitted because I succeed in picking apart the chain into its individual components and put them back together again in a way that is equally credible. And that justifies acquittal.'

'Let me tell you one thing.'

Jan flopped into the other chair and looked her straight in the eye.

'I don't give a damn about Haakon Holm-Vegge. He's only of

interest to me in so far as his case seems to have something to do with Hege's. To the extent that the explanation for sabotaging her is somehow connected to him. And it ...'

He leaned forward without relinquishing eye contact.

'... obviously does.'

'Then that's what we'll say,' Selma said, sounding upbeat. 'For the time being. However ...'

She unscrewed the lid of the bottle.

'Would you like a glass?' Jan snapped.

'No, thanks. The fizz disappears. But all the same ...'

She took a swig.

'I honestly think we should concentrate on the Trofodermin.'

'What do you mean?'

'I believe that bloody ointment is the culprit. Or, as a matter of fact ... I don't believe it, as such, because at the moment I've no idea what I should believe. But I have a hypothesis. A possible scenario, if you like. Can I use the board?'

Jan grunted his approval. Selma went over and wrote *TROFODERMIN* in bright orange on the glass screen.

'We're familiar with the ointment from the story of Hedda Bruun and the near-catastrophe in Italy,' she said. 'In September. We know that it contains Clostebol. We know there are athletes worldwide who have been caught doping with Clostebol in the past. If not very many of them. Some claim to have used the ointment for innocent complaints. From what I can see, that may well be the truth.'

Jan no longer seemed so stern. He was already more than halfway down his second glass of malt whisky, but seemed alert.

CLOSTEBOL

Black, this time, with a red ring around it.

'So we both choose to believe Hege. At any rate I choose to believe that Haakon has not deliberately taken the substance either. In the first place, because I knew him, and I quite simply can't get it to add up that he would cheat. Secondly because we know that he must have been exposed to the drug in the short period between last Monday and when he died on Friday. A minuscule, pointless, amount.'

'This is only a summary. We already talked about all this on Monday. You said you had a hypothesis.'

'Your list,' Selma said quickly, thumbing through to the notes on her own phone. 'Of people who knew about the episode in Italy.'

Rapid and slapdash, to avoid testing Jan Morell's impatience again, she wrote up all the names. She did not need to glance at her notes as she used the pen:

Bottolf Odda	Stian Bach
Reidar Farsund	Severin Pettersen
Hallgeir Hovd	Knut Nilssen
Astrid Beita	Mathias Strømmen
Mons Hansen	Arnulf Selhus

Selma turned to Jan and said: 'These ten people knew they were within walking distance of legal, over-the counter purchase of a preparation containing Clostebol during the trip to Italy. Hedda Bruun and Hege did also. Why aren't they included on your list?'

Jan shrugged and stared at her, looking discouraged.

'You think Hedda could have sabotaged Hege?'

'Not really, but I'd like the list to be complete.'

She added Hedda's name to the others.

'You and I know about it too,' he said angrily. 'Are we among the suspects?'

'No. We didn't find out about it until Saturday.'

Again Selma bit the steel pen. Once again she received a sharp rebuke.

'Which of these was in Italy in September?' she asked.

'All the trainers. Knut, Stian Bach and Bottolf Odda. The last of these for only a few days, admittedly, but after all he was the one who dealt with the incident when Hedda discovered what she had been given.'

He paused for a moment as he studied the list.

'And Astrid Beita. She was there too.'

'Why was she informed?' she asked. 'Isn't she the cook?'

'Yes. I don't know. Maybe she overheard something. This is at least the list of names my security consultant came up with.'

'Arnulf Selhus,' she said, putting brackets around his name. 'He wasn't there. Then how did he know about it?'

'There's not much that man doesn't know about what goes on in the Federation. As the Director of Finance, he might have been difficult to persuade when it came to the appointment of a new doctor. As you know, they didn't fire Stian. That would be expensive.'

'Reidar, Severin, Hallgeir, Mathias and Mons are all trainers. Two of them for the women, three for the men.'

'That's right. But what reason the trainers might have for sabotaging their own athletes is beyond my comprehension.'

'Wait up a second. Bottolf is the big cheese, then, and Stian the doctor who made a mess of things. And who, in my opinion, should have got the boot long ago. Knut is a physiotherapist. A kind of head physio, isn't he?'

'Well, a senior one, at least. And definitely the best of the lot.'

'Contact,' Selma said, stopping the pen on its way to her mouth.

'What?'

'Knut Nilssen does at any rate have all the opportunity in the world for physical contact with the skiers. It's in the nature of the work.'

'Eh ... yes?'

'If we consider that the substance is ingested through the skin, I mean. It would be easy for him to have done something like that.'

'Yes. Hege's sample was taken on 7 November. Out-of-competition. She was in Oslo. That was ...'

It took him less than thirty seconds of tapping his mobile before he went on: '... also Knut. Of course I don't really remember whether he treated Hege in the days before the drugs test, but I can find that out.'

'Do that.'

'But he can hardly have sabotaged Haakon,' he said in an undertone.

'Don't you think so?'

'Haakon only uses Anita. Anita Ulvestad. They're childhood friends, and Anita managed to sort his shoulder the last time it was a problem. He thinks she has miraculous powers.'

'OK. Not Haakon, then. So we're no further forward, unless you're willing to accept my theory about two different sets of circumstances.'

'Give over,' he said. 'The idea that two autonomous individuals got it into their heads to dope two different elite athletes on the sly is absurd. Of course there's a connection.'

With a sigh, Selma switched off the screen and crossed to the window. Jan was right. They were going around in circles. The list of people who knew of the unfortunate episode during the autumn run-up was virtually useless. First of all it was unthinkable that the story had stopped at the few who originally knew about it. It was unfathomable that no journalists had learned of Stian Bech's unforgivable carelessness, but Selma nevertheless refused to believe that all of the eleven mentioned on the list had kept the story entirely to themselves.

That sort of thing just didn't happen.

People talked. With their spouses. With close friends. In bed. In a drunken rant. Anywhere. As a means to ingratiate themselves. Make themselves interesting. *Don't tell anyone* was probably the most frequently broken request in the history of humankind.

Maybe someone had spoken to the press all the same.

Maybe there were journalists who knew about it, but had never managed to break the story. Selma tapped a speedy text message and sent it off.

'What was that?' Jan asked.

'Just some practical details. What could Sølve actually be after?'

'What?'

'Sølve Bang. Why is he so keen on this business with the tube in the air vent? He always rushes to the defence of the Federation. Good grief, he so often behaves as if he owns Norwegian cross-country skiing. Now he's even about to publish the definitive history book on the subject. If he felt evidence existed that Hege had cheated, why does he regard it as his mission to drag it into the public eye?'

'No idea. Sense of justice, perhaps.'

He sniffed and drained his glass in one last mouthful.

'Not that he appears to be especially honourable, exactly. As far as Sølve Bang is concerned, it's all about Sølve Bang. No one else.'

'Spot on. Previously, when he went to war in defence of the Federation, it was just as much out of self-interest. Does he have anything to gain from all the brouhaha that's being stirred up now? I mean with Hege, with Haakon, and with the IOC who might decide to exclude us ...'

Her eyes narrowed as she turned into the room again.

'There's something strange going on here ...'

'There's something strange about this whole situation.'

He gave a loud, protracted yawn, without covering his mouth.

'I must get home.'

'We'll never move any further forward until we find a motive.'

'We've found a whole heap of possible motives,' he said, getting to his feet and pressing a button on his mobile phone. 'That's exactly the problem. My driver will be ready in ten minutes. Sorry but I don't have time for a detour to Grünerløkka.'

'We haven't found many motives, Jan. Strictly speaking, we've only found two. One is that someone wants to destroy the careers of Hege and Haakon, either together or individually. The other is that someone wants to ruin the Norwegian Cross-Country Skiing Federation. What if this is all about something else entirely? What if ...'

'You can get to the bottom of that,' he broke in. 'This wager of ours isn't going in your favour at the moment.'

He opened the door and looked at her.

Selma had never quite made up her mind whether she liked Jan Morell or not. As a client he was pleasant enough. Open to advice, but with firm opinions. Smart at distinguishing between what he could force through and what he had to leave to her discretion. A prompt payer. When he exposed her, he was hard as nails. But also unexpectedly considerate, she had to admit. He could have sent the case straight to the police, and Selma would have been convicted as soon as she set foot in court. Instead he had chosen a punishment it was possible for her to go on living with. Only just, admittedly, but all the same. Jan Morell could be direct, bordering on brutal, in his dealings with other people, but he was also a benefactor, without showing off about it. After several years' acquaintance, and a few days of a kind of fateful union, she had however never seen him express love, or even any particular warmth, towards anyone except his daughter.

He obviously loved her dearly.

Maybe too dearly, if such a thing were possible.

What did she know.

Selma still couldn't decide what she thought of the man.

'Sorry to hear about that friend of yours,' she said, picking up her coat and bag on the way out.

'Friend of mine?'

'Yes. That photographer who's gone missing. Morten Karlshaug.'

'Oh, Klaus, yes. He's sure to turn up. As he always does. If I know him, he'll be lying in a yurt on the other side of the earth, having fun with a little Mongolian number. Klaus is a real womanizer and has never settled down with anyone.'

Closing the door that locked automatically, he made an inviting gesture towards the elevator.

'Why do you call him Klaus?' Selma asked.

'A nickname from childhood. Or ...'

Jan applied a stubby finger to the elevator button.

'More of a pseudonym, in fact. A bit unkind, but we've never called him anything else. He's sick in the head. I usually say it's reflected in his art. Wide-open landscapes as far as the eye and soul can see. He's award winning, you know. Internationally. He has taken the most beautiful photograph you could ever imagine from the top of Mount Everest. You've probably seen it, it was the year's ...'

The elevator pinged and the doors slid open.

'What do you mean by "sick in the head"?' she asked as she entered the elevator.

'He suffers from claustrophobia. Really hellish claustrophobia. So he got the name Klaus. He was only three when he accidentally managed to lock himself inside an antique rose-painted bridal chest. He lay in there for several hours, as far as I've been told. Was nearly suffocated and became totally disturbed. When we were young boys, once upon a time ...'

The elevator doors slid soundlessly shut.

THE BEGINNING

As a black Audi A8 with Jan Morell in the back seat swung out of the parking space in front of the Fornebuporten, Selma closed her eyes and sent up a silent thanks to higher powers.

He hadn't once mentioned the treatment she was about to start, according to a certificate from the Blue Cross. The paper had been delivered to him by yesterday's deadline, and he had accepted it in silence. He couldn't have given it more than a cursory glance, and that was worth her heartfelt thanks.

Of course no one at the Blue Cross could confirm that Selma Falck was actually attending a course of treatment for a gambling addiction. Quite simply because she was not undertaking any form of therapy. The random psychologist she had argued her way into a conversation with had been adamant. All he could stretch to was confirmation that she had sought him out. And that Selma Dorothea Falck, born 16 September 1966, had signed up for group therapy for a period of around four months.

In addition to receiving information about the website, *self-help.no*.

Selma peered at her mobile to see if Lars Winther had answered the text she had sent from Jan's office. He had.

Can't meet you tonight. Half past seven tomorrow morning suits. Same place as last time. L.W.

She stuffed the phone into her bag and started walking.

Intending to hail a taxi if she saw one, but first she needed a breath of air.

It was cold enough, and she turned up her coat collar against the north wind.

The psychologist had recognized her the moment she entered his office. He tried in vain to hide a smile when she gave her full name. Complying with Jan Morell's demand for proof that she had sought help was a humiliating low point in Selma's life. Which, after the events of the past few weeks, was not saying much.

It made no odds.

Everything was falling apart, anyway, she thought as she picked up speed.

Too many people knew. Or thought they knew. Jan had discovered Selma's secret, and that was the beginning of the end. Now the bloody psychologist knew about it too. And Lars Winther, even though, to be honest, he knew no more than that she wasn't averse to a game of illegal poker.

It had all gone so fast.

The contours around her dissolved.

For so many years her existence had been full of sharp lines. Her family separate. Her work in a different space. Friends. Handball, the best time in Selma's life, was rigidly framed by tangible medals and achievements for all eternity. And all these frames were populated by people.

Gambling was Selma's private space.

A blessed sanctuary where she was completely alone. For a long time it had also been an important source of income: some of the speculation in shares had been especially profitable. They were easy to live with, simpler than betting and cards. In every way. Jesso knew about a good deal of Selma's so-called wise investments, and had always admired her for everything in which she had learned the ropes.

The very first pure bet was also met with enthusiasm by Selma's social circle. She had been in London with a group of girls in the late winter of 1992 and managed to put a hundred pounds on Denmark becoming European Champions in football that summer. Since they hadn't yet qualified for the tournament, the odds were staggering. Selma had a vague notion that the blood-bath in the Balkans might also have consequences in sport, and risked all she could afford to lose. Only ten days before the final stage of the competition kicked off in Sweden, she was proved right. UEFA acceded to a request by the UN not to allow any involvement in sport by Yugoslavia, then ravaged by civil war. The country was disqualified and Denmark, runner-up in their group, was awarded the last place in the tournament.

And beat Germany in the final.

Selma travelled back to London and picked up a larger sum of money than she had ever had in her hands. Everyone knew about it. Friends and teammates laughed with delight. Jesso went almost mad with excitement. Selma's own reaction was both frightening and exhilarating, and she concealed it from everyone. Smiling broadly, she allowed herself to be congratulated, but kept the rest to herself.

The stimulation. The delightful, suffocating, intoxicating feeling that life itself was at stake when Denmark scored their second goal in the final. The amazing elation until the whistle blew and it was all over and she suddenly realized that her impulsive bet's highest value was not all the money she had won.

It was the feeling that something had been at stake the whole time.

From the moment she had handed over the hundred pounds in exchange for a receipt from a bookmaker in South London, she had felt it. Everything was exciting. What the UN would decide to do. Whether UEFA would follow it up. Whether Sweden would manage to beat England in their final game, which Denmark depended upon in order to progress. For weeks and months she had gone around with an unfamiliar, euphoric sense of being present in her own life. The entire time.

An interminable Olympic thriller of a final without any greater potential loss than one hundred pounds sterling. That brought a dizzying profit and an intense craving to do it all over again.

A taxi with a light on its roof came driving from the south on Snarøyveien. She flagged it down and crept into a compartment that smelled of pepper. The boy behind the wheel, he couldn't possibly be more than twenty-five years old, had fair hair and had pushed a pair of incongruous sunglasses on top of his head.

'Sinsenkrysset,' Selma said curtly. 'No, change that. Drive me to the Narvesen kiosk in Vogts gate. We'll drive on from there, I just need to do some shopping first.'

She leaned back in the seat and closed her eyes.

Everything was unravelling.

Selma herself was falling apart. She was trying to be a detective without the slightest idea of how to go about it. Her strength was to unpick evidence. Not to locate it. She was good at building a valid case from known facts. Not finding facts when she had no idea where they were hidden.

She simply couldn't do it. Her thoughts were going round in circles, they had no beginning or end, and they twisted around in a circular pattern she neither understood nor recognized.

Selma Falck was a trademark. A brand fashioned from memory and stringency, frames and straight lines. Logic. She was resilient and strong, intelligent and streetwise.

And she never gave up.

Now she was about to capitulate.

Somewhere in everything that had happened in this past short week, all the same, lay something she hadn't quite grasped, something annoying, a tiny stone in her shoe that she had never had time to stop and get rid of.

She just had no idea what it was.

'Deli de Luca,' she leaned forward and addressed the driver. 'Not Narvesen.'

'They're both at the same fucking intersection,' the ill-tempered driver said as he accelerated along the E18 towards the city.

THE CORPSE

H e wasn't ill.

Vanja had said that he wasn't ill.

Just affected, as she said. Influenced by an extremely traumatic event in his childhood that had never been cleared up. Nothing was really wrong with him. He had grown up. Behaved well. Never done anything worse than incurring two points on his driving licence. Obtained an education and got a job. A dream job, in fact. He earned good money, had a house and even friends. Sort of friends. He didn't really need them. The best thing was his work, because he was good at that, and going skiing.

He was still an expert skier, and he wasn't ill.

Vanja had said that, but Vanja wasn't here now to see how bad it was. All of it. Haakon's death, which made him sad, and Haakon's positive drugs test, which confused him and aggravated his headache.

Vanja was in pain herself.

It wasn't his fault.

'Cunt,' he snarled, and washed down four Paracet tablets with water.

It was a double dose, but his headache was really killing him.

The silence from the cell was bothering him too. Up here in the living room he had never heard anything, the work of installing the insulation had taken several weeks, but the absence of entreaties from the other side of the door when he had been down there cutting off the water supply earlier that evening made him more anxious than ever. He could have made the wall move, just to force a reaction. Or at least have looked in through the hatch.

He must go down. Just to check.

Always best to be on the safe side.

Not allowing himself time to change his mind, he got up abruptly and went out into the hallway. He opened the basement door and went downstairs.

It was still very quiet. Now that the water had been turned off, there wasn't even the sound of the low susurration from the pipes. He tramped extra hard across the floor, lifted the bolt on the hatch and opened it.

The man was asleep.

He was lying on his side on the bunk, with his legs at a strange angle. It looked as if he had decided to stand up, but hadn't had the strength and half of him had lain down again. One foot reached all the way to the floor. His arms were clamped to his chest, totally flat and crossed.

'Hey!' the silver-haired man called out.

It occurred to him immediately that he should disguise his voice. That was the plan. That was how he had written it down, in the manuscript, the precise plan that would ensure everything went smoothly, and that no one would ever find out who he was.

'Hello,' he croaked. 'Are you awake?'

Still no reaction in there.

'Bloody hell,' he said in a loud voice. 'Wake up!'

He couldn't open the door. It was far too risky. It could all be an act. Open the door and then, hey presto, the guy jumped up on his feet. Even if he was ever so debilitated after the days spent down here, desperation could bring undreamed-of strength. It was obvious that the man was desperate, and that was nothing to reproach him for.

Instead he hammered on the door with both hands. The cold metal made his fists smart. He stopped. Peered inside.

It looked as if the prisoner was dead.

But he couldn't be.

'Hello!' he bellowed, failing to remember that his voice should be someone else's. 'Are you sleeping? Get up! Now!'

Still silence.

His headache was on the verge of bursting his head now, and he felt he was about to lose his temper. He was so unused to this that he forgot his own intentions about taking the greatest caution and instead picked up a wooden ski from the stack behind the carpenter's bench, lifted the latch on the steel door and opened the cell where the prisoner was still lying as if he were dead.

The prisoner was dead.

He understood that immediately. The man had spewed up, it looked like; a disgusting, unrecognizable mass had seeped out of his mouth and nose. His eyes were only half closed, as he saw when he moved closer. His eyeballs were colourless and completely vacant, as if his life had departed through them in the end.

The man with the grey, thick hair began to cry. He walked over to the cadaver and laid it out on the bed. The legs were already affected by rigor mortis and the corpse would not lie flat.

He fetched a bucket of hot water and a few cloths. And then he carefully washed the naked body, changing the water and using a mild soap, baby soap, he cleaned the dead man before drying him thoroughly and dressing him in the clothes he had been wearing when he arrived.

Closed his eyes.

The man in the house with a cell in the basement cried and cried. When he was finished with the body, he sat with his back to the wall, the construction that was only meant to scare him, and sobbed with his face on his knees and his hands around his ankles. The cell with the movable wall was only intended to torment the man on the bunk, torment him the way he deserved and had to be tormented, before everything could be over and done with and they could call it quits.

He had not meant for anyone to die, and could no longer bear any of it.

THE CONFIDENCE

'**M**y gambling has cost me everything, Einar.'

The old down-and-out looked at her. He went on chewing a huge piece of ciabatta without saying a word. When he was finished, he drank the still-hot coffee in greedy gulps. Wiped around his mouth with the Mesta mitten.

'It had to happen some time,' he said, unruffled, as he picked up the pack of Smil chocolates.

'What?'

'Gambling doesn't pay off in the long run. If it did, there would be no bookies.'

'But ...'

'You've played for high stakes for years now, Mariska. High and often. You know, even though I was up shit creek at the time you were my lawyer, I wasn't stupid. Mental illness doesn't make you any more stupid than you already were. Quite the opposite, I'd say.'

Selma hid her face behind her cup. She felt an unfamiliar warmth on her cheeks, a slightly elevated pulse rate, as if she were seeking absolution for her sins from a priest and still didn't entirely know whether it would be granted. In the taxi on the way from Fornebu, the idea of confiding in Einar hadn't yet occurred to her. Neither had it while she sat in the vehicle feeling so miserable. Nor when she had bought some food for him, with chocolate and cola and everything she knew he'd like. Not even when the grumpy taxi driver had dropped her off at the Rema

1000 supermarket just beyond Sinsen subway station, had she envisaged the possibility that the sentence would ever be spoken: 'My gambling has cost me everything.'

She lowered her cup a little and went on: 'The house, Jesso and the children. I've put myself in a totally impossible situation, I've accepted an assignment I've no chance of solving, and so really have no chance of earning a sou for. What's more, I'm of no fixed abode at present.'

Einar Falsen smiled, cocked his head, swept a peremptory hand across the piles of stones and exclaimed: 'There's plenty of room here!'

With a low chuckle.

Einar himself had chosen to live as he did. In the first few years, after he was convicted and compelled to submit to obligatory psychiatric treatment, his friends and former colleagues had queued up to look after him. Three years in an institution had impaired his health. Nevertheless he was no longer regarded as presenting any danger to others and was released into a society he could only cope with by withdrawing from it. Countless attempts to move him indoors and give him dignity, as most people understood the term, had all ended in failure. Einar could not endure a normal existence. He began to roam about. One by one his friends gave up. For a number of years, however, he still had a few he could turn to when the winters became too harsh. And whenever he was physically ill, which happened only seldom. He could sleep on a settee for a night or three, before he set off once again, away from everyone who had once cared about him.

In the end he had only her.

She had never let go of her former client.

When she had approached him tonight, jumping from boulder to boulder beneath the continuous noise of the interchange, he had looked so peaceful. Tucked away under the concrete construction, with all his bags and baggage, he had sat in his sleeping bag reading the newspapers in the glow of a flickering, flaming torch. The yellow light had fallen upon his face, making it look even coarser. The wrinkles deeper, the eyes even darker. His beard wilder than ever. He had smiled at her, the usual reception, found a cushion and bin bag and welcomed her as the close friend he obviously believed her to be.

The secret had spilled out by itself.

'No thanks,' she said. 'I haven't yet fallen as low as that.'

'Tell me about it,' he had said, with a smile, as he dropped four pieces of chocolate into his mouth.

She told Einar about it. Told him all about it. Nearly all. Not about the footprints in the slush, that was still too recent, unexplained and frightening. But about everything else. About the beginning, the bookmaker in London, and about the end, the exposure when Jan Morell had come along to her office one Monday in November and reduced her life to rubble. She told him about everything in between, the years when hell-bent was the only course to take, and luck was usually on her side. In between it all she wove the story of her unsuccessful efforts to find out what had happened to Hege Morell. About Sølve Bang and hidden tubes of Trofodermin, about faint-hearted home helps and a Jan Morell who seemed increasingly knackered and surly with each day that passed without any progress. She confided in him about the embezzlement, about that galloping embezzlement, that unplanned, arrestable offence that had virtually snowballed all by itself, and that only an idiot would have thought she could get away with.

'You're not an idiot,' Einar said once Selma had unburdened herself. 'You're just stark, raving mad with gambling fever.'

'Don't tell anyone.'

He gave a wide grin. Selma noticed he had lost yet another

tooth since the last time they'd met, the right upper canine. The gap caused him to struggle slightly to pronounce the letter 's'.

More than an hour had passed since her arrival. Einar had lit his gas burner. Selma had brought a bag full of small gas canisters when she had still been on top of the world and could bring him more than coffee, food and chocolate. Six weeks ago, in fact. Now he had only two left, she noticed. One of these was now burning red and a beautiful shade of pale blue between them, and gave off a little heat when they curled their hands around the flame. The torch had burned down. The food was all eaten up. The traffic above their heads seemed more muted than she could ever recall.

'What do you want now?' he asked her.

'Want?'

'Yes. What would you like? What is it you'd like to happen?'

'I'd like to turn back time and quit helping myself to other people's cash.'

'You can't do that.'

'I'd like to win the bet with Jan Morell. I want to find some peace without having to resort to gambling on the sly. I'd like to find a place to live. I want people to stop contacting me. Today I had nineteen missed calls and twenty-nine text messages. Friends, former colleagues. Journalists. It's driving me crazy.'

'Mobile phones are the work of the devil,' he said, nodding. 'Incidentally, I'd start with the first one.'

'Win the bet?'

'Yes. If you manage to resolve the Chinese girl's case, a lot of the rest will fall into place. Then you'll have an incredible amount of dosh, get the rest of your debt wiped out, and will be able to make a fresh start. Get treatment. Drive out your demons. Concentrate on solving Hege Morell's case, that's what you should do.'

'I've tried, Einar. For a week, now. I'm just treading water. Or to be more correct, I'm going round in circles. This business of

Haakon's mysterious death, and especially the fact that he too had Clostebol in his body when he died, hasn't exactly made the case any simpler.'

'Forget Haakon. It's not those lesbian friends of yours who have engaged your services. It's that Croesus up on the hill there.'

'One case may well be connected to the other.'

Einar tugged off his mittens and curled his hands around the gas flame.

'That's of no consequence. If they're linked, then you'll solve both cases by finding out what happened to Hege. If they're not linked, then you're wasting a lot of energy and screwing up your own investigation by looking into Haakon's case.'

'But where should I begin?'

'With yourself.'

Selma looked up from the dancing, almost pulsating, gas flame. Einar leaned forward and placed a heavy hand on her lower arm.

'With yourself,' he repeated. 'You have to start by focusing on what you're good at. Give it a try, now.'

'I'm systematic.'

Silence reigned. A tram, empty at this time of night, rattled past along Muselunden to its berth for the night. A magpie had perched on a stone only two or three metres away from them, its coal-black eyes glinting with the reflections from the gas flame.

'And pretty smart,' Selma went on.

'You've got a phenomenal memory,' Einar added helpfully.

She nodded.

'Also, you're a good judge of human nature, even though you actually like to keep everyone at arm's length. At the very least.'

'I'm a good lawyer,' she said quickly, aware for the first time that the conversation was causing her a touch of revulsion.

'Yes. But that won't help you much in this case.'

Yet again there was silence between them. Only now did Selma notice that she was starting to feel cold: Einar had given her a brand new fleece blanket he claimed to have bought at the Nille store earlier that day.

At least it didn't smell too bad.

'Make use of what you're good at,' he said, almost impatient now. 'Use your systematics. Those analytical abilities of yours. Your memory. The fact that you're no stranger to human traits. Your contacts, for Christ's sake! You know everyone.'

'Yes, of course, but how?'

Einar gave a loud, almost theatrical, sigh. Scrambled up and out of his sleeping bag. The customary odour of dirty male overwhelmed Selma, and she had to struggle not to show it. He was wearing nothing but long underpants. He planted his feet inside a pair of safety boots and stood in front of her, legs straddled.

'What you've actually told me,' he said, raising his voice, as if standing in an auditorium, 'is that you can't find a motive for sabotaging Hege. To be even more precise, for each motive you're able to come up with, you can find counter-arguments that undermine its probability.'

Selma tucked the blanket more snugly around her.

'The most obvious one,' Einar continued, 'which we discussed as recently as the evening you accepted the assignment, is that someone wants to hound the Chinese girl off the ski trail.'

'Hege,' Selma murmured.

'Hege, right,' Einar replied, nodding his head. 'The Winter Olympics are round the corner, she's the favourite in most of the distances, and lots of people could benefit from Hege not lining up at the start of any of them. On the other hand ...'

He lost his balance for a second, and had to use a nearby boulder to steady himself. The startled magpie took flight.

'On the other hand, Norway doesn't only have the best female cross-country skier. We have four or five of the best. At least, we have plenty who could win. For a foreigner to get rid of Hege, it would have a limited effect. To put it mildly. There's a queue of potential Norwegian gold medal winners behind her. The foreigners would have to drug the whole gang of Norwegians to improve their own chances significantly. For a Norwegian skier ...'

He drew his unbelievably filthy fingers through his beard.

'Each and every one of them has a chance, in fact. They could all beat Hege Morell on a good day. At least most of them could. To run the risk of sabotaging a teammate would be crazy when you think of how uncertain the gain would be.'

Selma glanced up at him with increasing astonishment. He hadn't yet mentioned the mobile phone, tramlines, the CIA or a headache. Standing there with the crotch of his underpants almost reaching down to his knees, his ear flaps dangling and his beard sticking out in all directions, he looked exactly like what he was.

A raving lunatic.

Now and again she mentioned some of her cases to him. Anonymized, of course, and in a fairly superficial way. More or less to have something to talk about, especially when he was having one of his bad days and she wasn't feeling particularly chatty herself. He always showed interest, but was usually somewhat distant and measured. Except for when she told him about criminal cases. In the last five or six years she had practically wound up that side of her portfolio. The occasional old client might receive Selma's assistance, however, and these cases set Einar on fire. He became focused, full of questions and suggestions, and completely forgot that he was being bugged wherever he went or waited.

She had never seen him like this before.

'The conclusion is?'

He stared at her with one finger raised and his ear half-turned towards her.

'That no one is out to get her as a skier,' Selma said.

'Spot on! Then this is the question we have to ask: is anyone out to get her as a person?'

Selma opened her mouth but Einar beat her to it by answering himself.

'Hege Chin Morell has no enemies. No angry, rejected lovers. She is popular with her teammates, and not only because she's a good training pal. I've cut a few things from the newspapers this past week ...'

He crouched down towards a plastic bag and pulled up a substantial bundle of newspaper articles. It looked more like they had been torn out rather than actually cut.

'They like her, Mariska. They call her a gem. Honest and straightforward.'

'Those very words are not the sort of thing young people ...'

'Whatever! You know what I mean.'

He waved the papers in triumph.

'Hege Chin Morell is well liked. She is honest, fair, and considerate. A good winner. On the rare occasions she loses, she handles that well too. This past week, every single sports editor in the country has tried to dig up dirt on Hege. They haven't found a single thing. Quite simply because she doesn't have any foes. Not a single one.'

'So nobody was out to get Hege,' Selma said slowly, with the suggestion of a question mark at the end.

'No. And you've really known that for a couple of days. The problem is that you're not used to being so uncertain. You don't trust your own judgment.'

'But someone may be out to stop the Norwegian Cross-Country Skiing Federation. Or to harm them. Tarnish them.'

'Yes, that's one theory. And in that scenario, it's likely that Hege's case is linked to Haakon's. But then we have to ask ourselves ...'

All of a sudden he shivered with cold. He pulled off the boots and crammed himself back down inside the sleeping bag. Stiff and cautious, he sat down in his usual cavity, with his back against a stone shaped like the back of an armchair.

'It's fucking cold,' he said, hoisting the sleeping bag all the way up to his armpits.

The gas had burned out. He changed it for the last one he had and took a couple of minutes to light it, turning the burner up full.

'We have to ask ourselves: who on earth could have done such a thing? It would demand quite a lot, when you think about it. Elite athletes are careful. They don't just take anything from anybody. And to be completely honest, Mariska, we're really not suggesting that Swedes, Finns or Germans could come up with anything so radical.'

'The Russians, though,' Selma suggested.

Einar nodded.

'The Russians are just as crazy as me. They have people who could think of far worse things than this and get away with it. They have long experience of poisoning, and doping is, from a purely technical point of view, much the same. The KGB was awful. Its successor, the FSB, is getting even worse, if that's possible. They are entirely capable of undertaking sabotage such as this. Also, the Russians have far closer links between state and sport than the other countries I mentioned. But then again ...'

He tried yet again to obtain some heat from the burner. His hands came so close to the flame that he would have burned himself it hadn't been for layer upon layer of dead skin, grease and dirt.

'Do we really believe that?' he blurted out. 'In that case, they'd get rid of a couple of competitors, that's true, but it's still highly uncertain that we'll be excluded from the Winter Olympics.

Russia itself is being permitted to take part with clean skiers, despite there being evidence of systematic, state-sanctioned cheating prior to the Sochi games. A possible sabotage of two Norwegian skiers would have far too limited an effect for me to believe in anything of the sort.'

Selma's teeth were chattering. She crept under the baby-blue blanket and pulled the collar of her coat up over her ears.

'Anyway,' Einar added, with a grin, 'if the Russians are behind it, you'll never be able to prove anything at all. Not even you, Mariska.'

'I have to go,' Selma said, getting to her feet. 'It must be minus ten degrees.'

Einar held a finger up in the air. Checking.

'Eight,' he said brusquely. 'Sit down again, please.'

Selma remained standing. She tried to hop from one foot to the other, but it was difficult on the uneven ground.

'You have to be yourself,' Einar said softly. 'Even though your world has been turned upside down and you've lost everything you had, you haven't lost yourself. What did we talk about when you paid me a visit the other night?'

'Lots of things.'

'Qui bono, Mariska! Read *The Investigator's ABC*!'

He pulled his own copy out of the blue IKEA bag and waved it as he continued: 'We talked about searching for whoever gains from a crime. And sometimes more importantly: who loses most from it. Tomorrow it'll be a week since you took on this assignment, Mariska. You've spoken to the people involved many times now.'

He returned the book to the bag, pulled on his mittens and leaned back against the sloping stone.

'Who do you think would be punished most severely by Hege Chin Morell being caught doping?' he asked, looking her straight in the eye.

He maintained eye contact, something he could never normally do.

'Jan Morell,' Selma said, nodding.

'Who has, in contrast to Hege, of necessity acquired many adversaries, maybe even enemies, while building up a million-kroner company?'

'Jan Morell.'

'And who ...'

Only now did he look down. In the numerous bags and boxes around him, he knew exactly where to look. He found the same edition of the *A-magasinet* supplement that he had shown her earlier.

'Who actually says nothing whatsoever about himself when he is interviewed? In contrast to his daughter that everyone thinks they know all there is to know about?'

An answer wasn't necessary. Selma pulled off the blanket, which had become so full of static electricity that it had attached itself to her coat. Folding it up neatly, she placed it on a rock.

'Forget Hege,' Einar told her. 'Neither she nor the Federation is affected by sabotaging Hege Morell. It's the daddy who is the real victim, Mariska. The daughter is young and has loads of possibilities. The father is living out his dreams about skiing through his only child. He suffers most from what has happened. Her dad.'

'Sleep well,' Selma said. 'And thanks. Thank you very much.'

She leaned forward and let him whisper the accustomed words of farewell. In a reassuring voice, she answered as she had done for so many, many years: 'You did the right thing, Einar. The bastard deserved to die.'

THE MANUSCRIPT

601 INTERIOR, BASEMENT, OSLO, NIGHT-TIME

The MAN is busy building a wall. The basement is spacious and used for storing sports equipment and tools, some wood, spare tyres and a number of cardboard boxes. A gun cabinet is fixed to the outside wall. Ammunition is kept in a smaller cabinet beside a carpenter's bench, on which sits an old, worn teddy bear. One-eyed and with holes in one foot through which the stuffing is protruding. The MAN has mortar in a big plastic tub. He puts more breezeblocks on the wall, which is nearly complete.

MAN: What do you think, Teddy? Will it work?

The MAN is obviously used to DIY. He handles the trowel and blocks with speed and precision. Portrait pictures of three middle-aged men are hanging above the carpenter's bench. The MAN pushes the last block on the wall into place. He rubs his hands and goes over to the bear that sits underneath the pictures. Stops and looks at the photos for a while. Suddenly he points at the last of them.

MAN: You'll get to meet him, Teddy. He's coming to visit us soon.

The MAN moves his finger to the middle picture.

MAN: This one here will be an easier project.

The MAN shifts his finger to the last picture. Looks at the teddy bear and smiles.

MAN: This guy here, on the other hand, will be tricky. But we'll manage it all the same, you and I. Now everything will be paid back. We'll regain some balance, Teddy.

The MAN takes the teddy bear with him and heads for the stairs.

THURSDAY 14 DECEMBER 2017

THE ABOUT-TURN

Six hours of continuous, dreamless sleep.

Selma had been confused when the alarm on her mobile phone chimed at half past six. Darius had slept in her old, wonky bed without her noticing. Yet again she decided she would have to buy a new bed, but then realized once more that she wouldn't have time. Precisely an hour later, she was seated at a table near the back of the Åpent Bakeri café, with the whole place behind her and a latte in front of her.

Lars Winther came five minutes late.

His hair still wet, newly shaved and in a pale-blue button-down sweater with a white T-shirt visible underneath, he sat down on the other side of the table.

'Don't you want anything?' Selma asked.

'Came straight from breakfast. Anyway, the queue at the checkout was too long. What's this about?'

'You certainly get right to the point.'

'Yes, sorry. I've got a crazy amount to do.'

He glanced obliquely at an enormous diver's watch on his left wrist.

'Fine,' said Selma. 'What's really the situation at the Cross-Country Skiing Federation, then?'

Lars Winther put both hands on the table and pushed himself backwards a little. Smiled broadly. Started to laugh.

'Well, are you serious?'

'Yes.'

'How are things there? Have you read any of our coverage in the past few years?'

'Yes, that's why I'm asking. I know what you've written. I also know that at any time there's also a whole lot you don't write. For a variety of reasons.'

The man suddenly grew serious. Inquisitive, she saw. His eyes narrowed slightly, and he leaned forward again with a confidential air. Even lowered his voice.

'Of course there's a great deal we don't write,' he said. 'If only the public knew how much we have on prominent personages, government departments, organizations and institutions that we let drop. Maybe we can't really crack the story. We know, but we don't have sufficient documentation. Sometimes what we know is notorious enough, but the harmful effects of what we'd write aren't worth it, bearing in mind the relative insignificance of making it public.'

He sniffed and ran a long, slender forefinger under his nose.

'You also have all those stories that are more than spicy enough, but that despite it all come under the umbrella of private life and privacy restrictions. At other times we know, but have an editor who's scared to death that we're barking up the wrong tree. For example ...'

He drew his chair closer to the table. The noise of chair legs scraping across the tiled floor assaulted her ears.

'Arnulf Selhus, the Federation's Director of Finance.'

Selma nodded.

'Years ago, when he began at the Federation, I was fairly recently appointed to *DG*. I picked up a whisper about some shady business where he had been employed previously. In MCV, by the way. Jan Morell's company.'

Selma sat absolutely still.

'It's a long time ago, so I don't remember the details. At any rate, at the time I went to my editor and suggested I follow up the story. After all, Selhus was newly appointed as the Director of Finance in a sports organization. I thought it'd be interesting if ...'

'What happened?'

'He turned me down. All I had was one source and when I wasn't able to come up with anything more specific in the course of a couple of days, I was told to drop it. There was never any police involvement. There was never any story. What's more, and I think this was decisive for my editor at the time, when the opportunity arose, Jan Morell spoke well of the guy in public. Old Antonsen was of the opinion that there couldn't be anything behind it. The point is ...'

He smiled, almost shyly.

'The source was fucking solid. He was Selhus's immediate subordinate.'

'And you knew him well?'

He didn't blush, but went on to answer: 'To put it this way, I wouldn't have let the story lie today.'

A young woman holding a child on her hip and another by the hand tried to sit down at the table next to theirs. It wasn't easy – the three-year-old refused to take off his jacket, and the baby was screaming like mad. Lars Winther pushed their table half a metre to the left. They both moved their chairs accordingly. None of this helped.

'Have you ...'

Selma hesitated. She moistened her lips and chose to continue: 'Have you ever heard anything about a ... close shave in the run up to the season in Italy?'

'Eh?'

'An ointment? That the national team doctor had bought?'

'What are you talking about?'

Either he was the best actor in the world, or he certainly hadn't got wind of Stian Bach's gaffe.

'Jan Morell,' Selma said quickly.

'Yes,' he answered, sounding bewildered.

'What do you know about him?'

'About Jan Morell?'

'Yes.'

Last night Selma had been convinced.

That Einar Falsen was right, that she had finally discovered an angle of attack on what had really happened in Hege's doping case. The old down-and-out had seemed so convincing. So logical. It was Jan who was the intended target, not Hege. Selma had gone home to Løkka feeling relieved, in a state of near-euphoria.

Almost like after a successful night at the Poker Turk's place.

Her enthusiasm had evaporated in her sleep. This morning it had all seemed far-fetched. Distant, as if the conversation beneath the Sinsen interchange around a gas flame had been nothing but a sweet dream about succeeding again at last.

All the same.

She had to ask.

'I don't know very much about the man,' Lars said, frowning. 'If he's the one you want to know more about, you'd really be better asking someone who covers the financial news, such as *Dagens Næringsliv.*'

'He's quite prominent in the NCCSF as well.'

'In my opinion, not nearly enough! A man of his background and experience would be worth his weight in gold for the Federation. Ages ago, before cross-country had the arrogance to break away from the Norwegian Ski Federation and wanted to manage things for themselves, he was actually on the board. He was continually mentioned as a possible candidate for the post of president, but didn't want it. At least that's what all the rumours say. After Hege began to do well at the various ages and stages and looked as if she would have a career in skiing ahead of her, he more or less withdrew completely.'

'More or less?'

'Well, he's still involved, in a sense. His company is a pretty major sponsor, for instance. He's still the majority shareholder in MCV, isn't he?'

Selma nodded.

'Besides, he's someone who roams around in that milieu,' Lars went on. 'He's always involved when something big happens. Always has the official championship clothing. They think that's terrific, those boys. They stamp their authority in that way. Show that they belong. That they're on the inside.'

He grinned.

'You'll have to ask other folk about Jan Morell. But when it comes to the situation in the Crystal Palace ...'

He tossed his head. In the wrong direction, Selma noticed.

'... I could keep going all day long. Apart from creating fucking brilliant cross-country skiers, which isn't to be sneezed at, I have to admit, things are in a pretty sorry state up there.'

He took a deep breath and raised his hands.

'We'll take it point by point,' he said. 'A combination of formal and informal power.'

He held one finger up in the air.

'Fear-based leadership culture.'

Two fingers.

'Devoid of competence within the organization and its finance, including a total lack of understanding of the need for transparency and openness.'

Three fingers up in the air. This anecdote was obviously one he had told many times, and he spoke as if he was reading from a script.

'There you have the Federation's three main problems. Bloody hell, there you have Norwegian sport's three main problems! With a few honourable exceptions.'

'What's the worst?'

'Worst?'

'Yes, if you were in a position to change anything, what would be the most important aspect to tackle?'

'The informal structure of authority,' he answered after a brief pause for thought. 'Informal power is really dangerous. Nepotism, the old pals act. It exists everywhere, of course, probably in every workplace, and it's always negative. But in some locations it's more dangerous than others.'

'Oh? And then you mean ...'

'Power is a gift that gives you confidence. Through appointments or votes. If this is not to be misused, it has to be visible. There have to be mechanisms in the organization that make it possible to examine it. Look at it, control it and take it back if it is misused.'

Selma nodded. He now had the bit between his teeth.

'When configurations arise that are fuzzy or invisible, we lose that opportunity. Power is hidden. Power shouldn't be.'

He looked at her coffee cup.

'Don't you want that?'

Selma smiled and pushed the untouched cup towards him.

'Can you name some examples?' she asked.

Immediately the man grew slightly wary. The cup, halfway to his mouth, stopped for a second before it was put down again.

'What are you really after?' he asked.

'Since you don't know much about Jan Morell,' Selma said, 'what about Sølve Bang?'

Lars didn't blink, but Selma noticed a tiny movement on one eyelid, the involuntary and for most people imperceptible start of a blink. A quarter of a century's experience of lies and deception, both her own and that of others, gave her the confirmation she was looking for.

'What about him?' he said casually.

'Sølve Bang sounds like someone of that calibre. Someone who's not voted into positions that correspond to the situation they actually occupy. And the power they wield.'

Lars Winther folded his arms.

'I have a feeling I'm being interrogated,' he said. 'And I don't like it.'

'You've made good use of me in the last few days,' she said, with a smile. 'And to date you haven't told me much more than what I've been able to read in your newspaper columns.'

He pulled back his shirtsleeve to uncover his watch.

'I have to go.'

'Sølve Bang was your source,' Selma said. 'He was the one who gave you the result of Haakon's drugs test.'

Once again that minuscule twitch of his left eye, this time accompanied by an attempt to hide it as he lifted the cup and drank the coffee.

'Of course you can neither confirm nor deny what I'm saying,' Selma continued. 'I don't want you to, either. What I'm after is your opinion on why he is allowed to carry on like that.'

'Like what?'

'Do whatever he likes. Get hold of that kind of information. I learned about the drugs test on Monday, for very special reasons. Extremely few had access to it. Sølve Bang doesn't hold any position that would allow him to know, but he knew all the same. Why?'

'I really have to go.'

'OK.'

He stood up and began to shrug on his quilted jacket. Selma

looked up at him without saying anything. Only once he had slung the strap of his shoulder bag over his head did she add: 'Shame that you're going to miss out on everything I could have helped you with in the days ahead. Your choice.'

The journalist sighed. Remained on his feet.

'I have to know what your role is in all this,' he said seriously. 'You must be honest with me about what position you hold. I don't believe in this midlife crisis of yours. If you don't show me your cards, you can just forget about contacting me again.'

Selma took four seconds to weigh up the situation. She added five more seconds for the sake of appearances.

'OK,' she said. 'Sit down.'

He obeyed without removing his jacket.

'Off the record,' she told him. 'Everything I'm about to say.'

'OK.'

'Say yes.'

'Yes. Off the record.'

'Jan Morell wants Hege to go to the Winter Olympics,' she said succinctly. 'In order for that to happen, it has to be proved that she has been a victim of sabotage. In a sense, I've been hired to do exactly that.'

If he had only just betrayed his feelings earlier, and that with a flicker very few people would have noticed, he made no attempt to conceal his astonishment now.

'Sabotage? Do you seriously think that Hege Morell's been sabotaged?'

'I didn't say that. I said that Jan Morell believes so.'

'And you ...'

Selma gave a faint smile.

'Me? I've only just begun to come close to an understanding that there is a possibility of something of the sort.'

'You made four qualifications in that one sentence.'

'Yes. I did it deliberately.'

'But you believe there is a possibility?'

'Yes. And now that we've established the fact that I'm not tres-passing on your territory, we can both make use of each other. You scratch my back and I'll scratch yours.'

'Fine. What have you got?'

'Right now? Nothing. But I soon will have.'

They looked at each other. A little battle of the eyeballs that ended with him calmly lifting off his shoulder bag and unzipping his jacket. Looking around the half-full café, Tintin swept back his quiff.

'Sølve Bang is a collector,' he said softly. 'We've never really figured him out. Actually he's a bit ridiculous. Never before has anyone lived so well for so long on the basis of one sensational World Cup win. He takes himself too seriously. He's smug. But also so ...'

He rested on his elbows and leaned closer.

'... clever! Bloody hell, he's written a couple of articles in response to my strongly critical comments, and they are ...'

Again he took a deep breath and closed his mouth with a grim expression.

'... good,' he rounded off. 'He writes well, that goes without saying, but he's also knowledgeable and skilled in argument. Organized.'

'You called him a "collector".'

'Yes. This isn't something I know, Selma. But I think he collects information. Negative information. About people. He has some-thing on nearly everybody. Lots of people at least. For the past five years he has been working on this book project of his. The defini-tive history of skiing in the world's foremost winter sports nation.'

Suddenly he took on a thoughtful, almost startled expression. Glanced diagonally up at the ceiling.

'That book should surely soon be finished, shouldn't it?'

A little shrug.

'Anyway. In connection with his research he has gained access to most things and most people. Talked to individuals. Rooted around in the archives. Accounts. Minutes. And you know ...'

Now his smile was broader.

'People are keen on being on good terms with that book. As a journalist I know a lot of what people are willing to gossip about if they think it will be to their benefit. If they are scared.'

'So you think that he has ... pressured his way to informal power? Blackmailed his way to it, so to speak?'

'Well, maybe ... that's probably not how it works. It's more that he knows a lot, and can drop hints in a pretty subtle fashion. I tried to find out more about the guy's weird position last summer, but people are somehow ... yes, afraid of him. Anxious, at least. Difficult story to smoke out. And then we're into another of those points of mine.'

He seemed more enthusiastic now, and he pushed the almost-full coffee cup forward as he leaned even further across the table.

'People are scared up there. Management by fear.'

'How do you know that?'

'I'm a journalist. I talk to people. Let me illustrate ...'

He licked his lips before he began.

'Most people in the system are worried, fundamentally. Every time something happens, at least. They're terrified of the press. Of saying anything wrong, of saying anything at all, at least in public. Each time we fuck their arses, they get even more worried. And anxiety brings power. One person's anxiety gives other people power.'

He paused for breath and shook his head.

'Take Bottolf Odda,' he continued. 'In many ways he's a great guy. Jovial and friendly. The results during his period as cross-country president are good. Excellent, even. That's impossible to deny. On the other hand the Federation's finances are shaky, to put it mildly. And inaccessible. We have had to argue over every single fucking little receipt we've asked to see. In the first place, they spend more money than they've got, which would be a mortal sin in any other organization. What's more, it's downright difficult to see what they've spent their money on.'

'Wine, women and song.'

'Well, wine at least. Expensive wine. Which all the others and I wouldn't give a toss about, if this was an ordinary, private company. But they're not. They are custodians of a national cultural heritage. A cultural treasure, many people believe. Skiing is the strongest identity marker we possess. The folks up there lead an organization that depends primarily on volunteers. On mothers and fathers and aunts and grandparents who train the little ones, arrange races, set up trail nets all winter, cook waffles and hold jumble sales and ...'

He raised his hand.

'You know all about Norwegian sports, Selma. Hard, unpaid work. For fucking plenty of people.'

'Yes. Expensive wine and business class for the bosses might be loose change in terms of the bigger picture. But, as they say, it's all about the optics.'

'Exactly. And when this comes on top of now having two really nasty cases of drug-taking, in addition to that asthma medication affair, wouldn't you normally think that Bottolf Odda's coat is hanging on a shaky peg?'

He chose to answer himself: 'You would guess so. But believe you me, when the cross-country skiing conference is held at the beginning of June, Bottolf Odda will go to the speaker's rostrum and say a few well-chosen, reassuring words about everything painful and difficult. Then he'll spend a lot of time talking about the huge successes on the ski trails, after which he'll be voted in again by acclamation without any opposing candidate. Believe you me.'

'Unless we're disqualified from the Winter Olympics.'

Lars nodded.

'Unless we're disqualified from the Winter Olympics,' he agreed. 'But we won't be, no matter what happens in the cases of Hege and Haakon.'

'No?'

'No.'

'Why not?'

'Because the IOC is a spineless organization, rotten through and through,' he said, taking a slug of coffee. 'They won't exclude the cash cow. That would spoil the whole cattle show.'

Selma felt she needed the toilet, but didn't dare interrupt him. One thought had struck her. She tried to push it aside until she had time to examine it more closely.

'Do you mean that Bottolf Odda scares people?'

'Not the boo-scaring kind.'

Lars raised his hands and scrabbled in the air like a wild animal.

'More sort of ... network-scaring. The old boys club, as some say, and get smirked at. But they're right. It's all about the old boys, whether it's women or men involved. You know ... it's social bonds. They travel together. They come to decisions together. You can call it whatever you like, but it's all about decisions being made in back rooms. Outside the democratically chosen agencies. Beyond the rules and procedures. Someone has decided that Bottolf Odda should continue as president. And so he does. Unopposed. It's ...'

He drew a big ring around the coffee cup.

'As I said, it's about making sure you're on the inside. Those who are in the inner circle have to make sure they don't rock the boat. Be nice. Do as they're asked. Or else ...'

He pulled the cup to the very edge of the table.

'Loyalty, that's what they call it in fancy speeches. Cowardice would sometimes be a more suitable word. But what's the basis for this sabotage theory?'

'Nothing, in the meantime.'

'But ...'

'You have my word that you'll be the first to know. If there's anything to know.'

Her earlier thought refused to budge.

'Instead, give me a bit of help here,' she said. 'On Saturday, when that colleague of yours dropped a hint that there might be good reason to check whether Haakon had been drugged when he died ...'

Lars Winther covered his eyes with his hand.

'Yes, well, I'd rather not say anything more about that, thanks. At the risk of seeming disloyal to a colleague.'

'That was when Sølve Bang spoke up.'

'Typical of him. Without any real authority, he rushes to the defence of ...'

'Exactly. To the defence of the Federation. Saved the situation to some extent as well. But what has persuaded him to change his mind?'

'What?'

'He's obviously changed his mind. Or maybe I should call it his strategy.'

'Now I don't really understand what you mean.'

'On Saturday he reacted almost as a reflex, as he usually does. Springing to the defence of the Federation. Since then he has first of all leaked the information about Haakon's test to you.'

Lars stared blankly at her. This time his eyelid didn't flicker.

But he didn't protest either.

'Which was information the Federation would obviously

benefit from taking charge of making public themselves,' Selma went on. 'And secondly ...'

She took a deep breath and swallowed, clearly searching for the right words.

'Secondly, he has taken yet another opportunity to maximize this crisis.'

'How?'

'I can't tell you. Not yet. But he has done a 180-degree-turn since Saturday. From wanting to protect the Federation and the skiers to wanting to damage them all. What would be the reason for that?'

'Tell me what he's done! Then it would be easier for me to ...'

'No. But what could have happened?'

'No idea. What do you think?'

Selma was lost in thought. Einar had said something last night. When she had immodestly claimed to be a good lawyer, he had stated that this would not help her to make progress in the case of Hege Morell's drugs test.

He could well be right. But right now, with regard to Sølve Bang's curious turnabout, he was definitely wrong.

'When was that book to be completed?' she asked when Lars began to show some impatience.

'Sølve Bang's book project?'

'Yes.'

'I don't know for sure, but it has at least been postponed several times.'

'Do you know how much he gets for the job?'

'No. The contract is top secret. Statoil, of course, do whatever they like with such things, after all it's small change for them. For that matter, though, they're known to be generous when they first decide on something.'

'I have to go,' Selma said, standing up.

'Eh ...'

The journalist, taken aback, got to his feet. Selma grabbed her coat and gave a quick wave. She was already on her way to the door and had entirely forgotten that she needed the toilet.

Einar's advice was not as useless as she had despondently decided over muesli and yogurt on the cheese puff settee an hour and a half ago.

Selma Falck should start to rely on her own talents again.

It was high time.

DISCOVERING THE CORPSE

O f course he had tried to avoid roads with speed cameras. It had taken time. With the help of a program he had down-loaded to his iPad for twenty pounds, he had devised a circuitous route from Oslo to Larvik. Some of the cameras were unavoidable. He couldn't leave Oslo without paying a toll fee, so that would have to be left to chance. The speed cameras on Norwegian roads were not operational for more than a few hours each week, so he could trust to luck with them. He had driven long intricate detours involving trunk roads and secondary roads and the occasional farm track. A couple of times he'd been forced to turn around. The route he had chosen was far from ideal but he couldn't do anything but hope for the best. In order to cover his tracks even further, he had used his mother's old car. It had been stored in the garage with the number plates removed since her death two years ago, but fortunately he had kept the engine maintained. Practical work was his forte. DIY and tinkering with things. The registra-tion plates from his own Honda were easy to remove and attach to the ancient Toyota. With the help of black duct tape he had transformed a three to an acceptable approximation of an eight.

The journey took three hours with a corpse in the boot.

The body was heavy, and even though he was strong, he couldn't carry the dead man for any length of time. He wasn't keen to drive on forestry tracks either. Vehicular traffic was more easily noticed by people who were out walking.

He had come down to Lågendalen. When he drove under the E18 motorway at Bommestad, he began to pay more attention. He turned right at the second roundabout. Passed something that resembled a miniature version of the Alnabru bridge, before he reached yet another roundabout beside a retail centre and continued west.

It was years since he had been here. At his old job, someone had been talking about cycling the Farrisrunden trail. No one had asked him directly to come along, but the chat about the ride was so enthusiastic that he realized he was keen to join in. When he arrived, none of his colleagues was there. A spur-of-the-moment sail in the boss's new yacht had intervened.

He had cycled the sixty-seven kilometres, eaten dinner at a roadside café and gone home again with his bike on the roof of the car.

The forest north-east of Larvik was called Vestmarka. It was criss-crossed by paths and tracks, but he did not venture very far. Immediately after driving under the motorway again, this time travelling in the opposite direction, he drew to a halt. The noise of heavy traffic on the E18 seemed soothing. He had reversed the car a few metres on to a tractor trail just wide enough to accommodate the Toyota. It was raining heavily. The ground was soft and soaking wet, between pine trunks and the odd slender beech tree in flight from the famous forest further to the south-west. In the course of the ten minutes it took him to heave the body of the world famous photographer, Morten Karlshaug, down into a natural gully and cover him over, he didn't see a single soul. He drove out of the tractor track once again. The dead body could not now be seen from the road, concealed as it was by a thin layer of leaves and twigs and a couple of boulders he had managed to roll towards it. He broke a heavy branch off a spruce tree and used it to sweep all traces left by him and the car tyres as well as he could. Then he settled behind the wheel again and drove home.

The body had been dumped in an unattractive spot, far too close to the roar of a four-lane highway, nothing but a transportation route. A place to race through in search of the real hiking terrain further inside the forest. The cadaver was hidden, and most dogs would be kept on a leash so close to a built-up area.

There was nothing more he could do.

He drove to Oslo the same way he had come. Stopped in Kongsberg and cleaned the Toyota in a self-service car wash before he drove on, by now both hungry and thirsty.

He reckoned it might take days for the body to be found. If the snow came soon, it might even take all winter.

What he did not know was that the dead photographer was discovered exactly twenty-four minutes after he had left him. By a woman of seventy-nine, in rough seaman's boots and ancient oilskins, out in the horrible weather in search of some spruce sprigs to decorate her house.

She couldn't be bothered going very far. Just a short distance into Vestmarka, eight hundred metres from her own little house.

TRAIN OF THOUGHT

The traffic noise made it impossible to concentrate in the living room.

So Selma had sat in bed for three hours. The bedroom window looked on to the back yard. A former tenant had covered the glass in Christmas wrapping paper that Selma, for want of curtains and in the hope of leaving soon, had resisted the temptation to tear down. Only this morning had she discovered that the lopsidedness of the bed was due to the legs on the left-hand side being sawn short. What such an operation might be good for was beyond Selma's comprehension. With the help of two old volumes of legal statutes, she had succeeded in making the rickety bed somewhat level.

Darius had started to become more approachable.

His eyes were still blue and hostile, but he sometimes approached her to be petted. His tail usually stood erect with a tiny flourish at the top, something she had come to appreciate was a friendlier sign than when the tail was wagging. Since last Thursday he had caught another four mice, but no longer offered to share the deadly game with her. The cat now killed the rodents properly and left them at the front door, ready for disposal in the rubbish bin at the entry.

To her surprise, she heard him purring, curled up at her feet as she sat with her laptop on her knee in bright daylight tinged red by the Christmas paper on the windowpane.

If it had been easy to build a comprehensive picture of Hege Chin Morell by searching on the internet, her father was far more difficult to pin down. Admittedly, his name generated 153,000 hits on Google, but most were of no interest. The articles dealt primarily with his company, Morell Clear View. Annual accounts and rights issues. Contracts and expansion. New branches and the opening of offices in Asia.

Plus the occasional announcement about Jan's numerous directorships.

He was also frequently quoted after important ski races. Unfortunately he adhered to the usual parental clichés. Naturally, he was proud and happy. He assured everyone that Hege deserved her success. It was his pleasure to turn up, and his contribution was extremely modest in comparison with hers.

All spoken with a broad smile.

Selma had only found three in-depth interviews with him. The most recent was the paper version that Einar had shown her, a double interview in the *Aftenposten* weekend supplement. It dealt mainly with Hege. Almost only about her, as even the little that Jan Morell actually contributed was also related to his daughter. He talked about the good fortune of her adoption. About their shared passion for skiing. Father and daughter described her career, winning and losing and everyday life in the timber villa in Vettakollen. They mentioned Katinka's tragic death in passing. That also focused on Hege, who rather reticently spoke of her grief at losing her mother at the age of only eleven.

What Jan had felt when his wife died could at best be read between the lines. To be honest, there was little to find there either.

The oldest photograph was from *DG* and was ten years old, while *Dagens Næringsliv* had caught him making a speech when MCV had bought one of Sweden's largest consultancy companies and suddenly doubled in size as a consequence. This had happened in 2012. Selma read both of these articles twice over without becoming any the wiser.

In truth, Jan Morell was a very discreet man.

Selma still had no idea about his upbringing apart from that it had taken place in Kjelsås in Oslo. And that he had also been fond of winter sports as a child. This snippet of information had come from an article that wasn't directly about him, but about the opening of a new exhibition at the Ski Museum. King Harald had been present, and was pictured laughing in front of a showcase full of fibreglass skis from the late seventies. Jan Morell stood beside him, pointing at a pair of plain black skis with rattrap bindings.

These were the very Madshus-brand skis that financier Jan Morell had longed for more than anything else as a teenager. As the son of a single mother, he had to make do with secondhand wooden skis until he was an adult, as he told the ebullient king.

On second thoughts, it occurred to her that the text accompanying the photo did tell her something after all. What the word 'adult' conveyed was not terribly specific, but since Jan was born in 1962, he would not have turned eighteen until 1980.

Selma had been fourteen that year and had owned her first pair of fibreglass skis for a long time by then. Black and pale-blue skis from Skilom, she well remembered, and those were her second pair, now she came to think of it. At that age she had not known anyone who still used wooden skis.

At last she could write down something in the Moleskine notebook she had found in one of the boxes Darius had refrained from peeing in.

Poor?

She chewed the pencil.

You couldn't exactly be called poor just because you didn't have fibreglass skis. At that time, everyone had less money to spend than nowadays.

Without hesitation, she circled the word and scored through the question mark.

Single mother. Wooden skis, at least until 1980, despite his obvious interest in skiing. Jan Morell had grown up in more impoverished circumstances than most of his contemporaries.

Poor. She stared at the word.

It really told her very little. Her fingers automatically logged in to Facebook. She hadn't updated her page for the past four weeks. Her feed was, as usual, a blessed mixture of sports videos, offers of sports clothing and equipment, and stories about people she did not know at all and cared even less about.

It was about time she deleted the whole account. She wanted to eliminate people from her life now, not invite them in.

A post from Fredrik Solheim of *Dagsnytt Atten*, the six p.m. TV news bulletin, appeared. The scandals in the NCCSF were headline news on that evening's broadcast. The planned participants were not all yet confirmed, but Sølve Bang, the well-known author and skier, would certainly be one.

At last Bang speaks his mind about the current situation in the organization he knows better than most!

'Shit,' Selma said out loud.

Darius peered up lazily. The phone rang.

She snatched it up and glanced at the display before putting the phone to her ear.

'Hi, Jan.'

'Hi. Any news?'

'Not really. Nothing worth mentioning. What did you want?'

'I've managed to compile an overview of who was where at specific times. Of the ones on our list. From the Federation.'

'OK,' Selma said, trying to conceal how uninteresting she found this information. 'Send it to me, then, won't you?'

'I'll do that. I'd appreciate it if you'd call in this evening.'

'As I said, I don't have anything in particular to tell you.'

'You have to talk to Hege. She's stopped training.'

'I can't do anything about that.'

'Yes, you can. She listens to you.'

Selma continued to browse through the DG.no website on her laptop.

'It won't do her any harm to miss a couple of days training, Jan.'

'Yes, it will. She has a plan to follow. She's going to the Olympics.'

Selma did not answer. She surfed a little through the newspaper. *DG*'s main story was about the discovery of a corpse. In Larvik, it said, in a forested area near to the town. The police were as usual extremely reticent so soon after finding a body, but DGTV.no had made contact with an old lady in a sou'wester with her arms laden with spruce branches.

'Selma?' she heard Jan say.

'I'm here. Wait a minute, please.'

It was incredible that the police hadn't managed to shield the little woman from the journalists. This was a live broadcast, and she was willingly jabbering away. Alternating between smiles and expressions of horror.

'*You know, I go in here nearly every day,*' she explained enthusiastically as she looked up at the obviously far taller interviewer. '*All the way to Rømminga, often. I need to keep myself going, you know. But today I just wanted to get some sprigs of spruce so I didn't go far. The weather's so awful, but it'll soon be Christmas. It's so cosy with spruce branches as decoration, you see. And to think that I came across a body! That photographer, you know! The one they've been talking about on the radio and TV. I recognized him right away. Nearly trod on him, my goodness! It's so dreadful, this business. And it'll soon be Christmas too.*'

'Selma, are you there?'

'Yes. It looks like they've found Morten Karlshaug. Dead.'

'What?'

'In Larvik.'

'What the hell would Klaus be doing in *Larvik*? He was on his way to Mongolia, wasn't he? And ... do you know for certain that he's dead?'

'Are you close friends?' Selma interjected quickly, and as she did, a train of thought was set in motion.

'Childhood pals. We see each other now and again. Not often. He travels a lot. I don't meet many people in my private life. It's tragic if it's confirmed that Klaus is dead, but to be honest, I've got other things on my mind at present.'

A uniformed police officer finally came into view, turned the journalist away, and took the old lady with him. The camera wobbled slightly and the studio took over.

'Morten Karlshaug,' Selma said. 'Klaus. And Arnulf Selhus and you. You all hung about together as young lads, didn't you? Are you still friends with Arnulf as well?'

She closed her eyes. Rewound her memory back to the time when she stood in Jan Morell's home office with Hege. When they had looked at the big Karlshaug photograph of an eleven-year-old and her mother, and Selma had caught sight of a faded picture of three young men on her way back into the living room.

'*They were best friends*,' Hege had said at the time about Arnulf Selhus and her father.

'*Were*?' Selma had asked.

'*Were*,' Hege had answered. '*We have to go now*.'

She could actually hear Jan Morell lose his temper at the other end.

'That's really none of your business,' he replied sharply. 'As I told you, I've other things to think about at the moment. Will you come tonight?'

'Yes. But I'll need to let you know what time. You'll hear from me later. Have you picked up the news that Sølve Bang seems to be going on the offensive on *Dagsnytt* at six o'clock tonight?'

No reply. Jan Morell had simply hung up.

IMBALANCE

He hadn't checked the internet en route. Hadn't listened to the radio either. The speakers on his mother's old Toyota were broken. Instead he had attached earphones to his mobile and listened to an audiobook. *Augustus* by John Williams. It was absolutely impossible to follow. For three hours he had listened to a story in which all the names ended in –us, where the extensive gallery of characters changed their names continuously, and into the bargain the author shifted time and place with no sense of chronology.

It didn't matter. The point was to be distracted. His thoughts were in total chaos, and he knew his body well enough to be aware that his blood pressure was considerably elevated. His pulse too. It had remained under a hundred all the way from Larvik to Oslo, via byways he realized didn't matter in the least.

You couldn't move unobserved anywhere in the Western world these days. There was surveillance everywhere. His only hope was that no one had trained their binoculars on him in particular.

He was seeking equilibrium.

No one was supposed to die. That wasn't the intention. He hadn't died, after all. He had just been damaged. Robbed of what had been. What had belonged to him, what he had been born to and into. Only God had control of life and death, and everything had gone completely wrong. One person was dead. Another two were still alive.

'Imbalance,' he muttered as he drove the Toyota into the garage, removed the tape and put the plates back on the Honda. 'Imbalance. Imbalance. Imbalance.'

He drew a tarpaulin over his mother's old car, locked the garage and went into the house. On his way to the kitchen to make himself something to eat, he checked *Aftenposten* online on his mobile.

Man Found Dead in Larvik.

No. It should have taken time. It should have taken days. Maybe even all winter.

The man with silver hair walked unsteadily across to the small dining table in front of the window. Collapsed on to a chair and went on reading.

At present the police refuse to say anything other than that they suspect a crime has been committed. The body has not yet been identified, but DG.no has reported that it is the missing photographer Morten Karlshaug who has been found. South-East Police will hold a press conference about the case at seven p.m.

No. No.

He had such a thirst. His tongue was enlarged and was hanging out of his mouth; he pulled a face and staggered over to the sink. Letting the cold water run, he leaned into the stream and drank. He drank like an animal, lapping at the water; it spurted and spilled, and he struggled to swallow enough to quench this terrible thirst that could not be slaked no matter how much he drank.

The world was filled with chaos, and something had to be done.

THE BREAK-IN

Selma Falck knew that the penalty for violation of §325 of the criminal code was up to six years' imprisonment. By helping herself to Jan Morell's money without asking for his permission, she had fulfilled not only one of the alternative criteria that aggravated the embezzlement from a legal point of view, but all of them. Firstly, it was a considerable sum of money. Secondly, the money was cash that had been entrusted to her. In addition, the embezzlement had continued over a period of time. And to top it all, in the months prior to the embezzlement being uncovered, she had sent him statements for the credit balance that were not quite in accordance with reality.

To put it mildly.

Every single evening since Jan Morell had exposed her, she had thought about what punishment she actually deserved. A hundred years in hell was the answer she had arrived at, but based on current practice in the Norwegian legal system, she would most likely have been behind bars for well over four years.

Bearing that in mind, a mere break-in was a trivial matter.

She wasn't even going to steal anything.

With a smile on her face, she followed the elderly man who was taking such pains and going to such effort to unlock the door into the apartment block in Frogner. He thanked her nicely when she held open the heavy door for him, and said goodbye, unsteady on his feet, when he turned right in the entryway to shuffle up the stairs and into his own apartment. The kindly woman dressed in dark clothes with a knitted hat and large glasses continued into the back yard.

It was ten to six in the evening. Sølve Bang was in the NRK broadcasting building in Marienlyst, and would be there for at least another half-hour. At present he lived alone, she had discovered on the internet, and confirmed when she could see that his apartment on the second floor was shrouded in darkness. On Google Maps she had been afforded a bird's eye view and saw that there were balconies on this side of the block. Since Google only showed the facades overlooking the street, she was nevertheless far from certain that her plan could be put into action.

She had incredible luck.

The balconies were old and small, with wrought-iron railings in ingenious patterns. The windows must be from some time in the seventies, and the balcony doors looked even older. Fate had shown her further undeserved favour by placing the balconies quite near to a protruding old shaft of around one and a half times one and a half metres. She guessed it had been an old-fashioned privy in earlier times, and the gutter led down inside it along a half-metre-wide gap between the balconies and the shaft.

Blood rushed through her ears. She felt carefree, excited and self-assured. The adrenaline made her breathe through her open mouth, slightly faster than usual; she felt her heart beating, strong and gloriously rhythmical – at one and the same time, this was nothing at all and tremendously risky.

She scouted all around. Most of the curtains were drawn, with light showing in some places. No one was peering out. In the corner, where the gutter ended in a curve that sent the water down into a drain with a grate, she almost disappeared into the soft, sheltered darkness.

It took her less than two minutes to climb up to the second floor. She didn't even need to enter the first two balconies. With the help of the gutter, the shaft wall and the wrought-iron railings, it was an easy matter to clamber up unseen and cross the final obstacle. On Sølve Bang's balcony, she hunkered down and caught her breath.

If it was indeed his balcony.

Slight tension in her gut made her put her hands around her eyes like a screen and press her forehead to the glass door. The apartment block's entryway was situated exactly in the middle of the building with a stairwell on either side. Four apartments in each of them. The intercom apparatus at the door was organized in the same fashion. Two columns with four doorbells on each.

This should be his apartment.

Her eyes had grown accustomed to the gloom, and in the shadows inside, in what must be a living room, she eventually made out the subject of the massive photograph above the settee.

A young skier. Just a young lad. At top speed, clad in the red of the national team outfit, with blue shoulders and white lower arms, in a race that would give him his first and only World Cup triumph.

There were no decals on the window warning of a security alarm. She had thought through this potential problem in advance and decided she would have to take a chance. In the first place Sølve Bang was not the type to spend money on something that could not be eaten, drunk or boasted about. And in the second place she could make herself scarce long before anyone from the Securitas company turned up, the same simple way she had come.

Yet another intoxicating stab of adrenaline hit her when she realized that she wouldn't even need to pick the lock. The doorframe was ramshackle, and it was enough to jiggle it and then use the largest blade of the Swiss army knife she had brought with her, at the same time as firmly wrenching the door handle. Exactly like the door on Jesso's mother's summer cottage, where hardly anyone ever used a key to gain entry.

She stepped inside and closed the door behind her.

It smelled stuffy and reeked of Indian food. The living room furnishings were strikingly spartan. An old, worn corner settee was placed under the huge photograph and a winged armchair with a reading lamp stood beside the window. The atmosphere in here was old-fashioned and dismal. 'Dilapidated' was the word that sprang to mind. The stucco between the wall and ceiling was beautiful, but here and there it had disintegrated and no one had bothered to repair it. The plaster ceiling rose looked original and elegant, but the chandelier was missing. Three cables protruded from a brown, irregular hole in the middle where the hook had apparently fallen off. One wall was covered in bookshelves that seemed to have been built in ages ago. Books were crammed in all over the place, standing and lying, but she swiftly noticed that there was some kind of system in the profusion. Double doors were open into the next room, and if possible it was even more spartanly furnished. A desk was placed in the centre of the room, and on the desk sat a computer.

Selma stood absolutely still and listened.

She could hear the hum of traffic. Someone shouting out there on the pavement, as well as someone else laughing. A pipe began to rumble, but soon stopped. Inside the apartment it was deathly quiet.

She approached the computer and roused it.

The screen saver was an illustration in Sølve's last book, which had been published seven years earlier. The machine requested a password.

Selma leaned down and wrote *The Future of the Past*, the title of the book.

Wrong.

She tried *Forgotten Tracks*, Sølve Bang's breakthrough novel as an eighteen-year-old, but that brought her no further forward.

Until now she'd had unbelievable luck. The password, however, could be anything at all. Expensive wines. Exotic locations. Ski wax or dates or names of restaurants. As for herself, she used the same password everywhere except for her online bank account, aninejohannes123. Idiotic, she knew, and anyway, Sølve Bang had no children.

Don't think of the children. Change your password.

She let the machine go back to sleep.

The writing desk was actually a large dining table with no sets of drawers underneath. Everything Sølve might need for his work was on the desktop. A simple Canon printer. A stack of paper. A cup filled with pens and a mug of congealed coffee. Yesterday's copy of *Aftenposten* was lying beside it.

Since the bookshelves in the other room were exclusively for books, she would have to check the bedroom. He must keep documents somewhere. Sølve Bang hadn't had a permanent job all his life and must necessarily have lots of contracts lying somewhere.

She made for the door in the centre of the living room wall. It led into the kitchen, as it turned out. It couldn't ever have been redecorated since the apartments were built, and it seemed cold and bare. Even the fridge, freestanding and placed right beside a smaller door that Selma immediately assumed must lead to the servants' quarters of yesteryear, looked like an antique. At any rate, it must have been from the seventies, considering its dirty-brown colour.

At least there were plenty of drawers and cupboards in the kitchen, but Selma took a chance on him not having hidden his papers in there. Her elation at the risk she had taken in breaking in was now abating, and she began to get seriously nervous. She hurried through the room with the writing desk, out into a stub of a hallway. Stopped in front of the first door. Gingerly pushed the handle down and opened it wide.

The bedroom was chilly. An elastic band between the catches held a book clamped to prevent the window from closing. A digital alarm clock with oversized numerals on one bedside table bathed the room in a faint, icy-blue light. An unmade double bed was located beside the wall adjoining the living room. Disheartened, she opened the first wardrobe door, aware that it would take ages to search through them all.

The wardrobe was empty. She stood peering into the darkness for a few seconds before closing it and opening the next one.

It was empty too.

She couldn't understand this at all. It was beyond dispute that he lived in this apartment. Sølve Bang was always elegantly dressed and usually wore a tweed jacket or blazer. He had a wide variety of both, and it seemed obvious that the bed was in use.

This was a vain man's secret sleeping chamber, with a completely empty wardrobe.

Dispirited, she opened the third wardrobe, which had double doors.

There they were, jackets hanging on their own, and trousers neatly folded on hangers. The wardrobe was divided in two, with wire baskets stacked on one side. Socks and boxer shorts, singlets and T-shirts. All tidily folded and stored as if someone was employed to do so. Four pairs of dress shoes were rigidly lined up on the floor and brightly polished. One pair of brown, three pairs of black.

No loose papers. No cartons, shoeboxes or plastic trays.

Selma closed the doors and opened the next wardrobe, this

one too with double doors. One side was divided into ordinary shelves; the other was open with a wardrobe pole at head height. One solitary dressing gown hung there.

The shelves were loaded with ring binders. Probably twenty of them, maybe more, inscribed with their contents. Here were old manuscripts, dated and numbered. Tax returns and receipts, loan agreements and contracts. Sølve Bang was a man with a sense of order, Selma realized, and she stopped breathing when she spotted a slim sheaf of papers in a red plastic cover. It was lying on the second shelf from the bottom. Both the cover and the papers had holes punched for insertion into binders. They did not belong on their own on the shelf; this was something Sølve Bang had recently looked at. She grabbed the cover and removed the stapled-together sheets of paper.

It took Selma less than ten seconds to appreciate that she really had found what she was looking for. This was a contract, an agreement between Statoil (The Principal) and Sølve Bang (The Author) about writing the history of skiing in Norway (The Work). Selma located the relevant clause at once. After reading it, she used her mobile to take a photo of each of the five pages. Returning the pages to the cover, she put the folder back in place. As she was about to close the wardrobe doors, her eyes caught sight of the almost-bare wardrobe floor.

In the far corner, half hidden beneath the long dressing gown was a pair of ski boots. They looked brand new, but had been taken out of their box, which sat beside it.

Fischer, Selma read.

Fischer RCS Skate Boots. She stood staring at them and forgot to breathe. An involuntary gasp for air jolted her out of her paralysis, and she only just remembered to take a photo of the boots and the box before she let herself out of Sølve Bang's apartment.

Exactly the same way she had come.

THE BUS TRIP

Selma Falck had hardly ever had a headache in her life. Now it felt as if her brain was too large for her skull. An oppressive tenderness behind her eyes and at the back of her head made her ears ring, forcing her to keep clamping her jaws firmly together to counterbalance a difference in pressure that probably did not exist.

At the same time, there was chaos and a streak of light inside her skull.

A theory was taking shape, but all the pieces failed to fit.

She was growing increasingly convinced that Jan Morell was important. He had a central place in her imaginary jigsaw puzzle. Einar was right that it looked as if, of the two, Hege's dad was the one who took the doping scandal more to heart and was punished hardest. Unlike Einar, Selma had met both father and daughter regularly since the story had broken. The developments since last Thursday all pointed in the same direction. If Hege didn't exactly accept the situation, at least she hadn't continually dug down into the depths of despair. As her father had.

At the press conference just over half an hour ago, the police had confirmed that the dead body found in the forest outside Larvik was in fact Morten Karlshaug. Selma had read this on her mobile as soon as she had put enough distance between herself and Sølve Bang's apartment block, and could take off the glasses she usually wore when she was playing poker. They were from the eighties, big and heavy, and the lenses had a pale-blue graduated tint.

Of course, it could all be a coincidence.

Coincidences did happen.

Often.

Incidents A and B happening at the same time was not the same as A and B having something to do with each other. Nor that they had caused each other to happen or that A and B together had happened as the result of a common C. Correlation was not the same as causality.

Selma had to get hold of a packet of Paracet tablets.

Then she would go to Årvoll, she decided so suddenly that, without thinking about it, she put on considerably more speed. She could take the 25 bus from Valkyrien to Lofthus terrasse. Arnulf Selhus's address was accessible in the phone directory, and according to the map, it would take her only a few minutes to walk there from the bus stop.

She remembered the photograph in Jan Morell's home office, from the time when Hege had dragged her in there to see the portrait of her and her mother. A faded old snapshot of three young men was displayed by the door, big lads, one wearing a ski helmet that had once been red, white and blue. Arnulf Selhus, Morten Karlshaug and Jan Morell. Jan was the eldest and tallest of the three, and even in the photograph the most self-assured.

The alpha male.

At Majorstua she caught the bus in the nick of time after popping into a kiosk for some painkillers. It was now ten to seven, and the bus was only half-full. She found a seat beside the window almost at the very back. Leaned her head against the ice-cold glass. Closed her eyes.

Jan was punished through his daughter being caught taking drugs.

Morten was, from what the police had already claimed, the victim of a crime. He was dead.

They were both in the old photograph.

It could be a coincidence.

Probably it was just a coincidence.

All the same. Jan Morell's deficient childhood piqued her curiosity. Wealthy people, especially those who had come into their fortune through their own hard work, often used a difficult childhood to exaggerate their success. At least a modest upbringing. The hotel magnate Petter Stordalen sold second-rate strawberries in the town square for his strict father. This was something he harped on about, and he had even based his business philosophy on it. The investor Stein Erik Hagen came from a relatively prosperous family, but was fond of slumming it by calling himself a 'shopkeeper' even once he was well into his tenth million.

Jan Morell could, according to the little that Selma had found out about him, have been really poor. At least by Norwegian standards. Between an upbringing by a single mother without the money to buy her youngster proper skis, even at the end of the seventies, and a fortune of more than eleven million kroner, there must lie a fascinating story.

One that he had refused point blank to tell.

There could be good reasons for that, of course.

The bus pitched and swayed through Oslo. Her headache was easing. Her eyelids felt heavy, and she noticed that she kept sliding into some kind of doze. At one point she even dropped off, but woke when the bus braked suddenly at an intersection.

Some people were more private than others.

Jan Morell was a man who held the majority of people at arm's length. His childhood belonged to him, and there didn't have to be any other reason for him being reluctant to share it with anyone.

Well, apart from the king.

At the Ski Museum. In front of a showcase displaying black Madshus skis.

The third man in the photograph from the seventies was Arnulf Selhus.

If the Finance Director in the Norwegian Cross-Country Skiing Federation was walking around, hale and hearty, with not a care in the world other than that a real threat to its reputation was hanging over his organization, Selma would put aside her shaky theory. Two people from the same old picture being struck down could well be a coincidence.

Three?

Hardly.

She had to check.

What Sølve Bang had to do with the photograph on Jan's office wall was no longer a mystery. As usual, he was just out to safeguard himself, and didn't entirely fit into the picture, quite literally. That he might have trudged around in Vettakollen and Ormøya with ski boots on his feet, probably with no other purpose than to cause alarm, was nevertheless a mystery so complex that Selma found it best to lay it to one side. At least until later. Haakon Holm-Vegge, possibly knocked down and definitely dead with traces of a demonstrably ineffective dose of Clostebol in his body, didn't fit in anywhere either. Neither in the jigsaw puzzle Selma was trying to piece together, nor in the theory she was using as a template.

All the same, she chose not to let that stop her.

They were approaching Lofthus terrasse. Selma got up and stood ready at the door when the bus drew to a halt. She shivered in the cold. In the city centre it had been drizzling, but up here on the heights flurries of snow were blowing in from the east. Selma tried to shield her mobile from getting wet when she checked her direction on the map.

The house was only three minutes away.

A large villa painted with brown wood stain, in Selma's opinion definitely built in the early seventies, with a BMW X5 and a Honda Civic parked in the courtyard. Light shone from several windows, and as Selma turned off from the street, opened a squeaky gate and strode towards the entrance, two, maybe three, dogs began to bark inside.

It certainly looked as if someone was at home, and she rang the doorbell.

NEW PLAN

Everything was unbalanced.

He was too. He noticed that he lurched as he walked across the floor. He had a pain in his head, but only on one side. His right foot felt numb until he gave himself a hard slap on the thigh and realized that all the pain was situated on the left side.

He hated imbalance. Symmetry was vital.

He hadn't meant for anyone to die.

He was no killer, and that was why the plan had been designed as it had been. Earlier. The whole time, until the photographer hadn't endured his punishment and had died. Now everything was ruined. Because of the photographer's death, everything had gone awry. It couldn't be put right again, and life had become seriously lopsided.

He guzzled yet another glass of water. Moved into his bedroom, tore off his sweater and stuffed it into the laundry basket. Pulled down the roller blind and lay down on the bed, on top of the quilt, with his trousers on. His singlet smelled rank, he knew. He tried to breathe deeply and slowly, in through his nose, and out through his mouth.

Arms exactly the same distance from his body. Legs at exactly the same angle from his hips. Weight equally distributed on a point in the middle of the small of his back.

His breathing was already more regular. His pulse slower. He gathered all his concentration on that point in his back, the centre that held his body together and in place.

Balance.

It could be restored.

The photographer could not be brought back to life, but he could mete out the same punishment to the others. That would bring harmony. That would be fair.

As Vanja crossed his mind, he opened his eyes abruptly. She had left when he had needed her. Her absence disturbed him. He had been rejected, by her, as by all other women, when it had mattered most.

It hadn't been his intention for anyone to die.

'Cunt!' he snarled into the room, and quickly sprang to his feet.

He was still terribly thirsty.

THE MOELVEN HOUSE

The woman who opened the door might be about thirty years of age, only a few years older than Arnulf Selhus's ballet-dancing daughter Sophie. She also bore signs of being wife number two or three. A bit too blonde, a bit too thin and perfume that was slightly too overpowering. Her face was narrow and feminine, with a mouth on which she had at least demonstrated some restraint in her dealings with Botox.

'Selma Falck?' she blurted out.

The dogs were barking like crazy from the upper floor.

'Yes,' Selma said, smiling and holding out her hand. 'We haven't met before.'

'Eh ... no. Benedicte Selhus.'

Her hand disappeared inside Selma's. Her handshake was so limp that Selma couldn't stop herself. She squeezed it hard. A grimace of pain crossed Benedicte's face, and she withdrew her arm.

'What's this about?'

She was dressed in pale-blue, skintight jeans and a beige wrap-over cardigan in angora yarn on top of a chalk-white T-shirt. With an almost helpless gesture, as if she felt threatened and very small, she pulled the cardigan tightly around her and crossed her arms. Her narrow shoulders were pushed forward. She looked as if she was steeling herself for a plane crash, and made no sign of willingness to invite Selma in.

'I just need a word or two with Arnulf. If possible.'

'Do you know each other?'

'Not really. You see ...'

Selma flashed a broad smile, tilted her head and added vaguely: 'Norway's such a small country.'

'He's busy.'

'OK. Where is he?'

Benedicte Selhus hesitated. Her eyes fluttered slightly, and she tucked her pale-blonde, streaked hair behind her ear before pushing her hand back under her armpit.

'Quiet, boys!' she yelled in the direction of the staircase before turning back to Selma. 'He's really busy. Couldn't you just phone him? Maybe tomorrow?'

'It's a bit urgent, and I'd prefer to speak to him face to face.'

'Is there something ... wrong?'

Her wide eyes grew even wider, and Selma thought she could detect a touch of anxiety in them unwarranted by the friendly, even if obviously surprising, request.

'Not at all. It must be cold for you to stand there. Couldn't I come in for a minute?'

Benedicte looked over both shoulders. As if to gain some time, or to assure herself that no one else was there.

'Well, it's actually really inconvenient right now. Storm Teodor isn't feeling too well ... my son, that is. Ours. He's only three and his temperature shot up this afternoon. Can't you wait till tomorrow? Just phone Arnulf, won't you, and then you can arrange to meet.'

She forced a smile. It looked more like she had a sudden stomach cramp.

'You look incredibly like Olivia,' she added, very unexpectedly. 'Her in *Law and Order SVU*. Olivia Benson.'

'Mariska Hargitay,' Selma mumbled.

'What?'

'The actress. Mariska Hargitay. It's really very important for me to speak to Arnulf.'

'Phone tomorrow, then. That'll have to do. Have a nice evening.'

The door was shut. If not exactly slammed, it was impossible to read the situation as anything other than that Selma was far from welcome. For a few seconds she hovered on the little stone staircase as she digested their conversation.

Things weren't going well in the brown-stained, seventies house in Stølsveien.

Of course it could simply be because of a feverish three-year-old.

Or it could be about something else entirely.

She walked to the road. Turned around. A face vanished quickly from the window at the eastern edge of the house. The hinges squealed when Selma opened the gate and stepped out. She closed it behind her and plodded westwards.

After ten metres, she stopped. The neighbouring garden to the Selhus family was sheltered by a cedar hedge, but it was not so dense that Selma couldn't easily manage to squeeze through it. She jogged towards the low fence that separated the properties. Clambered over and ran with her back stooped to the corner of the brown house where Arnulf Selhus lived.

She knew these prefabricated houses well. In their time they had been built by Moelven, and came in modules measuring three times eight metres that were erected according to how large you wanted the finished building to be. Selma's parents had built one like this themselves, when she was seven and had to be hodman for her father when he built the foundations. The most striking thing about this model was the un-Norwegian, dark shutters on either side of all the windows. On the outside they were covered by grooved wooden panels. Inside, a hinged wooden board could be opened and closed at various distances from the window frame.

A simple, mechanical ventilation system, used both summer and winter, as Selma recollected.

The basement level was in darkness. The living room on the ground floor was easy to locate, since it had larger windows. Selma tiptoed as quietly as she could up the slope where the foundations disappeared into the earth, towards what she had calculated must be the kitchen window.

The ventilation was open. She heard voices. Crouching down, she turned her better ear to them. Her right ear.

'... not now. It's just not possible.'

Arnulf Selhus might well have been busy, but he was at least at home. Once again, Selma felt that welcome excitement, the intoxication of success, of having gambled and won.

'You could just tell me what it is, Arnulf!'

Benedicte's voice was softer than when they had met at the door. Appealing, like a little child's plea for help.

'No. You're not to think about this.'

'I don't recognize you, darling.'

Scraping noises, like a chair leg on the floor. Footsteps, perhaps, and silence.

A grown man crying.

Selma stood upright. Dreadfully slowly, to avoid scratching against the wall panel. She was bold enough to let one eye peer inside.

Arnulf Selhus sat on a bar stool, leaning across a kitchen worktop, with his head buried in his arms. Benedicte was caressing his back, trying to get him to lift his face. Her lips were moving, but she was talking in such hushed tones that Selma couldn't make out what she was saying.

But she could hear the weeping, and she saw his back shaking.

She saw that Arnulf Selhus was more broken-hearted than she had ever seen any man outside a courtroom.

Slowly and silently, she drew back from the kitchen window. Four metres away from the house she broke into a run. Across the lawn. She leapt over the neighbour's fence and squeezed through the cedar hedge. Out into Stølsveien. Stopped, clenched her fists.

'Yes,' she said under her breath, pumping her arms in triumph. 'Yes. Yes. Yes!'

The dogs had not alerted their owners by as much as a whimper.

Of the three men in an old photograph, all of them, within an extremely limited period of time, had suffered some kind of serious setback.

Nearly forty years later, and one had even been killed.

It was time to head for Vettakollen.

THE SHOWDOWN

'D o you hear what he's saying? *Do you hear*?'

'Not when you speak over him all the time.'

Jan Morell could be bad-tempered and obstinate. Furious, brusque and hostile. But Selma had never seen him like this. 'Off his rocker' was the phrase that came to her as she watched him pace back and forth across his own living room floor. Completely off his rocker.

Usually his robust figure exuded strength and authority. He was ten kilos heavier and five centimetres shorter than desirable, but compensated as a rule with his puffed-out chest, his steady gaze and acceptable placement on Kapital's annual list of Norway's richest individuals. Taken together, this gave him the self-confidence and peace of mind he needed in order to be how both he and everyone else regarded him: a powerful, competent and vigorous businessman.

Now his hair was sticking out in every direction. He loosened his tie and unbuttoned the top shirt buttons so recklessly that one of them sprang loose and fell on the floor.

'Of course, this is the responsibility of both the athletes and the Cross-Country Skiing Federation,' Sølve Bang pontificated from an iPad on which the evening news programme was streamed. 'And I have a distinct feeling that the Federation isn't taking this case at all seriously enough. They seem totally incapable of action.'

'Well, he's right as far as that's concerned,' Selma said. 'Do they do anything at all up in that ice palace of theirs? Other than "follow the procedures"? Which, strictly speaking, consists of sitting quiet as mice and waiting to hear what other agencies decide?'

'No,' Jan said, his face now red as a beetroot. 'But he's throwing petrol on the fire! And if he'd contented himself by criticizing the Federation, then I wouldn't say too much. But he's flinging both Hege and Haakon to the wolves! Listen! Just listen to him.'

'Shh!'

'The rules are crystal clear,' Sølve Bang said calmly. *'Every athlete has an independent, objective responsibility to remain clean in accordance with WADA's guidelines. If they don't, no mercy is shown. That's how it is, and that's how it has to be if we're to have the slightest chance of combatting this odious practice. As far as Hege Morell is concerned, she is rightfully suspended while the case is considered, but we haven't heard a cheep from the NCCSF about regretting the incident. Nothing about distancing themselves from Hege Morell's use of banned substances.'*

'Use of banned substances!' Jan shrieked as he tossed his tie aside. 'It's really unclear whether she has "used" banned substances at this present time.'

The quote marks were drawn with both arms, wildly gesticulating in what threatened to turn into an attack of apoplexy.

'Sit down,' Selma said in a friendly voice. 'I've got a lot to tell you.'

Jan Morell had almost thrown himself upon her when she had appeared in Vettakollen at the back of eight p.m. He had run off at the mouth as she removed her outdoor clothes. Dragged her into the living room and literally pushed her down on to the settee before pressing 'play' on the iPad. Roaring so loudly that she had been forced to cover her ears.

'*The worrying aspects here are on a number of levels,*' Sølve's radio-friendly voice continued. '*The management of this crisis that has occurred is one of them. However, the important thing is that we take a closer look at how the situation has arisen at all. It should not be possible for our two best skiers to take drugs of any kind without the Federation knowing about it. Either they have known what Morell and Holm-Vegge have been up to, and if that is true, then the whole organization ought to be shut down...*'

He paused for effect. What he was saying was so extraordinary that neither his fellow participants nor the presenter seized the opportunity to speak.

'*...Or,*' Sølve Bang continued just as calmly as before, '*the situation is that they haven't known. In that case, the scandal is equally great. For then, once and for all, they will have shown their incompetence, their lack of control and their total inability to create systems that produce clean, honest sports. And not least to implement these systems in a manner that prevents scandals such as the one we are now facing.*'

Jan's expensive suit was crumpled. He stood in the middle of the room, with his arms lifted slightly from his sides and his palms showing, His usually so well groomed, combed back hairstyle was bedraggled and he had acquired a forelock. It didn't suit him at all, especially since it revealed a bald patch on the crown of his head.

'*Now I think we should calm down a bit here,*' said a voice Selma recognized as Lars Winther's. '*I agree with Bang that there's a lot to indicate serious deficiencies in the NCCSF. And his presentation of the objective rules are correct, as far as I understand them. All the same, I believe that this case has so many elements to it that we should take some time to get to the bottom of what has really happened before we rush to any final judgment. About the Federation, but especially about the two*' *athletes involved. Their cases have a number of differences, and there's reason to believe that ...'*

'Differences?' Sølve interrupted. *'What differences? They're both elite athletes. They've both used Clostebol, a banned substance. They're both Norwegian. I call that two virtually concurrent, composite cases.'*

'What should happen now, then?' the presenter asked.

'Norway should withdraw from the World Championships this season,' Sølve Bang said, slightly more agitated now. *'The FIS, the international ski federation, should immediately appoint an independent committee to investigate this. Norway's Cross-Country Skiing Federation should be gone through with a fine tooth comb, on every level. As far as finance, doping, and administration are concerned. Everything.'*

'That would surely mean we won't have a cross-country team in PyeongChang?'

'In the worst-case scenario, yes. But if we are to save this sport at all, this most Norwegian of all cultural expressions, we must take up the evil by the roots. Without delay.'

Jan stopped the player.

'He's not fucking real,' he said, sitting down heavily on the settee directly opposite Selma. 'I've regarded him as a friend. A close acquaintance, at least. Then he first makes a grubby blackmail attempt, and then he throws Hege in front of a bus on national radio.'

'He's feathering his own nest,' Selma told him.

Jan was not listening. He sat slumped on the settee, trying without success to tidy his hair. The bags under his eyes were bigger than before, and his mouth had stiffened into a half-severe, half-despairing, grimace.

'Are you listening?' Selma asked.

'What?'

'Sølve's feathering his own nest. He's trying to wriggle out of a contract. For the book.'

'What book?'

'The history book. About cross-country skiing in Norway.'

'Oh, that.'

Jan sank back on the settee.

'Didn't you hear what I said?'

'He's going after my girl,' Jan said softly. 'That slimeball will ...'

'I'll take care of Sølve.'

At last he looked up.

'Take care of?'

'Yes. He has a clause in his contract that means he'll win big if Statoil withdraws as the Federation's sponsor. If they break with them and find it damaging to be associated with them. More specifically, he'll avoid repaying three point eight million kroner.'

Jan looked at her in confusion. Finally he left his hair in peace and sat up straight on the settee.

'Will he be rewarded if they withdraw? How ...'

'No. He'll just avoid having to deliver the manuscript, however, and keep the advance he's already been paid. All of it.'

'How ...'

Selma sighed and caught his eye.

'I don't know much about books, because I don't read many. But I know a lot about contracts. And I've read up on what is called artistic licence. When an author is going to write a commissioned work, you never have any guarantee that the book will be as the customer wants it to be. That the person who has purchased the author's work will also receive it when it's finished, in other words. It therefore sounds reasonable that a customer who's loaded, in this case Statoil, lets the author keep the fee even if the company isn't satisfied with the end result. Or if they no longer wish to be associated with the contents of the book, which in this case is the actual dilemma.'

'I'd never have gone along with that.'

'No. But then it's not MCV that has commissioned the work either.'

'How can you know that the contract has such a clause?'

'I can't tell you that. Just trust what I'm saying, Jan.'

'But ... if Sølve Bang receives the money whether it's published or not, why is he bothering then to ...'

Again he collapsed back on to the settee, clutching his hand to his head.

'I don't understand.'

'You're tired,' Selma said, smiling. 'To be blunt, I don't think there *is* any book.'

'It's to be published before the Winter Olympics. In less than two months.'

'Yes, but I don't think it exists. At the very least, it's far from finished, I suspect. From what I've discovered, it's been postponed several times, though I don't know why as yet. But I can imagine the reason. Sølve Bang is notorious for having writer's block.'

Jan looked apathetically at her.

'He publishes one book each decade,' Selma went on. 'Approximately. They're usually well received, and sell well. Abroad too. But very few people can live for ten years on one book. Between publications Sølve Bang often lives from hand to mouth.'

'He lives in Frogner. In a massive apartment!'

'Yes, massive and dreary. That's not the point. The point is that he has to pay back three point eight million kroner if he doesn't deliver that damn manuscript. The contract is clear on that. If he doesn't complete it within the deadline, the money has to be repaid. But if this scandal is allowed to grow, then Norwegian cross-country skiing won't be something that Statoil will want to be associated with. Identified with. Neither here at home nor overseas. Then they won't want any manuscript, none at all. Sølve will be pretty well off the hook and gets to keep most of the money. Which has probably all been spent, anyway.'

Jan still seemed as if he couldn't quite grasp what she was talking about. Selma stood up. She crossed to his side of the polished concrete coffee table, crouched down and placed her hand over his.

'Let me take care of Sølve Bang.'

He looked at her without answering, but didn't pull his hand away.

'It really was Morten Karlshaug they found,' she said quietly. 'Dead in the forest. Killed, in all probability. And I must ask you something in connection with that.'

'I saw that,' he mumbled, rubbing his face with his other hand. 'Fucking sad. Ask away.'

'There was no unfinished business between you?'

'Me and Klaus? No. Why do you ask?'

'Wait a minute. But between you and Arnulf Selhus there's been some kind of ... falling out?'

Now he no longer wanted her near. He got to his feet, strode over to the drinks cabinet and poured some whisky into a tumbler.

'I can't fathom what this has to do with your assignment,' he said brusquely. 'And the relationship between Arnulf and me is none of your business.'

He drank half the contents of the glass, poured in more and crossed to the empty fireplace. Leaning his elbow on the mantelpiece, he took another gulp.

Selma approached the drinks cabinet. She opened it and took out the decanter. The golden liquid twinkled behind the richly embossed glass.

'I've never tasted alcohol,' she said softly.

'Why not, actually?'

'I just never started. Trained too much. Wanted to go too far. Later I discovered I needed to be in control. Of myself. More than most people, in fact.'

Jan smiled for the first time since Selma had arrived.

'You're right there. Combining compulsive gambling with alcohol would be catastrophic.'

'What's the worst thing that could happen to you, Jan?'

Selma was still holding the decanter. She lowered her gaze. Turned the beautiful decanter around. Shades of deep yellow and brown danced and vibrated behind the intricate pattern on the crystal. He did not answer.

'The very worst thing,' she repeated.

'Losing Hege.'

'Yes, but after that.'

'For Hege's career to lie in tatters. In other words, I'm living a nightmare.'

Selma nodded.

'Have you enemies, Jan?'

'Of course I have.'

'Bitter foes?'

'More than likely. I don't spend much time thinking about that sort of thing. I apply my energy to MCV instead. It goes without saying that I've broken a few eggs along the way.'

'Can I have a look at your office, please?'

He had raised his glass, but froze on the spot.

'Why on earth?'

'Can we?'

Selma made a peremptory gesture towards his office door.

'Preferably not,' he muttered, but all the same he put his glass down on the mantelpiece. 'Come on, then.'

The last time Selma had been in Jan's home office, it had smelled of aftershave and furniture oil. Now there was a faint residue of cigarette smoke in the room.

'Klaus took that picture,' Jan said, pointing lethargically at the large photograph of Hege and Katinka. 'I like it.'

'It's fantastic. But this one here ...'

Jan was standing with his posterior against the substantial writing desk in the centre of the room, his arms crossed and his eyes fixed on the portrait of mother and daughter. Selma stood just inside the door, pointing.

'This is you, Morten Karlshaug and Arnulf Selhus, isn't it?'

Yet again the corners of his mouth curled into something resembling a smile.

'Yes. It was taken just before I met Katinka. It was in the newspaper, after a cross-country competition in Marka. I was seventeen, and the others a year younger.'

'Had you been together throughout your childhood?'

'Yes, in a way.'

'In a way?'

Jan came across to her. Studied the picture. His stubby finger touched the ski helmet.

'I got that skiing cap from Kupper'n himself,' he said. 'And wore it out. I wore out a cap, Selma, wore it until it fell apart. That was what my childhood was like.'

'I've noticed you don't talk about it.'

'About the ski helmet?'

'About your childhood.'

'My childhood is a closed chapter. Has been for a long time. Come on, let's go back.'

He pushed her ahead of him out of the office and closed the door emphatically behind him.

'You must speak to Hege,' he said imperiously. 'That's why I asked you to come.'

'Where is she?'

He stopped and surveyed the room, slightly confused, as if he had only just noticed his daughter's absence.

'Maggi!' he shouted.

The kitchen door slid open immediately. The scared, slight figure took a couple of tentative steps into the living room.

'Where's Hege?'

'At the cinema.'

'At ... the cinema? Without telling me?'

Selma wanted to let him know that his daughter was twenty-four years of age, but held back the comment.

'Yes,' Maggi said submissively.

Jan dismissed her back into the kitchen. The door slid shut.

'Sorry,' he murmured to Selma. 'I've wasted your time.'

He fetched his tumbler from the mantelpiece and sat down again.

'No,' Selma said. 'You haven't. But now you're going to answer my questions.'

As he sipped the whisky, he glanced at her over the rim of the glass.

'That depends what they're about,' he said.

Selma perched on the edge of the seat. Straightened her back and let her hands grasp her knees.

'You said the worst thing that could happen to you, apart from Hege dying, would be her career being destroyed. Why is that?'

His frown made his eyebrows join together.

'That should be obvious. She's my only daughter. I love her. She's the best female cross-country skier in the world. A successful career will open up the world to her. What's happened now ...'

He swung the glass in a haphazard arc.

'It makes everything difficult for her. Impossible. She will always be known as the one who cheated. Who fell. This will follow her for the rest of her life. It's not a fate you wish for your only child.'

'Why didn't you have a skiing career of your own?'

'That can hardly have anything to do with this case. I really don't have time for this.'

'What would be the worst thing that could happen to Morten?' Selma said quickly. 'Klaus, I mean. To die? Was he particularly … afraid of dying?'

Jan shrugged with one shoulder.

'No more than the rest of us. Death is probably what we all fear most of all. If we're not terribly ill or aged. Sometimes even then, I expect. But as far as Klaus is concerned …'

He gave a faint smile.

'Klaus would actually have chosen to die rather than be locked inside anywhere. Many people believe that claustrophobia …'

The rest of the whisky disappeared, and he got up to pour some more.

'… is a kind of worried scepticism about confined spaces,' he went on as he headed for the drinks cabinet. 'But it's not really just an aversion. Most of us are capable of feeling that, with heights and tunnels and enclosed cupboards. For Klaus, we're talking about sheer panic. Really deep, destructive anxiety. I never saw it at its worst, because he always went around … in a state of readiness? Isn't that what the psychologists call it? Always plan a few moves ahead, to avoid placing yourself in a position where you could be locked in.'

'He's been to Mount Everest. How did he manage that without being able to sleep in a tent?'

A brief little guffaw, an appreciative glance over his shoulder as he poured the whisky.

'Smart thinking! He managed without one. He got Bergans to make a special tent for him, with two transparent walls. Which was a bit of a challenge, as far as I understood. To obtain the same extreme qualities as the professional tents, in transparent material. But it worked. And he managed it.'

'Do you mean that quite literally? That he would have preferred to die?'

'Yes. Or to be honest, it would have killed him. After a while, at least. But where the hell are you going with all this?'

Selma did not answer. She was still perched on the edge of the settee, her back ramrod straight. She felt the heat from her hand penetrate through her trousers. Wrote out a mental index card and filed it away in the right place.

'Selma?'

'Now it's important that you're exact, Jan. Do you seriously mean that Morten Karlshaug could have died from being locked inside somewhere?'

'Yes, I really do think so. I mean, I've never seen him completely shut in anywhere, but we hung about together for years. He was always the one who had to know where all the doors were situated. Windows. Escape routes. On cabin trips and building sites, school basements and all the other places that young hooligans might think of going into in the seventies.'

Again Selma was a million miles away.

This time Jan let her be. She suddenly realized that he was studying her.

'You've formed a theory,' he said slowly. 'What's it based on, and what on earth does it have to do with a photograph in my office?'

'Arnulf Selhus,' she said in a loud voice. 'What's his greatest nightmare?'

Jan's face closed down again.

'No idea,' he muttered. 'But he's acquired a gaggle of children through three marriages. Five or six, I think. Losing them is probably his worst fear, just as much as for you and me.'

'But apart from death?'

'Don't know, as I said. I no longer know him.'

'You did at one time. Both when you were young, and ten years ago when you got a job for him as Finance Director at the NCCSF. Did the break with Arnulf come before or after you put in a good word for him?'

Jan stood up and looked at the clock. Drained his glass in one gulp and slammed it down on the polished concrete table.

'This has nothing to do with the case, Selma. You'll have to go.'

'I'm pretty sure Hege's been sabotaged.'

'What?'

'I'm pretty sure...'

'I heard what you said. But why do you say that? What have you found out?'

'I'll tell you when I have more to go on. If I'm to make further progress with this, I really need you to answer my questions.'

He grabbed the glass and began to move towards the drinks cabinet again. Changing his mind, he called out to Maggi. She stood in the living room three seconds later.

'Did you buy Pepsi Max, as I asked you to?'

Maggi nodded.

'A bottle and two glasses, then. With ice cubes.'

She hurried from the room. Selma felt the usual prick of shame at never voicing any protest about Jan Morell's behaviour towards the Polish home help. During her first visit to Vettakollen, almost exactly a week ago, Maggi had seemed upset about the doping allegations and flustered about everything that was going on. However, at that time she had clearly felt at home in the timber villa. She had been quiet and friendly and showed Hege motherly concern. Now she was cowed, scared and jittery.

You're not very nice to her, was what Selma wanted to say.

But she didn't. Instead, she sat in silence, waiting until Maggi returned with glasses and a litre and a half of Pepsi Max. The ice cubes made it fizz explosively when she poured out the cola, since she forgot to tilt the glass.

'Sorry. Sorry.'

Her skinny legs rushed through the living room, into the kitchen and returned with a cloth. The spilled liquid had formed dark, irregular blotches on the highly polished concrete table.

'Sorry,' she said for the third time, as she wiped up the spill and then made herself scarce.

'Why did you get Arnulf Selhus the job at the Cross-Country Skiing Federation?'

Selma picked up a glass and wiped the bottom of it on her trouser leg.

'Because everyone deserves a second chance,' he said sullenly.

'What had he done wrong?'

'It's nothing to do with you.'

Selma sighed. She stood up. Stood for a few seconds staring at him. He stared back, his expression that of a sulky teenager.

'You know me as an easy-going woman,' Selma began, still on her feet. 'Most people do. Very few have seen me angry. No one has seen me cry since 1986. I hardly ever swear, I smile a lot, I have a pleasant manner. I seldom voice my opinions, other than in legal matters. I'm popular, Jan. I'm looked up to, and not just because I'm in better shape than most twenty-five-year-olds. I'm very well known, idolized by many and well liked by most. And proficient at my job, irrespective of how hair-raising the embezzlement was. No matter how many lies about my own penchant for thrills and gambling I've whispered in my own ear down through the years. I'm competent. I'm smart, Jan. That's why you chose to enter into this bet. I'm Selma Falck, and it's Selma Falck you chose to get you out of your life's worst ...'

Katinka crossed her mind, and she checked herself.

'... second-worst crisis. Ergo you agree with me about most of what I've just said about myself.'

Still their eye contact was firmly locked.

'But if you think for a moment,' she went on, a bit louder now, 'that I can't lose my temper, and that I can't speak my mind straight out ...'

Her hand shook when she leaned over to pick up the glass. She didn't care. She drank half the contents before she put it down again, and continued: '... then you're terribly mistaken. And now I'm angry.'

She felt the trembling subside. Her cheeks were burning. Jan Morell sat there on the leather settee, more relaxed than he had been all evening, with something that was beginning to look like a smile at the corners of his mouth.

'Smirk away,' she said, fuming. 'Be my guest. Sit up here in this pathetic, fading timber palace with its tasteless furnishings and acre of ground while you rot away in your sorrow-filled widow-hood.'

His eyes narrowed. Not much, but she noticed it. He drew his thighs slightly closer together. Hoisted himself up a little on the settee, but still maintained eye contact with her.

'If, on the other hand, you would like to find out who sabotaged your daughter, and if you want me to tell you what I think has happened, and what might be about to happen, then you must ...'

She let herself drop down on to the settee. Took a deep breath and slammed both fists on the table as hard as she could. A freezing pain shot up from both pinkies, all the way to her shoulders. The concrete hardly made a sound.

'*Bloody hell, pull yourself together! And answer my questions!*'

'OK.'

'OK?'

Her hands were incredibly sore.

'Maggi!' Jan roared at the kitchen door. 'Bring two bags of frozen peas!'

It took less than half a minute before Selma was sitting with a bag of peas tied to each hand with dish towels. Maggi tied the last knot and disappeared just as fast as ever.

'He stole from me,' Jan said calmly. 'Arnulf Selhus. Exactly like you. And exactly as with you, I felt he deserved another chance. Just not at MCV.'

'There seem to be a lot of people who steal from you,' Selma said, her pulse stabbing rapidly and painfully on both hands.

'Not so very many. And I always find out.'

'What did he do?'

'Sent me fake invoices. Sent them to the company, that is. Which on MCV's behalf at that time is to say Finance Director Arnulf Selhus. From himself, to himself, but disguised as genuine debts. He transferred just over three million kroner to his own account by authorizing invoices that looked bona fide.'

'What were the conditions?'

'Conditions?'

'To avoid reporting it to the police. I had to fulfil loads.'

'He wasn't able to repay the money. He was recently divorced and had a new baby on the way with his new wife. A lot of changes, and the youngest son had contracted leukaemia. But I have a promissory note. A claim for the entire sum will be made if he commits another crime. Also, he knows that I'd have him fired from the Federation on the spot. And that it would be impossible to get another job. At least within finance, which is his field. One incorrect entry from that guy, and he'll lose everything in his possession. He knows that, so I expect that the NCCSF actually have the most compliant, thorough and meticulous finance director in the world. From that point of view, I've done everyone a favour.'

'This was before I became your lawyer?'

He nodded.

'Just before,' he said.

'How many people knew about the cheating with invoices at that time?'

His head rocked from side to side.

'Well, only a few. But what one person knows, nobody knows, what two people know, everybody knows. As they say.'

'How many? Just a ball park figure.'

'Three or four people anyway. His two immediate subordinates in the finance department, at the very least. They knew of the agreement I came to with him as well, unfortunately. I probably wasn't very quiet when I had it all out with him. In fact, *DG* had picked up a whiff of something for a couple of days. I smoothed it over by praising Arnulf in public. It did the trick at that time, but to tell the truth, on a couple of occasions in subsequent years I've had questions about what happened. Such specific questions that several people must actually know the story by now. As I said, what one person knows, and all that. But what has all this to do with Hege?'

The dark stains on the concrete table were drying out. Selma's hands felt progressively worse.

'She's not who it was intended to damage,' she said. 'It was you.'

'Me?'

'Yes.'

'But ...'

'Someone's out to punish you. To punish Morten Karlshaug, Arnulf Selhus and you.'

'But ... how can you ... What would ...'

'I don't have many answers at the moment. But I have a whole raft of questions. I want to ask one of them right now. And you have to answer. Honest and true.'

The hair had fallen over his forehead again. His lip was damp with perspiration. He nodded.

'Did the three of you ever do anything serious to harm anyone in your youth? In your childhood? Something really serious? You, Arnulf and Morten?'

His mouth had dropped half-open. His lips were dark-red and moist.

'No,' he said sharply. 'We did a lot of crazy things, but never anything serious. Never anything illegal.'

He did not blink. Not a flicker on his face. His eyes were fixed on hers, and she was the one who had to yield in the end.

Never before had Selma Falck come across such a good liar as Jan Morell. He was even better than she was.

'I see,' she said. 'If you think of anything, give me a call.'

She stood up. The bags of peas fell off. When she bent down to pick them up from the floor, it hurt her right hand so much that she wondered if she'd broken something.

'Let me get them,' Jan said. 'Do you really mean it? That it's all just window dressing? That Hege's been sabotaged in order to damage me? Are we talking about some sort of revenge, then? Some kind of ...'

'See you later,' Selma broke in, as she headed for the door.

'Someone like that would have to be mad,' Jan said as he helped her on with her jacket. 'Totally mad!'

'Let's hope you're wrong,' Selma replied curtly, opening the front door. 'Let's hope, sincerely and wholeheartedly, that you're wrong, Jan.'

EINAR FALSEN

'There are so many gypsies here,' Einar whispered.

He was well hidden inside his sleeping bag, nestled in a hollow surrounded by four boulders, when Selma arrived.

'It's swarming with them!'

'Not at all,' Selma said quietly. 'There are no Roma people here now. None at all. Just you and me.'

'And loads of gypsies.'

He seemed terrified. The stink was worse than ever, and the hole left by the recently disappeared canine tooth was almost certainly infected. The distinct swelling and his sickly breath indicated that he ought to see a dentist pronto.

That was not going to happen, as Selma well knew.

'Let's sit you up a bit,' she said, taking hold of his armpits.

'They're coming! They want my space. The gypsies are going to kill me, Selma.'

'Look what I've got for you, Einar!'

She didn't like giving him alcohol, and did so very seldom, but she always had a hip flask of Brandy Special in her handbag. To be on the safe side. For occasions such as this. Brandy Special was what he always wanted. Never anything else.

She opened the flask and held it out to him. His hands were shaking when he grasped it. Guided it to his mouth. Drank. He drained the flask, with brief pauses in between times. Neither of them spoke until he finally returned it with a groan.

'Good, Mariska. That did me good. Can I have some more?'

'No. Lie down now.'

He lay back between the rocks.

'They'll take me,' he whimpered. 'Go away!'

His arms were waving in the air.

'I'll look after you, Einar.'

'Will you?'

'Yes, I'll sit here and watch over you. You need to sleep.'

'You can borrow my Nille blanket. The light-blue one. I haven't used it, so it doesn't smell too bad. Here ...'

He tried again to scramble up into a sitting position.

'I'll sort it myself, Einar. You get some sleep. I'll stay.'

'You'll stay,' he said, smiling, and Selma saw that the mucous membrane in his mouth was a deep shade of red. 'You'll stay with me. Thank you.'

His eyes slid shut.

Selma put her hand on his cheek, between the unruly beard and his eyes. He was burning hot. She took out three Paracet and sacrificed the Pepsi Max she had in reserve in her bag.

'Take these,' she said, handing him the tablets and the bottle.

He put the three pills on his tongue, washed them down with cola, and smiled cheerfully.

'Make sure the gypsies don't get me,' he muttered.

Einar Falsen should be in hospital, but Selma knew he would never go. During all his years as a free spirit and down-and-out, she had only once managed to persuade him to accompany her to see a doctor. He had fractured a finger. There had been an unbelievable commotion. The idea that the radiographer might microchip him to gain control over his thoughts had come like a bolt from the blue. The entire time until Einar was to go in for an X-ray, he had behaved reasonably well. In exemplary fashion, in fact. Done as Selma told him and allowed the doctor to examine him. Answered questions.

It had ended with the radiographer taking a week's sick leave and had given Selma a horrendous task to prevent criminal charges being brought.

'Just go to sleep,' she whispered.

Einar really ought to be in hospital, but that wasn't going to happen. On the rare occasions when he was really unwell, or when the winter was unusually harsh, she had found a place for him in a shelter. He had stayed there for three days at most, and all he did was to watch episode after episode of *Law & Order SVU* in the common room until he left as soon as his legs could carry him.

Moving him would be pointless. He could sleep off the infection and the madness, as he had done before, or else he could die in the course of the night.

Einar Falsen had once been a police officer. An extremely capable police officer. At the beginning of the noughties he had led a special group combating the sexual abuse of children. The internet had seriously begun to be an arena for crimes, and the battle had to be intensified. A man was brought in following a formal complaint by two devastated couples in Romsås. Their children, a boy of five and a girl of eight, had shown a worrying change in behaviour in the past few weeks. Both had in the end told them in snatches what the detainee had done. The children knew him only as Uncle Bjørn.

Uncle Bjørn had given them lots of things. But he had also taken a great deal from them, and when the police received the complaints, they conducted an immediate search of the man's residence. His name was actually Anders and he was in his early forties. Single and childless.

His apartment could have been used as an operating theatre. Sparkling clean. Neat, tidy and without as much as an innocent porn magazine in a drawer in the bedside cabinet. In the basement they found nothing but two pairs of skis, an old kicksled and four winter tyres. The man also had a computer. It contained not the slightest trace of viewing the increasing number, and borderline legal, pages of spicy adult entertainment.

Which in itself was so suspicious that Einar refused to give up. Uncle Bjørn was arrested on a Friday afternoon, a well-known move to get around the rule then in force about making an appearance for remand in custody within twenty-four hours. They could stretch it out all the way to Monday before going to court. On Sunday evening the police had still drawn a blank. The stories of the two Romsås children, unclear and slightly disjointed, were sufficient for an experienced policeman like Einar Falsen. But they were miles from guaranteeing a remand order. Far less a subsequent prosecution.

Then Uncle Bjørn's grandmother phoned.

It turned out the suspect had a grandmother aged eighty-seven, sprightly and of sound mind, to judge from her voice. She had been given Einar Falsen's name at the duty desk. She had been looking for her daughter's son all weekend, and had finally learned from a neighbour that the police had been there and picked him up.

She could well imagine that a lovely man like Anders would be able to help the police, but might it be possible to let him know to get in touch with her as soon as he was finished with them?

Einar Falsen had a sudden idea. He wondered whether it might be the case that Anders kept some belongings at her house? Yes indeed, the grandmother proudly confirmed. After all, she had plenty of space, she'd been a widow for twenty years, and Anders was her only grandchild. He was such a good, considerate boy. He often visited her, and if Anders needed his yellow suitcase, then the police could most certainly come and collect it.

An hour later, at half past nine on the Sunday night, a rather despondent Anders sat in an interview room with Einar Falsen, wondering if he would be able to go home soon. A young police-woman came in with a large, heavy, bright yellow suitcase that was placed on the table between Einar and Anders.

Einar asked the prisoner for the code for the lock.

Anders broke down. Einar broke open the lock. The case was crammed with VHS videos and Polaroid pictures. It would take days to go through all the home-made videos, not least because the investigators had to take regular breaks from what they had to watch. However, Einar had immediately picked up a bundle of photographs.

One of them was of his own daughter, in a pose he had never been able to forget since then. Anette was maybe eight years old in the picture. She would have been eighteen if she had still been alive, but Anette Falsen had committed suicide two years earlier. She had never told anyone about what had happened to her and had, despite her parents' tenacious efforts, vanished into a fog of drug-taking and despair before, unable to take any more, she had hanged herself.

Einar, who ever since his daughter's death had seemed a tad unstable to some of his colleagues, killed Anders on the spot. The policewoman could later say that she had stood as if paralysed, and that the whole incident had taken less than a minute. She had heard the noise, she related in the witness box, a loud crack as the suspect's neck snapped.

The next morning, Selma Falck was appointed Einar's lawyer.

Selma could never leave Einar.

The Nille blanket and a pillow were clearly visible on top of the IKEA bag, and she grabbed both of them. She made herself as comfortable as possible among the big, reddish-brown stones. She took out her phone. Einar didn't move a muscle. He must be already in a deep sleep. Selma wanted to watch a film, but discovered that she had only eight per cent juice left. Einar's power bank was somewhere in the bags strewn around him, but it felt wrong to rummage through his belongings. She stuffed her phone back in her bag and began to talk instead.

She talked about Jan Morell. About his daughter, Hege. She told of the break-in at Sølve Bang's apartment, about Lars Winther's photo of her on her way into the Poker Turk's. In a low, singsong voice, she spoke of everything she had experienced in this past week. Of Maggi, whom she liked, and Benedicte Selhus, whom she thought a sad figure. She talked about someone out there in the night, whom she thought had avenged himself on three boys in an old photograph. She spoke of Haakon, who would be cremated tomorrow, at a funeral that, after the events of recent days, probably wouldn't take place in a crowded Trefoldighetskirke, the Trinity Church, in the presence of royalty. Only close family and a few friends would be there. And in a completely different venue from the one originally planned, in a possibly vain attempt to keep the press at bay. She talked about her frustration at not being able to understand what Haakon had to do with Hege's case. Maybe she had been right all along: everything was coincidental, but at the same time she couldn't quite put his case out of her mind.

She didn't mention her own children.

She thought of them, all the time, and felt a painful gnawing in her diaphragm that never let up, and of her sorrow that they no longer even sent her hateful text messages.

She refused to think about Anine and Johannes, and spoke instead about a man in ski boots who had first frightened Hege, then her, by openly trudging into a property in Ormsundveien that no longer belonged to her.

Selma had been talking for three hours on the trot. A lot of it had been mentioned several times over. Some of it she had forgotten to say. She was shivering and her teeth were chattering, but she kept going and, at regular intervals, took her hand out to feel whether Einar was still alive.

She thought Sølve had been the one who had done the tramping around. He had the right ski boots in his wardrobe at home, there were images of the tracks, with an object for comparison just as Einar described in *The Investigator's ABC*. Sølve Bang was a cunning bastard who thought of no one but himself. He had girlish hands and toddled around like a penguin, and Selma should really phone her old teammate from the Bækkelaget Sports Club who was now Director of Communications at Statoil. She would tell her about the deception, he wouldn't get away with it, but why Sølve Bang would traipse around in other people's gardens with ski boots on his feet was still beyond her comprehension.

'His feet are too small,' Einar grunted.

'Who?'

Selma leaned towards him.

'I thought you were asleep,' she said softly, with a smile.

'I'm resting. And Sølve Bang has small feet. You've said that twice. The pictures you took in Vettakollen were of footprints made by shoe size forty-six or something like that. At least that was what you said an hour ago. But you've been rambling a lot. You've got terribly mixed up, Mariska. My goodness ...'

He struggled up into a sitting position. His eyes were no longer quite so glassy.

'The gypsies have gone!'

'Yes, we're the only ones here. And now I have to take out my mobile, Einar. Just for a second.'

'Wait a minute,' he said quickly, producing a huge aluminum bin lid from one of the crevices behind him.

He used it as a shield for his head and torso.

'Just a minute! You have to promise you'll only take a second!'

Selma looked through it until she found the photo of Sølve Bang's ski boots. Using her thumb and forefinger, she zoomed in on the cardboard box beside them.

'You're right,' she said in an undertone. 'These are size forty-one.'

'Is your phone gone?' Einar whimpered.

Selma switched it off and put it in her bag.

'Yes.'

The bin lid clattered as he wedged it between the rocks again.

'People like that turn up in every case,' Einar told her, and touched his mouth. 'Fuck. I've got such bloody hellish toothache. Or where my tooth used to be, at any rate. My whole mouth, actually. You don't have any more booze?'

'No, not here. I can come back with some more tomorrow.'

She glanced at her watch.

'Today. Later today. What did you mean by "people like that"?'

'People like Sølve Bang,' he said in a resigned tone, struggling to find a more comfortable position.

His movements were even more sluggish than usual. He still kept blinking his eyes in a grimace of pain, and he was fighting to get his tongue to cooperate when he spoke. But he was better. He was present again.

'There's always someone who turns up to obscure the picture,' he said. 'To mess things up. And who turns out to have nothing to do with the case in hand. It happens in every single investigation. It's only on TV that the detectives stay on the motorway. A straight road, sort of thing. Full steam ahead to a solution and a far too rapid confession. In reality, there are always a few unnerving dead ends and people who suck all the energy out of you without it leading to anything. People like that and liars, Mariska, are an investigator's worst enemies. People who make themselves look important. Push themselves forward. People who lie about things that don't really matter too much. That at least the police don't give a toss about. Infidelity and smoking hash. Fuck off, I say. If people would only tell the truth to the police and the courts, we'd have a far more impressive clear-up rate and zero miscarriages of justice.'

'Who can have left the footprints in the gardens, then?'

'I'll bet it's the same person who's after the boys in the photograph.'

'But why?'

'I don't know. Maybe it's nobody. Maybe just a random skier. Looking for a cat or something.'

'Yes, it certainly was somebody. I just can't fathom why.'

'Maybe the first time was sheer chance. He wanted to check how Hege was doing. And then he caught sight of you. Through the window. And got worried that the renowned Selma Falck was now on the scene. You have a reputation, you know. But as I write in *The Investigator's ABC*, such things often cause an investigation to grind to a halt. Forget those fucking footprints. Now I think I really do need some sleep.'

He shook a pillow that had once been white. Now the colour was indefinable, a brownish-grey batik pattern. Einar plumped up the pillow and laid it down between the stones.

'Maybe he didn't like the idea of you working on Hege's case. He's probably heard of you.'

'Everyone's heard of me. But why ...'

'I need to sleep,' Einar told her, and stretched out.

He closed his eyes and tried to find a comfortable position where he could find rest.

'You don't need to watch over me now,' he whispered. 'The gypsies have gone. I did the right thing, didn't I? It was right to kill him?'

Selma had scrambled to her feet. She folded the pale-blue blanket and placed it on a stone so close to him that he would be able to reach it without getting up.

'You did the right thing, Einar. The bastard deserved to die.'

THE MANUSCRIPT

701 INTERIOR, THERAPY ROOM, HOLMENKOLLEN, EVENING

Spacious room with physiotherapy equipment. A WOMAN is lying face down on a massage table with her arms by her side. Outside it will soon be completely dark. The wind is howling, and branches of the birch tree outside are striking the window. A MAN dressed in white with black Crocs on his feet is quietly walking around the room.

MAN: November already. Soon be time for the opening of the season at Beitostølen.

WOMAN (muffled from the table): Yes, if I can get this hamstring sorted. It's still bothering me a bit.

MAN: I'm sure we'll be able to sort things out. This is the third treatment. Nothing is torn.

The MAN opens a drawer, takes out a tube. Squeezes out a good dose of cream into his left hand, puts the tube back in the drawer, locks it and approaches the table.

WOMAN: It felt better after the last time, but it's still a bit tight. Here.

The WOMAN touches the back of her thigh, and pinches it.

WOMAN: What are you using?
MAN: Some oil.
WOMAN: Can I see the bottle?

The MAN grabs a large bottle of massage oil from a bench. The WOMAN raises her head, looks at the bottle, and lies down again. The MAN pours some of the oil into his hand, mixes it with the cream he has already squeezed out, and starts to massage her. Vigorous, slow strokes. The WOMAN moans from time to time, but is otherwise completely silent.

702 INTERIOR, CORRIDOR, HOLMENKOLLEN, EVENING

The same MAN walks through a bright, long corridor. Art on the walls. Glass walls at both ends of the corridor. The DIRECTOR OF FINANCE dashes out through an office door, nods briefly and rushes towards a door marked with an icon for the men's toilets. He enters. The MAN sees that the office door has been left open. Hesitates for a moment, before his face takes on a determined expression. Goes in and closes the door behind him.

703 INTERIOR, OFFICE, HOLMENKOLLEN, EVENING

Close-up of the MAN's hands. Writing down two series of numbers on a Post-It. Puts an official document back in a drawer, heads quickly to the door as he stuffs the note into his breast pocket. Looks relieved, almost triumphant, as he steps outside, as if something he had thought might be difficult has turned out to be straightforward. He leaves the door open and hurries away in the opposite direction from where the DIRECTOR OF FINANCE had disappeared.

THE POKER TURK

The doorbell rang.

Darius wailed with displeasure and jumped down from the bed. Selma scrambled out of a deep sleep and the cosy quilt. She grabbed a T-shirt and hopped into a pair of trousers on her way to the door. The only person who knew she lived here was Jan Morell.

'You could just have phoned,' she said as she opened the door.

'Hello there!' said the Poker Turk.

He was holding up an old car key.

'The Amazon,' Selma said, sounding confused.

'Yip. It's parked in Hesselbergs gate. In front of number six. Just down the road from here. With brand spanking new winter tyres. I changed the spark plugs too. And the oil. The brake fluid. More or less a full service. Plus I installed a DAB adapter. The FM band is dead nowadays, you know.'

He gave a broad grin. His brilliant white teeth were all at sixes and sevens inside his mouth.

'I realize you're a bit short of money,' he said, winking. 'Pay me back when you can afford it. Or not. All the same to me.'

Selma tried to shake herself properly awake.

'It can't stay here in Løkka,' she told him. 'It'll be stolen. Would you like to come in?'

He shook his head.

'Have to go. I fitted an alarm as well.'

He handed her the key, which had acquired a fob.

'You just press here ...'

A long, slim index finger sporting two silver rings showed her how the alarm functioned.

'And here when you're locking it. Alarms aren't terribly effective, but they're better than nothing. And you'll need the car now and again. A nuisance to pick it up from my place every time. Will I see you soon?'

Selma was still struggling to stay wide awake.

'Sure,' she mumbled. 'Thanks a million.'

'Anything for you, Selma. Anything for the best lawyer in the world.'

With a toss of the head, he thrust his hands into his jacket pocket and rushed down the little staircase, past the mailboxes and out.

KARMA

This wasn't how the manuscript was supposed to end.

Not like this.

The man with the thick grey hair snatched up the sheaf of papers and hugged them close. Several pages escaped his embrace and fell to the kitchen floor. He bent down and tried to pick them up, but dropped several more. And then even more. He released his grip, and let the nearly 150 pages cascade to the floor.

'Not like this,' he said in despair, searching for the final pages in the chaotic pile of paper. 'Not like this. Not like this. Not like this.'

They were supposed to meet up, all of them. In section twelve. The very last episode.

Jan Morell, Arnulf Selhus, Morten Karlshaug and himself. They were to come together when the three of them had received their punishment. People should pay the accurately devised, exactly allotted, and surgically precise penalty they deserved. He had spent two months measuring it all out – they would learn how everything could fall apart and the world go to hell while it still went on spinning as if nothing had happened.

As if everything was just as before, even though nothing actually was.

He had discovered their weaknesses. Their greatest fears. Jan Morell's was obvious to anyone who paid attention. Morten Karlshaug himself had spoken of his unbearable claustrophobia in an interview in the *New York Times* in 2011. It had been harder to find out what Arnulf Selhus was most afraid of, but rumours circulated about him just like everyone else.

In the end he had been certain.

They would sit down when it was all over, according to the manuscript, around the circular kitchen table. No one would have the superiority that sitting at the top of the table would confer. Not even himself. They should all be equals when they met. All four should have suffered the same loss, felt the same pain.

The manuscript was finished and everything should proceed as he had decided.

The last episode was a chamber play.

He couldn't find the end. The pages had all got mixed up. They had slid out, he tried to push the pages together with his palms, but they were jumbled up. Became crumpled. Furious, he snatched at the papers, put them on the kitchen table, one and two and three at a time, in a mishmash strewn on the tabletop, and it was impossible to locate the final pages.

The perfect conclusion.

The manuscript was entitled *Karma*, and it was all about balance.

About equilibrium in the universe. About justice, about no one getting more than they deserved, neither of happiness nor torture. They should discuss things. All four of them; he had spent an entire week on the dialogue in the concluding section of the manuscript. It dealt with what they had done, insisting that no one could get away scot-free. With the interaction between actions and consequences, a logical argument of the natural world that was impossible to escape. He had marked the kitchen table with the points of the compass.

E, W, S and N: he had inscribed them with painstaking accuracy where the compass had shown where the letters should appear.

Karma.

Action. Deeds. Implementation. But primarily the motive behind the choices you made in life. The consequences that flowed from them, the response the circumstances gave to an individual's behaviour.

His motives were noble. He wanted to bring balance. For forty years he had meekly accepted his fate. He had been robbed of his life when only seven years old, and nevertheless continued to exist without complaining. No protest. With head bowed, he had always done as he should. His duty. He was skilled at his job, but never said much. His life fell silent when everything went wrong, and remained silent as he grew up. He sought solitude wherever it could be found. He went fishing. Hunting. Always alone. He had borne his sorrow, accepted his loss and played as well as he could the cards life had dealt him.

His reward had come late, but it had been worthwhile.

He was so little when it had all happened. Everything became chaos and darkness, and all of a sudden he was moved away. He had no idea who they were, the three boys he had seen in the woods. The three nameless skiers who had sealed his family's fate one day after Christmas in 1977 had long ago been reduced to faceless, vague contours. The only thing he remembered after all those years was a ski helmet, until a photograph in a newspaper, almost exactly forty years later, gave him the answer to the question he had never quite dared to ask.

Fate decreed it. The black Madshus skis in the Ski Museum, with the King and Jan Morell laughing in front of the display case, was his reward for all those silent years.

A memory had been unleashed.

It was pure karma.

A fortnight of thorough searching later, he had found the names of the other boys, in a photograph in the National Library database, where there were complete annual volumes from the time when *Dagsavisen* had been called *Arbeiderbladet*. Jan Morell was even wearing the ski helmet and looked unmistakable.

The boys looked happy in the picture.

One of them was laughing. The others were smiling. They were grinning at the photographer after completing the Grenaderløpet ski race from Hakadal to Asker.

The man with the shock of silver hair sat down on one of the chairs.

N was written on the table in front of him.

North, where according to the manuscript he was supposed to sit, but the script was now a mess, and he couldn't find the ending.

It had all been karma.

Nearly everything. It had been so easy. So unexpectedly easy. Even the bank account numbers that he hadn't quite known how to get hold of, had beckoned to him like the working girls in Bankplassen when the Finance Director's door had been left open. It had taken him less than a minute to find the list of accounts for the entire Selhus family; it had been in the top, lockable drawer of the desk. Which had been left unlocked.

The man was only going to pay some accounts, after all.

Karma.

He already had Haakon Holm-Vegge's bank details, from the repayment of a casual loan during a trip eighteen months ago. If the auditor or anyone employed in the finance department, contrary to expectation, didn't uncover what Arnulf had apparently done, then the punctilious, argumentative skier with a bachelor's degree in economics would very likely sound the alarm.

If even he overlooked Arnulf's transgressions, then the man with the grey hair would rouse the sleeping dog himself. He would alert Jan Morell.

Anonymously, of course.

Creating the fake invoices had been a piece of cake.

Everything was fate, everything was karma, and he had bought two tubes of Trofodermin and brought them back from Italy when he had learned, following the near-catastrophe with Hedda Bruun, what the ointment contained. He had only just made a start on the manuscript then, but he had realized that he would find a use for the cream. Karma.

Three treatments with the ointment on Hege Morell's thigh had turned out to be sufficient.

Karma.

He had placed the second tube at the bottom of Hege's sponge bag prior to the World Championship weekend in Lillehammer. He had hoped for a random search as soon as the result of the urine sample was made known.

Unnecessary, as things had turned out. And stupid. But no harm done.

Selma Falck was a far greater disappointment. She was the only real challenge fate had sent his way in his work of regaining balance. Following a ski trip on Norefjell the day Hege was exposed for all the world to see, he had gone up to Vettakollen to witness Jan Morell's pain. To savour the anguish in the timber villa. He had waited until the journalists got fed up and packed up. Endorphins were pumping through his body as he witnessed the despair in the living room behind the vast panorama window. He had challenged fate by walking all the way across the lawn, but none of the people inside had spotted him.

Selma Falck should not have been there.

She was clever and dangerous.

He had seen her leave, together with Hege, who had been alarmed by the footprints. The ski boots were uncomfortable to drive with, but someone had stolen his trainers while he was out on the slopes.

Selma Falck had taken photos, he saw from his hiding place at the foot of the garden. He had sought refuge there when the two women got up from the settees. She had followed his footprints, but not all the way down to where he stood in the shadows holding his breath.

Karma.

Since then he had collated a folder of material on her. Considered including her in the manuscript. Hesitated, and decided against it. He had seen her house. Seen her son, he assumed, through the window on the upper floor, and an old woman in the kitchen, cooking pancakes for supper.

He had gone there on his roller skis. In December he went for lengthy runs every other day and could just as easily make use of the excursion. He had visited her house to get a look at her, but she wasn't there. However, he knew where she lived and had almost written her into his manuscript.

His back had never given him any problems, but in order to look after the prisoner in the basement he had taken some sick leave.

'Not this,' he moaned, slapping his hand on all the paper in front of him. 'Not this. Not this.'

Everything was off balance, because the prisoner had died. No one was meant to die.

With Haakon's surprising accident, fate had taken a staggering turn, but the man with the silver hair had no idea what had occurred. Nor did it concern him.

Karma, he thought, and grew livid at the thought of Haakon's mother.

Vanja Vegge.

'*Cunt*,' he shrieked in a falsetto.

She had let him go. Turned her back on him when he needed her most. Rejected him, the way he was always overlooked and rejected by women.

By women he came close to, quietly and always in vain.

By his mother, who had let him move away with his father, far away from everything that was familiar and true.

By Vanja Vegge, when he had finally found someone to talk to. Someone who understood him and listened instead of turning away.

'First-class cunt,' he said loudly and harshly in order to bite off a rage so red it made him dizzy.

Leaving behind the chaos of paper, he went down into the basement and opened his gun cabinet. He took out his big game rifle and crossed to the ammunition chest. Grabbed what he needed.

For a minute or two he stood examining the pictures. A large cross was drawn above Morten Karlshaug's face. That morning, he had hung up a picture of Vanja Vegge beside the three men.

He ran his finger between the photographs. Back and forth. In the end he slammed it down on Arnulf Selhus's forehead.

'You first,' he said. 'Then the others.'

THE FUNERAL

A shabby, sparse crowd of people stood outside the little chapel at Østre Gravlund graveyard. It had stopped raining. Fortunately the temperature had still remained on the right side of zero degrees Celsius. All the same, a bitter wind accelerated through Groruddalen, making the mourners at the funeral turn their backs to the north.

It was all over, and two members of the press had managed, despite all the secrecy and bringing forward the appointed time, to find out about the diversionary tactics. The photographers, however, kept a respectful distance from the bleak, box-like building.

Vanja Vegge and Kristina Holm were clutching their order of service leaflets as the coffin containing Haakon's remains was carried out to a waiting hearse. Psalms had been sung and speeches delivered. Haakon was described as a fantastic partner and father, a considerate son and a brilliant skier of several years standing.

No one had mentioned anything about doping.

Selma had felt ill throughout the service, as she always did at funerals. It was as if the glass globe around her, the barrier that made it completely impossible to be entirely present in other people's lives, grew larger and thicker on occasions such as this. Naturally, she knew the etiquette. She did everything correctly. Squeezed hands that had to be squeezed and embraced anyone who needed that sort of thing. She had been out in plenty of time and knew that she couldn't leave until Vanja and Kristina indicated that they wanted to go home. All the same, it was as if all her muscles were urging her to leg it. Death had an insistent proximity, she knew; it created a forced sense of fellowship, an awkward intimacy that only made her feel a strong compulsion to escape as quickly as possible. Besides, funerals were not the place to be when you didn't even have the ability to cry.

The funeral reception had been cancelled, thank God.

Haakon's mothers looked so diminished. Even Vanja who, in addition to being too heavy, was also tall and stately, had withered away entirely in her unfamiliar, dark, monochrome clothes. First the shock of their son's death, then the viewing on Monday and the memorial ceremony in Maridalen the following day: it had all become too much for them both.

Although their sorrow would never end, their mourning had by now worn them out completely, Selma thought.

Elise stood like a pillar of salt beside the hearse. Her father had his arm around her. Little William was held in his grandmother's arms and was laughing. He had been given a new fire engine for the occasion, fortunately with no sirens. Selma couldn't understand why they had brought him with them. He was far too young to be able to remember anything of the service, and it couldn't be good for him to see his mother in such a state of collapse as she had been inside the chapel.

At last the coffin was safely inside the hearse. Those nearest went across and laid a final hand on the coffin lid. Selma withdrew as far as possible, back into the throng that could barely number more than forty or fifty people. Not a soul from the Cross-Country Skiing Federation, as Vanja had refused to invite them. Selma's hope was that the close relatives had by now had their fill of hugs, and that she could just shuffle off to her Amazon without having to say her goodbyes. She had parked on the other side of the E6 and Strømsveien, and it was quite a distance to walk to the closest footbridge.

She very nearly succeeded. The hearse rolled slowly away en route to the crematorium at Alfaset. Elise's father, sister and two brothers escorted Vanja, Kristina and Elise to the relatives' car park beside the chapel. Selma turned up the collar of her coat and pretended to accompany a group of elderly women who seemed to be walking in the same direction as her.

In the corner of her eye, she noticed that Elise had broken away from the family group.

And was heading straight for Selma.

The impulse to break into a run was almost irresistible. Instead, she stopped and turned towards the brand-new widow with a sympathetic expression on her face.

'You were wrong,' Elise said sotto voce, as she came to a halt.

'About what?'

'Haakon *was* unfaithful. I'm not going to tell anyone else. Vanja and Kristina, Mum and Dad, they don't have to know. But you were wrong, you see.'

Elise was also bereft of make-up today. Her pallor was almost transparent. She was the only one in the entire mourning procession who was dressed in light-coloured clothes – a beige coat, pale brown trousers and a mohair scarf in the same shade as her coat.

It all matched perfectly.

'I'm sorry to hear that, Elise.'

'Sure. Do you want to know who it is?'

Certainly not, Selma wanted to yell, but instead she put her hand on Elise's arm.

'This is neither the time nor the place,' she said gently. 'If you like, I can call in on you some day next week. Then we can have a chat, just you and me. It's probably all a misunderstanding, and ...'

'Sophie Selhus,' Elise said, slightly too loudly.

A married couple Selma recognized as Vanja and Kristina's neighbours across the hall, walked past arm in arm. They stopped and stared for a second, before the man dragged his wife onwards.

'The ballet dancer,' Elise added.

Quite unnecessarily, as Selma was well aware who Sophie Selhus was. Her brain had taken an unexpected, sudden nap.

'What did you say?' was all she could utter.

'Sophie Selhus. Haakon has always thought her so *beautiful*.'

The word was spat out in a cloud of contempt.

'He's given her presents. Very expensive presents. Including an iPhone X and a MacBook.'

'How on earth do you know that? What in ...'

Selma shook her head ferociously. Her brain needed a jump-start.

'Look here,' Elise said, her short-lived anger turning to tears.

She held out her own iPhone.

Selma looked at the display.

It showed a map, with the location of several Apple devices.

'*Find my iPhone*,' she muttered. 'I don't understand ...'

'There,' Elise said, pointing. 'Stølsveien. That's where the new laptop is. At Sophie Selhus's house. I've been longing for a new MacBook for a year now. Haakon said it was an unnecessary extravagance. And then he goes and buys one and gives it to ...'

She flung out her left hand to cover her face and bowed her head.

A switch was flicked on. Selma took a deep breath and stood there without saying a word. Without thinking. She tried to set her brain loose, to let her thoughts fall into place where they should be, all by themselves. She had plenty of them, far too many; for more than a week now she had constructed theories and built plans and tried to force everything down into a template where they didn't fit.

A picture was emerging.

'That function,' she said abruptly, trying to make eye contact. 'Hey, look at me, please.'

Elise let go of her own face and looked up.

'Does it work only when the device is turned on?'

The girl nodded.

'It has to be connected to the internet.'

Selma gulped, cleared her throat and took Elise's hands in hers.

'So that location means it's switched on right now?'

'Yes, it would be on the list if it was switched off, but not visible on the map. I discovered this yesterday. Early this morning it was disconnected, but now it's in use again.'

She sobbed.

'She's using it now, Selma. In the middle of Haakon's funeral.'

'Haakon hasn't given Sophie Selhus a laptop,' Selma said quietly, slowly and clearly, without letting go of Elise's hands. 'He wouldn't have registered the machine to himself if he intended to give it to her. You're going crazy with fear and grief, Elise. Sophie Selhus is an adult, she can probably set up a computer herself and anyway, she lives in an apartment in Vika. Not at her father's house. Think about it, Elise. You're totally mistaken. I'll sort all this out, but you have to believe me. You're feeling bad enough without ...'

'Is that true? Do you promise to ...'

'Yes. See you later. I must run.'

She was already five metres away, dashing at top speed towards her car.

THE FIXER

If Karsten Kvelde had worked for an American, he'd have been called a fixer. At MCV, his title was 'security consultant'. In reality, he was Jan Morell's private detective.

Most of what Karsten Kvelde did was legal. When, on some rare occasion, he was forced to stretch a rule or break a law, generally in the form of hacking, he was unusually proficient at covering his tracks. He had been employed at MCV for eight years now and hadn't aroused as much as a single suspicion. Far less a complaint. Generally he found his work at MCV lacking in challenge, sometimes bordering on humdrum. He was a trained police officer and had a degree in business economics from Norway and in computer engineering from the USA, and had earlier worked as a security officer on an oil rig in the Gulf of Mexico as well as a refinery outside Cape Town. At the age of forty he had received an offer from Jan Morell, which, from a pecuniary point of view, had been impossible to refuse.

The assignment he had been given yesterday by his employer had once again been disappointingly simple. When he approached his boss's office, as usual immaculately dressed in a dark suit, white shirt and with black Brunello Cucinelli shoes on his feet, he was carrying a leather documents case under his arm. It contained ten sheets of paper. He knocked on the door of the top-floor office in the south wing of the Fornebuporten building and entered when he heard permission granted.

Jan Morell glanced up from his work and gave a peremptory nod.

'Did it go OK?'

'Yes,' Karsten Kvelde said, placing the case in front of his boss before standing with his hands behind his back on the other side of the desk. 'Would you like a verbal summary?'

Jan opened the case and flicked quickly through the papers before closing it again.

'Yes, please.'

'Everyone on your list knew that Hedda Bruun had almost come into contact with a banned substance after a mistake made by the national team's doctor at the gathering in Italy. So, they had easy access to an illegal drug bought over the counter. I've charted their movements, finances and any other circumstances that might be felt relevant.'

He coughed quietly behind a closed hand.

'The five trainers have been everywhere with the national team since Italy. No irregular trips, meetings, flings or anything.'

He raised his eyebrows and paused for a moment.

Jan nodded briefly and made an impatient gesture with his hand.

'Bottolf Odda was in Italy at the gathering prior to the start of the season,' Karsten Kvelde continued. 'He also went to the opening of the cross-country World Cup in Ruka in the last weekend of November, but was in Norway during the competitions in Davos last weekend. It was planned that he should go, and he had a couple of important meetings arranged there, but because of your daughter's drugs case, he stayed at home.'

'Anything else out of the ordinary?'

'Nothing.'

'Go on.'

'Astrid Beita, the cook, hasn't been on any trips since Italy. Normally she just travels during the most important championships. The Olympics and the World Championships. Allowing her to travel to northern Italy was really a sort of … reward. She lives with her husband and two teenage children in Tåsen. Works part-time in a catering company. Her husband's a plumber, nothing irregular about their finances.'

Again he cleared his throat. Jan Morell had opened the documents case once more. He sorted out the sheets of paper that dealt with the ones Karsten Kvelde had already run through.

'Knut Vetle Nilssen,' he read from the next sheet. 'Born 23 August 1970.'

'Yes. Unmarried, lives in Maridalen. He's been on partial sick leave since ...'

'Wait. Is his middle name Vetle?'

'Yes. That's usually a Norwegian form of "junior", isn't it? Maybe not so common to use it as an adult?'

Jan raised his right hand without taking his eyes off the sheet of paper.

Karsten Kvelde remained dutifully silent as Jan read it.

'Currently on sick leave,' he mumbled.

'Yes. He went with them to Beitostølen, but has been in Oslo since then. He's worked part-time, roughly fifty per cent, up at the Federation. His sick leave is coded L02, which means "Back symptoms/problems". Paradoxical for a physiotherapist, perhaps. And a yoga practitioner.'

He allowed himself a little smile, but it disappeared in a flash.

'Sometimes he has half days,' he continued. 'Occasionally he works every second day. He's treated all the senior skiers, of both sexes, all autumn. Apart from Haakon Holm-Vegge. Haakon preferred someone else.'

'Apart from Haakon,' Jan repeated in a murmur. 'I already knew that.'

Karsten Kvelde waited. Jan went on sitting with the same sheet of paper in his hand. For a long time, before suddenly relegating it to the bottom of the pile, asking: 'Stian Bach?'

The security consultant smiled.

'He keeps going the way he started. No sign that he's been relieved of any duties or reprimanded in any other way for the incident down there. Apart from that the newly appointed doctor, Vibeke Stenshaug, makes his job somewhat easier. There hasn't been more to do, to put it that way. I can't find anything unusual about Bach's finances. He earns one point eight million kroner a year at the Federation.'

'Bloody hell,' Jan said, still without looking up.

'In private practice, as a pulmonologist and specialist in internal medicine, assuming he had a public office, a man of his age could rake in double that sum.'

'Pulmonologist. I could just imagine it, yes. Women?'

'Not from what I was able to find out in twenty-four hours. Married to a nurse, three children in their twenties. Lives in Smestad in his own childhood home. I can certainly take a closer look at him, but what I can't find out about romances in twenty-four hours normally isn't worth knowing.'

At last Jan looked up from the leather documents case.

'The regrettable thing about you is that you're so dependent on that fucking computer of yours,' he said. 'If you had a network of contacts like Selma Falck has, and the same instinct she has for how this infernal country of ours is screwed together, I wouldn't need that woman at all.'

'Thanks,' the detective replied curtly, unsure whether Jan Morell had paid him a compliment or not.

'What about Arnulf Selhus?' Jan asked, extracting the last sheet.

'This season, Arnulf Selhus hasn't been on any of the national team's trips. In all likelihood, he doesn't usually go either. He learned about the affair in Italy because a new doctor had to be appointed pronto. Although I don't know for certain, I expect he protested about it. There was no need for any additional doctors, and they're expensive. I assume Bottolf Odda had to tell him the truth.'

'Finances?'

'A bit strained, but fairly tidy. He's acquired too many children over the years. The eldest is twenty-six, and the youngest only three. Storm Teodor.'

Again a fleeting, restrained smile.

'Naturally, I've not gone in and had a look at the Federation's finances,' he went on. 'That was beyond my remit. However, I've looked at Selhus's own transactions during the past few months. Everything there was above board. Barely keeping his head above water, as I said, but just managing. And then there was maybe one little item.'

'What was that?'

'He received a payment from the Federation at the end of November for seventy-five thousand kroner.'

Jan gave him a sharp look.

'And?'

'It was paid back six days later.'

'And?'

'I assumed therefore that it was a payment made in error. It all went through so quickly that he hasn't gained any interest to speak of for a sum of that size. It looks a bit like an unauthorized loan of some kind, but as I said ...'

'Six days. Payment in error. Unauthorized loan.'

Jan Morell picked up a black Mont Blanc pen. Tapped it lightly on the leather documents case that he had now closed. The detective felt a certain discomfort at the change in his boss's face – an angry flush had become visible beneath the perpetual tan. The pulse on the right side of his throat was noticeable and it was far too fast.

'The payment was also made into a savings account,' he added. 'Not to his current account.'

'A savings account? Are you sure? If it had been an incorrect entry from the Federation, it would surely have gone into his current account? Why would the Federation even have had access to his savings account number at all?'

That had been four question marks in rapid succession, and Karsten Kvelde chose to answer them all by first shrugging his shoulders.

'It was his savings account. If you like, I can take a closer look at the whole thing.'

'Do that,' Jan Morell almost barked at him. 'At once.'

The security consultant nodded and made for the door. Not until he had closed it behind him did it dawn on him that he had forgotten to tell Morell about Arnulf Selhus's trip to Milan with his wife ten days ago. She worked part-time in a boutique in the Paleet shopping arcade in Karl Johans gate and was attending a fashion show in Italy. Karsten Kvelde slowed down a little, but finally set his mind at rest by remembering that everything was written down in the papers his boss had in his possession.

And walked on.

Jan Morell was left sitting on his own, doing nothing but staring out the window for almost half an hour.

Arnulf Selhus had wasted his second chance, and that had to have consequences.

It would have consequences, Jan Morell decided, and stood up to look for an old agreement and promissory note. That Arnulf had obviously had cold feet and paid the money back after a week didn't improve matters in the slightest.

There was never room for a third chance.

Never.

THE ALL-POINTS BULLETIN

It was exactly twelve noon when Selma Falck started the engine of her red Volvo Amazon with black roof and leather seats. She switched on the radio: it was preset on channel P2. She put the car into gear, rolled out of the parking space and listened with only half an ear. Until the news bulletin was almost over.

'*In connection with the death of the cross-country skier Haakon Holm-Vegge, the police are on the lookout for ...*'

Selma turned up the volume.

'*... a Peugeot 206. The colour may be red or burgundy. The car was seen in Maridalen on Friday evening, and police would like to make contact with the owner. Information can be given to the nearest police station or by phone ...*'

Her mobile rang.

Selma put a hand into her bag on the passenger seat. The engine lost power as she fumbled to find her phone and she had to increase speed over an intersection without changing gear.

'Selma Falck,' she said, clamping the phone between her ear and shoulder.

'It's Lars Winther here.'

'Hi. I'm busy right now, driving my car without hands free. Could I call you back later?'

'We still have an agreement, don't we? That I'll get your story when the time comes?'

'Yes. But now ...'

'Haakon's clothes were contaminated.'

'Eh ... what?'

'Forensics have detected Clostebol on his clothing. His underwear.'

Selma almost forgot to turn off from the E6 down on to the Store Ringvei ring road. At the very last minute she wrenched the wheel to make the exit road, to furious honking from a car behind her.

'What do you actually mean by that?' she asked, switching her phone to loudspeaker.

'His underwear was impregnated with Clostebol. I have it from a reliable source in the police. Most likely they won't publicize it yet, but I know they're searching for a number of items of clothing he had stored in the Glass House. Since his wife ... his widow, I mean, is at the funeral, they don't expect to get that done until this afternoon.'

'I'm on my way from there just now.'

'Oh. Eh ... condolences. You were his godmother ...'

The mobile slid down from the dashboard.

'Wait,' Selma said loudly, struggling to get hold of it without having to take her eyes off the road.

It was impossible, and she drove blind on the ring road at ninety kilometres an hour for three whole seconds.

'Now,' she said, out of breath, as she put the phone on her lap. 'Can you hear me?'

'Yes. According to what I've heard, his wife has already had everything Haakon had stored in his locker up there delivered to her.'

'But what does that mean?'

The phone crackled as he gave a hearty laugh.

'That Hege's not the one who was sabotaged, as you theorized, but Haakon! It looks like that, at any rate. He's had his clothes smeared with Clostebol, for fuck's sake! In some substance or other, I don't know which one yet. But we can trade information, Selma. The reason I'm phoning is that I want to ask you about ...'

Selma saw that she was driving at 110 kilometres per hour. An environmental speed limit of 60 had been introduced on 1 November. She braked hard.

'I'll call you later,' she said, and hung up.

Over the course of two days, she had watched a picture slowly take shape. It was no longer just the edge pieces of the jigsaw puzzle that fitted, but the beginnings of a legible picture.

And now it had started to dissipate again.

THE TIP-OFF

As Lars Winther emerged from the *DG* building in Akersgata and began walking towards Grensen, he heard someone shout his name. He stopped and wheeled around.

'Agnes,' he said, smiling at the petite twenty-three-year-old with blue hair in high pigtails.

'Hi there,' she said breathlessly. 'I've found out who sent the text message tip-off about Haakon Holm-Vegge. The editor said you'd just gone out, so I ran to catch you up.'

Lars opened his eyes wide.

'Have you? Good work. How on earth ...'

'Do you really want to know?' she interrupted.

'Eh ... no. Who was it?'

She put her hand down into the back pocket of her black jeans and took out a note.

'Arnulf Selhus,' she read out. 'Director of Finance at the Norwegian Cross-Country Skiing Federation. Here are all the details. Address, phone number, you name it. The guy is probably good at finance, but he's hopeless at covering electronic tracks.'

Lars Winther stared open-mouthed. He gawked at her for so long that she waved the note in front of his eyes.

'Don't you want it?'

Snatching it, he hugged her, lifted the young woman up in the air and planted a big, loud kiss on her cheek.

'Thanks!' he said loudly, laughing.

'Hash tag MeToo,' she answered, beaming from ear to ear.

THE STORY

Selma had turned off from Trondheimsveien and driven into the square in front of the old Aker hospital. She stopped her car at the deserted taxi stand and let the engine idle. Just as she was about to phone Jan Morell, he called her.

'Jan,' she said.

'Selma,' he replied.

'You have to tell me something,' she said. 'It's important.'

'Yes. I'd nearly forgotten. But not quite. It was only one incident among so many other cock and bull stories from that time. And I'd no idea that it might be him. I've met him countless times, Hege uses him you see, but I hadn't a clue that he was the same person as the seven-year-old from that time.'

'What ... what on earth are you talking about?'

'What we did. Klaus, Arnulf and I. You asked if we'd done anything ... illegal.'

'No. I asked if you'd done anything serious towards anyone. Something that could make someone want to ... punish you all.'

'Yes. I was thinking about illegal acts. There were quite a few of those. We pinched a few things here and there, especially me. Vandalized property. Never anything major, but ...'

'Jan,' she broke in. 'What did you do?'

There was silence at the other end. Several times she could hear him take a deep breath, and then not quite know where to begin.

At last the words came tumbling out.

Selma Falck listened to Jan's story for eight whole minutes without interrupting. She put her phone down when he was finished, put the car in gear and then drove as fast as she could to the brown Moelven house in Stølsveien.

THE EMAIL

The front door was slightly ajar. The dogs were not at home. Neither were Benedicte nor little Storm Teodor.

It was of course illegal to enter another person's property even if the doors were lying open. It was not acceptable to walk into other people's homes without ringing the doorbell or announcing your arrival in some other way. It certainly wasn't a good idea to creep about in a strange house in order to look around, but Selma Falck had done all of these things.

And she was now pleased she had thrown caution to the winds, as Arnulf Selhus's family was spared an extremely traumatizing discovery.

He had been shot in the head.

With a gun far more powerful than necessary, in Selma's considered opinion. The entry wound at the back of his head was obvious, and the bullet had taken a bite of the man's face on its way out. At least a third, it looked like, but since the body had fallen forward and lay with the face turned to one side, it wasn't easy to say if anything more was gone. Blood and brain matter had sprayed out over the desk, over the MacBook and also some distance over the white-painted wall the desk was pushed up against. At the far edge of the desk lay an almost intact eyeball.

Until last Monday, Selma had never seen a dead person. Now she had seen two.

This was an execution.

She felt remarkably unmoved.

Resting pulse rate. Clear head. Steady hands as she took out her phone and called the police. Her voice was calm when she introduced herself, explained where she was and what had obviously happened at this address. There was no question of suicide, she said on her own initiative, and if they could hurry, that would be brilliant. Since she was aware the conversation was being recorded, she also added that she had come to have a chat with the now-deceased Director of Finance at the Norwegian Cross-County Skiing Federation, and had heard a suspicious noise. Somewhat indefinable, but disturbing all the same, and it had made her want to check that the occupants of the house were all right.

And so one problem was solved, she decided, as she returned the phone to her coat pocket.

The room was small, maybe ten metres square, and clearly served as a combined guest room and home office. An olive-green settee was placed on the one long wall, while the small desk was on the gable wall furthest away from the door. Only a small, rectangular basement window far up beside the ceiling let what little daylight there was spill into the room.

Flesh and blood had spurted forwards and upwards. Therefore Selma ventured a little closer to the corpse, but at least she didn't step into any of the mess. If asked later why she hadn't just gone out and waited for the emergency services to arrive, she would just explain that she had wanted to check if the man was really dead.

Anyone over the age of ten could ascertain from a distance of five metres that this was a death, but she would blame the fact that she had been so upset.

If anyone, contrary to expectation, might ask her.

There was another computer in the room. A white Dell tower PC sat on the floor beside the right leg of the desk, while the monitor and keyboard were pushed out to the edge of the desk itself.

To make room for the MacBook, Selma realized, as she stepped even closer. The machine actually did not belong in here. It belonged to Haakon Holm-Vegge. To be sure of her case, she dug out a ballpoint pen from her bag. Even though the portable machine had a touchpad below the keyboard, it was apparently connected to an external mouse. At least a slim Magic Mouse lay on the right-hand side of the laptop, slightly slanting, ten centimetres from a dead, clenched fist. He must have let it go before he was shot.

Selma used the pen to touch the mouse.

The machine woke from its slumber.

The screen lock wasn't even activated.

Her eyes ran over the screen image, legible even through the spatters of blood and something Selma assumed was brain matter.

Bingo.

The machine belonged to Haakon. It was never intended for Sophie Selhus, exactly as Selma had argued. The greyish-yellow marker on the left side showed that the sent box was open and in the email, Haakon was entered as the sender.

Arnulf, Selma read.

Now you really must cut this out. For over a week I've been patient and waited for you to come up with this 'explanation' of yours. I can't be bothered any longer. I want to be in the clear if any complications crop up concerning this money. DG and several other media outlets have been out to get the Federation for a couple of years now, and sending money at random to people not due to receive it doesn't exactly look very good. Isn't that what they call 'system failure'? I am really furious with the whole lot of you. We skiers are slogging our guts out to produce results year in, year out, and all of you up there in the Crystal Palace can't even keep the formalities in order. I'm not the only one who's starting to get really

annoyed about all the mors you make. You demand everything
from us skiers. That we win. That we think of community and soli-
darity rather than taking out the rewards that the best of us would
actually like as security for the rest of our lives. That's all very well,
but then in return we should have a well-ordered organization.
BLOODY HELL, Arnulf! I'm going to tell Bottolf when I meet him.
He's going to Davos at the weekend, but as soon as he's back I'm
letting him know. This was a matter of more than 53,000 kroner.
And it was with me for a whole week! What if I hadn't discovered
it? And told you? What would have happened if there had been a
sudden inspection of the accounts or something? Typical if it had
been one of us athletes who had to take the rap for your sloppiness
yet again, just like with Martin and that asthma medicine the
Federation was so fucking sure about. It's just as unprofessional to
dish out money to people who're not due to get it. You'll be hearing
from me. Haakon.

The unknown avenger had hit the bull's eye. He had discovered
what Arnulf was afraid of. In Haakon, the avenger had also found
exactly the right piece in a game so ice-cold that Selma caught
herself feeling impressed. She was gripped by an irresistible urge
to delve deeper into the computer.

She heard sirens in the distance.

It was logical that Arnulf Selhus had needed to get hold
of Haakon's laptop when the twenty-six-year-old died. It had
been used to write emails about something that would cost the
Director of Finance money, job and career if it came to light. Jan
Morell gave people a second chance. Never more than one, as he
had made crystal clear to Selma several times in the past week.
He would not have been interested in excuses.

But maybe explanations.

Selma wasn't entirely sure, but Arnulf had obviously not dared
to take a chance on talking his way out of it all.

The sirens were approaching.

Without hesitating, Selma grabbed the mouse. Clicked on the trashcan.

It contained two emails, both from Haakon to Arnulf.

Arnulf had been busy deleting traces of his correspondence with Haakon when he himself was killed. He was trying to save the situation when he suddenly died.

'But why now?' she whispered to herself. 'Why did he wait for almost a week?'

The doorbell rang.

Selma unbuttoned her coat, grabbed the tail of her black blouse, picked up the computer mouse and wiped it clean. Put it down on the desk without touching it again, and used her own pen to nudge it towards Arnulf Selhus's dead fist.

And left the room.

The police couldn't be more than a couple of minutes away. She hurried to the front door and stopped dead when she saw who was standing in the doorway.

'Lars?'

'Hi ...'

'Arnulf Selhus is dead,' she rushed to tell him. 'He's been shot. In the head.'

The tall man took a step back. He inadvertently lost his footing and his balance on the steps. With an impressive manoeuvre, he seized hold of the railings and managed to avoid taking a tumble. He stared at Selma with a gaze that confused her.

The man was terrified, she realized.

'Not by me, you idiot!'

'Who ... who did it, then?'

'I don't know for certain, but I ...'

An old burgundy-red Peugeot 206 stopped outside the gate. A slim, blonde woman in joggers, running shoes and an all-weather jacket emerged from the driver's seat. She opened the boot and grasped the leads of two English setters that then scampered ahead of her towards the gate. When the woman caught sight of the two individuals on the doorstep, she came to a sudden halt.

Selma darted across the courtyard.

'Benedicte,' she said, with no idea how to continue.

She put her hand on the bolt that held the two parts of the gate together and closed it. Her hand was still aching, and both little fingers had turned dark-blue overnight.

'Have you spoken to Arnulf?' Benedicte Selhus asked, with an apologetic smile. 'He's still at home, isn't he? He's usually at work at this time, of course, without a doubt, but he was so pleased when I called him about a laptop I'd found that he came home to pick it up. He got a new one last week, you see, but it had disappeared. Did you get a chance to talk to him? Sorry I was a bit abrupt yesterday.'

She reached out for the bolt. Selma's hand was still covering it. A stab of pain passed through her sore little finger when Benedicte tried to push her hand away.

'Can I come in, if you don't mind?' she said, and an irritated frown appeared between her eyebrows.

'Where had the laptop been?'

The setters whimpered.

'Sorry, but could you let me through to my own house, please?'

The police patrol car appeared from a northerly direction. The blue lights swept ever-closer and were already casting ice-cold reflections on the wet asphalt only twenty metres away from the two women. All of a sudden the sirens were cut off as the car parked. Lars Winther had also come down to the gate by now, and Benedicte Selhus's eyes darted in fear from the two interlopers to the patrol car and back again.

'Benedicte,' Selma said, holding her tightly by the arm. 'Where did you find the laptop?'

'Under Storm Teodor's bed! Silly Arnulf hadn't turned on the screen lock, so Storm Teodor had hidden it and had a great time. There were no games on it yet, but he had learned how to access NRK-Super. He's actually very advanced for his age, and had managed to plug it in and everything, and ...'

Selma released her grip. Three policemen marched towards them and the wail of another siren pierced through the bleak grey afternoon.

'Arnulf was over the moon,' Benedicte said, looking at the police. 'I found it this morning when I vacuumed the floor. He thought it had been stolen. But ... what's actually going on here?'

'Who owns that car?' one of the police officers asked brusquely as he approached.

He grabbed his shoulder and said something Selma couldn't catch over the police radio.

'My husband's son,' Benedicte said, by now as disconsolate as she was confused. 'We've borrowed it for a couple of weeks because the dogs make such a mess in our expensive cars in this disgusting weather.'

She drew the dogs closer to her and burst into tears. The noise from the approaching police cars was unbearable, and she called out in despair: 'Could someone please tell me what's happening?'

THE SHOT

S elma enjoyed being with Lars Winther.

They were using each other. He was useful to her and she to him, and there was nothing more than that between them. They were bound to each other by an unwritten contract that either of them could break without any advance warning.

She wished it could be like that with everyone.

'Here,' she said, handing him a C4 envelope she had taken out of her bag before they drove off. 'Give that to your wife. Didn't you say she works in the news section?'

'Eh ... yes. What is it?'

'A description of how Sølve Bang is trying to swindle Statoil. A blow-by-blow account, fully documented.'

'Eh?'

'Just give it to your wife, won't you?'

It had taken them quarter of an hour to make their escape from Stølsveien. If it hadn't been for the officer in charge recognizing her, they would probably have had to stay there all evening. A female officer, the youngest of all the police personnel that had swarmed on to the property in the course of only a few minutes, had taken Benedicte away in a car, leaving her murdered husband behind.

'You drive really fucking fast,' Lars Winther said, seeming both anxious and impressed.

Selma responded by driving so recklessly on the roundabout at Sinsenkrysset that she nearly scraped the side of a tank truck.

'It was your choice to come with me. Try again, please.'

Pulling on the safety belt, he made another attempt to phone Jan Morell on Selma's mobile.

'Straight to answerphone now too,' he said. 'Do you understand anything at all about this case?'

'Yes.'

'Can you explain to me what's happened, then?'

Selma shifted gear and accelerated as soon as she had passed the speed camera where the motorway continued over a bridge above Nydalen.

'Not really.'

'Not really?'

'Only if it's all off the record.'

'It *is* all off the record. Of course it is. This story exploded well beyond the remit of the sports section long ago. I really just want the lowdown on whatever has to do with the NCCSF, but maybe it's impossible to separate that from ...'

'Everything and nothing,' Selma interjected. 'This case has absolutely everything and decidedly nothing to do with the NCCSF.'

Lars leaned towards the passenger door and stared at her.

'Enlighten me,' he said softly.

'I'm afraid I don't have the full picture as yet.'

'So give me what you have.'

Selma sniffed, changed gear and noted that she was driving at 102 kilometres per hour. Without allowing that to make her apply the brake.

'Both Hege and Haakon are innocent. From a sports law point of view as well. Neither of them personally ingested Clostebol, either by accident or because they wanted to cheat. They've both been sabotaged. By two different perpetrators, and with two different motives. One wanted to avenge an old injustice. The other wanted to save his financial situation, his work and his reputation. His whole existence, in other words.'

She shook her right hand gingerly.

'I've got such a terrible pain in that finger,' she muttered before raising her voice to continue: 'The rumours about Arnulf Selhus, the ones you wanted to dig up at the time you didn't get permission, were true. Jan Morell has held that fact over his head like a sword of Damocles for all these years. Until now, when someone knew how to make use of it.'

Lars appeared increasingly bewildered. He switched on the recorder function on his own mobile and held it up with a quizzical look at Selma.

'Only for my own use,' he said. 'No one else will be allowed to hear it.'

'Fine,' she said, nodding. 'But I can never be quoted on anything. Besides, I stress that there's still a lot I don't know. Some of what I'm saying is pure guesswork. Such as, for example, that Hege's positive test came about as a result of her being massaged with an Italian ointment normally used for cold sores and rashes.'

'What?'

'Trofodermin,' Selma said, enunciating clearly and emphasizing every syllable. 'It's sold over the counter in Italy. Remember the name. It's a medication that will be written into the history of Norwegian skiing in flaming letters. Believe you me.'

'Troformin ... what?'

'Trofodermin. I'm also willing to bet a fair sum of money that the police will find out that Haakon's underwear was smeared with the same cream. All cross-country skiers have their own lockers up in that grand palace there ...'

They had turned off the Store Ringvei ring road towards Slemdal, and she nodded forward, up over the hillside.

'... and it's never been much of a challenge for intruders to open them.'

'So Hege and Haakon both having traces of Clostebol in their bodies is unrelated? It's all ... a coincidence?'

'Again,' Selma said, narrowly averting a skid before the car went out of control, 'both yes and no. The national team's physiotherapist, Knut Nilssen, applied the drug to Hege and killed Arnulf. In turn, Arnulf was responsible for giving the drug to Haakon. Of course, I don't know why, and now that he's dead it's difficult to ask him. All the same, I'll bet it was all an attempt to get Haakon to focus on something other than being an unappointed patrolman at the Cross-Country Skiing Federation. Far more difficult to take on that role if you have a doping charge on the go. Maybe he even killed him. It remains to be seen what the police find out regarding that car he borrowed from his son. Now that they have a specific vehicle to examine, they won't take long to discover whether the car has been in Maridalen at that particular time. And if it's been involved in any kind of collision. But you know ... The worst thing about it all ...'

She heaved a sigh. She was growing increasingly restless as they began to climb the hill and close in on the timber villa in Vettakollen.

'Try one more time,' she told him.

Lars gave it another go.

'Straight to answerphone,' he said apologetically. 'What are you actually afraid of?'

'Something frightening enough to take a random man like you with me to investigate,' she said. 'The worst thing about it all is that there was no intention for anyone to die at all. I think, anyway. I'm pretty certain.'

'I still don't understand any of it. Not a single smidgen.'

Selma did not answer.

'We'll go over it all again later,' she said, driving on in silence.

They approached the house where Hege Chin Morell lived with her dad and her Polish substitute-mum. The gardens grew larger. The trees taller and the fences longer. The clouds were so low above Oslo that Selma felt she could touch them. On an impulse she dropped her speed and parked on the hard shoulder about a hundred metres from the bend where Jan Morell's extensive property began.

Without saying anything, she stepped out of the car. Lars Winther followed suit. They had parked on the south side of the road, where a steep slope led down to a colossal example of functionalist architecture. The owner had improved the outlook by cutting down the trees at the bottom of the plot. Selma stopped unceremoniously and looked across it.

Under the lowering sky, nestled beside the narrow, black fjord and surrounded by slate-grey hills, the lights of Oslo twinkled. Her city looked best from a distance, she thought. A big city that was easiest to live with beyond the city streets. She inhaled the clear, cold air deep into her lungs and felt an indescribable urge to sleep.

They both heard the voice.

Harsh, commandeering, but nevertheless so far away that neither Selma nor Lars could make out what it said.

'What the fuck was that?' Lars exclaimed, as he broke into a run up towards the bend.

Selma slung her bag back in the car and followed him without bothering to lock it.

'Don't come any closer than that!' the voice roared, and Lars stopped suddenly in the middle of the road.

Selma went on. Up the hill, into the little cul-de-sac, right up to the tall Serbian spruce hedge that demarcated the Morell family's property. She ran across to the two roughly carved obelisks that differentiated the driveway from the road.

And stopped all of a sudden.

Jan Morell stood in the middle of the lawn. With his hands partly raised in the air, like a reluctant villain in a Western movie. The voice called out again.

'You're going to say it. You're going to say that you killed my brother.'

'I didn't kill your brother,' Jan answered slowly in a loud voice, as he took a couple of paces forward.

Selma couldn't see the person he was speaking to. She flipped off her high-heeled boots. The ground felt ice-cold through her thin tights, but now she could move soundlessly on the gravel that was laid in the driveway and in a narrow border along the entire hedge and around the tree trunks to prevent the growth of weeds. She also let her coat slide to the ground as she approached the most distant statue, skirted around it and crept into the hedge.

Knut Nilssen was at the foot of the garden. She registered that he was left-handed. The butt of the rifle was leaning on his left shoulder, allowing him to catch sight of her easily if he hadn't already been prepared to shoot, with his left eye fixed on the gun sight.

'Say it!' Knut Nilssen bellowed his command once again and came closer.

His thick, silver-grey hair fluttered in the wind.

Jan raised his hands a bit higher.

'I didn't kill him. We didn't kill him. We tormented him, and I broke his skis. I'm really sorry about that. Terribly sorry, Knut. Put down your gun, and then we can ...'

Knut walked another three steps forward, without lowering his weapon.

'You killed Arne. *You took everything I had from me. Say it!*'

Now he was screaming. Selma tried to move closer, but she had no idea what she could do. Her brain was empty. She wasn't cold, felt nothing in fact, but was struggling with all her might to come up with a plan to do something in this absurd tableau in which Jan Morell might be shot at any moment by a big game rifle on his own frozen lawn in the month of December.

The elk emerged from the woods.

The elk heifer of Vettakollen. A city elk, one of the animals that fed on old apples and carrots left out for them in big gardens. She was used to people, but wary and alert all the same. She was seventeen months old and had managed on her own since spring. No bull had covered her in autumn, she stayed close to the residential area, and human beings had never done her any harm. She didn't like them, but she was curious and extremely hungry. There were carrots here. Usually there were carrots here, and apples that were still juicy and sweet lying on the ground.

'Say it!' Knut Nilssen bawled as he came even closer.

The heifer froze on the spot, Selma saw, but she did not turn away. There were now only about twenty-five metres separating the two men. Knut couldn't possibly miss if he pulled the trigger.

Jan should have done as Knut asked. Jan ought to say it, Selma thought, he must say what he had to, and hope it would be enough. She opened her mouth to shout, but her voice had gone, and the elk heifer was on the move again. Slowly, with a characteristic, majestic gait, the animal stepped across the grass, heading straight for Selma. The carrots and the apple tree were in the middle of the distance between them. Knut still stood with his rifle ready to fire, left-handed, with his body turned towards Selma and his right eye shut.

'I killed Arne Nilssen,' Jan Morell said.

Selma would never be able to recount what happened next in the huge garden on the Morell property that December evening, with rain in the air and a north wind blowing.

The elk was about to step into the line of fire between Knut Nilssen and Jan. It kept moving. And took yet another step.

'I killed your brother,' Jan Morell shrieked, more desperately now.

A shot rang out.

A sharp, menacing report from a Browning .308 rent the air as the elk heifer reached the carrots. The bullet stopped exactly halfway towards its intended target. The elk was hit in the head and fell down dead. The man who fired the shot lowered his rifle. He remained standing in surprise and confusion, still holding the gun, when a woman tackled him, partly from behind, partly from the side, in stockinged feet and with a force he'd never thought possible for a female. The shooter fell. He dropped the rifle, tried to struggle to his feet, but a man came running and launched himself at him as well, and Knut Vetle Nilssen realized he would not be able to escape.

'Pick up the gun,' Lars Winther roared. He had a wrestler's hold on the shooter's neck.

Selma scrambled to her feet. She was shaking. She threw her arms around her body and knew that if it hadn't been for a head-on collision on a handball court in 1986, she would have burst into floods of tears on the spot.

The elk lay lifeless under the apple tree.

Jan Morell picked up the rifle. Emptied the chamber and removed the bolt with accustomed movements. He shoved the ammunition into his pocket and placed the rifle and bolt down on the ground. Then he tore off his cardigan and wrapped it around Selma.

'I think I've won,' she said, her teeth chattering loudly.

'What do you mean?' Jan Morell asked.

'Our bet,' Selma said, only just managing to force a smile.

THE CHRISTMAS PRESENT

Elise Grønn had just closed the door behind her parents when the doorbell rang again. She looked discouraged as she turned back into the hallway – more than anything she wanted to be left completely alone. It had been difficult to convince her parents, which she could understand to some extent, but now they really would have to cut this out.

A strange woman stood on the doorstep.

She was young, dressed in a police uniform, and her handshake was firm when she introduced herself and asked to come in for a minute. She meant it quite literally, and stood right inside the door.

'We found it in your car,' she said softly as she handed Elise a small package.

A Christmas present. The paper was red, with tiny silhouettes of golden angels. The ribbon was also golden, and tied a bit too loose. A card almost as big as the package was attached to the bow.

'What's this?' Elise whispered.

'A Christmas present from Haakon to you. We're not really supposed to hand over anything until all the tests have been completed, but I thought ...'

Elise looked from the package up at the young policewoman, taller than her, with blonde, boyishly cropped hair.

'I lost my husband last year,' the stranger said. 'Nine days before Christmas Eve. So I thought ...'

She swallowed and forced out a smile.

'Haakon was actually knocked down. We're not making it public yet, but it won't be long till we do. I shouldn't really tell you this, but we now know that it was Arnulf Selhus who was driving the car. We've yet to find out whether he had planned the accident.'

'Nine days before Christmas? Did your husband die nine days before Christmas Eve?'

'Yes.'

'Then it was exactly a year ago today.'

'Yes.'

She lowered her eyes. Spoke to the floor.

'I still don't know all the details of his death. Secret service.'

Yet another smile, almost a grimace.

'So I thought you'd want to know as soon as possible. And to have this.'

'Thank you.'

'My pleasure,' said the officer, with a brief nod as she exited through the door that slid shut behind her by itself.

Elise opened the card.

To wonderful Elise from hopeless Haakon, with a promise to be a better husband and father. At least to be around more. Love you. PS: Sorry the cellophane is broken! I wanted to show you I could actually set it up all by myself. Your darling Haakon.

She walked slowly into the living room. Sat down on the big grey settee with the pale-pink cushions and opened her Christmas present. It was an iPhone X, exactly what she had wanted. Switched off, but fully charged, and with a red paper heart stuck on either side of the box to replace the broken seals.

Tears began to trickle down her face, but at the same time she picked up her old mobile from the wooden tray on the footstool and tapped in her sister's number.

She wanted William to come home at once.

SUNDAY 17 DECEMBER 2017

It was now the third Sunday in Advent.

One week left until Christmas Eve, and Selma Falck had bought a little plastic tree for 199 kroner at the Clas Ohlson store. Complete with twinkling lights, it stood on a circular mat that concealed an unsightly stain on the laminate beneath the window.

Einar Falsen sat on a red settee from the sixties, looking around, with a bag of cheese puffs in his left hand. Darius was curled up contentedly in his lap.

'It's really cosy here, Mariska. I could even think of living here, you know.'

'I'll soon be on the move,' she said, smiling, as she sat down beside him and handed him a glass of cola. 'I can see if you can take over the place.'

She had switched on the TV. The flat screen had given Einar a shock as soon as he had shuffled into the living room, but Selma had pulled some fine chicken wire over it in advance, attached with parcel tape at the back. It filters all the radiation, she had told him, beaming, and Einar had accepted the contrivance with more or less good grace. It was seven p.m., and the theme tune for the *Dagsrevy* news roundup was playing. Selma unscrewed the lid of a bottle of Pepsi Max and turned up the volume. The headline story was still the drama at the Norwegian Cross-Country Skiing Federation, Arnulf Selhus's murder and the chaos surrounding the drugs tests on Hege Chin Morell and Haakon Holm-Vegge.

As it had been for three days on the trot.

A lot had already emerged. Until now, the police had been extremely reticent, but *DG* seemed to have incredibly good sources with knowledge of what had actually taken place. So good that Oslo Police District had finally recognized that they would have to take the lid off a little, if they weren't to appear continually on the back foot. To date they had only used spokesmen who were lower down the pecking order. Tonight they had sent the Chief of Police in person, appointed to the post only three months earlier.

She was interviewed immediately after an attempt had been made to summarize the case, in a report that most of all resembled a compendium of the last few days' editions of the *DG* newspaper.

'*The Police Chief of Oslo, Hannelore Lorentzen. Do the police now understand how this story all fits together?*'

The interview was live.

'*Yes,*' she answered, looking the interviewer straight in the eye. '*Of course we don't have all the details, but we're beginning to gain a broad overview. As it turned out, at the perpetrator's house we found ...*'

A tiny hesitation, but her gaze was still steady.

'*... documentation that sheds light on what was planned and how it was carried out. And the motive behind it all.*'

'*What kind of documentation?*'

'*It's too early to ...*'

She broke off, picked up a glass of water and took a drink. Her hand was trembling ever so slightly as she put it back down again.

'*There was actually some kind of manuscript,*' she said.

'*A manuscript?*'

'Go girl,' Selma said, lifting the bottle of Pepsi in a toast. 'Now we're taking the culture of openness seriously!'

'No point in keeping it secret,' Einar replied, nodding, as he crammed cheese puffs into his sore mouth. 'This stings like fuck, but it's good!'

'Yes,' the Police Chief said. '*The accused has written a manuscript in recent months about what had happened and what was going to happen. This documentation is now being examined carefully. In many ways we can say that it forms a unique ... confession. We've also made other very interesting finds at the accused's house. Against the background of these, we believe we can now say with certainty that the thwarting of the intended murder at Vettakollen and the civil arrest of the accused may well have prevented additional murder attempts to the one at that location.*'

'What? Who, then?'

Hannelore Lorentzen grasped the glass again and took a long drink.

'*I would like to request you to respect the fact that, out of consideration for the ongoing investigation, we cannot give any further particulars.*'

'Vanja,' Selma said under her breath. 'Lars Winther whispered in my ear that Knut Nilssen planned to kill Vanja too. That will come out soon enough.'

'*Several media outlets have today claimed that the death of Morten Karlshaug is also linked to this case. Can you tell us anything more on that subject?*'

The Police Chief picked up the glass again, but put it down when she realized it was empty.

'*I can only confirm that, as of today, we have a strong suspicion that we are talking about the same perpetrator.*'

'Knut Nilsson, then?'

She nodded almost imperceptibly.

'But what on earth was his motive?'

'I can't say anything further about that at present.'

She hesitated for a moment, and then continued: 'To all appearances, we're dealing here with some kind of vendetta. Concerning something that happened a long time ago. I can't tell you any more than that.'

'As far as Haakon Holm-Vegge's death is concerned, have you come any further to reaching an explanation for that?'

'We have discovered that a burgundy-red Peugeot 206, driven by the now-deceased Arnulf Selhus, was in Maridalen when Haakon Holm-Vegge ran off the road and had an unfortunate accident. More than that I can't say, other than that the cause of death has been ascertained. He drowned.'

'Can you also say something about the drugs tests on the two athletes, Hege ...'

The Police Chief raised both hands.

'As far as that is concerned, a great deal of technical investigation remains to be undertaken. We will not comment on that aspect of this complex case for three weeks at the earliest.'

'But the Norwegian Cross-Country Skiing Federation has already confirmed that they intend to request that Anti-Doping Norway rescind ...'

Now she shook her head and interrupted him again.

'I can state that those involved in the upper echelons of sport already believe they have documentary evidence showing that the two athletes were sabotaged, and therefore are innocent according to the organization's own regulations, but the purely criminal aspects are for the police to deal with. And we have nothing more to add in relation to that. As yet.'

'Do you believe that Haakon was knocked down?' Einar asked as he turned the bag of cheese puffs upside down to find that it was and would remain empty.

'Well, a situation did certainly arise that got his dander up. On the film clip we see him lashing out at the car with his pole. It could have knocked him off balance, at the very least.'

'But did Arnulf Selhus drive up to Maridalen that night in order to kill him?'

'We'll probably never know. What we do know for sure, however, is that Arnulf actually bought three tubes of Trofodermin when he was in Milan with his wife a fortnight ago. The police said so this morning. In all likelihood it will turn out that he was the one who tried to make it look as if Haakon was taking drugs. He had access to the locker room; he had the means as well. If Haakon were still alive, his focus would probably have been one hundred per cent on exonerating himself from a charge of cheating. Not running to Bottolf with a complaint about a payment made by mistake that had already been cleared up. Discrediting your accusers is a strategy as old as the hills.'

The TV was now broadcasting interviews with various representatives of Norwegian sport.

A children's ski coach in the Heming IL sports club was very shaken, and the treasurer of the BUL sports club was almost speechless at what had happened. Three fourteen-year-olds on skis in Granåsen were more concerned about the arrival of snow in Trøndelag.

'But what do *you* think?' Einar insisted.

'Well, Arnulf may have been in Maridalen just by chance. He had the dogs with him, and they had to be walked regardless of the weather. Maybe he drove there because he knew Haakon would be in that particular area. I've always thought that Vanja's son shares too much information, and he had put out a selfie on Instagram before setting off on his training session.'

She made to pick up her phone, but caught herself just in time.

'#notbadweatherjustunsuitableclothes and #notexactlyawimp.

Plus #allalongMaridalen, so there was no doubt about where he was going.'

Sighing, she shook her head.

'The police will get to the bottom of it.'

'Yes, I suppose so. The Selhus guy is dead anyway. Got his comeuppance, if I may say so. And that Knut Nilssen, too. He seems even crazier than me, from what they write about him. Waited forty years and then ... Bang! You know, if you set out on revenge, then dig a grave for two!'

Einar gave a toothless grin.

'Is that a snippet of Buddhist philosophy?' Selma asked with a smile.

'No, James Bond. Are we eating anytime soon?'

'The pizza's in the oven.'

'Jan Morell!' Einar called out enthusiastically, pointing at the screen.

The reporter's voice was talking to an image of Jan Morell as he approached the entrance of the NRK building in Marienlyst.

'Financier Jan Morell, father of Hege Chin Morell and himself the victim of a murder attempt last Friday, is very critical of the NCCSF's handling of the case against his daughter.'

Cut to Jan Morell, now making his way along NRK's internal corridors.

'An extraordinary general meeting for cross-country skiing should be called,' he said firmly.

'He looks totally exhausted,' Selma whispered. 'He seems diminished, somehow.'

'Is it correct to call him a financier?' Einar asked. 'Isn't it just a fucking enormous consultancy company he runs?'

'Shh.'

'*This case has demonstrated that the systems surrounding athletes, when it comes to the danger of being innocently caught by the doping regulations, fall very short. We have seen that the Federation has no procedures or culture designed to look after their athlete's interests when anything goes wrong. Personally, I'm of the opinion that the doping regulations should be changed. The athletes quite simply cannot live with an almost total absence of legal safeguards. The Norwegian Cross-Country Skiing Federation may be of a different opinion. But they must, as soon as possible, work out and implement systems that in the first place will prevent cases like the one we have just witnessed, and secondly take care of the athletes when things go wrong. For this to happen, they must gather some courage. In order to stand up to the inflexible anti-doping bureaucracy. That Anti-Doping Norway and WADA are fighting a battle we all support, countering the practice of cheating in sport, must not mean that they can escape fair criticism.'*

Jan ran a stubby finger under his nose before he went on: *'As we know, courage is difficult to come by when you don't have the aptitude for it. That's why it's imperative to clear out the whole tier of management at the Federation. And it will be entirely natural to start with the Cross-Country President, Bottolf Odda.'*

'Do you intend to take the initiative in such a process yourself?'

'Yes. Definitely. But first of all my daughter has to be accepted back into the national team. She's going to take part in the Winter Olympics in PyeongChang.'

A grim, faint smile appeared before the broadcast was cut off.

'Jan should never have said that,' Selma commented, shaking her head. 'It could be detrimental to Hege. Mark my words!'

In the next item, Bottolf Odda was seated on his office chair in the NCCSF's iconic building in Holmenkollen, leaning back casually. He had taken off his jacket and had his hands folded over his corpulent belly.

'What this case shows very clearly is that our systems function.

Exactly as they are supposed to do. No one can guard against criminals.'

'But shouldn't you have held open the possibility that Hege Morell was telling the truth when she protested her innocence?'

'We have supported Hege in every possible way. Naturally, we don't have an investigative apparatus, and we are bound by the laws of sport to follow a certain protocol in such instances. Which have now led to the case being cleared up.'

'But surely it wasn't the NCCSF that cleared ...'

'As I said,' Bottolf Odda broke in, *'we don't have anyone employed at the Federation in an investigative role. That would have looked good, wouldn't it? But we have initiated and followed the necessary procedures to have the charges against Hege Morell withdrawn.'*

'So she's welcome back into the national team?'

'Of course.'

Now he was no longer smiling.

The oven pinged from the kitchen. Selma switched off the TV and got to her feet.

The doorbell rang.

'Wait,' she shouted as she ran into the kitchen, took the pizza out of the oven and emerged into the hallway again.

Opened the door.

'Hello,' Jan Morell said. 'How are your hands doing?'

He was wearing the same clothes as they'd seen on the TV. He was carrying a slim leather portfolio under his arm.

'They're sore. But I'll survive.'

Selma left the door open and headed back into the living room. Jan Morell followed her. He stopped suddenly when he saw an elderly man in long, grubby underpants sitting in Selma's living room. On his head the man wore a big hat with earflaps sticking out on either side. The horrible cat was on his lap, glowering at Jan.

'Meet Einar,' Selma said casually. 'Einar Falsen. My best friend. Would you like some pizza?'

'No thanks. I just came to give you this.'

He pulled off his gloves and pushed them into his pocket. Opened the zip on the portfolio and took out a sheet of paper.

'A bank remittance for thirteen million kroner,' he said, handing it to her.

She took the slip of paper.

'Oh, Christ,' Einar exclaimed.

'Thanks,' Selma said. 'Couldn't you just transfer the money, though?'

'More fun this way,' he said, a smile playing at the corners of his mouth. 'I wanted to meet you. I've cancelled the rest of your debt. You're free, Selma, free to do whatever you want.'

'You can have this in exchange,' Selma said, taking a document from her back pocket. 'My legal practising certificate. Hege's case is wrapped up, and among the conditions you set for not reporting me was that I should give this up. Of course, I'll deal with the formalities. That's just a piece of paper, after all. But more fun, as you say. Symbolic.'

Jan stared at the certificate.

'Keep it,' he said. 'The bet was about Hege. You saved me as well. Regard the certificate as a bonus.'

'No,' Selma said. 'You're right. I should never land myself in such a situation again. I'll manage OK, Jan. It's obvious I'm cut out to be more than a lawyer. Take it.'

He did as she said. Stuffed the paper into the portfolio and zipped it closed.

'Then I'm off. If there's nothing else I can do for you?'

'Are we going to eat that pizza before it gets cold?' Einar wailed from the settee.

Selma put her hand on Jan's arm.

'Two things,' she said in an undertone. 'You could be a bit nicer to Maggi …'

He blinked.

'And then you can get me a date with Morten Harket.'

Jan Morell laughed out loud. His laugh engaged his eyes and mouth and lungs and vocal cords. Selma had never heard him laugh like that, and he laughed for a long time.

'I'll certainly try the first,' he finally said. 'But when it comes to Morten Harket, even I have to throw in the towel.'

Jan Morell was still chuckling when Selma closed the door behind him and returned to Einar.

'Now,' she said, rubbing her hands. 'Pizza. With pineapple on top, the way we both love.'

'Love,' Einar said, nodding, and Selma couldn't recall the last time she had felt so happy.

Happy and free, it dawned on her when she stood in the middle of the living room, looking around in this horrific arsehole of an apartment.

Jan was right.

Selma Falck was free to do whatever she wanted.

The twenty-third Winter Olympic Games were over.

Norway had never performed better. The small country on Europe's northern periphery set a new record for the total number of medals won and became the best nation in the world. Not only for the 2018 games, but also in history. Fourteen gold. Just as many silver. Eleven bronze, and in addition so many places in the top ten that no one could be bothered counting.

Hege Chin Morell was also in PyeongChang.

When she wasn't selected for the opening event, the ten-kilometre freestyle, she began to realize how things stood. Before she was sabotaged, she was undoubtedly the best skier in the national team. In a test run in the same event three days before departure for the Olympics, she had beaten the runner-up by four seconds. None of her efforts were good enough. Too much time had elapsed, according to her trainers. They were unsure, they claimed, and there was fierce competition for places. Two fits of rage from Jan Morell and yet another refusal to let her start later, Hege understood that she would never again ski for the Norwegian national team.

Her decision to quit was made on the flight home. She wrote a message on a napkin and asked her father to drive her up to the Cross-Country Skiing Federation HQ. There, she calmly walked in, borrowed a roll of tape from the receptionist, and hung the napkin on the door of Bottolf Odda's office.

When she strode out of the Crystal Palace, with determination in every step, towards her father's car to drive home to Vettakollen, she didn't yet know that she would never again strap on a pair of cross-country skis.

Instead, she became a doctor and moved abroad.

EPILOGUE

THURSDAY 29 DECEMBER 1977

Bloody, shitty brother.

Arne wasn't allowed to leave his side. Their mother had been uncompromising when, earlier that day, she had crammed the lunchbox into the rucksack and screwed the lid on the Thermos so tightly that Arne had struggled to take it off again when they took a break at Sinober: 'Don't leave your brother. Do you hear me?'

Mum had rumpled the hair on both of their heads, even though Arne was taller than her now. In addition, Vetle had to endure a smacker of a kiss on his cheek before their mother had knotted the blue-and-white Kjelsås football scarf more firmly around his neck and pushed the two boys out the door.

'Do you hear me, Arne? Don't leave your brother, and be home by six.'

Vetle didn't yet have a wristwatch, but he knew they were very late. Far too late, he felt. Darkness had crept across Nordmarka ages ago, because even though the sky was clear, the days were at their shortest now. The temperature had dropped in the course of the afternoon, and Vetle's feet had started to freeze in earnest. The ski boots that had been passed on by Arne were still far too big for him, so he had swapped the woollen socks for thin ones when his mother wasn't looking. It was bloody awful going around in ski boots that slid with every push-off. In all secrecy, behind the row of garages below the apartment block, Vetle had forced his feet into his old boots that were far too tight.

The skis were brand, spanking new.

Fibreglass, and the first pair of unused skis he had ever owned.

Vetle was only seven years old, but he had skied since the age of two. With his brother's well-used planks, in Arne's old boots and ski clothes. Heavy wooden skis, always too long, with scratches, dents and blunt edges.

The Christmas-present skis felt like feathers under his feet. Like air and next to nothing, even though these were also long enough for him to use for a number of years. His big brother had received black Madshus skis. Arne had fastened them on in the middle of the living room even though he was fourteen years old and had acne and a weird voice. Their father had carried up the long, slim parcels from the basement late in the evening, when they all thought that Christmas Eve was over and done with; none of their greatest desires had been fulfilled and the seven-year-old was struggling to keep his disappointment in check.

You shouldn't be ungrateful.

It wasn't nice.

And then there were new skis after all. Vetle's pair was burgundy-coloured. 'Bonna' was written in bold letters on the bindings. Norwegian skis. Burgundy wasn't as cool as black, but the skis were made of fibreglass and the only things he wanted in the whole world. The brothers got a pouch of Swix ski wax to share from Uncle Bjarne, that too a welcome gift that turned up late, when all hope seemed to be gone. Arne had stood in the narrow hallway, waxing both pairs of skis until the wee small hours.

Since then, the boys had scarcely been indoors.

Vetle and his big brother were among the first youngsters in the entire neighbourhood with fibreglass skis. When the fathers in

Jupiterveien as usual arranged a race in Langsetløkka on Boxing Day, the brothers had won in their age groups. It was all because of the fibreglass, the other youngsters had grumbled, but their dads had shushed their backbiting away, firmly declaring that it was the man on the skis that mattered.

Always the man on the skis.

They had been awarded diplomas and hot blackcurrant juice, and Kent from the furthest away of the Myrer apartment blocks was permitted to try out the Bonna skis. Vetle's dad had struggled to hide his pride when he drew his youngest son towards him and said: 'Maybe those skis were worth the money, my boy. But they were certainly highway robbery, so you take good care of them. That applies to you too, my lad!'

The final words were shouted in Arne's direction.

'Take care of those skis! They cost an arm and a leg!'

His big brother was fooling around. He stood with his left ski on the ski run and used his right to kick off on the well-prepared outside edge, almost like with an enormous skate. He took off at top speed down the slight slope down towards the clubhouse.

'Stop that nonsense,' their father roared. 'Ski properly! You're damaging the skis. And the ski run!'

It had been such a wonderful evening. Just Vetle and Arne, Mum and Dad. Their relatives had all gone home. The apartment was still conventionally decorated, with a glittering tree, a Bethlehem star in the living room window, and elves, angels and candles everywhere. The family huddled around the little kitchen table and ate leftovers as their father teased their mother so mercilessly that Arne even blushed. Vetle himself just felt warm and happy and even managed to persuade everyone to play a board game, *The Missing Diamond*, once they were replete. In fact, Vetle was the one who found the sought-after cardboard disk, the one with the biggest diamond of all, before he won by flying straight to Cairo on the third night of the best Christmas he had ever experienced.

Bloody, shitty brother.

Vetle hadn't seen him for ten minutes at least. Almost unnoticed, Arne had picked up speed as they approached the residential area and the car park where they would unfasten their skis and walk the last four hundred metres or so home to their apartment. Mum had promised that they would have cheese toasties with ham and Dole pineapple. Dad had said they would be allowed to watch a movie, *Tante Pose*, on TV. The film was ancient and boring, but Mum laughed so uproariously every time they watched it that even Arne would bring his supper with him and sit on the floor in front of the TV to watch.

Vetle's feet were too cold for him to keep up when Arne increased his speed. He had tried, but had to fall back just where the ski run turned a bend that was long enough for Arne to have vanished completely when Vetle finally skied all the way around.

It must be at least seven o'clock by now. Maybe later. There were hardly any people on the ski trails and the cold had begun to eat its way from his tight ski boots up towards his calves and thighs. His mittens were damp with perspiration that eventually turned to ice. His fingers were tingling. He had started to totter, he noticed, and he was gasping for breath as he struggled to ski properly. The way Dad had taught him. The way Arne did. Swaying, swinging, with effective diagonal movements so rhythmic that it wasn't even particularly strenuous. He wanted to ski like his hero, Ivar Formo, but he couldn't manage to do it.

What's more, he could hear something.

Voices. Loud voices and laughter that didn't sound happy at all. The laughter of big boys, the kind there were a lot of in the school playground, and that often made Vetle hide behind the bike shed and stay there for the whole of the break. From the trail he was on he could see another clearing near the forest, where the sound was coming from. A couple of pairs of skis, Vetle thought for certain, maybe three. Or four. It looked as if there was a new, proper ski trail up there past the spruce tree that had fallen on a boulder and that sometimes looked like a dead man. If you screwed up your eyes a bit. In the darkness it was as if the snow was incandescent, with a faint, bluish light that only looked attractive when he was with someone. Preferably Dad.

The voices did not subside.

Vetle wanted to go home. He sniffed and trudged past the new trail. It wasn't far now. Arne was probably already at home. Maybe Dad would come to meet Vetle on the track; he would certainly be angry that his brother had left the wee one behind. At least Mum would be. Mum would be furious, and had probably got Dad to put on his coat and go out to fetch Vetle who was all alone in a world that would soon be full of houses and lights, but nevertheless could still be scary and dangerous.

He came to a sudden halt. Just ahead on the ski trail, maybe fifty metres or so, three boys came whizzing out of the forest. They were laughing and yelling and didn't look back. None of them caught sight of Vetle, but Vetle recognized the first of them, the biggest one: a fifteen-year-old with a knitted helmet in red, white and blue. He wore that hat all winter, the boy from Brannvaktveien, even though those helmets were really only for speed skaters. He was in the tenth grade, the class that actually didn't exist, and everyone knew what sort of people were in there. The guy had Kandahar bindings attached to a pair of clunky, tar-coated wooden planks.

He was bloody good at skiing all the same. He came flying out of the deep snow and swerved perfectly on to the main trail.

Vetle stood like a statue and watched the three boys disappear from sight.

He could hear a wailing noise from the forest. Quite faint, but distinct nonetheless. It was someone crying, Vetle thought, a boy crying as Vetle had never heard anyone cry before. Arne never cried, he was far too big for that, but this was Arne, it was Vetle's big brother who was blubbering so loudly, the seven-year-old was absolutely positive of that without really understanding why, and he turned abruptly with the lightest skis in the world and went back to the freshly made track towards the undulating slope on the east side of the ski run. Annoyed, he trudged quickly upwards, without sliding his skis, using the fishbone technique when the hill grew steeper. The trail didn't go far. Just up to the steepest part, where it flattened out in a little clearing, a fissure on the mountainside beneath spruce trees heavily laden with snow and a naked, spindly beech.

Arne was sitting there.

Vetle's big brother sat on the snow, on his backside, with his back leaning against a bare mountain ridge. He had lost his cap. His mittens were gone. He was curled up, with his head on his knees, and Vetle could see that the laces on one of his ski boots were untied.

The sobbing suddenly stopped, but Arne did not look up.

'Go away,' he said quietly. 'Go home.'

'But ... your skis ...'

One of the Madshus skis was lying diagonally in front of Arne, an arrow pointing straight at Vetle. The other one was planted in the snow. It was broken. The break cut the logo in two, and it said 'Mads' on the larger piece and 'hus' on the pitiful half-metre left hanging down towards the ground, still only just attached to the rest of it.

'Dad will be mad at you,' Vetle said softly. 'He'll kill you.'

'Go. Go home.'

'They were really dear, Arne. And you have to come with me. Mum said that you weren't …'

'You have to go home,' Arne bawled, looking at him at last. 'Go home! And don't say a bloody word about this to anybody! Don't you dare, Vetle! Not to Dad, not to Mum, not to …'

He drew breath in a gasp and shot his arm out into the darkness, towards the new trail that led down to the ski run, towards the residential area, all the houses on the plateau south of the lake at Maridalsvannet, where the ice-covered water could only just be made out through the spruce trunks that had been studded with snow diamonds since long before Christmas.

Arne pointed towards Oslo and screamed: 'Get yourself home! Swear you won't say anything!'

There was something strange about Arne's eyes. They were shining and slightly faded at the same time. It was difficult to see clearly in the semi-darkness, but a strange expression had come over his brother's face.

'I swear,' Vetle mumbled.

'Go!' Arne bellowed again.

Vetle went. He gave his brother a final glance as he pressed on his poles and set off across the short expanse of snow. He said nothing. Asked no questions. He skied the kilometre or so to the car park, colder than he had ever been in his little life. He removed his skis and rubbed them clear of snow before tying them together with his poles and hoisting them over his right shoulder. Vetle went home to his mum, and there was no chance of cheese toasties or *Tante Pose*, but on the contrary a tonguelashing because he had come back three hours late. Without Arne. Who looked as if he would never come back.

And then night fell.

Vetle hadn't said anything. He got undressed, brushed his teeth and shrugged at all their questions. Mum cried and moaned, Dad coaxed and threatened, but Vetle had made a promise. Even the policeman who came, in a stiff uniform and a captain's cap he folded and pushed under his epaulettes when Mum opened the door, couldn't persuade him to change his mind. The grown-ups would find the tracks, Vetle thought sleepily, and he wouldn't give away anything that would make Arne angry.

'He left me behind,' was all he could say.

Arne was a good big brother, even if he had left him behind, and Vetle had sworn not to say anything.

Vetle took his teddy bear and went to bed. No one came to say goodnight. Dad had gone out with three other men, all neighbours. Mum had other mums visiting her. The last thing Vetle heard before he fell asleep with Teddy in the crook of his arm was women's voices from the living room. If he hadn't been sleeping so incredibly heavily after his long ski trip, he would probably have heard more and more people coming into the little apartment where a star hung in the window and the Christmas tree lights were not turned off even though it was night-time. If Vetle hadn't fallen asleep so quickly, he might well have padded across to the window, as he sometimes did when Arne hadn't yet come to bed and he couldn't sleep. Then he would have seen that it had started to snow. He would have noticed the wind that picked up and packed the snow into soft frames around the windowpanes. Vetle would have struggled to see the streetlamps, only fifteen metres away, for all the whirling, dancing snowflakes that in the end turned to driving snow in a blizzard no one had forecast.

But Vetle was fast asleep.

When he woke the next day, it was a completely different mum who ran her hand through his hair, over and over again. It was a mum who had lost her voice, and with eyes that resembled Grandma's. And in those eyes, in the pale-blue gaze that Vetle would never forget, there was something that even then caused his life to collapse in ruins, but that he only learned to put into words many years later.

Reproach.

It was the day before New Year's Eve and the beginning of a new and dreadful time.